D0410510

Brimstone

Also by Richard Masefield
Chalkhill Blue

Brimstone

Richard Masefield

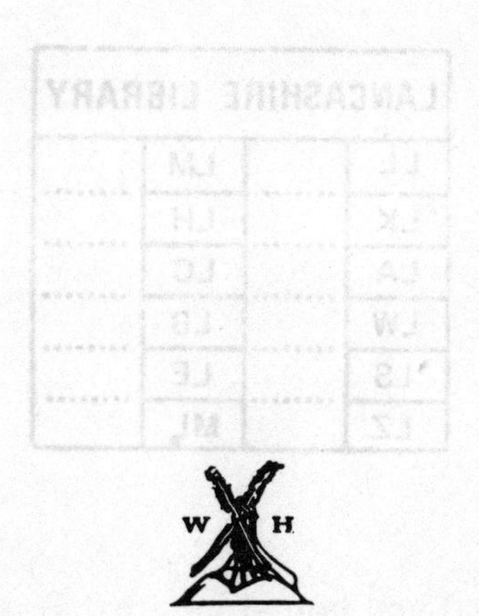

HEINEMANN : LONDON

William Heinemann Ltd
10 Upper Grosvenor Street, London W1X 9PA
LONDON MELBOURNE
JOHANNESBURG AUCKLAND

First published 1987

ISBN 0 434 45261 0

Printed and bound in Great Britain by
Mackays of Chatham

Acknowledgements

I am especially grateful to Mr Keith Richardson for sharing with me his knowledge of eighteenth-century England. Also to Geraldine Horwood, Joyce Robinson and Fred Goldsmith for much invaluable information on the subject of horses. For help with my researches outside England I am further indebted to: M and Mme Pierre Bartagnon, Paul Lemaistre of the Musée at Fécamp, Mme Andrée Pinel, Nathalie Varnière, Christine Wilson, the Librarian and staff of the Mitchell Library in Sydney, Bill Apps of Parramatta, Edward and Dawn Oliver, Elizabeth Biggs and Peggy Harding in South Africa, Charles Stirrup, Hugh Taylor, Caroline and Rhona Upcher.

Finally my thanks are due to the following for their no less valuable contributions to background material: H. K. Bagnall-Oakeley, Dr Noël Carr, Rosemary Clarke, Raymond Cocks, Andrew Crozier, Agnes Macmillan, Sir Peter Masefield, The Rt Hon Lord Shawcross Q.C., The Reverend Michael Thompson, The National Maritime Museum at Greenwich, the Librarians and staff of the London and Seaford Libraries.

FOR MARY, CLAIRE AND ROBERT

In memory of a very fine man,
REG DAVEY

BOOK 1

(1793–1798)

Chapter One

From the chalk headland to the east of Sellington Gap the sea shimmered crimson and gold, fine as tiffany silk. Every ripple, every pebble beneath it stood out with crystal clarity in the early sun; and from the naked figure in the shallows a vastly attenuated shadow sprawled out across the beach to the foot of the cliffs. For Aaron Corbyn, who would never be a tall man, his own giant profile was a source of some considerable satisfaction. Of all things in life he took for granted, and there were a number, his own body was not one. It had always pleased him – and never more but when someone else regarded it. Tossing the wet red hair back from his brow, he raised an arm to stripe the cliff with its shadow – one finger extended, pointing up the chalk face to the place where he knew the girl to be concealed. He laughed aloud. Aye, and not only a girl to watch him, but a dentical little tight-arse of a parson's daughter into the bargain!

Aaron had descried Miss Rimmer's slim figure tripping down the cliff path long before she herself had come to realize the nature of her trespass and dodged backwards out of view. And for upwards of ten minutes thereafter he'd observed the yellow straw crown of her bonnet protruding like an outsize horse mushroom from the grasses and wildflowers that fringed the clifftop, occasionally fidgeting to right or to left as if for an improved view of the theatre below, patently unaware of its own visibility from the water.

Not that any such evidence of feminine hypocrisy could surprise a young cynic like Aaron. For all their exhibition of modesty and decorum, he made certain that all women were holds-full of prurient curiosity. Wanton by nature, prudish by grace! Why ten to one the parson's daughter had never before beheld a grown man in the natural state of Adam, poor child. He glanced briefly to where his hobbled horse still stood beside the churned and ravished track up from the beach, before returning to the immediate business of washing, of removing the worst of the gunpowder-smutting from his face and forearms. Time enough to send the girl on her way, he thought, before old Ashby's flocks arrived to scuff over the evidence of their night's work. And if a perspective view of his masculine endowments should serve to improve on her education meantime, to divert her from the state of the track, then so much the better, thought Aaron Corbyn.

It had been barely light when he entered the water, with the retreating fishing smacks no more than a series of triangular silhouettes cutting through the first pale ribbons of daylight. But as the sun rose triumphantly on a new summer morning, their rusty sails had taken its colour, bleeding dramatically through shades of flame and saffron to the palest gold. And Aaron's heart had leapt at the brave sight of them safe out from shore again; the fisherfolk of Crowlink and of Sellington once more about their daily business – and not a dram of spirit nor a shred of tobacco between them to link their craft with another more lucrative trade.

"Wave 'em ta-ta for me will you, ye young raddle-pate!" the Horsemaster, Tolemy Harris, had cried as he hauled himself back into the saddle and pirouetted his pony for a parting word. "Tidy little bout, I'd say. Tidy but not gaudy, as the Devil would 'ave it when 'e painted 'is arse purple and tied up 'is tail with a yellow ribbon!"

Harris's small discoloured teeth showed pale in the darkness. "Come up to Lullington 'safnoon if you've a mind, moosh – and we'll chew the quid some more over a nice little drop of wet, eh?" And without waiting for an answer, he'd flourished a pistol the size of a young cannon and cantered off to join his convoy of laden pack-horses. Leaving to his latest apprentice the routine business of clearing the tub-boats and seeing the ewe flocks down to cover the more incriminating of their tracks.

In his mouth Aaron could still taste the bitter flavour of the husser-an'-squencher, the powerful concoction of hot beer and gin with which Tol Harris insulated his tubmen for repeated immersions in an icy sea. As he now stooped to splash the water up onto his own body, the young man felt pain in the muscles of his arms, across his neck and in his shoulders where the ropes that yoked the heavy four-gallon kegs had scored the flesh. A numb ache in his thighs and pectorals from the biting coldness of the Channel. Pain, and pride in pain. For ever since childhood he'd relished any kind of attainment which related directly to the force of his own will, rather than to the advantages of a privileged upbringing. Aaron was drawn naturally to rebellion and as a child was seldom out of mischief – riding horses too strong and too spirited for his slight frame, scratting with bigger and older boys who regularly thrashed him for his presumption, behaving with outrageous familiarity toward a series of young women who knew better, and even stood taller than he. By the age of eleven he'd dislocated a shoulder and twice knocked himself insensible in hunting accidents. At thirteen his nose had been broken in a bare-knuckle fight with a carter's lad three years his senior. At fifteen, soon after the death of the mother he worshipped, he'd contrived to collect a dose of the pox from a fire-shipped whore on the West India dock at Newhaven. Yet through it all he'd remained in good earnest, learning from his mistakes, building on his triumphs, never for an instant doubting his right to success. Within a twelvemonth of acquiring the French gout he'd succeeded in curing it himself, by means of abstinence and judicious applications of Dickman's Mercurial Salve. The following September Aaron had joined the Newhaven fishing fleet for the daring, and most profitable, rescue of hundreds of French emigrés from the port of Dieppe. And now at the age of nineteen, in this Year of Our Lord of 1793, he felt justifiably convinced that he could race a nag, trim a sail, or turn-up a woman as expeditiously as any young fellow in Sussex.

On the resumption of war with France that February, Aaron had shown no hesitation in petitioning his elder brother to allow him to respond to King George's appeal for young landsmen volunteers – to buy him a commission in their father's old regiment. A request which Brother Rafe most unreasonably refused to grant him. There were others, however, and Aaron had known where to find them, who'd not scruple to turn this or any war to favourable account. At the commencement of hostilities, all British government concessions on spirits and tobacco had been automatically withdrawn. Tariffs on tea and fine fabrics were sky high again, while the resources of the local preventivemen had been depleted beyond all pretence of effectiveness by the recent call to arms. Clearly there were adventures to be had and profits to be made by the man bold enough to override a petty restriction or two. And Aaron was nothing if not bold.

The young man laughed again, his eyes returning to the cliff. But now the time had come to shift his little peeper from her position of eminence up there amongst the knapweed and the daisies. For who could say that the shepherd Pilbeam and his boy were not already moving their folds, or even now driving the flocks down toward the Gap?

South Down wool to purchase contraband, little South Down hooves to cover its passage. A double duty that the Sellington flocks had owed Tolemy Harris and his kind ever since the notorious Mayfield Gang had first set the fashion for commandeering sheep to such purpose from the folds of Bopeep Farm over at Alciston. There was even an old rowing-shanty to celebrate the event. And on a sudden wicked impulse Aaron now began to chant the words, cupping his hands to fling them up the cliff to where the girl still lay.

'Little Bopeep has lost its sheep
And don't know where to find 'em . . .'

He'd felt the need to do something reckless, that was all – to shout and whoop at the success of their night's work. To celebrate the chinking guineas and bright India silks in his saddle bags – to shock, and to shatter the peace of a respectable Sunday morning . . .

'Ah, but leave 'em alone,
And they'll come home
A-tagging no tales behind 'em!'

. . . to race up the beach, bollock-naked, and see the parson's daughter take to her slippered heels!

* * *

It was just when Ellin Rimmer had finally convinced herself that her presence was unsuspected by the younger Mr Corbyn, that the gentleman had commenced serenading her with the verses of that odious tavern song! The circumstance was mortifying to say the least of it. And by the time the young man's intention to leave the water had become apparent, his female spectator was preparing for flight.

It was her own ridiculous fault of course. Ellin admitted it frankly as she worked her way back through the wet grass on elbows and knees and tentatively rose to her feet. Impetuosity and immoderation were her most constantly besetting sins. Papa had ever maintained it. And Papa she knew to be right, for she hadn't a moderate bone in her body. To say the truth, the most circumspect female could scarce be blamed for accidentally discovering a morning sea-bather in an uncivilized coastal region such as this where the clifftop prospects were so sudden and unexpected. But having discovered him, the barest glimpse should have been sufficient to precipitate a true lady in a dieaway swoon, or at very least to turn her steps resolutely in a contrary direction. But sad to relate, the parson's daughter had observed neither of these elementary statutes of decorum.

It was true that on first perceiving the young man in the water Ellin had stepped back mighty smartly – pausing but for the briefest moment to ascertain that he really was devoid of garments. Her motive though – honesty again compelled her to acknowledge it – had been rather one of caution than of delicacy. It was further true that she'd exclaimed "Shocking!" and "For shame!" to a passing herring gull, and with a creditable show of conviction. But the fact that in the next instant she hastened to find herself a conveniently concealed view of the beach, had tended to rob even that exclamation of its respectability.

As a matter of record, it was her lamentable impetuosity that had guided Ellin's steps to Sellington Gap at this early hour in the first place. Her official commission had been to the farm dairy, to collect the milk and butter for the parsonage household. But on an exploratory venture to the Gap the previous afternoon, she was so impressed by the theatric ruggedness of the chalk cliffs that she resolved straightaway on a sketching expedition thither for the first fine morning that offered. She had already gathered from the farmer's daughter, Ann Ashby, that her father's flocks were driven down from their folds early each day to drink from a spring at the foot of the cliffs. And Ellin had only to discover a stunted quickthorn by the side of the cliff path to have the idea for her composition all complete. A perspective view of an arcadian shepherd, with two or three romantically shaggy sheep drinking from a pool nearby. Indeed what could possibly be more agreeable? In the background those positively *gothic* cliffs, and in the foreground of course the deformed little thorn tree. Mr Gilpin, she felt sure, could not help but approve it.

Not that Ellin had ever met with that master of the picturesque in person. But as a subscriber to the Chichester circulating library, she'd long been familiar with his essays on romantic composition. 'For what could be more artistic and melancholy in a foreground,' Mr Gilpin had decreed, 'than a tree with a dead arm, a drooping bough or a dying branch? Indeed for some scenes it is essential.' So naturally, when the succeeding morning had dawned fair it had been to the twisted thorn tree and not to the farm dairy-house that Ellin had repaired, armed with her sketch book and crayons and a cheerful resolution to exceed all previous efforts in artistic melancholy. On this second sabbath of the month the service in Sellington church was to be an afternoon one. Which guaranteed that Papa would be safely closeted with his sermon for the best part of the forenoon. Her time was her own, and the commission to the dairy could wait!

But then after all to come upon an inharmonious pile of clothing in place of her expected sheep. And beyond that – gracious heavens! – a totally naked young man! For melancholy and for gothic effects the thing was ruined, utterly! Yet notwithstanding . . .

From her hiding place Ellin could scarcely be unaware of the beauty of the chain of golden ripples that his slim body dragged out across the surface of the water. Ripples lapping to the distant shores of her own experience to release feelings she could not define. No girl of her time could claim ignorance of the male physique. Every public hall, every gallery and formal garden displayed its complement of dying Gauls and Apollo Belvederes. But in Ellin's experience these classical nudities had all been of parian marble or cast plaster, austere and white as chalk. Whereas the youth in the sea was coloured most beautifully, one had to confess it, red and pink and gold. Smooth limbs gleaming wet. She envied them their naked freedom. An arm outstretched to catch the glow of the early sun; and the remarkable red hair that proclaimed his identity, darkened by the water to a rich mahogany, plastering the young man's face and neck and the base of his belly – where other still more remarkable features depended . . .

Ellin sucked in her lower lip and caught it in her teeth. This then was the flesh one committed sins with! Neither red nor gold as it now appeared, but dusky like a ripened fruit. She leant forward for a less obstructed view, staring intently, unwilling to miss a detail. And it was at that moment that he caught her, shamelessly cupping his hands to shout up to her that ridiculous chantyman's ditty! Bopeep indeed!

Yet still she'd stared, unable to move until she saw him splashing through the shallows to his horse – and then, alas, too late. By the time she recollected herself and made shift to retreat, she could already hear his hoofbeats on the path below. And before Ellin could decide what best to do he was virtually upon her, reining in, wide astride and – Judas God! – still naked as a savage!

"Your servant, Ma'am."

His manner quite ludicrously gentlemanlike for one so entirely without clothes. Though even through the palpitating heart of her confusion, something incorrigibly curious in Ellin continued to examine him – noting the young man's skin to be after all as white as any statue, fine textured, blue veined across the chest and upper arms . . .

"Your servant," he repeated, now grinning like the head of a bass viol. And since for the moment Ellin could envisage no suitable form of address for an unmarried lady confronted by a naked man, she turned speechlessly instead to run as fast and as far from him as she possibly might.

"Hey there!" he called after her – the rude young jackapes! "But why run now, Sweetheart, after such a teasy wait? Stay rather, and let patience be rewarded!"

But Ellin was already halfway to the thicket of blackthorn and elder which separated the cliff path from the lower farm track. Behind her she could hear a peal of horrid laughter, to be followed by the rhythm of the pony's hooves again – first trotting, then gathering to a canter. In her imagination she pictured his wet red hair rising and falling with the motion of the horse, his naked arm outstretched again to pluck her from the turf, as with a sob of terrified relief she bolted rabbit-like into the bushes.

* * *

Aaron remained, still chuckling, to watch the girl emerge from the far side of the thicket and strike up the track towards the Ashby farm. She'd torn her scarf on the thorns by the look of it, and as she ran her bonnet bounced on its ribbons against the dark ringlets at her back. Yet even in her flight he had to allow there to be something unusually appealing about her. The type of Judy that normally left him cold she was, the little parson's daughter. Too insubstantial by half for Aaron's idea of healthy womanhood – pippin-breasted, and with a flat little boy's arse very like beneath all that bowed and bunched up sashing.

'A faint hearted little totty-head who'd see danger in a bowl of milk!' That's what he'd thought when he first caught sight of her. But after their confrontation on the cliff just now he wasn't so entirely sure. The small compressed mouth gave little enough away. But for all her obvious embarrassment her grey eyes had been steady, and in them a look of provocation; a thing unvoiced yet clearly stated. A parson's daughter she might be, but no plaster saint he'd warrant! For Aaron recognized the look as one he'd intercepted scores of times at town assemblies and country fairs, and in the dark backstreets of Newhaven port. Why the jade was dangling after him, he'd take his oath on it!

* * *

Ellin could still hear the echo of his laughter as she hurried up to Bury Farm and to the place where she'd concealed her milk jug amongst the brambles – red as a cherry still, and not entirely from her own exertions. She was affronted she assured herself, *utterly affronted*! Whatever her own fault in the matter, Mr Corbyn's had been infinitely and inexcusably greater. On that there could be no dispute! At the discovery of her presence any kind of a gentleman must certainly have hastened to immerse that offensive part of himself in the water, to remain there in discreet concealment until such time as the lady could conveniently withdraw. But flagrantly to parade it before her as Mr Corbyn had. To pursue her from the back of a horse, to laugh at her – God save us! – and himself as naked as a needle. 'Twas simply not to be borne! Why, if she had not been fearful of missing her target and making him laugh at her still more, she'd have been in fifty minds to take up a piece of chalk from the track and fling it at him there and then. Yes she would. To fling it at the odious beast with all her might and strength! Ellin rummaged her inadequate vocabulary for stronger adjectives to describe him. Not only odious neither, but insufferable, *abominable*! 'Twas amazing how abominable she found him!

But then as she very shortly discovered, violent feelings are notoriously apt to violent turns of direction. And before Ellin could make further headway with her execrations, a traitorous dimple impressed itself entirely unbidden in either pink cheek, and she too began to laugh.

Chapter Two

The congregation withinside Sellington church that afternoon was larger and even noisier than it had been for the previous two weeks of the new parson's incumbency. For one thing, in Sellington as elsewhere in England, the faithful had been exhorted most particularly that Sunday to petition the Almighty for victory over the heathen French. And for another, word had by now spread even to the outer boundaries of the parish that the Reverend Saul Rimmer was a regular brimstone of a preacher.

Of Chichester, where Ellin was raised, it was often said that while half the town slept the other half went about on tippytoe for fear of waking them. It was very much that kind of a place. In the cathedral there the ladies' whispered conversations rustled as discreetly as the silks of their petticoats. And before being rusticated to the far side of the county, it had never occurred to the Reverend Rimmer's daughter that divine service could be anything but dull. The frankly uninhibited behaviour of his new parishioners came then as something of a pleasant surprise to Ellin. From her aisle position a row back from the pulpit, and without turning or raising herself in her seat as so many of her neighbours seemed to be doing, she could comfortably observe upwards of a score of worshippers.

'And really,' she thought to herself that afternoon, 'with the exception of the Corbyns and that rabbity little parish clerk, they might as well be sitting at their own kitchen tables for all the heed they're paying to the altar or to poor Papa!'

Foremost exponents of this relaxed and refreshing attitude to churching were the prosperous Ashby family, who occupied between them the entire front pew on Ellin's side of the nave. At its far distant end where the light from the green glass window struck full on their heads, two of the younger members of the family were currently absorbed in a game of hucklebones. Next to them their nine-year-old brother strove unsuccessfully to restrain the bobtail puppy he'd borne with him to church, admonished from the near side by his elder sister Annie, who in turn was employed in constructing a cat's cradle for the squalling baby on her step-mother's lap. The two men of the family, meantime, were embarked on an earnest discussion of the latest French war and its likely effect on their livelihood. A dialogue which, despite its private intention, was all too audible to the girl directly behind them. For both men were blessed with ten-acre-field voices patently unsuited to interiors of any kind.

"What queers me, Dad," young Tom Ashby was declaring in loud and plaintive tones, "is if this be a just war, as Mr Prime Minister Pitt would 'ave us believe it, then why do we 'ave to part with our wool so blooming cheap these days at English markets?"

His father, Sam Ashby, passed a meaty hand over the unbecoming flaxen wig that occupied so great a part of Ellin's forward vision. "Because wars'll be just for Sussex flockmasters when hens make holy water, that's why!" he returned in a thunderous whisper that carried the blasphemy clear through the chancel arch to the ears of the new incumbent at the altar rail. "But there, the Frenchies'll still pay a fair price for our wool, boy, ye can be sure of that," he added comfortably.

"But Dad, we've no ought to sell abroad now, surelye? With you a parish officer and all?" Tom's great frame contorted visibly beneath the strain of contracting his lungs. "Not now Mr Pitt would 'ave it as trade with Frenchies be no better than corresponding with the enemy, so to speak."

"God damn your tarnation Pitt!" At full volume Farmer Ashby's voice automatically silenced all other conversation in the church. "We know all about your poxy Pitts down 'ere, we do!" he bellowed. "This kiddy's father were only the bleddy Member for Seaford, weren't 'e? And did 'e look after our interests 'ereabouts like a proper Member should? Did 'e, my arse! Why that old Pitt never so much as showed 'is nose in Sussex above once or twice in seven year. So what the bugger does a son of 'is think 'e knows about the price of Sussex wool, even if 'e is the bleddy Prime Minister? Answer me that, Sir!"

"But Dad, I only thought . . .'

"You thought! And did you for sure, ye great dallop? Well, you know what thought did doan't ye, Tom Ashby? Only lay abed and shat 'isself, didn't 'e? *Thought* 'e were up!" The farmer laughed heartily, his good humour restored. "No Sir, the Pitts of this world would soon make a tidy 'avoc of our loose trade in wool if we were fool enough to let 'em try."

And if any doubts had lingered in Ellin's mind as to the extent of local involvement with the contrabanding trade, this last overhearing must certainly have removed them. The Ashby family were the most successful independent farm-holders hereabouts, as the girl Annie had informed her on her first visit to their dairy. They enjoyed grazing rights over miles of coastal downland, with enclosed arable acres in the Sellington valley and two or three other sheltered combes between Went Hill and the Cuckmere river. The final decay of the Wenhams of Chalkdean, their overbred and ultimately overspent landlords, followed as it had been by a series of helpful land enclosure bills, had vastly improved the Ashbys' standing in Sellington. And if Ann Asbhy omitted to add that much of the capital for their expansion derived from generations of illicit wool-exporting, Ellin was too intelligent an observer not to have guessed at it. Any girl of her time would have to be stone deaf indeed not to have heard of the wool-traders, the legendary 'owlers' of Kent and Sussex. Blind too not to have remarked the quantities of trampled horse manure which littered the track up through the Ashby farmyards from the beach. And dense into the bargain not to have speculated over the square oilskin package in evidence that very morning beneath the cheese bench of the dairy Ann Ashby supervised.

"Ask no questions, Ma'am," the farmer's daughter observed mildly, catching the direction of Ellin's glance as she herself had dipped for her milk, "and we'll tell you no lies." And she'd wiped away the surplus and handed her the brimming jug with a confidential wink.

Not that the Ashbys were by any means the only folk in Sellington to supplement their earnings from such business. 'As mischievous and impenitent an assembly of souls as any you might hope to have the cure of,' had been the description of the Sellington parishioners that his Lordship the Bishop had settled on as most likely to commend so remote a parish to a commencing vicar of Saul Rimmer's evangelical persuasion. And casting around her in the church Ellin could see the evidence for herself, or suspicioned that she could, in eyes shadowed from lack of sleep and hands black-grained as no mere rickyard or trawling ground could leave them. Night-blacking? The livery of the professional contrabander? Was that what grimed their fingers and clogged their broken nails? And the young man in the sea that morning? Was it night-blacking that he'd been washing from his face and hands when she first beheld him? And was he as guilty as the rest? With a reminiscent little thrill of excitement Ellin stole a glance at the empty seat across the nave from the Ashbys. On her return home from the dairy she'd destroyed the sketch she'd made of that interestingly gendered figure, and after no more than the briefest refreshment of her memory of it. But the original? Would he still ride down to church, she wondered, with his brother and his aunt already seated and the stall-gate so firmly closed against him?

At that very moment Ellin's ears caught the sound of iron-spelted boots on the flags of the aisle behind her. His boots? Could they be? A brisk stride certainly, and hardly that of a heavily built or long-shanked man .. Something cold fluttered in her stomach, and swiftly she opened her prayer book to read at random, forcing her eyes from line to line. 'I will keep my mouth as it were a bridle while the ungodly is in my sight . . .' Earlier on the cliff, fascination had for the moment blinded her sense of decorum. On no account must it be allowed to do so again.

The ringing footsteps approached, drew level with Ellin's pew and halted. 'I held my tongue and spake nothing . . .'

"Ah, little Miss Bopeep is it not? So I have caught up with you at last!"

In spite of herself she started, and then became conscious of an interested lull in the conversation around them. Yet with her eyes downcast still she could not help but observe his boots – so highly polished, and elevated she noticed at the heels, rising to smallclothes of ivory buckskin that fitted to a hair, skin-tight even to the falls . . . Hastily Ellin returned her gaze to the prayer book. 'I kept silence, yea even from good words, though it was pain and grief to me . . .'

But he refused to spare her. "And would you disregard me, Ma'am, when before you were so attentive?" He continued relentlessly. "I've been counting on your opinion of this new rig of mine, to try against the last in which you saw me, strike me if I ain't."

As she raised her head reluctantly to meet them, Ellin saw that his brown downward-slanting eyes positively glowed with malicious enjoyment. Eyes that spared nothing. 'Like hot embers,' she thought. Hot embers which were shortly to kindle within her an overwhelming temptation to give the fellow the setting-down he so richly deserved.

"In that case you must give me leave to reassure you, Sir," she heard her own voice pronounce with as cool a show of indifference as ever she could have hoped, despite the tight constriction in her throat. "For I am persuaded that the suit you now wear is infinitely more becoming to your figure."

And too late then to disown the remark however she might wish it. The young man's red brows were already up. And to crown the whole, what must he do next as she hurriedly returned to her prayer book but distinguish the pair of them with a burst of profane laughter, as unrestrained as on the cliff. With Sam Ashby and his progeny blatantly revolving in their seats to consider them the better. And in the lower-deck of the pulpit, she knew it even without looking, Papa's white-surpliced figure fairly fluffed up with astonishment and disapproval!

"Lord bless us, but by my word the child has a squeak under her bonnet after all then," the young rogue triumphed, unabashed. "Though for my life, Miss Rimmer, I swear you do me an injustice. Nay, we must make some further trial of the case, I insist on it. And I'll lay odds that my former suit may yet impress itself upon you a deal more favourably!"

With which unexampled audacity the odious youth made her his salute. An elaborate scrape with a full bow, performed to admiration with one hand on the pleated ruffles of his shirt. "Madam, your most obedient . . ." before moving on to assume his seat at the vacant end of the Corbyn pew.

"I acknowledge my transgression and my sin is ever before me. Hide Thy face from my sins and blot out all mine iniquities . . ."

Ellin Rimmer's puritanical little father had always occupied the place within her of her own recalcitrant conscience. And the sound of his voice precipitately launching the congregation into the first of their afternoon scriptures recalled her, still blushing, to her duty.

"Dearly beloved bretheren, the Scripture moveth us in sundry places to acknowledge and confess our manifold sins and wickedness . . ."

Unlike Aaron Corbyn, Ellin had never loved or grieved for the woman who'd brought her into the world; for her own mother had survived that event by less than two weeks. Throughout childhood her companions had been limited to a succession of dull-witted nurses and maid-servants. Her father had no taste for social diversion. His duties in Chichester as Chaplain to the Bishop brought him all the intercourse he desired, he said, with the sybaritic society of that place. He saw no reason to expose a child as susceptible as his only daughter to their levity and pleasure-seeking. Nor could he approve, or afford, a private seminary for her education – instructing her himself instead in an obscure corner of the Bishop's Palace in all he considered it seemly for a mere female to know of penmanship, history and mathematics. Which was why Ellin found herself at the age of eighteen without a single close friend or confidante, without relatives (aside from some unknown cousins in the northern county of Yorkshire), indeed with no one but Papa himself to whom she might direct her affections.

"We ought at all times humbly to acknowledge and confess our sins before God, yet ought we most chiefly so to do when we assemble and meet together to render thanks for the great benefits we have received at His hands . . ."

But naturally there'd been compensations. There always are. In the first place Ellin had never been averse to her own company, or to that of pet rabbits and rag dolls And for the rest? Why, for a subscription of a shilling a quarter, the public circulating library at Chichester had provided her with as wide a variety of acquaintance as anyone could hope to meet. Papa had never discouraged reading for instruction – had even condescended to make extracts in her behalf from Mr Fordyce's *Sermons to Young Women*, and to recommend Mrs Champone's *Letters on the Improvement of the Female Mind* for her daily readings. And if he was unaware that she'd also devoured the scandalous *Tom Jones* within the privacy of her bedchamber, together with the gothic horrors of *The Castle of Otranto* and scores of the romantic and sentimental novels that have ever been popular with lonely young ladies – then what the eye didn't see the heart could hardly be injured by, his daughter most reasonably assumed.

"Almighty and most merciful Father, we have erred and strayed from Thy ways like lost sheep . . ." The General Confession, the necessity of reorganizing one's thoughts and one's skirts into an appropriate posture, had inevitably brought that exasperating young Corbyn across the aisle into sharper focus again.

"We have followed too much the devices and desires of our own hearts . . ." Although, considering that the Absolution and Remission were so shortly to follow, there was really very little to be gained at this moment, Ellin thought, from actually forbidding oneself to think of him . . . And now that it was dry his hair was certainly an extraordinary colour in comparison with his brother's plain brown wig beside him, or the discreet black lace of his Aunt Drusilla's tippet and veil. A most outlandish and improbable hue. 'Coquelicot' you'd have called it in a fabric – drawn back over his collar, turned up and tied with a silk ribbon into a thick red queue. As a fact there was something so materially different about that hair, about the velvety slimness of the kneeling back, such a wide distinction between them, that it was hard to credit him with the same parentage as the man in the pew beside him.

It had been obvious to Ellin from her first attendance of the little downland church that the Corbyns were the only family of gentle birth in the parish. The nearest approach to the Quality it could now offer. For despite the fact that they'd come later to the area, farmed less acreage than the Ashbys and owed lower church tithes to the parson, there was about them all, even the red haired Aaron, a visible stamp of consequence and good taste that no Sussex-bred farmer could imitate. They were not of the land, these Corbyns, but of that growing class of parvenu gentry to which the English professions owed so much. The brothers' maternal grandfather, Godfrey Heathcote, had practiced as an attorney it was said and later as a judge, before his retirement and subsequent death in Sussex. Their mother had been something of an heiress by local standards, their father an heroic army captain. And for all Mr Rafe Corbyn's eccentric involvements in physic and the practice of surgery, for all his brother's wildness, no one disputed the family's right to a foremost stall in Sellington church.

The Corbyns' manor house of Chalkdean was in itself a local landmark, and one that had impressed Ellin most particularly when she and her father had driven the two miles thither to sup tea with the doctor and his aunt. Even Papa, who'd always advocated the severest restraint within his own doors, could not but admire the spaciousness of the Chalkdean vestibule, the excellence of Mr Rafe Corbyn's library and surgery. Mistress Drusilla had been most flattering on the occasion in her willingness to discuss the shortcomings of rural society with a mere parson and his daughter, her elder nephew full of politesse. But from the moment that she'd first beheld him through the long window at his aunt's back, Ellin's fancy had lighted on the *younger* Mr Corbyn as the very model of eligibility (as prescribed by any Tatler story or romantic novel worth the name).

"Ah, but I see that you've espied my brother, Miss Rimmer."

Following the direction of her gaze, Mr Rafe Corbyn had tactfully foreclosed his aunt's lecture on the superiority of Tunbridge Wells as a watering-place over Cheltenham and Harrogate, and steered the discourse to a topic of more immediate interest to his female guest. That his brother had been out riding on the estate was apparent from the young man's spurs and whip. The fact that he had some other more pressing object in view, all too obvious from the manner in which he strode past the window without a glance to spare for its occupants.

"And I fear that we must excuse Aaron his devoirs this afternoon," Rafe Corbyn was saying. "He is still of that trying age you see, Miss Rimmer, that professes to prefer stables to drawing rooms, saddles to elbow-chairs, and almost anything so he'd have us believe to the felicities of a lady's tea-board. Not but we haven't some hopes of reforming him yet," he added. "Is that not so, Aunt?" To which the dignified Drusilla had responded with a sniff.

He was an estimable character, this gentleman physician. A conscientious practioner it was said, who even had the assurance to perform an occasional cure on some or other of his downland patients, which was, after all, more than most of his profession achieved. And as such a fine resource no doubt for any rustic community. Regrettably unexciting though as a man, Ellin concluded – past first youth, too full of gravitas to be at all romantic. And more to the purpose, a deal too elevated besides as master of the Chalkdean estate to fall within the province of an aspiring parson's daughter.

No, there was no denying it. In the face of all his uncouth manners and suspicious behaviour, it was still the younger Mr Corbyn who drew her interest. Ellin peered out from between her fingers at that outlandish queue of hair while her father recited the Absolution.

As a matter of no great surprise it was the elder and not the younger Mr Corbyn who delivered the second lesson in the church that afternoon. The sobriety of his manner and appearance in marked contrast to the blustering self-consequence of Farmer Sam Ashby, the previous lector. But Ellin had not heard above one word in ten in any case. Long before then she had returned in her imagination to a private romance in which Aaron Corbyn, suitably reformed, had played a leading role. Only to be tiresomely interrupted again by the thin reed of her father's voice, this time giving out the text for his sermon. "Revelations Nine, verse seventeen." To be followed by the sound of the upper pulpit door snapping shut behind him.

"And thus I saw the horses in the vision. And them that sat on them had breastplates of fire and jacinth, and out of their mouths issued fire and smoke and brimstone!"

Ellin's own delicacy of bone and feature was a good deal less appealing in a middle-aged clergyman. Nor was it at all enhanced by the wire-rimmed spectacles. Nor yet by the Reverend's antique physical wig, with its side-bushes of discoloured horsehair sticking out over either ear. Indeed poor Papa resembled nothing so much as a lady's marmoset, his daughter irreverently decided, as he gripped the purfled rim of the pulpit and crouched forward to deliver his address. "By these three was the third part of mankind destroyed. And the rest repented not of the works of their hands, nor of their worship of devils and of idols of gold and silver and brass . . ."

If only he could see himself though as she could, chittering down at them all so angrily from his marmoset's perch! But of course he never would, not her Papa. 'And I only hope to goodness he'll leave off before Armageddon at the least – and all those dreadful descriptions of congealing blood and frogs leaping out of people's mouths,' thought Ellin, to whom the subject of the text was all too familiar. That her father should progress, however, from general to specific condemnations had not occurred to her. For on previous occasions he'd been content to leave it to the consciences of the sinners themselves to find a personal application for his words. So when he fixed an unequivocal eye on the Ashby pew beneath him, to repeat at point blank range: "Idols of gold and silver I say! Yea, and trade with those enemies of peace in France who fear neither God nor man, nor the Devil himself!" his daughter was quite as astonished as any of them.

Worse was to come. Not only did a local preacher dare to mention the unmentionable; but even before the enormity of his blunder fully registered with his churchwarden and principal tithe-payer in the pew below, he went on to compound the error with more of the same. "Thou defyest the laws of thy God, thy King and thy Country to follow the wickedness of thine own imagination!" he cried, the lenses of his spectacles flashing fire from the candles of the upper pulpit. "And I tell thee that unless thou repentest of thy lust and deceit and turn to the Lord. His hosts shall smite thee with pestilence and tempest and earthquake! He shall scorch thee with flames, reap thee with sickles, crush thee in the press of the wrath of God, and cast thee down into the lake below which burneth with fire and brimstone and is the second death!"

"Strap me! Sounds like a cure for the pox!"

The comment was clearly audible to Ellin across the aisle, even above Ann Ashby's giggles and her father's paroxysm of outraged coughing from the pew in front. But the Corbyns when she looked presented almost as impassive an appearance as before. The good doctor sat staring ahead of him still at the marble tablet on the wall that commemorated his parents' lives. His arms firmly crossed, his face immovably grave. The veiling that swathed his aunt's tall Theodore hat beside him trembled but to the barest degree. And had it not been for the reflex of a hidden muscle at the angle of the younger Corbyn's prominent jaw, the origin of the remark might yet have remained obscure.

Whether or not Papa himself had heard was impossible to determine; for by now he was fairly gripped within the force of his own eloquence. "And ye who wilfully connive at the transgressions of these bold and naughty men," he accused, adjusting his lenses to the wider perspectives of the congregation, "ye who imbibe their smuggled liquor and clothe thy womenfolk in their silks of purple and crimson . . .!" He pointed a bony finger at the uniformly drab mulls and Norwich crapes of his female parishioners. And again Ellin caught the ripple of a muscle in that same lean jaw across the aisle. ". . . I tell thee that the sin of avarice hath defiled thy immortal souls, to fit thee only for the Lord's wrath. Nor have thee the least power within thyselves to avert His dreadful day of reckoning . . ."

At which the queue of flame-coloured hair jerked back. Oak creaked, buckskin creased and stretched – and in another moment the younger Corbyn was on his feet before them all.

"Say you so, Parson?" he flung up at the impassioned little figure in the pulpit. "Then hear me when I tell you that at this rate your own reckoning will likely come a deal sooner than Judgement Day! We've long been out of patience with Methodists and tub-thumpers in these parts, Parson. So take good heed. What we've no patience with we shift, Sir, you may be sure of that! In one moment and out the next, Sir, quicker'n a curate's fart through the seat of a rush chair!"

In the interval of stunned silence that followed, the sound of the young man's boots again rang briskly down the aisle; and as he approached them the standing rabble in the doorway divided like the Red Sea to let him pass through and out into the graveyard beyond.

Chapter Three

Miss Drusilla Corbyn could never have conceived of driving out to church with anything less than a team of matched bays to draw her. Indeed if her elder nephew had not shrunk from such ostentation, she'd have mounted a postillion and liveried footman as well. As it was, while the younger Corbyn applied his spurs and stirred the chalk dust outside the church with his departure, the chaise-and-four in which his aunt and brother were to return home stood waiting still beside the tapsel gate. An old-fashioned German landau, so large and high at the box that its coachman could not only see over the churchyard wall but himself appeared above it, jack-boots and all. Not that his visibility at such an elevation could be said to add anything much to the dignity of the Corbyn equipage, bald and hatless as he was, slouched forward with his neck sunk in his collar and his lower lip thrust out morosely.

Coachman Gabel Turner had been with the Corbyns too long and served them too faithfully not to consider himself above reproach. Only the coachman of an earl or a countess might drive uncovered, as well he knew. But time enough for his own hat, Gabel reasoned, when the Master and Mistress were safely bestowed in their seats. It was shady enough beneath the old Spanish chestnut at the gate meantime. And he'd be danged if he'd hatch vermin under a swelty tye-wig only to improve her ladyship's view of him from the church door. Danged if he would!

She was there now as it chanced, her Ladyship. Turner could already see her on the step. And for all his bold internal scorn, his whip hand stole out to feel for his coachman's hat beside him on the box. In starting trim, out first as ever, her Ladyship – disallowing Master Aaron's tarrifications that is.

"Trouble?" the coachman enquired glumly of his bays, automatically settling the symbolic hat about his ears and easing himself down, stiff jointed, to meet the Mistress at the gate. "A chancy boy, Mus Arrun. Always were, and I daresay always will be. 'Arness yourselves to that young article, my beauties, and you'll meet trouble 'ead on I give ye my word. Aye, and before you've drawn 'im ten clear paces."

Meanwhile and true to form, Mistress Corbyn was down the church steps and already halfway to the gate, marching like a grenadier in her tall hat and burgundy velvet – her gaunt and inflexible figure answerable in every way to the will that propelled it.

'Bad a skin as I ever saw 'er in,' the old coachman decided, catching a glimpse of the expression beneath her swaying veil as he flung back the door of the chaise and stooped to fold out the step to his mistress's advancing foot.

'And my mistake I'm sure,' he advised himself bitterly, as she flounced back onto the seat without a word of acknowledgement or even so much as a glance in his direction. 'Your 'umble-condumble should've lifted your Ladyship's bum-pads for ye, I collect?' With which he'd latched the door to stand and await the Master.

From her position in the open landau Drusilla Corbyn was herself unable to judge her nephew's progress, due to the convolutions of its folded hood. But Turner could see him right enough, standing in the church doorway in conversation with the new parson – with old Sam Ashby snorting down his neck from behind, red as a scalded hog.

'And taking some of the strut outter the both of 'em, or I'm no driver,' the coachman concluded on a milder and altogether prouder note. 'Proper young gentleman for dip'matics, our Mus Relph, and always were.'

* * *

Rafe Godfrey Corbyn hurried down the path to the waiting conveyance in the knowledge that he'd already kept his aunt waiting for longer than was either courteous or prudent. But in all conscience he could hardly have left the church without some kind of reparation for Aaron's ill-mannered behaviour, however much the canting little parson might have invited it. He could even feel sorry for Saul Rimmer and others of his misanthropic persuasion. 'And not least at Bury Farm this dinner time,' Rafe thought with an involuntary smile at the prospect of the parson's traditional attendance with his daughter at the Ashbys' Sunday board. 'A riding, drinking, hearty fellow who sports a hunting coat beneath his surplice. That's more like Sam's idea of an enlightened country parson. And after a sermon of that kidney, 'tis odds on he'll chew this one up and spit him out with the beef gristle! And then think twice about victualling him and playing Squire to his Rector in the future, I'll warrant!'

But Rafe's amusement was short-lived. One glimpse through the carriage door of Aunt Drusilla's disapproving burgundy knees had seen to that. "Thank you, Gabel. We'll be off home then shall we?" he suggested with a wink at his old fraud of a coachman, adroitly swinging himself up onto his high box as if he'd never heard of rheumatics. 'And now we'll have it,' he thought resignedly.

'And now 'er Ladyship'll justabout *create* – soonasever we clear the 'ouses,' thought Gabel Turner, flicking the whip with a certain fatalistic relish. "Git up there then, you old craturs. Box your tarnation trotters!"

But Drusilla Corbyn, teased beyond sufferance, was unable to contain her sense of grievance for anywhere near so long. "Well now, Sir?" she demanded above the rattle of the swingletrees, and even before they'd negotiated the first narrow bend between the parsonage and the duckpond.

"Well, Aunt?"

"Well what have got to say for your brother's latest masterpiece, I should like to know?" Miss Corbyn threw back her veil as she spoke. Years of impertinence from her younger nephew had permanently predisposed her against him. And now her sense of outrage was only too apparent. It twitched at the mittened fingers in her lap. It heaved at the necessary reinforcements of her bosom and tapped out at the toes of her narrow Chinese slippers.

Facing her across the carriage, Rafe prepared himself for a long drive home. "Upon my honour, I liked it no better than you,

Ma'am," he offered. But was permitted to say no more until Aunt Drusilla had given vent to the intolerable pressures which had been building up beneath her stays from the moment of his brother's exit from the church.

"Honour, did you say?" She was a little deaf, and always spoke loudly herself to compensate. "And what of your brother's famous sense of honour? You'll never persuade me, Sir, that he even knows the meaning of the word! And what of *my* honour, pray, as a lady of rank? Ridiculed I tell you! Disgraced I say, and before a passel of sniggering punch-clods!"

"Now Aunt, you must allow . . ."

But Drusilla was in no frame for allowing, either explanations or interruptions. "You've spoiled that boy with too much lenience," she insisted. "I daresay you'd prefer not to hear this, Nephew; but 'tis plain as day to me that if he'd been indulged less and thrashed more often since his mother's death, he'd be something less random and unmannerly now. Though on reflection," she added without pausing for one, "whatever you may think Rafe, I myself misdoubt if anything could entirely civilize that young savage. There's a deal too much of my own scapegrace brother Michael in him for that."

"Saving your pardon, Ma'am, but I do believe you exaggerate the case. You always have, you know, where Aaron is concerned."

Despite every resolution to the contrary, Rafe felt sufficiently nettled by the injustice of his aunt's remarks to reply with some asperity. "I assure you that my brother's faults are by no means beyond the reach of amendment. And if his manners have been spoiled by indulgence, then I think you must acknowledge that it was Mamma who was chiefly at error. For you know that from his first infancy she never could deny Aaron anything."

But already he'd said too much. Rafe saw it at once in the change of expression on his aunt's strongly marked features from righteous indignation to something altogether more disturbing. She smiled – with Aunt Drusilla a mere extension of her long upper lip.

'And confound it man, here you sit priding yourself on your rationality and moderation,' Rafe admonished himself, 'only to act the turncoat on young Aaron and on poor Mamma the moment your own emotions are engaged. So much indeed for false pretensions!'

"But heaven pity you, my poor nephew," his aunt was now declaring with every further evidence of satisfaction. "To have to suffer that worthless cuckoo-child stealing away so great a part of the love your own mother owed you, and from his very cradle too." Leaning across the carriage she laid a sympathetic hand on his knee. "That young man has never taken me in. I've never been blinded to his true character – no Sir, not for one minute! But my dear sister-in-law was such a simpleton in some matters. I fear Elizabeth never saw as I did how infinitely more deserving was her firstborn child." She patted his knee lightly and with a coyness that ill-became her. "Worth fifty of the younger any day of the week, I've always upheld it."

"You flatter me, Aunt." It was Rafe's turn again to smile in acknowledgement of the compliment and of the point she'd gained over him; at the same time taking advantage of a sudden jolt of the chaise to dislodge the importunate hand. "But I think you apprehend that's not what I inferred. I simply meant that Mamma permitted Aaron too great a licence while I was abroad at Cambridge and in London.

"In any event," he added on a deliberately more businesslike note, "my brother shall receive a first rate trimming, for his churlishness before we sit down to luncheon this afternoon. On that you may depend."

"Flimflam!" The lady sat back again and lowered her veil significantly, conscious of the rebuff. "I'm sure we may depend on your easy nature to bring things to an all too amicable conclusion, if that's what you mean. You're a good man, Rafe, I make no doubt of it. But I hope I may also say frankly to you and without offence that in my experience most good men haven't the sense that God gave *geese*!"

'And for the matter of that, most good women are 'eadless ones, I'd say,' Coachman Turner reflected from the box. And as if to confirm him in the wisdom of that maxim his mistress remained near static and, save for an occasionally prolonged sniff, quite remarkably silent for the rest of their ascent of Sellington Hill.

From his passengers' viewpoint the progressions of cottage thatches and windblown hedges that passed between the landau's hoods as they climbed the hill were doubtless unremarkable enough. But for Gabel the wider prospects that his box seat afforded were an invariable source of inspiration. As the team strained to draw the heavy vehicle up to the Gibbet Crossways at the summit, his pessimistic habit fell away. Unconsciously he straightened his spine and sucked in his pouting lower lip. But for the gulls and the carolling skylarks he was the highest mortal creature for miles around. 'On the lid o' the world,' he thought. For though he felt its enchantment to the very depths of his Sussex soul, the old man could no more have framed the feeling in words than flown up into the sky himself with the larks.

Behind him the flint track fell sharply to the village – to pealing church bells and darned Sunday-best. Below that to the new slate roofs of the Ashby farm and the chalk cliffs beyond it. But ahead of Gabel's team, to right and to left, the downland lay open to the heavens. The lead horses required little enough guidance for this familiar run – nothing beyond a brief halt at the top for wind and the application of the skid, and thereafter an occasional shortening of the reins to check their homeward pace; leaving their driver free to reflect on the sagacity of a God who'd shown the remarkable good sense to save his best designs for the Sussex cart-track between Sellington Hill and Chalkdean Manor.

To the eye of the most seasoned traveller it must still have been a landscape on a splendid scale; a panorama of rolling chalkland, scooping and rising, rippling in the breeze like something alive. The slender bent grasses which gave it movement were already bleached by the summer sun, and on Middle Brow and the further slopes of the Cuckmere valley where the sheep had yet to graze them the hillsides were washed with gold. But for one who'd known this high chalk country all his life, as Gabel had, its greater interest lay in the variety of living things it harboured; in a tapestry of creeping herbs which took millennia to weave, in the insects it attracted and the birds that fed on them. Birds were everywhere, patrolling the turf, rising up under the carriage wheels – speckled titlarks by the hundred, wheatears hovering like giant butterflies on rapidly beating wings. And on a distant slope of Friston Dencher a covey of bustards. 'Sussex turkeys', as the locals knew them; great clumsy creatures that took sixty yards of furious flapping to clear the ground, and thus proved an easy prey to coursing greyhounds – or to keen young marksmen like Master Aaron.

The old coachman shook his head, thrusting out his lip again and automatically returning to his melancholy frame as the landau left the open downland for its descent to Chalkdean. 'Shouldn't wonder if they'll all be adone before long, the way that young rapscallion's catering after 'em, poor things,' he thought gloomily. 'And never a tarnation turkey left for folks to gark at.'

* * *

Disapproval of Aaron was quite the fashion in the Corbyn chaise that afternoon; manifest not only in Drusilla's periodic sniffs and Coachman Turner's sorrowfully shaking head, but also in a contemplative frown on the face of its remaining occupant.

Viewing the elder Mr Corbyn through the shortened perspectives of her own extreme youth, Ellin Rimmer had failed to do him justice. There was indeed little remarkable about his face – nothing shockingly hot or pleasurably disturbing in his sensitive brown eyes, nor yet the slightest tinge of 'coquelicot' in his plain brown wig. Yet he was tall and well set on his limbs. The breadth of his shoulders and swell of his calves owed nothing to fashionable padding. And on the right side of thirty still, he was a deal more youthful in his impulses and energies than a girl eleven years his junior could ever conceive possible. Not that Rafe himself was in the least addicted to personal conceit. Appearance he believed was of little consequence in the order of things. As a physician he saw the sense of keeping his person clean and free of vermin. As a gentleman of some local standing he acknowledged a duty to cut something of the figure his income afforded. Otherwise he was as free from vanity as any man alive. And had his aunt felt inclined to voice her opinion just then that her nephew's frown, the contraction of strong brows over a good prominent Corbyn nose, was most becoming to his physiognomy, Rafe would have been considerably surprised.

As a fact the perennial problem of his younger brother had brought many a becoming frown to Rafe Corbyn's face over the past years. In 1789, returning briefly from London for his Grandfather Heathcote's funeral, Rafe had solemnly promised his mother to see Aaron safe from harm. Soon afterwards she too had died of the same epidemical fever, poor lady, having taken the infection from her father. But bound still to the London hospitals for a further year of anatomical lectures and surgical application, Rafe had found his undertaking next thing to impossible to keep. At fifteen, denied the love and influence of the mother he'd adored, Aaron had run wild – casting beyond the manor estate for diversions that involved him in bull-baiting at Lewes and whoring at Newhaven, and in horse-racing on the downs anywhere that nags and sporting gentlemen could be brought together. And all his brother's cautionary letters, all their aunt's complaints and injunctions, had been insufficient to keep the boy from bad company and all manner of riotous escapades.

On Rafe's return to Sussex as a qualified physician the following year, his brother's official apprenticeship to the Chalkdean bailiff was judged advisable. Aaron would become an agriculturalist, he decided, to bring his wayward energy to bear on the management and modernization of their grandfather's estate. And when in February of this year of 1793 the domestic revolution in France had escalated to an international conflict involving Britain, he'd no hesitation in refusing the reluctant young farmer his application to join the military.

Like many enlightened men, Rafe himself had applauded the fall of the Bastille to the French mob four years earlier. 'A magnificent act of liberation from tyranny,' was how he'd described it in one of his many encouraging letters to Aaron soon after their dear Mamma's interment. Tom Paine had been a Lewes man after all; and in his undemonstrative fashion Rafe had rejoiced to read the articles of the new French constitution with Rousseau's, Paine's and Thomas Jefferson's grand ideals at their head. 'Men are born and remain free and equal in rights' – the words struck a sympathetic echo in his own soul. And through all the disillusionment and bloodshed that followed, he'd remained opposed to war with a country that was striving still for liberty.

"Brother, even if I was prepared to let you go, it could never be to a war I consider misdirected, you must see that?" he'd appealed to Aaron on the first occasion he refused him. And he hadn't added, since there seemed no sense in doing so, that he also thought the boy a deal too like their father to derive anything but harm from military influence.

Michael Corbyn had been a soldier all his adult life. Even after his marriage to their mother he'd declined to sell his commission; forcing her to share his lodgings at Shoreham until the expectation of a child had sent her back to Chalkdean. Rafe still had a vivid memory of his father in his crimson and silver uniform and white-cockaded hat, stooping to lift his solemn little boy beneath the arms and toss him in the air. A man as full of charm and red haired energy as Aaron had become. He'd seemed like a god to his nine year old son, the summer he returned to sire Aaron and throw his father-in-law's ordered household into such a state of uproar. But in later years – prompted by Aunt Drusilla, who'd always detested her impecunious brother – Rafe came to see his father as he was, as callous, irresponsible and immature. And with such knowledge had come resentment for the martial ethos that fostered such defects in its soldiers (and which in the end had permanently removed his father from this mortal coil whilst marching in close-order up a certain Bunker Hill outside the erstwhile American colony of Boston in Massachusetts).

No indeed, he'd been right to refuse Aaron on that and all the other times of asking. The only pity being that in denying the boy his chance of a King's Commission, he appeared inadvertently to have driven him further into the disreputable arms of Tolemy Harris and his free-trading associates. Out of the smoke you might say, and into the smother! Rafe stretched his long legs and sighed, avoiding his aunt's accusing eyes to stare out at the passing landscape.

As they continued their descent the Chalkdean estate came up to meet them, enfolding the landau within the steep banks of its drive. Just now they were close-mown, save for an occasional stand of foxgloves or flowering willowherb which the sentimental haymakers had spared. But later there'd be scabious and harebells on the banks, delicate blue blossoms which bowed to every passing cart and chaise before falling in their turn to the scythe that would make way for the primroses and cowslips of the spring. Seasonal delights which followed one another in due sequence whatever the year, whatever the national state of peace or war. And would doubtless continue to do so, Rafe reflected, whether Aaron settled down to farm or joined the King's volunteers, or chose to risk his neck-bone running freight through Sellington Gap. A reassuring thought.

As the drive began to find a level, its banks gave way abruptly to the greenish trunks and spreading branches of the sycamore avenue the last of the Wenhams had planted to protect his house from south-easterlies off the Channel. For a moment or two even Aunt Drusilla's bilious expression had assumed a mellow aspect beneath its canopy. But not for longer.

"I make no doubt you'll find your brother in the stables," she enounced, waiting only for the top of the manor garden gate to appear alongside before rising to her feet. It was a privilege she'd always demanded, the right to anticipate her nephew's employees and make them seem dilatory in her service. Part of the secret of her dominance. For with whatever celerity he hurried back to open the carriage door and fold down the step, poor Gabel was never swift enough to beat her to it.

"For all the good your notion of a trimming is like to do any of us," Drusilla flung back at her nephew as she sailed up the garden path, brushing the lavenders with her skirts on either side. "Oh yes, I know you too well, Sir. By the time you've finished wrapping it in clean linen for him, I'll lay the scoundrel won't know whether he's been taken to task or congratulated on his restraint!" A remark that required no answer. And indeed his aunt had already swept on through the stone portals of the doorway and out of sight before Rafe could think to offer one.

For practical considerations of drainage and ventilation, the original Saxon stead and the Wenhams' later medieval manor at Chalkdean had both occupied sites a little above the combe bottom, with their cottages, stables and outbuildings disposed in the hollow beneath them. And despite innumerable improvements and additions in subsequent centuries, their basic configuration remained the same. Thus it was that from Drusilla's garden gate the landau continued its descent past the east frontage of the house and the door of Rafe's surgery to the coach-house and stables below. The manor itself was without architectural pretension. A clutch of mossy roofs and twisted Tudor chimneys rambling back from the four tall gables of russet brick that overlooked the garden; with oak timbering jostling the knapped flintwork of the drive front and windows of every shape and dimension adding to its air of comfortable confusion. The stables, on the other hand, had been entirely rebuilt to modern specification when Godfrey Heathcote first purchased the estate from the Wenham trustees – laid out around an open yard with ample haylofts above the stalls and dormitories for the grooms and stable-lads over the coach-house.

They'd always been a favourite haunt of Aaron's, the Chalkdean stables, for he valued his horses above all other possessions. And even before the carriage turned in through the yard entrance, Rafe could hear his brother's familiar whistle above the din of iron-shod hooves and wheels on flintstone cobbles.

Chapter Four

He found the young rogue in sleeves and weskit, busily scrubbing the sweat from his black hunter Nimrod with the remnant of a woollen tammy. The horse's saddle-blanket and Aaron's own expensive coat lay together, tossed carelessly over a stable door. And approaching them across the open expanse of the yard, Rafe felt unwarrantably stuffy and overdressed of a sudden in his snuff-brown fustian and beaver hat – disadvantaged as ever when forced to confront his brother on his own proving ground.

"Aaron!"

The strength of his own voice surprised him, for he'd intended only to silence the exasperating whistle. "Brother, I believe you know why I'm here," he amended on a quieter note. Only to be goaded into a further display of irritation by the boy's deliberate failure to react. "In the name of God, Sir, do me the favour of attending at least when I speak," he heard himself bluster – sounding all too distressingly like their aunt on a number of similar occasions. And then perforce must stand and wait with his two fists jammed in the pockets of his coat, while the other took care to remove every last fleck and speck of lather from the horse before finally vouchsafing him an answer.

"Tell me, Ray, why is it that you atheists find it so damn difficult to leave God out of things?"

An escaping lock of bright red hair described an arc like a sabre slash across Aaron's face. His eyes were narrowed to slits as he squinted up into the sun, his skin taut and faintly freckled over the cheekbones. A chain rattled in a nearby stall and Nimrod shuffled on the cobbles. "And if you're thinking to read me a lecture on my conduct in church this morning, then I'd say you were in no case for that either." Aaron's voice flat-toned and ironic, as always when addressing his brother. "Not when I've heard you declare a dozen times that the world's divinities are little more than monuments to its peoples' weaknesses. Save your breath, Ray, there's a good fellow. I vow we've all of us had a bellyfull of preachifying for one day.

"And if that ain't the truth now, Nimrod, then I'll be shot," he added as an aside to the restive horse.

That his brother's words had struck a chord of truth, Rafe could hardly deny. It was a fact that his own sense of logic could no longer permit him belief in a merciful deity whose scheme of Creation included the kind of miseries he'd witnessed as a student and a physician – stinking gin cellars and syphilitic children on the streets of London, undernourishment and rickets in village hovels, epidemics everywhere to carry off one child in three. Aaron was right. He had no time for a god who could fashion such vulnerable creatures as men and then proceed to scourge them with pain and fear, threaten them with damnation and bribe them with the hollow promise of immortality. And for what purpose? 'Why for His own glorification,' said the theologians – to demand the acknowledgement and worship of these faulted creatures and bask like some great reptile in the warmth of their praise. Yet the observance of Christian ritual was something of another case. And if Rafe permitted himself the small hypocrisy of Sunday churching, it was because he allowed for its benign influence on communities like Sellington. He could not agree with the radicals in Paris and London who clamoured for the extermination of religion. Because he saw, as they apparently did not, that the great majority of mankind depended on the hope of an ultimate paradise to face the harsh realities of life on earth – to console them for all those innocent babes, young mothers, sons and husbands who died annually of the croup, of child-bed fever or of smallpox. To worship a god created by Man, in fact, in the image of his own most desperate needs.

Watching the repeated strokes of the body-brush on the horse's already shining flanks, Rafe tried again to explain the thing to the boy as he had so often in the past.

"All right, Aaron," he acceded, "in fairness I'll admit 'tis true,

I'm in no way to sermonize on religion. And nor would I claim to be better than the man who can. But at least I recognize my duty I think, to see beyond my own beliefs to those that uphold others; and I beg you to do likewise, Sir. For like it or not, Aaron, you have a responsibility to discharge to those less fortunate than yourself – an example to set in your behaviour here on the estate. Aye, in the church too. And perhaps more to the purpose, in your dealings with that blackguard Harris and his crew. Do but consider, Brother; they're contrabanders, lawless and desperate fellows! 'Tis not only wrong to associate with them now with talk of French invasion in the air, but the duty of any loyal Englishman, I'd say, to oppose them."

"Ah duty! You did say 'duty', Sir?"

"You know I did. The duty of an Englishman."

"Duty then, so now at last we come to it!" In the act of replacing Nimrod's saddle, Aaron spun round to face his taller brother. "And do you agree with the parson, Ray, that the trade which has stood between our villagers and the poor rates these two hundred years is nothing less than a sin of avarice? Do you tell me that it is my duty to set an example in the face of this mythical invasion, when you and Aunt Drusilla and little Parson-devil-dodger himself have all taken a share of moonshine in your time, and without ever a sight of the receiver's fine? And what of our dear aunt's preference for green hyson tea? How is it she comes by it so reasonable, would you say? And what is it that you fine English gentlemen smoke by the fireside of an evening? Wild tom-bacca, Brother? Or dried rabbit tressles?"

"Aaron . . ."

"And tell me as a fact, Brother-dear, with your hand on your virtuous heart; have you never bottled off a tub of geneva or of rum for your own table? Nor taken a dallop or a keg for your doctoring in the place of coin? Well, have you or have you not?"

"That's all beside the mark as well you know – and after your behaviour this afternoon, Aaron, I warn you I'm in no humour to be wilfully misunderstood."

"But on the contrary, Sir, I understand you all too well. You said it yourself, when it comes to the pinch you're no better than the rest of us for all your moralizing. You're all jaw, Ray, like a sheep's head. And for my life, I have no appetite for such lean fare!"

With which he gave the horse's girth a final wrench and sprang back into the saddle, scattering bantams in all directions as again he applied the spur.

Yet all things reviewed, Rafe thought, there was nothing so very original or even unnatural about a youngster like Aaron becoming involved with the local traders. All moralities were relative, he reminded himself, as he retrieved his brother's coat from the stable door and prepared to face Aunt Drusilla alone across the starched and undoubtedly smuggled Roanes linen of her luncheon table. Whatever he'd said to Aaron, in Sussex such ancient commerce was scarce to be considered a crime by any but a Revenue man, even in wartime. And in every likelihood his brother would grow naturally beyond the influence of Tolemy Harris and his kind. He was not a vicious youth – teasy, damnably so, but in no way vicious. In many ways Aaron was still little more than a wilful adolescent, Rafe told himself, missing his mother still for all his brave assurance. But given time and a brother's good counsel, he felt sure the young rebel would relapse eventually into virtue.

* * *

As he turned Nimrod up from the drive and onto the steeper slope of Friston Hill, Aaron stifled conscious thought, abandoning himself to sensation. Above the trees on the exposed southern flank of the hill a barrage of heat and light awaited them, he and the horse. It drew them up into a redolent atmosphere of thyme and sunbaked turf, combining with the after-effects of a sleepless night and the spirits Aaron had consumed to give him an exhilarating sense of expansion. As if inches counted for nothing. Higher, taller, bigger now than his brother – that's how he felt.

He controlled Nimrod instinctively and with the minimum of effort, thundering over the brow and headlong into the valley beyond. Success with a horse, as Aaron saw it, was a simple matter of domination. Your will over his. For as with his remote ancestors who danced in the antlers of the deer they'd slain, there was something primitive in Aaron Corbyn that strove to claim for himself the power of each of the stallions he'd broken. At the top of the second hill he drew rein, sufficiently reassured by his own performance to entertain an affectionately disrespectful image of

Brother Ray on the broad old slug of a Welsh cob that he rode.

'Like a bottletit on a horse-turd,' thought Aaron, 'for all his years of riding!'

If his own outburst in church had ruffled Rafe's fine sensibilities, he'd fully intended to make reparation. Even to endure their aunt's sniffs and frosty silences over Sunday luncheon if needs must, for the sake of eating in peace with the brother who now represented all the family that was left to him. But at his first glimpse in the stable yard of those fond reproachful eyes, a familiar surge of defiance had driven Aaron to resaddle instead.

Poor old Ray – worthy and conscientious enough for a score of empirics and college physicians. Ray, who'd forgotten more Latin and Greek than Aaron would ever know, yet who was still as blind to the obvious as he'd ever been. With all his long academical training his brother couldn't seem to grasp that it was the game of life that counted, not the rules people invented for it. The same ruthless game of hazard it had always been right down the ages, old as the itch. What was virtue in plain fact, what made of and where to be found?

'What can it avail to drive forth a snail? – Or make a sail of a herring's tail...?' Another old country rhyme they'd both of them learned at their mother's knee. Aaron smiled bitterly and reached up to drag the confining ribbon from his red hair, to shake it out in the wind and sun . . . *'Or books to compile of manners and style? – Vice to revile and sin to exile? – To teach or to preach as reason will reach . . .?'* What were responsibility and respectability after all but cloaks for the naked truth? Aaron had no illusions or sentimental notions, no time for abstract ideals or profundities. In life there was but one obligation, and that was to oneself. But one important choice to be made, as old Ray would doubtless discover some fine day. You chose either to win in life, or to lose.

Aaron himself had learned that lesson long since in the rough competitive company that so often beckoned him beyond the confines of his brother's estate. And notably on the famous downland racetrack that now lay beneath him at the foot of the hill.

For years the best young riders of the district had met on this track on appointed Sundays through the season to try their mounts against Tol Harris and his crew; with sporting gentlemen from Lewes and Brighthelmstone to lay odds on their chances of success, and quite as much gold like to change hands in an hour or two of racing as in a whole morning on the local corn exchange. A treacherous three mile downhill course it was, snaking through the chalkhills from the Horsemaster's own headquarters on Lullington Heath down to the reedbeds of the Cuckmere river near three hundred feet below – deserted this Sunday, save for the rabbits and fat little South Down sheep that shared its grazing. Deserted, but not for Aaron. Because as he and Nimrod joined the track at the great left-hand curve that swept it down through Charleston Bottom to the river, he encountered his own combative spirit time and again powdering past him in the contrary direction. More often than not he'd won his races in recent years. More often in fact than any other rider since Tolemy Harris had quitted the field. A basis for the bond between them.

The spirals of blue smoke that betrayed the position of Harris's camp in the hills had been visible to Aaron almost from the moment he'd left Chalkdean; and now as he entered the settlement itself, a seductive odour of woodsmoke and savoury onion stew issued forth with the dogs to greet him.

"Geemeny! The red devils've come for us!"

A grotesquely wrinkled old woman looked up from her cooking pot to wave a wooden spoon at the youth with the flaming hair. "What's it like in 'ell then, Raddlepoll?"

It was an old joke between Tol's mother and Aaron, and she followed it with a high-pitched cackle of appreciation at the cheeky fig o'Spain gesture he flourished at her over his shoulder, thumb thrust out obscenely between two forefingers. "Come back and fetch it for yesself if you've a mind, dearie. I'll warrant you'll not find old Dorcas shy!"

The site of her son's headquarters had been well chosen, set like a fortress in a high fold of the hills that sheltered its shacks and shanties and primitive bender tents from the winter wind. A rare pocket of loamy topsoil meant richer grazing, deeper rooting hawthorns and elders here than elsewhere in the downland. Evidences of the place's earlier cultivations were still visible on its eastern slopes, in the raised 'lynchet' banks of some ancient field system. But its present occupants raised only horses and game fowl, and the children of their casual liaisons.

Tolemy Harris himself had first come to the Heath as a competitor in its racetrack steeplechases, in the days when his name had been plain 'Thomas' and his horse-dealing trade pronounced by many 'horse-*stealing*'. The come-by-chance child of a Sellington girl and a travelling tinker of that mysterious Rómani race which Sussex folk identified as 'Egyptian', he'd early been rejected as a half-bred by both his parents' communities. A Gypsy to the villagers, a Gaújo to the hedge-people and neither fish nor fowl to either, the young Harris had learned perforce to make his living between them. At the great Rómani fairs of Heathfield and Crowborough he'd soon become a familiar figure in an outlandish floral tailcoat with a row of silver crown pieces shanked for buttons, trading stolen horses artfully coped and coloured to disguise their distinguishing marks. Later he'd taken to jockeying for the sporting gentlemen on the downland racetracks of Lewes and Alfriston and Lullington Heath, and to supplying mounts and pack-horses to the contrabanders of the Sussex coast. From which it had been but a short step for a man without loyalties to providing horses for their natural adversaries – for the Revenue men, for the magistrates of Lewes and the officers of the garrison towns of Seaford and Newhaven.

As a horsemaster of local repute, Harris had no hesitation in accepting a post as an Assistant Riding Officer in the pay of His Majesty's Customs – to ride with the hounds, as it were, while continuing to supply the hares with their best possible means of escape. Until such time that is as it suited him to inform on the contrabanders, to be instrumental in breaking up the gangs that were then operating out of Sellington and East Dean – preparatory to taking over their landing trade for himself.

Riding up through Harris's camp with a pack of yelping lurchers at his heels, Aaron's interested eye tallied the unmistakable signs of the Horsemaster's success – in the gleam of gold and the lustre of silk, a glimpse of turkey carpeting through a crooked doorway or an Arabian bloodhorse carelessly picketed out amongst the sturdy gypsy ponies. Connected by its notorious racetrack and a network of lesser downland tracks to half a score of favoured landing places along the coast, and within easy reach of the old coach road over the downs to Lewes, the Heath was well placed as the centre of an operation as extensive in its way as that of the old Hawkhurst Gang in Kent. With his contrabanding and

Revenue contacts, Harris had soon recruited his own gang and established himself in a fair way of business with the merchants of the City of London. And of recent years it had been said that his pony trains left Sussex for the capital more frequently than the stage-coaches; with bribed men in the toll-houses along the way, and sufficient French spirits already stored in his fences' entrepôts at Lambeth and Stockwell to keep the entire city comotose for a month.

In equivalent circumstances Arthur Gray, the leader of the Hawkhurst Gang, had erected for himself a vast and splendid mansion at Seacox Heath. But the riches of Croesus himself could never have induced a Harris to build.

"There's summat unaccountable in the mortar that works into your cistern and buggers you in the end, moosh," the Horsemaster had once confided. And it was no matter of chance, Aaron realized, that the very hub of Tolly's trading empire as he now approached it was suspended between four huge red-painted wheels. Never mind the vehicle's patent unsuitability for the narrow downland tracks, or the rust that caked its axles and skid-pans, or the nettles that flourished beneath it. The enormous eight-horse stage waggon in which he dwelt was clearly as much a symbol to Tolemy Harris as the Egyptian title he'd adopted. In his choice of a home, as in his forename, he inclined to his father's nomadic heritage. Ready to hitch up and move on, or so he claimed, at any time he chose.

Between the curved rad-shafts of Tolly's waggon a ladder stairway ascended six steps to the triangular flap of its entrance. A sloe-eyed child in a brocaded waistcoat, straining to hold up another little smaller than herself, watched Aaron unblinkingly as he dismounted to kick the dogs aside and tether his horse. But he was well enough known on the Heath by this time, and no one stepped forward to challenge his entry.

From within, the waggon's external superstructure of ash hoops and tarred canvas was entirely concealed by a lining of antique tapestry; a vaulted tunnel of flowers and trees and crowding figures, with medieval ladies upright on one wall and standing on their wimpled heads on the other. Aside from a small window-flap callously hacked through the priceless Flemish fabric at the back of the vehicle, it was without ventilation. An extravagant number of candles in silver sconces added the reek of burning tallow to an atmosphere already heavy with the odours of brandy and tobacco and unwashed bodies. And everywhere Aaron looked he saw their yellow flames reflected in gilded ornaments and coloured Venetian glassware – dancing across polished surfaces, diffused in the slippery satins of the cushions that littered the floor, and in the counterpane of crimson silk that draped the Horsemaster and his near companions sprawling among them.

"Corbyn! Ye young son of a whore!"

Light cascaded like crimson water from Tolly's proud paunch, the most obvious measure of any man's success in a time of flat bellies and staring ribs. He heaved it at Aaron beneath the silk in a crude salute. And in the act of transferring its bulk from the girl on one side of him to she on the other, he paused politely to extend an invitation to his visitor.

"'Op in with us, moosh, if you've a mind, and make a proper team of it!" He twitched the counterpane aside to reveal an heroic spectacle of corpulent vigour. A tangled Laocoön group lacking only the rearing serpent, and that not entirely.

"Come on, ye young jockey," the Horsemaster coaxed, "and let's see you take this little filly 'ome to the post, eh?"

"What? and risk spoiling her mouth for your bit?"

The girl moved languorously, and in the candlelight her skin gleamed with a fine sheen of perspiration. But Aaron was never the man for another's leavings. "No Sir. I'll make shift to break my own nags if you don't mind," he said with studied impudence. "Aye, an' prick 'em home too, Sir, with my own cock-spur!"

Tolly's laughter shook the waggon. "My eyes and limbs! Bust me if the kiddy ain't as sharp as a packet of needles!

"Up out of it then, Livvy," he added as an aside to the rejected girl. "And fetch the young gentleman a nice bit of bait on your way, girl. I'll swear 'e's 'arf as thin as a rasher of wind. Drop of O'Davey wouldn't go amiss neither, Liza. Gee-woot then – move your poops!"

He gave the nearest buttock a nostalgic pat as the two girls rose sullenly to obey. And then gathering the counterpane in about his own impressive haunches, he beckoned Aaron to join him on the floor amongst the cushions. "Well set you down 'ere halong of me, boy, and listen to your old Tolly cast your future for ye like a proper Rómani chál."

Harris' idea of a nice bit of bait was the best part of a leg of lamb as it transpired, succulently tender as only thyme-grazed mutton could be, and more than likely originating from the Corbyn's own teg flocks on the adjacent hills. The curiously named 'O'Davey', on the other hand, was of a clear quality and fiery potency that nothing of local origin could begin to imitate.

"Middling little old drop that. A woman may 'ave the drawing of you, moosh. But thank the Lord with a bottle or a tub 'tis the other way about, eh?"

Tolly quaffed a bumper of the spirit in a single draught, and then began to search out the residue from his beard and moustache with the tip of an athletic red tongue. "Oh-der-vee," he enunciated, relishing the triple Gallic syllables with the final traces of their namesake. "Know what she is, d'ye kiddy? Or 'ow we come by 'er?" A pair of small eyes folded within the fatty creases of his face considered his visitor shrewdly. Sharp black little animal eyes like a weasel's.

"*Eau de vie* – 'Water of life'. Cognac in this instance distilled from the second pressing – beach-hugged up from La Rochelle to Fécamp, I'd imagine, and thence across direct?" Almost more than anything, Aaron hated to be patronized.

"Right y'are – Faycom's the place for wet goods, and that's a fact." Tolly belched appreciatively. "Best little old port for contraband. No light'ouse, d'ye see? And there's where you'll double your fortune pal, take it from Tolly. 'Tain't no kind of fortune-telling trick to see that."

"I'faith, and do you say so? And all out of *eau de vie* and mutton-sweat, would you have us believe?"

"Outter *gold* Sir!"

The Horsemaster interrupted himself in some reminiscent exploration of his own anatomy beneath the counterpane to flourish a massively ringed paw at Aaron, laden with golden hoops and signets. "Gold, no bounds! Fencing-cullies can't pay enough of it these days for Frenchy goods, wet or dry – and Frog-eaters'll sell ye anything you fancy justabout, and for a quarter 'er natural worth, just so long as ye pays 'em in British gold angels."

The hand disappeared. "And plenty of room in the deal for lining your own side-pockets," Tolly added casually. "I'd say that were eyeproof."

Aaron lowered his pale lashes to mask the gleam of interest in his own eyes. It was true of course. The four year financial crisis across the Channel, with successive devaluations of the Franc, had put gold at a premium in revolutionary France. Robespierre's National Convention needed a constant supply of bullion for minting the coin to pay its troops in the Low Countries and elsewhere. And despite Pitt's recent Traitorous Correspondence bill, there were men at Westminster even now publicly applauding such gainful trade with the enemy. It was the time for bold action and quick profits, not for timid insularity. As Tolemy said, anyone with eyes must see it.

"If we could but make sufficient runs before the Duke of York beats 'em in Holland," Aaron meditated as if to himself, toying still with the steam of his glass. "Or our new warships bottle 'em up so tight in their harbours that not even so much as a fishing smack would get through to them . . ."

"There now, didn't I allow the kiddy were sharp? Now you've got the fore-'orse by the 'ead, moosh. More runs and more gold for all – that's it in round numbers. And a man of our own in Faycom to set us up, eh? There's a thought to look at. A boy with a French tutor in 'is past and a bit of knowledge of the fine world, comprenny? Be the making of any young squab, that would."

The eyes of the two men met, naked now of all pretence. When an idea attracted Aaron he gave it his full attention.

'And time enough for tidy morals when I've a wrinkle or two more in my own arse,' he thought pragmatically. Unlike his brother, he'd always believed in an afterlife, in his own immortality and the ultimate choice between heaven and hell that it implied. It was simply that Aaron felt brave enough, far enough away from death still, to look the devil in the face for a while yet before surrendering himself to moral rectitude. Time enough for Rafe's good deeds when he was as old as Aunt Drusilla, as fat and well greased on other men's cupidity as Tolemy Harris, lolling like the Cham of Tartary in all the smuggled splendour of his stage waggon.

Chapter Five

For upwards of a fortnight Ellin had entirely deprived herself of clifftop excursions. For her a signal achievement. And on the inevitable day when inclination finally conquered resolution, she contrived to lie abed later than usual at least, to arrive with her sketchbook and crayons no earlier than the Ashby flocks.

But this time the tide was out. In place of calm reflective water a landscape of rocks and pools and limp brown seaweed now lay unattractively exposed, combining with the dying hawthorn, half a dozen beached herring boats and any number of milling sheep to make the whole subject impossibly busy. And long after the shepherd and his dogs had driven the last bleating ewe from the beach, the little pastellist on the cliff above strove valliantly on to impose some sense of order to her first hasty delineations. As an afterthought she'd resorted to some fashionable 'morbidezza' shading here and there, then to a little softening and blurring with the fingertip, and finally to a sudden impulse to tear the thing from the book, screw it into a ball and fling it out over the cliff.

'If the beastly thing refuses to co-operate, then it deserves no better,' she maintained. 'That's it and all about it!' But before she closed the book she ran a crayony finger down the serrations in its margin, which were all that remained now of her two attempts at the view. If only she could as easily tear her memory of the first of them from her mind!

Since the Sunday when he'd so scandalously berated her father from the nave of his own church the younger Mr Corbyn had attended neither morning prayers nor evensong. Although, each time her glance alighted on his empty seat in the Corbyn stall,

Ellin's incorrigible imagination had made up the deficiency by supplying all the wanting details of costume and figure and queued 'coquelicot' hair. With great civility the boy's aunt, Miss Drusilla Corbyn, had called at the parsonage only the previous week to enquire of Miss Rimmer's health and press on her a basket of wasp-pitted greengages from the Manor garden. But as the lady's condescension on that occasion had not extended to entering her house, and since no further invitations to tea at Chalkdean had been forthcoming, Ellin had been driven to speculation as to the whereabouts of the younger nephew – and to village gossip, second-hand through the parsonage maidservant. Suggestions were rich and various. Caleb Fowler at the forge had heard it of Mr Turner the Chalkdean coachman, that the young master had set forth on a visit to his Uncle Barnabas in Tunbridge Wells. Whereas the landlord of the Lamb tavern had had it from a fisherman, who'd had it of a riding officer that a brick-topped lad of young Corbyn's description had been seen on the Bourne turnpike at Dicker Common, flying like a mail-rider toward London. While old Mrs Pyecroft, who'd known Master Aaron as she said since he was catering about in long frocks, was telling anyone who cared to listen that he'd run off to join the Military for sure – and all against his brother's intentions.

Against the racket of a tumbling barrel-churn in her dairy, Ann Ashby gave credit to a still more outlandish suggestion. "Glory, gone for certain, as the milkmaid said to 'er swain be'ind the cattle shed," she informed Ellin with a good natured smile. "Gone away abroad m'dear, surelye. Mustn't say where, must we? But tell you what, if but the 'arf we 'ear of be true, Ma'am, that young rogue'll either come back a rich man, or else a guillotine's 'ead shorter than 'e were before!"

Though of all the explanations for Aaron's absence, Ellin reflected as she returned the crayons to her drawing box and began to retrace her steps, Ann Ashby's must certainly be widest of the fact. In France Robespierre's dictate: 'Terror without virtue is evil – virtue without terror is helpless' had become the slogan of the Terror itself. In the Place de la Révolution in Paris, in Nantes and Toulon and in most of the great cities of the new Republic, its execution machines – its dreadful 'guillotines' – were reaping their own gruesome harvest this summer. No surely, wherever Aaron

Corbyn had disappeared to, whatever his involvement with the local contrabanders, he could hardly have been rash enough to embark for France of all places at such a time?

In the weeks following her second unsuccessful sketching expedition, the public newspaper reports of events across the Channel had tended to confirm Ellin in this conclusion, and her father in his conviction of man's essential baseness. Forty, fifty, a hundred heads a day for the baskets through July and August and on into September. And when it had become further obvious that local trade with the executioners not only continued but showed every evidence of expansion, the Reverend Rimmer's outrage acknowledged no bounds.

"Lord, discover their plots, discomfort them and shake their babel down!" he privately exhorted the Almighty when he awoke in the night to the sound of hoofbeats or creaking cleat boards. And publicly, the strench of brimstone ever in his nostrils, he'd thrown himself into a series of weekly sermons which, while continuing to enhance his popularity as a gratis Sunday entertainment, effectively excluded him and his daughter from all other forms of social intercourse with his parishioners. The Ashbys no longer bade them to Sunday luncheon at Bury Farm. At haymaking, day-labour was so unaccountably scarce that the crop on the church glebe could hardly have been got in before its seed dropped, had it not been for the team Mr Rafe Corbyn sent over from Chalkdean to mow and carry for the parson. Meantime Jeemes Elphick, the parish clerk, became notably less willing in the performance of his duties. Likewise the parsonage maidservant. And even the sick were increasingly apt to drift into sleep or unconsciousness, Ellin noticed, when duty prompted Papa to a parochial visit.

Papa himself was undeterred. Since the death of Ellin's gentle young mother in bearing the child of his body eighteen years before, the main force of all his human passions had been diverted to the service of the Lord. A Lord cast in the mould of his own frustrated needs. For hours on end he'd kneel on the bare boards of his study floor, mortifying the flesh but indulging the spirit, scandalizing the Supreme Being with his endless catalogues of the vices of mankind. In fact so exclusive had become these discourses between Minister and Maker, that little in the way of merely human commerce was found necessary. For relaxation Papa might sit and smoke his pipe or pinch at his snuff-box whilst reading from the Good Book or the Sussex Weekly Advertiser. But he seldom thought to seek out the flesh and blood companionship of his daughter across the hallway, or in any way to compensate the poor girl for the society his solitary habits denied her.

Poor girl indeed! No conversation but of the most banal kind with the maidservant, Mary Codsall, or with Annie Ashby down in her dairy; no society of her own level. Distrusted by the villagers without, Ellin's existence within the parsonage was circumscribed most drearily by domestic necessity. By the planning of frugal meals in endless succession, the feeding of poultry, the repair of garments she'd already repaired time and again before. On weekday evenings there was the labour of teaching the intractable Mary to cipher and say her catechism, spoiling their eyes by candle-light. On Sundays mandatory church attendance. But no romance – no opportunities anywhere for enlarging her stock of experience! For all her means of access to the circulating library at Lewes or the assembly rooms at Seaford or Brighthelmstone, those towns might have been as distant to her as the Indies. Which left only her drawing crayons and an ill-tuned spinet for recreation.

Indeed the only really interesting incidents in Ellin's life these days were those generated within her own imagination – on her way to the dairy perhaps, in the phantasy of another sudden encounter with Aaron Corbyn, returned from heaven-knows-where to add a little zest to her dull existence. With a deliciously guilty pang of pleasure to live over those earlier extraordinary meetings with that infamous bad character on the cliff or in the church. Or to follow a known contraband trail on one of her lonely walks, imagining herself concealed in the darkness, risking life and maiden state to see the night-riders pass by. Or at home in her own parlour to harrow herself as best she might with newspaper reports of desperate emigrés shipwrecked along the coast at Seaford, or of the former Queen of France locked up in a tiny cell in the Conciergerie prison in Paris.

It was from one of her father's newspapers, sent over second-hand from Chalkdean, that Ellin learned in mid-October of the pathetic hauteur with which Marie Antoinette had ridden down the Rue Saint Honoré to the guillotine, her sunken cheeks rouged in a final gesture of the frivolity for which she'd always been notorious. A drama at last! A romantic tragedy of truly gothic complexion which surely demanded solitude and lowering landscapes to do it the proper justice?

For once the elements obliged. By noon that day a cover of dark nimbus clouds shadowed the valley, promising rain and deepening the hills on either side to a dramatic indigo. All through luncheon the wind rattled and battered at the parsonage windows. And immediately the meal was over and Papa had withdrawn to his study, Ellin pulled a weather-cloak around her shoulders with an old hooped calash to cover her bonnet, and sallied forth with theatric resolution into the gathering storm. The wind was a sou'westerly off the sea, salt-laden and whirling with autumn leaves. Violence to match the force of her own emotions. It roared in her ears like the sound of a great crowd, pressing the yellow grass-bennets in towards her, agitating the sheep bells on the higher slopes into a mad music of their own. With a satisfactory thrill of horror Ellin imagined the French Queen facing the roar of the press, the jangle of the tumbril's bells as it rolled her on over the cobbles to the blade that would shear her life away. Heaven have mercy on her!

As the image faded from her mind, the wind forced the tears from the corners of Ellin's eyes in two long streaks, up over her temples and into the disordered brown hair that blew about her face. Tears for a foreign aristocrat? A lady she'd never seen nor even particularly admired? Or was she weeping for herself – for the feelings a young man had promiscuously stirred in her and then uncaringly abandoned?

Either way, the rain obliterated those foolish, self-indulgent tears, when a few minutes later it came slanting in from the Channel.

When Ellin returned to the parsonage, forced home by the inadequacy of her mantle and slippers in the face of a genuine cloudburst, it was to the sound of raised voices within her father's study. Papa had company. Not, as she later assured herself, that she had the slightest intention of overhearing. It was simply that the voices had been so very loud. While the necessity of pausing on the hall drugget to remove one's wet bonnet and muddy slippers must inevitably bring one into close proximity of the study door . . .

"But d'ye reckon there be regular 'arm in this 'ere night-trading, Parson?" a querulous young Sussex voice was demanding from within. "More 'armful than swearing and that, would you say?"

"Harm? Harm, YOU IGNORAMUS!" Ellin's father exclaimed in the largest capitals. "Oh Lord, *when* will this generation learn? Their ears are dull of hearing! Their eyes they have closed, lest at any time they should hear and see and understand! Why there's SIN, boy," he railed, "mortal sin I tell you in such wicked and unlawful trafficking!"

"There now – and is that the truth? Well the Lord 'ave mercy on us poor sinners then, Mus Rimmer. For there's precious few 'ereabouts as 'aven't an arm and a leg in the trade, and I doan't deceive ye. Grand folk and all, Sir."

Patently there was one soul in the parish who'd taken Papa's admonishments to heart. "Why there's a Frenchy lugger'll 'eave to yonder before morning, if the sea bain't too rough for 'er," the young voice recklessly divulged, eager now for confession and absolution. "And a tub or a dallop aboard 'er for pritnear all of Sel'ton village, and Jevington and Wannock besides I reckon. And sinners all, d'ye say?"

"Tonight boy? Did you say *tonight*, and here at the Gap?"

Ellin's father swept the other's question peremptorily aside with two of his own. "Tell me truly now as ye hope for salvation, are you positive 'tis for tonight?"

Waiting for the answer, with her mantle gently dripping on the hall tiles, Ellin thought with a shiver of the stories she'd heard of smugglers' informers – of 'peaches' and 'tag-tails' – and the gruesome fates that befell them. I'faith the fellow within must be out of his five wits even to think of springing such a revelation – and on Papa of all people!

A thought which simultaneously occurred to the speaker himself it would seem, as he now floundered on into qualification and denial. "Ah, no be fair, Mus Rimmer – no I never said tonight for sure, strike me if I ever! Tomorrow – as like it'll be tomorrow as tonight, Sir, being as it's so tempesty and all. Or Saturday sennight for aught I can tell. I can't tell ye nothing for sure, Mus Rimmer, baggered if I can!"

"Be still boy – you've said enough."

For all his obvious deficiencies, Papa was not a total fool.

"Remember what joy there shall be in heaven," he added a little more charitably, "over the one sinner that repenteth." And his daughter outside in the hall conceived a hopeful picture of him reaching over to pat the wretched 'tag-tail' on the shoulder.

"Turn thee from thy wickedness and thy sin shall not be thy destruction. The Lord is deep in His judgements and rich in His mercy. And I have no doubt, fellow, that you have ledgered enough in your account with Him this day to preserve your miserable soul from the flames."

"But you're never agoing to interrupt our Traders, Parson, *surelye*?"

The rising panic was obvious in the young man's voice even through a panelled oak door. "All forbid ye should interrupt 'em, Mus Rimmer, for I'll tell you straight I'm a dead man if ye do, Sir! A coffin case for sure!"

Though as bad luck would have it, the conclusion of this interesting exchange was lost to Ellin in the necessity of removing herself to the parlour fire forthwith, as the servant girl Mary Codsall appeared at the stairhead with an expression of frank curiosity on her face. Voices in the hall and the latching of the front door a few minutes later confirmed the visitor's departure. And running barefoot to the window, Ellin was just in time to catch sight of Zebediah Fowler, the blacksmith's noodle-pated youngest, loping up the hill through the rain.

"And oh please God, don't let Papa interrupt them," she beseeched with her face against the cold glass, watching until that foolish and frightened young man had disappeared through the archway of his father's forge. "When all is said, Lord, 'tis really no more than a little contrabanding. Not as bad as thieving, d'ye see? And if the traders themselves must answer for that as a sin, may we not safely leave them to do so on Judgement Day?"

But compared to her father, who lived piously, prayed constantly and had likely forgotten how to sin, Ellin's credit with her Maker was not of the best. In fact as far as meritorious behaviour was concerned, she knew herself to be head over ears in debt. And in all fairness she could hardly blame the Almighty for siding with His ordained minister, when Papa's excited voice summoned her from the parlour door to assist him with harnessing the horse for an errand of urgent business with Mr Justice Collier in Seaford.

"But Papa, 'tis raining hammers and hatchets outside," was the only objection she could think to offer. "T'will be quite dark in an hour or so, and you'll be soaked in the bargain."

"My dear child, 'tis our right judgement and not our bodily comfort that must ever guide our actions."

From behind the thickened lenses of his spectacles her father's eyes, grotesquely magnified, travelled slowly from her own draggled tresses to the dripping hem of her mantle and the set of bare pink toes which protruded beneath it. "And I trust we may endure a shower of rain on the business of the Lord," he added in the sarcastic voice that through her childhood had always proved so devastating to his daughter's petitions, "with at least as much fortitude as the foolish virgin who ventures out without umbrella or pattens, without even an adequate pair of boots to her feet? "In any case," he cleared his throat self-consciously and adjusted the linen bands at his throat, "I am persuaded that it would be best if we took the curricle."

"*We*, Papa?"

For Ellin it was to be a day shock full of surprises. But her father, as impatient of explanations, as intolerant of opposition as ever, was anxious now only to be on his way. "I have reason to suppose that there may be some unpleasantness in the village tonight," he muttered, gesturing irritably for her to retrieve her slippers from the fender and cover her naked feet. "T'will be safer for both of us I think if we rack-up overnight at the Tree tavern in Seaford, at least until this business is concluded. And if Codsall's fearful of remaining in the house alone, you may send the girl to fetch her mother down to sleep on the kitchen settle for the night."

"Papa, that would be folly!"

In all her nineteen years Ellin had never presumed to contradict her parent so flatly, nor with such energy. "But don't you see? Ten to one Mary already knows all she needs to of that young Fowler's business with you this afternoon. Why I'll vow the pair of you might have been heard in Chalkdean for all the trouble you took to lower your voices!"

And having said so much, she had to say the rest. "Papa, I beg you would listen!" She crossed the room impulsively to lay a hand on his thin arm. "If you allow that girl to leave now on any pretext, she'll have half the villains in Sussex out, I guarantee it, before we've even put Betsy to the shafts."

There were still times when he attended to her. When she reminded him perhaps of the wife he had lost. And God knows she had to try. "Oh do but consider, Papa!" she said, forgetting herself so far as to shake his arm in her agitation. "Do you not imagine the authorities would already have acted against these men if they could? But they're too weak, Sir, you know they are! Why there's not a dozen armed officers to the Preventive Force in Seaford. Less than eighty men all told in the entire garrison. And with contrabanders by the score in every port and village down the coast!"

He stared at her in silence while the rain lashed the parlour window; and for a moment surely there'd been uncertainty, even vulnerability, in the great pale eyes behind the lenses? But the Reverend Saul Rimmer's views on life and duty had long been formed without recourse to reasoning. And now he flinched away from the intimate pressure of his daughter's hand, to force the ready quotation – the mystery of God Himself – between them.

"Through the blessings of Heaven they shall be extirpated from the face of the earth. Yea, even if they number ten thousand or ten thousand thousand! They repent not of the works of their hands, nor of their idols of gold and silver. And so shall they be cast into the brimstone pit!"

And staring back into those fanatical unapproachable eyes, as she had so often in the past, Ellin acknowledged defeat.

As usual it had fallen to her not only to bridle and blinker Betsy, but also to direct the involved procedure by which the mare was backed to the shafts and harnessed there. For Papa was one of those impractical people who declined to master commonplace manual skills, including the proper adjustment of neck-collars and saddle-pads and the intricacies of straps and buckles which connected them within a harness. Indeed had it not been for the sheer impropriety of doing so, Ellin fully believed he'd have delegated the reins and the whip to her as well. For in truth her father was little fonder of driving a horse than he was of riding one.

The Rimmer's curricle (the very humblest vehicle from the coach-house of the Bishop's Palace in Chichester) was a battered two wheel chaise of the type officially designed 'rib-chair', but more usually known as 'wear-arse' in view of its total innocence of any kind of spring. Despite its greased hood and driving apron, it afforded its occupants little enough protection from the elements. And even before the Reverend Rimmer and his daughter left the village, the rain had begun to penetrate their outer garments. Peering out through the miniature waterfall that cascaded from the roof, Ellin could see moving shapes behind the windows of the cottages. Here and there the glimmer of a rush light or the pale blur of a watching face. Faces she recognized; Mercy Langshaw two doors up from the parsonage, Mrs Tinsley and old Goody Pyecroft. Women whose husbands and sons could be down on the foreshore even now for all she knew, awaiting the lugger from France. And did *they* know what their parson was about as his shabby little chaise toiled up the hill through the rain? Had Mary already spread the word down the cottage backs? There was something sinister about those watching faces which suggested to Ellin that she had. And despite the worsening weather of the higher slopes, she felt a real sense of relief when the last cottage window slid away behind them and out of view.

At the Gibbet Crossways on the top of the hill they'd turned westward for the long descent to the valley of the Cuckmere, and to Seaford. The vast downland panorama below them, which in a more clement season had inspired the Chalkdean coachman to such near-optimism, was now converted to a battlefield for the opposing elements of earth and sky. Curves and contours which formerly seemed maternal and serene, now crouched like monsters in dark and threatening attitudes. Winds that had caressed now clawed and buffeted, shrieking defiance at the man or conveyance who dared to brave them.

Ellin, as ever, was prey to conflicting emotions. She thought with real alarm of tearing roof fabric, of Betsy falling to break her knees and overset them all on the slippery downhill track. In every shadow and thorn tree at the wayside she seemed to see the hostile faces of the women at the cottage windows. Yet all the time at the very heart of her apprehension, something wild and self-destructive in her was exhilarating – glorying even – in the violence of the tempest.

Oh Ellin! Immoderation, impetuosity – those old besetting sins! Guiltily she glanced at her father's face, expecting disapproval; but discovering to her surprise an excitement equivalent to her own.

'And there you see, he is not so unlike you after all,' she told herself triumphantly. 'Bless us, even Papa has feelings that defy restraint!'

Before Ellin could adjust, though, to such an interesting and novel notion of her parent, a violent lurch of the vehicle recalled her to the immediate dangers of their descent to the river. It was too early in the season still for the flint carts to have done their work, and the way was mired and rutted, awash with running water. With the full weight of the curricle and its occupants bearing down on her breechings from behind, the unfortunate Betsy skidded and stumbled down the slope, occasionally sliding bodily with all four hooves together. And hanging onto the hood supports for dear life, it was as much as Ellin could do to keep her seat.

"That's it, Betsy, there's a girl," she whispered encouragingly at the mare's bunching quarters. As she watched from beneath the hood the Cuckmere river came slowly into view, snaking across the valley floor pewter-grey in the twilight. "A little further, girl, just a little. We're almost there."

On the far side of the river lay Walls Brow and the yellow glimmers of the easternmost habitations of Seaford Town. But to reach them they must first cross the long earth causeway that spanned the river marshes. Ellin's eye ran eagerly ahead to measure the distance. Half a mile? Perhaps a little more? Her glance swept over, snagged, and then reluctantly crept back to something obtrusive on the distant river bridge. A cart, was it? Or a group of cattle? As Betsy slithered the final yards to the foot of the hill the thing took substance; and for the second time that afternoon Ellin reached instinctively for her father's arm, all her apprehensions now come to focus on the phalanx of waiting horsemen that blocked their path.

"Papa!" She clutched at his wet sleeve, shaking it again in frantic emphasis. "Papa, look! Do you not see them?" But of course his spectacles were fogged with moisture, he surely must have missed them?

"Horsemen Papa, a dozen at the least. Rein in – oh rein in here and stop the chaise!" He must stop, he had to! What could she do to make him listen? "Papa please, please pull her in!"

But it was as if he'd gone deaf as well as blind, because again he shook free to slap at the horse's wet back with the slack of the reins; then reached for the whip to lash her forward toward the bridge.

Chapter Six

It was a nightmare, their progress down the causeway; an old terror of Ellin's of a sudden come to life. On the nights when she'd lain awake in the darkness of her little closet in the Bishop's Palace at Chichester, forbidden even the comfort of a rush light – or when sleep itself had admitted the spectres she'd fought so hard to exclude, she had felt as she felt now. In her dreams there'd been no recognizable landscapes. Nothing but a sense of helpless propulsion toward some waiting horror, like the condemned Queen of France in her rolling tumbril. But now in the remote and rainswept gloom of the Cuckmere valley she perceived a horrid and familiar pattern. The realization of every childhood fear. The drumming of the rain on the curricle's roof, scarce heard for the past mile of the descent, now sounded deafening in her ears. The rank odour of the river mud revolted her. The wet fabric of her garments chilled and chafed at her skin. And all the time the segment of causeway framed within the arch of the hood grew shorter, the looming obstruction ahead ever darker and more menacing.

Now Ellin could distinguish individual figures on the bridge. Men who seemed too heavy for the mounts they sat, hatted and muffled to the cheekbones against the rain. Coloured gypsy ponies, head to head and nose to tail, their pied and spotted markings merging in a solid barricade of horseflesh. Closer still she could see heavy oaken cudgels resting on the animals' withers. Weapons which removed all doubt as to their riders' intentions.

'Highwaymen,' thought Ellin, fighting panic. (Real panic now without a trace of illicit stimulation.) 'Saints preserve us!'

And still her father worked the whip to urge them forward.

Between the advancing chaise and the waiting horsemen on the bridge, at a point where some earlier deluge had eroded its surface, a swathe of moving floodwater crossed the road. One more obstacle, as it now appeared, than the wretched Betsy was prepared to tackle.

By the time her passengers had recovered from the suddenness of the mare's decision, it was to find that the other horses had broken ranks to enter the water from the far side – so close already that Ellin could distinguish the riders' features beneath their blacking disguise. Although strangely, at the moment they emerged as men of flesh and blood, the worst of her fears evaporated. To commence with they were not a large group, no more than five or six of them at most. And if their leader was impressive for his girth and for the 'Egyptian' cast of his profile, the rest she thought looked far from easy in their role as highwaymen – their black-daubed faces comically blotched and blotted by the rain.

'And are you still a child, Ellin Rimmer, to be afrighted by phantoms and bogeymen?' she demanded stoutly of herself. 'Gypsies and hedge-people from Lullington Heath, that's all they are as well you know. Common ignorant fellows who're bound to respect a parson's neckbands and a lady's gender when the cards are down.'

And thus emboldened, Ellin was actually preparing to lean from the chaise and request of the nearest piebald face that he would kindly remove himself and his horse from their path, when her father's harsh voice pre-empted her.

"Stand aside there," he commanded at pulpit volume. "Avaunt I say, or by God we'll run ye down!"

Unimpressed by such a threat from an entirely stationary vehicle, the leading horseman merely extended a casual hand to secure Betsy's bridle and turn in his own steed alongside her.

"Proper lamentable weather for travelling, Parson," he observed. "Best see you safe across I'd say, and then turn ye back for 'ome, eh? Afore your little maid 'ere can catch cold?" With which he proceeded to propel a crabbing and recalcitrant Betsy on through the flood toward the bridge and the turning place beyond it.

"Unhand us, you villain! Unhand I say!"

Ignored by his corpulent escort, and now it seemed to be denied all possibility of access to Mr Justice Collier and the military garrison of Seaford, the Reverend Rimmer lost no time in applying to a higher authority. "Confound them! Destroy them! Stretch out Thy hand to smite them, oh Lord!" he wailed into the wind and the rain, half standing in his chariot to brandish his whip like some latter-day Joshua. "Cast them into the depths, I say!" And without waiting for the deliberate processes of Divinity, he launched himself forward to deliver the first blow.

To the parson's horrified daughter it seemed as if the thongs of his horsewhip had acquired some godgiven power of their own. For any normal circumstance the deficiencies of Papa's aim would have ensured that he spent his fury on the curricle's wheels or shafts, or on poor Betsy; on anything in fact but his intended target. But as it was, she watched the whip unfurl with an unerring accuracy – in over the man's high collar, up under the brim of his hat – powerless to prevent it as with a sound like a pistol shot it bit into the unprotected flesh of his cheek.

"Gorr-damme!!"

A split second later the man emitted a great bellow of pain. And as he leapt in the saddle to jerk up on Betsy's bridle, both horses plunged in white-eyed panic.

It was all over in something less than a minute. In a brief confusion of splashing water the animals were brought in hand, with the chaise slewed broadside to the current and its driver still gaping in wonderment at the miraculous provision of the Lord. Over in one sense, but only beginning in another. For as Ellin saw the man rein in and raise his hand and stare at the blood on his fingers, her old sense of nightmare returned.

"Ye never oughtter adone that, Parson." The man turned slowly, wagging his truncheon like an admonishing finger as he heeled his pony back through the water towards them. "That ain't Christian, Parson," he said, his black eyes glittering, "b'aint Christian at all!"

Whether or not he'd actually intended her father a violence with the weapon, it was obvious that Papa himself expected it. And as the man kept on coming toward him another new aspect of his character was revealed to Ellin. Papa's courage was as much moral and as little physical as could be, it seemed. Because already his skinny thigh was trembling like the dodder-grass against hers; and his voice when he spoke was high-pitched with alarm. "Don't you come near me now, don't you dare!" he warned shrilly. "I'll see you in Hell if you so much as touch me – in Hell you dog, depend upon it!"

"Ah, and I'll see ye rubbed down with an oaken towel, Parson, as I'm a living man." And on he came out of the shadows, his terrifying blood-boltered face above them now on a level with the chaise hood.

Cornered, afrighted, marooned as he believed in the eddying floodwater, the little parson struck out again blindly with the stock of his whip, this time to deal the horseman a glancing blow on his riding boot a little above the stirrup. It could hardly have pained him greatly. But under the circumstance the slight smart that the man felt through the polished hessian had been quite enough to call down the full force of his vengeance.

"A pest on you, ye rumbustical old bugger!" he roared. "Take that then, Sir, in fair exchange, and that for your confounded belver!" The heavy oak bat descended with terrific energy on the parson's own stockinged shin. And then again a fraction lower at the same moment that the little man began to scream.

Ellin heard the bone snap at the first blow, felt the agony of the second; and with an incoherent cry of rage that swept before it every other feeling, flung herself straight out of the chaise and into the arms of her father's assailant.

"Whoo-op! Steady up Toby!"

Unable to control his horse, to protect himself from her flailing fists and at the same time to bear the girl up from the flood, the man settled for an opportune fumble of her breasts while Ellin's own weight dragged her down the animal's wet flank and feet first into the river.

"Lud bless my soul," he exclaimed, "I reckon she've set 'er 'eart on catching cold no matter what."

'And oh go and butter your wig!' thought Ellin feebly, expended now and weeping for sheer mortification as they lifted her from the water to set her back beside the moaning ruin of her parent. Someone had retrieved her floating bonnet, and someone else the reins. They placed them in her trembling hands; and then together in a body led Betsy on to cross the bridge and turn beyond, to retrace her path across the causeway and back up the rainswept hill.

The men spoke little to each other and to their captives not at all. But by then Ellin was too wretched, too sickeningly aware of the effects of the road on poor Papa, to care greatly what they thought or did. And when their leader turned back out of the dusk to address her at a point where a track branched off to Chalkdean, she peered out at him dully, her mind too clogged with spent emotion to produce any one of the appropriate reactions.

"Take 'im to Chalkdean, Missy, there's my advice," he offered, pointing down the waggon-track with his truncheon. "Gentleman there's a fair 'and at bone-setting they do say, for all that 'e's a college doctor.

"And as for you, ye old fool," he growled at her father, leaning in to fill the chaise with brandy fumes, "stick to saving souls from 'ere on in, eh? An' recollect old man, if you peach on us now you're like to find yesself in your own graveyard afore long – put to bed with a shovel and six feet of Sussex clay for your counterpane." He flourished his truncheon in the parson's ashen face. "No soldiery, Parson, comprenny? Or you're a dead man!"

And in final emphasis of the point he brought the weapon down again, this time square across the mare's quarter-strap, to send the curricle lurching off into the darkness of the track to Chalkdean.

* * *

By no stretch of imagination could Rafe Corbyn's library at Chalkdean Manor be considered the most comfortable place in which to spend a wet October afternoon. It was ill-lit for one thing, uncarpeted for another, with an inadequately small fireplace for such a large room and a damp north facing aspect. Moreover, much as a lining of calf and morocco bindings might be felt to add distinction to such an office, neither the musty smell nor the sombre appearance of so many books contributed anything at all to its cheerfulness.

From her repeated sniffs and restless shiftings of position, Drusilla Corbyn certainly gave little impression of comfort in her seat by the library fire. And a less generous nature than her elder nephew's might have imagined her sole purpose in remaining there to be one of distracting him from his own pleasure in the place. But Rafe knew his aunt better than that. In the forenoons, while he treated house patients and those still hale enough to beat their own path to his surgery door, or addressed himself to his pestle and his pharmacopeia, she seemed content to spend her time badgering his domestics into efficiency – with all the routine demands of laundering, baking and preserving to occupy her. On fine afternoons, while he viewed the estate with his bailiff or rode abroad to his tenants and cottage patients, his aunt derived obvious satisfaction from the trim flower gardens she'd created around the house – from her own aptitude for bullying plants, weeds and gardeners into like submission. But on inclement afternoons such as this, when no urgent cases summoned and rain confined the pair of them within doors, Rafe understood it to be satisfaction of another kind that Aunt Drusilla sought.

That the Chalkdean household relied upon the lady, and had done ever since she'd volunteered herself to take the helm after her sister-in-law's untimely death, was beyond dispute. Rafe's respect and gratitude were hers by right. And yet she wanted more from him, he'd always sensed it. As a frankly undesirable woman whose appearance and financial independence were neither of them sufficiently handsome to secure a husband – ignored by a feckless brother, provoked by the nephew who most resembled him, disliked by the servants, even abandoned by Nature itself with the coming of her climacteric – Drusilla Corbyn found herself in urgent need of some affection. And it was for this elusive commodity that she sought her elder nephew's company, endured the discomfort of his library.

Rafe understood and even sympathized. But affection is necessarily a reciprocal emotion; and sadly Aunt Drusilla's capacity for appreciating any interest that did not run parallel with her own was strictly limited. She flattered herself that little of consequence escaped her notice. Yet for all her practical skills she lacked human perception to a quite astonishing degree – imagining as a case in point that the act of bringing her lace-mending to her nephew's miserable fire must in itself deserve his approbation; and in her efforts to capture his attention entirely overlooking the fact that it was she and not Rafe who required the reassurance.

Whether he was reading or entering the estate books or studying the latest medical treatise from London, she felt perfectly entitled to sniff and to fidget her feet on the foot-warmer – to interject remarks on the weather, the war, or indeed anything that sprang to mind. And Rafe could well imagine tonight's terse entry in her journal:

> Spent a companionable afternoon in the library with R.
> Finished repairing second-best mechlin lace collar.

Without the faintest suspicion, he felt certain, as to how sorely and consistently she'd tried his patience.

"Bless us, Nephew, the hour is come and what d'ye think?" Her latest interruption as the whirring of the library clock gave notice that it was about to strike.

"I fancy, Aunt, that you're about to tell me what to think," Rafe said wearily. "Is that not so?"

But such gentle irony was lost on Aunt Drusilla. "Five of the clock and no tea," she exclaimed obliviously, laying down her mending and unhooking the spectacles from her cap. "So now I shall have to ring for myself after all, I suppose?"

"Well do by all means, Aunt, if you feel inclined."

"Inclined, Rafe? Did I hear you aright? Because if so I can assure you 'tis no simple matter of inclination. Why if you will insist on these barbarously early rustic luncheons, then you can hardly deny us a little necessary sustenance in the afternoon I think? And here is the hour come and gone, Sir, without so much as a whiff of hyson – and when I bade William most particularly to serve tea in the library at five. Upon my soul I declare there's no object in keeping servants if they're so little to be depended upon!"

It was an old tune of his aunt's played on a well-worn fiddle. And although Rafe thought it doubtful she could have missed the footman's entry with the tea-board at that very moment, she'd risen anyway to grasp the tasselled pull and to ply it with a vigour that would have done credit to any parish bellringer.

"So *here* you are, William!" She released the bell-pull only when satisfied that every servile ear in the household must have heard it and apprehended her displeasure. "When I confess we had quite given up hope of meeting with you this side of supper. Well, set the board down, man, now that you've finally bestirred yourself to bring it, and let's see if Madam Hannah has at least contrived to measure it out correctly."

'And yet I do believe she really cares for Chalkdean,' Rafe thought magnanimously, while his aunt stalked forward to take charge of the beverage that the excisemen and smugglers had between them rendered so indispensible to the English. And in the tail of the same thought he was again reminded of Aaron's latest and most serious dereliction. Aaron in some enemy seaport, in La Rochelle or Fécamp, freighting tea and tobacco and *eau de vie* even now in defiance of the law, and of his brother.

'And how could he have cared so little for his family, for the Corbyns' good name, to have so compromised us? And despite every inducement to lead a useful life here in Chalkdean?' he demanded of the bound philosophers of his bookshelves and for quite the hundredth time.

"Your tea is poured, Rafe," said Aunt Drusilla.

'So you see I am determined to shift for myself, to stand on my own two feet, Ray,' Aaron's most recent letter from France had unrepentently declared. 'And whatever you may make of my trading adventures, remember this, my dear old stumble-stone – I take myself for what I am, accountable to Aaron Corbyn and to no other, be he saint or sinner, Englishman or Frog-eater . . .'

"I said your tea is poured, Sir."

Like many people with imperfect hearing, Drusilla Corbyn hated having to repeat herself. "And considering the time it's taken to reach us," she added sourly, "I make no doubt 'tis more than halfway cold already."

Rafe had barely relieved her of the dish, though, before footman William reappeared at the door with an expression on his simple face that betokened a crisis more desperate even than a part-chilled teapot.

They found the parson's daughter where William had left her, draggled and disarrayed beneath the red-glazed physician's lamp in the porch of Rafe's surgery; and the parson himself in a still sorrier state, slumped in the curricle beyond. The little man shrieked like a wired hare when they lifted him down, and fainted clear away at Rafe's initial attempt to relieve him of his blood-stained stocking. It took three of them to reduce the fracture, nonetheless – with William at the shoulders, and Gabel Turner's steady hand requisitioned from the coach-house to hold the upper limb in place. And Aunt Drusilla, scorning convention to direct the lamplight for her nephew, while at the same time making the most of the occasion to impress on them all the outrage of her sensibilities.

"Oh these times, these intolerable times," she declared theatrically. "A man of the cloth to be so cruelly used. Our own rector, what is more, and Chaplain to the Bishop! 'Tis a hanging matter, Nephew – a hanging matter I tell you, and nothing less!"

On examination, it appeared that his assailant's second blow had misaligned the parson's broken shin to force a bone splinter through the skin, opening a way for the necrosis that so frequently condemned such injuries to eventual amputation. Before splinting and bandaging, Rafe had therefore deemed it a wise precaution to wash the wound with alcohol. An old and proven method which it was said the naval surgeons had borrowed from the Arabs. And one which in this instance was not without its ironic aptitude, he thought wryly. For as it chanced he'd used a French cognac for the purpose from his brother's smuggled store. While from Miss Rimmer's breathless account of events – before they'd packed her off with a maidservant for a change of clothes – it seemed more than likely that the man who'd arranged for its import was also personally accountable for the wound it now salved. But what action to take against the villain? That was the question.

"Why good heaven, Sir, I wonder you could ask! You must send William directly to the justices for a warrant to arrest the rogue," his lamp-holder unhesitatingly asserted over the unconscious body of the parson. "There's no other course open."

"But recollect, Aunt – the fellow's face was blacked. We have no certain proof 'twas Harris. And even if the Rimmers should contrive to identify him positively, I doubt very much there's a jury in Sussex who'd convict such a notable free-trader on their evidence."

"Nor a single local man of principle it would seem, to oppose him in his villainies. Well I confess I thought better of you, Nephew." Aunt Drusilla averted her large nose from the reek of the brandy and sniffed disparagingly. "Or could it be, Sir, that you fear he'd cry rope on someone closer to home? Is that it,

Rafe? Someone you'd see us all damned to protect from his own selfish folly?"

Bending to his complicated eighteen-tailed bandage, Rafe was aware of the lamp jerking impatiently above him, knew she was watching him waiting for his answer. But how to explain the complexity of the thing to a mind as narrow as his aunt's? How to make her see that to use an incident such as this as a means of forcing an unwilling authority to action, could be to ignite a powder keg that had the power to blow half the communities of the downland to Kingdom Come? Easy enough for Aunt Drusilla to talk of magistrates' warrants and hangman's nooses, to set the officers of the law against the contrabanders and then to sit back and watch the bloody outcome like the Quality at a cock match. Easy for one raised as she'd been in a fashionable spa town like Tunbridge Wells. Easy to ignore the injustices of a society in which a farm worker must be ready to support his family on thruppence a day, and expect to hang for the theft of a single sheep from a flockmaster like Sam Ashby who owned three thousand. A society in which any convicted contrabander must die on the gallows or in Botany Bay, on the word of a judge who privately relished smuggled brandy and purchased it with his legal fees at every opportunity!

'And do you agree with the parson, Ray, that the trade which has stood between our villagers and the poor rates these two hundred years is nothing less than a sin of avarice?'

No indeed he did not. There was more to protect here than his brother's skin, whatever his aunt might choose to think. Not that Aaron's life, on the other hand, was to any degree less important than the others'.

'And I'll make him justify it yet, the young blackguard,' Rafe thought determinedly. 'I'll send to him in France through Ashby or the Heath, that's what I'll do. I'll write this very night to demand he use his influence to stop this violence . . .'

"So you intend to do nothing, I suppose," Aunt Drusilla interjected. "To see your own vicar assaulted and afrighted half to death without lifting so much as a finger in his behalf?"

"No soldiery!" The parson's voice cut in before her nephew could supply an answer. A thin falsetto quavering with alarm.

"No soldiery, Corbyn, or I'm a dead man!"

His eyes as they flickered open were remarkably devoid of faith or righteousness – smaller without their lenses, yellow-tinged to confirm Rafe in his diagnosis of a liverish constitution. 'Like the eyes of some wretched hunted creature,' he decided, 'seeking only to protect himself from further persecution.' And ignoring his aunt's objections, he hastened to reassure the pathetic little man as best he might.

"There'll be no further attack from the men who waylaid you, Reverend," he said firmly. "On that you have my word. I've lived and worked with these people for the greater part of my life. I know what carries with them and what does not. And you're right, of course, where contrabanding's concerned, military interference can only serve to make things worse. But there are more ways than one to skin a cat, Sir, and if you will entrust me to try what can be done I believe I can promise you your future safety, and that of Miss Rimmer.

"Meantime I must insist you remain with us here in Chalkdean," he added quickly before Drusilla could gainsay him. "What you most need now is natural rest. 'Tis certain you'll be in no fit state to travel without risk of fever for at least a fortnight. And there's no reason I can see why the young curate from East Dean should not be persuaded to take the services at Sellington until such time as you're fit for duty."

Nor did the parson's daughter offer the smallest objection to Rafe's preferred policy of diplomacy over force. On the contrary, having once reassured herself of her father's fair prospects for retaining his limb, the girl's relief was all too obvious.

"Believe me, Mr Corbyn, I did everything possible to dissuade Papa from this undertaking in the first place. Short of physically restraining him, that is. But when his mind is set, you know, he can be quite as stubborn as any mule in harness," she further observed, with an unaffected frankness that greatly endeared her to her listener. "And if as you tell me he now sees the folly of provoking these ruffians on their own stamping-ground, then I can only attribute it to your own wise counsel, Sir, and beg to thank you for it most sincerely."

She made him a delightful picture. A profile as delicately cut as an Italian cameo, turning to him with such flattering attention from the chair his aunt had but recently vacated by the library fire, smiling to discover two dimples simultaneously. A girl out of the common way, he'd always thought so. And nothing the worse, it would seem, for her own part in the affray on the causeway. Divested of her wet clothing and dressed now in an old fashioned looped-up polonaise that had once been his mother's, she sat with her dark hair loose about her shoulders like a simple country maid's; and the firelight and the rose coloured stuff of the gown leant warmth to the pallid tones of a throat and breasts that were paler by far than any mere countrywoman's. A lovely girl, the veriest pattern of innocence and sweetness!

It was little short of a miracle, Rafe thought, that such freshness could have survived so dour a parentage and upbringing. Yet could she really be as naïve as she appeared, he wondered, this little parson's daughter? And was she such a stranger yet to life that Ellin Rimmer failed to realize her own most captivating appeal to the man who now beheld her?

Chapter Seven

Some seven months later one morning in May of 1794, the subject of her own appeal was in fact uppermost in Ellin's mind. It was an oppressive overcast day following a week of brilliant sunshine, and bringing with it that sense of human restlessness that so often accompanies a sudden change in the weather. Standing at an open casement above-stairs at the back of her father's parsonage, Ellin was gloomily aware of the clutter of furniture in the bedchamber behind her. A curtainless bed, a chair and a table, threadbare druggets and dingy mock-india paper – familiar, depressing, dull to a degree. And in the tarnished dressing glass her own reflection, jaded, pallid as a ghost.

"Prisoner of Lochleven," she declaimed, playing with the idea of a portrait sketch from the mirror. But today even the prospect of a crayon study failed to recruit her spirits. The appeal was absent from the subject itself, were it ever so well drawn. And with a melancholy sigh she turned back to her contemplation of the scene below her window. Down in the churchyard, and in the narrow glebe paddock alongside it, the green evidence of God's plenty was everywhere burgeoning forth from swollen stalks and bursting buds. Flowering already, wafting its perfumes on the still air through a great symphonic chorus of birdsong. Throstles and linnets, blackbirds and robins, singing their little hearts out. And a cuckoo calling from somewhere in the elder coppice beyond, to mock Ellin in her isolation.

On the summer day she'd arrived in Sellington life had seemed so full of romantic possibilities. 'And now another spring is come, and all but gone already,' she thought with a pang of disappointment. 'Passing you by, Ellin Rimmer, just as life itself is.'

After the excitements of her adventure on the causeway, Ellin had looked forward to her daily visits to her father at Chalkdean Manor, and to her inevitable meetings there with its owner. Mr Rafe Corbyn was reserved still be be sure, still a thought too gentlemanlike for his visitor's romantic taste. But his patience with her ungrateful parent, his unfailing kindnesses and his skill as a physician could not be denied. When his patient had been returned home to Ellin's care at Sellington Parsonage, she had missed their daily meetings most unaccountably. From that moment snow in January, rain in April, unending domestic chores and sickroom duties competed with each other for sheer dreariness in the pages of her journal. And to Ellin's further chagrin, the rapidity of her father's recovery made frequent visits from his physician unnecessary through the months of his recuperation.

Papa was walking now with the aid of a stick. The bone had knitted and the wound healed over within a matter of six weeks, and without any kind of infestation. A marvel his daughter attributed entirely to Mr Corbyn's aesculapian arts. It was obvious, nonetheless, that events of the previous autumn had injured her father in other ways. The symptoms of physical cowardice that she'd first detected in him on the day of that fateful confrontation at the Cuckmere bridge remained evident throughout his recuperation. Day after day Ellin had watched them torment him, seen the shame in his eyes and heard it in his constantly complaining voice. Until on the morning they'd discovered Zebediah Fowler's body on the beach at Sellington Gap, she witnessed the final routing of his conscience.

The boy's skull had been smashed like an eggshell. And the village spoke with one voice. Even Zeb's own father, repeating the phrases mechanically like a church response. "'E must've fallen, poor lad. Aye, slipped and fallen from the cliff . . ." Though Mary Codsall, dusting and scrubbing with a zeal that was new to her, had declined to look Ellin in the eye. And Ellin herself perforce recalled another young man, and the rhyme he'd chanted at her from the very beach on which they'd found poor Zeb.

'. . . But leave 'em alone and they'll come home, a-tagging no tales – *a-tagging no tales* behind them!'

As for Papa, from that day forward his condemnations were

directed exclusively toward the Jacobins, the Anti-Christ in France. At the end of February, on the day appointed as a national fast to ensure God's protection against the French, he'd hobbled up the pulpit steps to denounce a nation which, as the orator Verginaud had already pointed out, had developed a depraved taste for the blood of its own offspring. Yet in comparison with his earlier sermons the rhetoric lacked either passion or conviction. And listening to him from her seat on the aisle, Ellin was forced to acknowledge that the evidences of humanity she'd once so longed to discover in her father, now served merely to undermine her respect for him without in any way increasing her affection.

She sighed again, moving further into the window to inhale the living atmosphere of the world beyond; drawn instinctively to something musky and unsettling in the blend of perfumes that rose to her from the may blossom and wild parsley in the glebe hedgerow, and from the pendulous male candles of the old Spanish chestnut. For Ellin's sheltered adolescence had provided her with no means of identifying the smell of regeneration – that most primal pungency of life, present not only in pollen barm and sappy spring growth, but in the seminal emanations of all animal masculinity including man. Nor could she have realized precisely what it was that disturbed her about the upright sheaths of the Arum lilies by the church wall, or the stiff purple spadices they disclosed. Nor what attracted her to the frantic mating dance of the Brimstone butterflies above them. Yellow pollinators of yellow spring flowers, spiralling upwards through the shadows like sparks on a current of air. She knew only that when she stood at her window to breathe in the scents of this fomenting Eden, she ached with an inexpressible ache for something better and bolder and more beautiful than God or life had ever seen fit to offer her.

No thought of Aaron Corbyn, or of any other man, had yet entered her consciousness. But when that unmistakable individual suddenly appeared from the Lord-knows-where, riding down into the green Eden below her window, Ellin recognized him straightway as the missing Adam. So he was home! And already it seemed as if her own restlessness had been nothing more than impatience for his arrival. All at once her spirits shot up ten degrees – all questions of the young man's involvement with the Trade, or with poor Fowler and his death, thrust hastily aside.

Not that she cared for the rogue to suspicion her interest, not for the world! At the first glimpse of his red hair Ellin stepped swiftly back into the shadows of her bedchamber, out of range of the humid brown eyes that had twice so discomposed her.

'Though it could hardly signify if he *did* happen to catch sight of me,' she fraudulently assured herself. 'In my own house, standing at my own window – why nothing could be more natural!' And rather than go against nature, she began to edge forward again for a second viewing.

In the brief time it took Ellin to dispose of her scruples, their object had dismounted, and was presently engaged in securing his horse to a ring in the churchyard wall not twenty paces from the parsonage gate. His improbable hair, the first thing one noticed always, had been cropped short. Too short now to tie, but coaxed forward over his brow instead in a tousled 'Brutus' style which gave full liberty to its natural curl. With his usual disregard for convention he'd ridden forth without topcoat or hat, without even a token *chapeau-bras* to clamp beneath his arm. Yet for all that, he might have stepped out of a French fashion plate for the elegance of his appearance. His neckcloth was of black silk and expertly tied, while in contrast his calamanco weskit was more brilliantly yellow, more daringly abbreviated than any Ellin had beheld – so short in the waist that a handsbreadth or more of white lawn was clearly visible beneath. The bold black and yellow theme was carried even to the breeches, tiger-striped from hip to knee like the hose of some medieval courtier; and on down to the gold tassels and gleaming black leather of his riding boots. A young popinjay if ever she saw one. Yet a man now, a youth no longer.

But by this time the horse was secure. 'And in a moment he's bound to look up and see me,' Ellin thought with a little anticipatory thrill of excitement, forcing herself to remain where she was in full view of the churchyard. She tossed her head. 'And anybody may blame me who likes,' she pronounced defiantly, 'but I'll not be moved from my own window on account of a coxcomb like that! Why in the world should I be?'

Although at the same time she'd made sure that he would not

catch *her* looking, not this time – gazing out instead over the chestnut tree to the rising slope of the hills behind the church; and arching back but ever so slightly the better to define the outline of her small breasts when viewed from beneath.

Even in the flush of their spring growth the downs looked pale against the luxuriant foliage of Sellington combe, speckled and splotched like a great bolt of white-spotted muslin with the fleeces of their grazing flocks.

'So count the sheep, tally them in pairs as the shepherds do,' Ellin instructed herself on a sudden nervous impulse. 'How does it go now? Come along, you remember . . . Wintherum wontherum twintherum twontherum *wagtail*, that's it! And that's ten. White-belly coram dar diddle *den*, that's twenty. And who cares if he is watching?'

For watching her he certainly must be by now – looking up, covering his surprise with the expression of smiling impertinence she knew so well. Fancying himself so great! 'Etherum atherum shootherum cootherum *windbar*, thirty.' Willing her to turn her head and look down – as if she'd ever dream of giving him the satisfaction. 'Windbar, thirty, then bobtail, bopeep . . . No, not "bopeep", you gull! What in folly's name are you thinking of, Ellin Rimmer?' But now she'd broken the rhythm, lost the words. 'Lost her sheep, and can't tell where to find 'em . . .

'Start again Ellin. Come along, Wintherum wontherum . . .' She was trying so hard to tally them, doing her best not to look. But with Ellin, doing her best just never quite seemed to answer. And when at last she came to steal a peek, the merest little glimpse from the tail of her eye, it was to discover the wretched man part-turned away from her in conversation with a second figure – with a woman of all undesirable creatures. A strapper of a female half a head higher than he was, whose great suet dumplings of breasts instantly proclaimed themselves to be those of the farmer's daughter, Ann Ashby.

Not that anything could have persuaded Ellin to so much as pass the time of day with that posturing young dand down there, not if he'd begged her on his knees, she assured herself. And that being so, what possible object could there be in blaming providence for Annie Ashby's appearance on the scene?

'Because if Aaron Corbyn cares to pay court to a trumpery

overstuffed baggage of that girl's type,' Ellin informed her glaring reflection in the dressing glass, 'then good luck to him I say. For certainly 'tis of no great consequence to *me*!'

* * *

Aaron's own view of providence just then was predictably a shade more charitable. Not for him his brother's habit of restraint; for unlike Rafe he seldom swam against the stream of his own inclination. He needed a woman and providence had very obligingly supplied him with one. Cause and effect, as simple as life itself. Since the death of his beautiful and beloved Mamma and her replacement by the censorious and horse-faced Aunt Drusilla, Aaron had taken every precaution to avoid those feelings of *tendre* that so inconvenienced men in their dealings with womenkind. Deliberately he'd unhitched the appetites of his body from the tiresome emotions they drew in their traces. And now his brother Ray was the only soul on earth he truly cared for, aside from himself, that was.

For Aaron there had always been girls like Nan Ashby and he barely distinguished between them, unselective as a Tom sparrow. This one was a handsome enough wench he supposed in her own blunt-featured way. His eyes moved openly over her body. 'A fine big gal,' as men called her behind her back, and sometimes on it. 'Plenty there, lad, to hold on by!' To meet him the farmer's daughter had sprugged herself up in printed muslin, with a beribboned bonnet and a scarlet band knotted around her neck in the latest callous female fashion *à la guillotine*. She'd stopped short, though, of having her back hair shorn *à la victime*, thank heaven. Because for Aaron, this girl's most obvious visible attractions were the rope of flaxen hair that drooped across her shoulder, and below the braid, upthrust to meet it, a pair of magnificent white bubbs. Upthrust and squeezed together in a double cheeked parody which only a rig, he told himself, could fail to recognize and respond to.

But first there were the rules of courtship to observe. A little charade which even notoriously loose-rumped strammels like Nannie demanded of their swains. And who, when all was said, could play that game better than Aaron? Always at his most gentle in anticipation of acts of violence – like the cat in the popular simile, patting with soft paws at the plump little mouse he intents very shortly to devour.

"Well now, and have you missed me, Nan?" he enquired – eyelids, gingery lashes drooping, sprawled back against the wall to slowly massage his own braced thighs with the flat of his palms. No woman's body half as interesting to Aaron Corbyn as his own.

"Miss you? Oh lor, Sir, like we'd all miss turnpike gates!" She smiled, not at Aaron but at the ribbed bark of the chestnut, fiddling clumsily all the while with the switch of her fat yellow pigtail.

'Oh yes, a thorough good natured girl,' he thought, 'who'd as likely lie down if you only begged her to sit!' And did old Sam her father know the half of what she got up to between supervising his milkings for him. Did he, hell! For all the farmer's personal flexibility of outlook in matters of wenching and wool-trading, Aaron knew he took his status in the village a deal too seriously to countenance a hedge-whore for a daughter. No, if Annie's reputation had got back to Sam Ashby's ears she'd have borne the marks of his riding whip across her plump shoulders ere this, he had no doubt of it.

As he watched the girl fiddling and tugging at the braid, twitching it up from her breasts to stroke her freckled neck, up to her lips and back to her breasts again, Aaron could feel the tensing of his own saddle muscles beneath his palms. But he'd not reach out for her, not yet. First he must sing for his supper, because that was the rule of the game.

"And did you think I'd forgotten you?" he said nonchalantly, kicking at a loose pebble with the toe of one polished boot. "Did you think I'd come home to Sussex without a *cadeau* in my pocket for my own sweet Nan?"

She laughed aloud. A gurgling provocative sound from deep in her throat. "Doan't you come that with me, Aaron Corbyn. I know 'ow many beans make five all right. And I'd say you've as like forgot me as many times as you've danced Moll Peatley's jig with they bloodthirsty Frenchy mamselles we 'ear tell of! And as for your 'cadow'," she added slyly. "If 'tis what you're showing in the front pocket of they gimsy marrer-striped breeches, Sir, then I'll lay odds I'm not the only Judy you've brung it 'ome to neither!"

"Lord save us! Whatever next will the woman say? And are we onto Moll Peatley's jig already, Nannie?" Aaron raised his two hands and his eloquent brown eyes in mock horror. "Why Madam, your temerity fair takes m' breath away, I do declare! But won't you leave me in my breeches even for the time it'd take you to peep under the flap of my saddle bag? For my life I swear I've never known a girl so mighty quick to go to work and slow to claim her wage."

And he stepped after her, light and taut-strung as a dancing master, while Annie rushed excitedly ahead of him to the horse. The gift he'd brought her was a gown-length of exquisitely ramaged Lyons velvet. A pattern of violet convolvulus vines on an amaranthine ground, cut from a bolt in his Fécamp warehouse and tossed into the cabin of his lugger for their crossing the previous night. As the girl unfolded the fabric with childish delight, rubbing it against her cheek, draping it voluptuously around her like a toga, Aaron indulged in a moment of self-congratulation. Whatever Pitt's government or Brother Ray might have to say, the truth was that the import of such goods stood to benefit a great many more people on both sides of the Channel than they could ever harm. In their manufacture, work for those French weavers who'd survived the seige of Lyons the previous year, and whose art might otherwise be sacrificed to war. In their freighting, bread for the starving *pécheurs* of Fécamp, whose herring boats had long since been requisitioned by one protagonist or sunk by the other. In their landing and porting, a living wage for the men of Sussex who'd always depended on such trade.

In the months that had passed since the overhauling of the rabid little parson on the Cuckmere causeway, Aaron had returned but thrice to England. In November he'd come promptly enough on receipt of Rafe's letter. Although less, as a matter of fact, out of any sense of fraternal duty or concern for the Rimmers' well-being, than to convince his Lullington associates of the need for further investment in their operation. With the French exchequer's rising demand for gold and more shipping than ever in the Channel, the English fishing vessels which had handled the bulk of the trade since the outbreak of war, now found themselves increasingly at risk of interception, if not by the Revenue then by

Admiralty cruisers or French corsairs. Meantime, poverty and massive unemployment in the Normandy fishing ports had opened the way for a new French-based industry of an unprecedented scale. On his arrival in Fécamp as Harris's agent the previous July, Aaron had been greeted virtually as a saviour.

Within a matter of days the mayor had issued him with a licence to trade from the port, provided only that he select his master and crew from the redundant Fécampois. Within a month he had secured the lease on a vacant warehouse on the Quai Vicomté. And by early November he'd not only chartered and equipped his own *chasse-marée*, but felt sufficiently emboldened to arrange for local coasters to deliver substantial quantities of brandy and geneva to Fécamp. Awaiting only a necessary capital investment from the merchants of London, by way of Lullington Heath, to commence trading at the ridiculously youthful age of twenty as a master smuggler in his own right.

Aaron had himself been aboard his own maiden run out of Fécamp the following month; returning to France to commission a second vessel from the proceeds of that venture. A custom-built lugger, gaff rigged and shallow keeled to give any Revenue cutter a run for her money and if necessary to beach directly onto the shingle. And by the completion of that craft in February, trade between Fécamp and the Sussex coast had already been sufficiently stimulated to compel the Lullington Horsemaster to extend his pony caravans and recruit additional tide-porters of his own.

In April Aaron had received a second letter from his brother, this time to inform him of reports in the Sussex Weekly Advertiser which not only detailed large movements of contraband through Crowlink and Cuckmere Haven, but even hinted at some sinister connection between the illicit traders and the sudden death of the Sellington youth, Zebediah Fowler. Reports, Rafe maintained, which could only serve to draw attention to the increasing blatancy of the trade, and eventually to stir the preventivemen to action. So once again Aaron had returned to the unwholesome atmosphere of Harris's bow-top waggon on the Heath. This time to discuss alternative landing places where contraband might be roped and derricked up the cliffs – to plot new overland routes for the caravans which avoided the local villages and made directly for safe-houses further inland at Hailsham and East Grinstead.

And then afterwards at Chalkdean, for the sake of poor Ray's nicety of conscience he'd forced himself to take another dose of his brother's moralizing with as good a grace as possible, while he looked out from the library over the familiar roofs of the stables below and planned a more rewarding assignation with Sam Ashby's nubile daughter.

But now here was Nannie herself thrusting gratefully against him, cocooned still in the luxurious embrace of his gift from France, looping the fabric around him and pulling it in to bind them close together. And now of course was the time . . .

Aaron freed himself to stoop swiftly, then gradually to straighten. The girl flinched and drew in her breath, hauling on the velvet noose.

"Gawd'amighty, you young belswaggers you're all the same," she murmured appreciatively. "My word you are!"

"And you, Ma'am, as variable as an April sky." (Although in truth he'd found her willing accessibility just faintly disappointing.) "So where shall it be, Nan? In the shaw again, behind the church? Or must we imitate the Hellfire brethren, my love, and improve on our acquaintance down here amongst the gravestones?"

Her neck smelled of perspiration and warm hair and cheap jessamy perfume. He rubbed his cheek against it as she had rubbed hers against the fabric; and then without moving his head raised his eyes deliberately to the rigid figure of the other at the casement above them – the little parson's daughter spying again, watching all along.

'And now for shame, Miss Rimmer, where is your blush? Staring so guiltily as if it were your petticoats I was lifting – your little pipkin, Miss, beneath my fingers!'

* * *

Without direct intention Ellin slipped silently down the parsonage stairs, through the kitchen and out-kitchen and into the green stillness of the world beyond. She felt curiously weak, fearful of proceeding yet unable to remain behind; drawn after them by an urge stronger than all Papa's warnings, more potent by far than the murmurings of her own pliant conscience. Eve reaching out for the apple, Pandora fumbling for the gilded catch of her casket.

Poised on the edge of revelation, she could not have held back to save her life.

By the time she reached the churchyard they'd already cleared the stile behind it. To follow she must stoop beneath the drooping garlands of the hawthorn. Waist-deep in nettles and flowering parsley, she tracked them by the broken stems their feet had trampled, listening like an animal for the rustle of their movements up ahead. A natural spring at the base of the scarp beyond spilled down from its pool to feed the stream by the churchyard wall, and ultimately the village duckpond. Ellin could see the dark gleam of its water through the leaves, already suspicioned where she'd find them.

In the centre of the coppice a massive oak sprawled out over the water to spread its serpentine limbs above the elder trees; a rarity in the downland and a monument to its own age, for such trees grow but slowly in the chalk. Between them the shade of its canopy and the convoluted platform of its roots had created a little glade about the pool. A leafy fold in the skirts of the downs, where village children came to fish for roach or tench – and on occasion Ellin herself, to sketch or search for cress and water mint where the sun struck through. Or simply to ponder her own reflection in the water, leaning where Annie now leant against the mossy trunk of the oak . . .

. . . Annie with her back to the tree, holding up her skirts and petticoats, her knuckles white at their hems. And Aaron Corbyn's booted feet already stamping the ground ivy that grew at the oak's roots, crushing its blue flowers, filling the glade with its bitter hopbine odour.

And Ellin herself, so very still, with the breath burning in her throat and eyes only for the mounting violence of the man's assault.

* * *

For Aaron too Ann Ashby had lost her personality. If he thought of her at all it was merely as a receptacle, an object of sensation as immaterial in herself as the blackbird that chuckled its foolish warning from the branches above them, or as the folds of the expensive velvet cloth around her shoulders. For it was not her need but his own that impelled him. A force which sprang not from Nan, but from the strength and energy of his own body, from the springtime itself and from his plain delight in both.

The girl's mouth gaped open, a dark shadow beneath him. But Aaron's own lips were pressed tight, his eyes wide and unfocused. Every sense enslaved now to a single anticipation – drawing in, pressing down, irresistibly gathering for the leap . . .

Ah now! And NOW . . . to leap and leap again! The milt spouting, springing out of him like some marvellous winged creature. Great now, greater than any damn female – all the lifeforce within him soaring for its freedom!

Only to take the leaden shot as it must at the very apex of its flight. To gasp and convulse, and to flutter still convulsing down to earth.

* * *

Returning later to his horse with as little after-course of courtesy or gratitude to the jade as might possibly be contrived, Aaron felt no more than any man might feel at such an ebb – a sense of heaviness and diminished force. As if the little spurt of cuckoo-spit he'd left within her body had contained some buoyant energy of its own. Yet not entirely spent. No, never that. Because for Aaron the mastery of weakness brought with it another kind of satisfaction – to feel his pulse slowing and his breath return to normal, to stride the strength back into his limbs, with no thought now for the woman that he'd used. And never a glance for the other, crouching in the undergrowth by the path with her small hands clutched to her breasts.

Chapter Eight

"I acknowledge my transgression and my sin is ever before me . . ." For Ellin it was the literal truth. In the past – and even after her encounter with Aaron Corbyn in his natural state of Adam – she'd been largely successful in separating her knowledge of the act of generation in animals from that of men and women, who walked upright and behaved toward each other with such formal courtesy. But now she'd tasted of the fruit of knowledge. And now there could be no blaming of chance or circumstance for the prurience of her own nature. Ellin had flirted too long with petty misdemeanours not to recognize a cardinal sin when she committed one. That she'd known what Ann and Aaron were about in the shaw behind the church did not admit of a doubt. Deliberately she'd followed the pair of them to witness their fornication. God, she knew, was duty-bound to punish her.

And so he had. Night after night in wakefulness and in sleep libidinous images had been sent to afflict her. To her bed a familiar daemon – a taunting red-haired incubus who jerked and writhed and battered at her senses, his pale thighs splayed and straining, flushed with gold and licked with crimson fire. To her nostrils the bitter fragrance of trampled ground ivy. To her ears that thrilling final gasp of masculine surrender, incessantly repeated. To the recesses of her own body the humiliation of a physical response – a guilty vice, through teasing flame-tipped fingers and hidden springs of pure sensation.

"By night on my bed I sought him whom my soul loveth. I sought him but I found him not." Inevitable perhaps that it should be so, with so little still to occupy her mind and her emotions. Yet even

in the light of day, even about her duties in the parsonage and the village, Ellin found that these alarming retrospections were unwilling to leave her be. She could hardly see a shirt hanging out in the breeze but that she must imagine some muscular masculine inspiration beneath its flapping tails. In church, at the thanksgiving for Lord Howe's naval victory over the French, she raised her eyes gratefully to the altar, only to commit an act of comprehensive mental sacrilege with the sinuous semi-naked figure on the cross above it. And down at Ann Ashby's dairy-house, strive as she might to see Annie as Papa would have done in her shoe leather – as a Jezebel or a Babylon whore – she could feel nothing but envy for the things the girl had known and felt. Shamefully, while she listened to Ann's amiable chatter and watched her dairymaids slap the yellow butter into shape, she could still picture her holding up her skirts for the man with her broad back to the oak. Even the butter itself recalled the flutter of lascivious wings, of the yellow 'butter-flies' that were named for it, palpitating up through the oak leaves to the obscene stamp of Aaron Corbyn's tasselled boots.

Now that she understood the nature of that primitive mystery, Ellin could enjoy no ease. She found herself obsessed, drawn unwillingly toward it like a bird to a serpent. No longer attracted solely by the person of the younger Mr Corbyn – for had it been so, the temptation would hardly have persisted so fiercely in his absence. She'd scarce have recalled the hands of that ruffian on the causeway still with such indecent clarity. Nor would she have been so acutely aware of every brawny labourer or fisherman who so much as laid an appreciative eye on her. Aaron had vanished again from the locality. But before doing so he'd awakened in her something that had only stirred before. And if any man should attempt to try her further on one of her lonely perambulations through the countryside? 'What then, Ellin Rimmer?' the insidious serpent hissed. She had always known herself to be morally weak. But now Ellin shuddered to contemplate the abyss that yawned beneath her feet.

"Lord, Thy rod is constantly upon me for the purposes of my correction."

But the Almighty's design for Ellin was not merely to scourge her with the consequence of her sins. He had, it would appear, an additional purpose in mind. As revealed to his unworthy handmaiden one sunny September morning after church, when Rafe Corbyn sought her out amongst the gravestones.

"Miss Rimmer, good morning." He came up with her by the old Wenham altar-tomb, and both bowed as custom dictated. The gentleman physician also uncovered, to hold his buckled hat awkwardly before him. Surprisingly awkwardly, Ellin thought, considering how many such conversations there'd been between them.

"Your father looks better than ever," he said. "We'll have him running yet, I daresay." And heavens, what a difference a smile made to the man's face!

"Thanks to you, Sir, and to your ministrations."

He was formally bewigged, dressed plain as a Quaker as always. 'But a nice big upstanding sort of man for all that,' Ellin remarked in confidence to herself. 'Half a cubit taller than the brother at the least. Longer in the leg, and something heavier in the chest and backseat too from what one can observe . . .' She lowered her gaze advisedly, abashed by the familiar turn her thoughts had taken.

He cleared his throat. "But Miss Rimmer, I must tell you that I have not waylaid you simply to pass the time of day," he said. And as Ellin looked up at him the hat performed a deliberate revolution between his hands. "In truth I have come to seek your guidance on a matter of some moment," he added heavily against the clamour of the Sellington church bells.

"*My* guidance?" She could no longer contain her curiosity. "But how can I help you, Sir?" And surely he couldn't mean to declare himself after all? And to *her*? And here in the graveyard with his aunt awaiting him in the chaise and her own father watching the pair of them so narrowly from the church porch?

"The warmth of my regard for you these past months cannot entirely have escaped you, I fancy. Or can I have been mistaken?" An irregular pink flush variegated his not unpleasing features.

'And oh Judas he *does* mean to,' she thought wildly, and hardly yet knowing whether to feel shocked or gratified. The rich Mr Corbyn at her own gate! And ready to credit her with some secret expectation of the event into the bargain. When all the time she'd been repining for his worthless brother – a contrabander as everyone now supposed, shamefully established like the traitor Tom Paine in enemy France!

"Indeed, Sir, you are entirely mistaken. I do assure you that no such idea entered my head," she replied with a show of calm she was barely equal to maintaining; for rightly she now perceived her own future to hang in the balance. Within the space of a few exchanges they'd become partners, she and this square-figured and undeniably eligible man – partners in the ritual measure of courtship that one so often encountered in the pages of romantic fiction, or rehearsed over to oneself in imagination.

"And forgive me," she added in the faintly teasing manner permitted of romantic heroines, "but is it any marvel that I failed to anticipate your regard, Sir, when your behaviour toward me since before Christmas has been so perfectly formal and correct?"

His colour deepened, became moist, and the tortured hat brim completed another slow turn. Yet to do him credit Rafe Corbyn had given no ground. His brown eyes held hers still with a stoic persistence. Downward-slanting eyes like his brother's, she noticed (and how strange that she'd never done so before in all the time she'd known him!).

"Then I see that I too must apologise for my woeful lack of comprehension in such matters," he was saying in that soft deep voice of his. "For truly I believe that my affections have been settled on you for these many months past, my dear Miss Rimmer. And if I have been over-scrupulous in repressing them, you must apprehend that it was rather for fear of offending you than from any want of sincerity."

And then again and at last the corners of those rediscovered brown eyes had lifted. And how much younger he looked, she thought, smiling so. How much genuine warmth there was to her Mr Corbyn's character when only he allowed it to shine through!

* * *

'Needles and pins
Needles and pins
When 'e gets married
'Is trouble begins!'

The arrival of the bridegroom's equipage (complete with that vital protagonist, his aunt, his coachman and his stout cousin

Barnabas from Tunbridge Wells) was announced from the top of the churchyard wall by a row of chanting village children, swinging their legs excitedly while waiting for the signal to scatter. A cue that Mistress Drusilla had been more than willing to provide, reaching up to rap on the back of the driving seat with the be-ribboned nub of her walking staff.

"See them off at once, Coachman – and use the whip if needs must!" she commanded in a tone of voice which in itself served amply for the purpose, while at the same time distracting poor Gabel for long enough to get the start on him in the race for the carriage door.

"And if you can't make yourself useful in that respect, you might at least contrive to be punctual in releasing me from this uncomfortable vehicle," she added, rattling the handle triumphantly in token of her victory. "You're getting old, man, and I'm sorry to say more sluggardly and indolent with every day that passes. 'Tis high time you pensioned him off, Nephew." With which she flung on ahead of them through the tapsel, to leave the gate yawping and bucketing on its central pivot like a frisky colt.

"And who'd My Lady find then to bear with 'er naggings and 'er jagglings, 'er everlasting gumtions and tarrifications?" the old coachman demanded of his persecutor's fast retreating rear. "Contrary as Twitcher's donkey, she be!" He shook his head, the tears of rage and frustration starting in his faded blue eyes. "Twitcher's donkey, that's 'er Ladyship – mad in a minute and for everlasting kicking out at the wind!"

Rafe laid a sympathetic hand on his shoulder. "Now then, Gabel, you know that's no way to speak of your mistress," he said mildly, and largely for the benefit of his cousin. "Miss Corbyn has had a deal, I may say a vast deal, to concern her during these past weeks of preparation for the wedding and for my wife's coming to Chalkdean. It has placed a severe strain upon her nerves, and I fancy we should all of us be ready to make her due allowance. Is that not so, Barnabas?"

It was an over-simplification of the case, as Cousin Barnabas and the irascible old coachman undoubtedly knew as well as he. Because of course it was plain that the lady's present agitation extended well beyond wedding feasts and bridal furnishings. Plain to all that Aunt Drusilla was altogether too possessive in her affection, too jealous of her own status within the household to regard Rafe's betrothal as anything but a personal threat.

Rafe, who understood her better than anyone, anticipated the reaction and had done his best to soften the initial blow.

"You know that I shall be forever grateful to you, Madam, for the concern you've shown for us all since my mother's death," he was at pains to assure her. "And I think I need hardly say that there'll always be a home for you here at Chalkdean. You already like Miss Rimmer I'm sure, and there is no reason I can see why from our wedding forward we should not all of us go on together in perfect harmony."

"That, we must conclude, is because your wits have gone a-begging," had been My Lady's most unreasonable rejoinder. "You're so simple, Nephew, that I believe you'd have to look in a pond to see if it was raining or no! And, much as one regrets inviting attention to the shortcomings of a member of one's own sex, I consider it no more than my duty as a relative to point out that the girl's unqualified for you by birth, by fortune or by accomplishment." (Such duties Aunt Drusilla would never shrink from.) "A fortune-hunter, Rafe, and a mere parson's daughter at that!"

On which occasion, as on so many others in her life, Rafe's aunt had said too much. He told her so as a plain fact and they'd parted foes, avoiding all discourse on the subject, until the first official bawling of the banns had prompted her to a further catalogue of dissensions. This time she'd judged it prudent to avoid personal references to the bride-elect, addressing herself instead to the scandalous rumours that must attach to a match so hastily made up, and to the sheer impossibility of assembling a civilized wedding party at such absurdly short notice. But in the end of course she'd acquiesced, as Rafe had known she must when faced with an ultimate choice of falling in with him or quitting his household. Although in so doing, Aunt Drusilla could scarce have made plainer her belief that domestic tranquility as her nephew knew it at Chalkdean was already a thing of the past.

'Needles and pins
Needles and pins . . .'

So why must he marry, and why so precipitately? For duty?

Was that the spur? With his brother abroad and his own age approaching the meridian? Was he taking a wife only for the sake of the future, for the duty he owed to Chalkdean itself? To be sure his sense of duty had always been one of Rafe's most prominent characteristics – his principal reason for becoming a student of Hippocrates himself when he could well have afforded to pay a surgeon, a bonesetter and a journeyman apothecary to do the work for him. Perhaps the tendency was inborn? If not, a shatterbrained mother, the influence of an elderly grandfather and Aaron for a younger brother must all have played their part in encouraging its development; not to mention his own observations of weakness and dependency in the streets and hospitals of London. He saw it as the duty of every educated man to rise above the baseness of his nature, to advance himself and others less fortunate as far as he was able. And now marriage, Rafe, by the same token?

Old Gabel certainly thought so.

"I never did know a wedding but that the women folkses 'ad to go and make a middling boffle of it," he muttered resentfully, as the gaze of all three men accompanied Mistress Drusilla in her martial progress up the church flags. "But doan't ye go paying no 'eed to 'er Ladyship's orations, Mus Relph. For 'tis time you were in double-'arness an' no mistake, before some danged young female goes and gets ye into mischief without." The coachman frowned and heaved a feeling sigh. "You need a boy, a son Mus Relph, and a good wife to go with 'im and all. Reckon any man with a fork to 'is leg would tell you the same."

Indeed there was every good reason for a man of Rafe's age and bachelor status to take a wife. And not even Aunt Drusilla could accuse him of advancing the date of the wedding for any motive baser than that of obliging the young lady herself. For had he not deliberated the action for something above nine months, for the time of a full-term gestation, before framing his proposal? And would he not have been willing even then to constrain himself to a like period of betrothal for the sake of the proprieties, had not Miss Rimmer seemed so positively anxious to have him without it?

"I am sensible of the compliment, Sir, and I do believe that perhaps we were meant to marry," she had reflected with that beguiling blend of naïveté and frankness that was so peculiarly her own. (And in innocence, no doubt, of the convention by which a lady was expected to refuse a gentleman on first application.)

"You must forgive my presumption," she'd continued a little breathlessly. "But if you really do consider me worthy, Mr Corbyn, and feel equally resolved in your own sentiments – then might it not be prudent to speak to my father now, while you already have so great a part of his attention?" And those delicate curving lashes of hers had lifted to direct him to the bespectacled figure of the parson, peering myopically at them from the church door.

It would be an exaggeration to say that Rafe was a prude, but in his academical studies at Cambridge he'd absorbed and concurred with the ideas of the classical philosophers, of the Neoplatonists who were still so entrenched in that university, of Shakespeare and Milton and of the great pre-revolutionary French thinker François Voltaire. Later he'd consulted the medical authorities – Celsus, Stahl, Hoffman and John Brown. And all he noted agreed in the view that to be healthy in mind and body, to advance his higher faculties, the enlightened man must first achieve self-mastery.

'*Animum rege, qui nisi paret, imperat,*' as Horace put it: 'Rule your passion, for unless it obeys, it governs you.'

What's more, Rafe's own fleshly encounters in university jelly-houses and London clubs, his adolescent discoveries of the emotional peaks and troughs to which even a twopenny whore could subject a rational male, had confirmed for him the wisdom of two thousand years. In the most ordered and civilized existence occasional gratification of the senses was permissable, even necessary. Few were exempt. But unconstrained indulgence debilitated, dulled the intellect. 'Carnality reducing the bright beacon of human intelligence,' as Cicero described it, 'to little more than a guttering flame.'

"I feel sure that Papa will already have guessed at our business in any case," the parson's daughter had mischievously declared that day in the churchyard, "if only from the extreme formality of our expressions. And should he also approve your proposal, Sir, as I venture to suppose he may, then I must tell you that for my own part I'd not wish to delay its celebration for a single unnecessary day. I'd wed you tomorrow, Mr Corbyn, and that right gladly, indeed I would!" Her laugh had been sweet and surprisingly low. "So there Sir, you have my answer!"

Unlike his aunt, whose clothing gave off a faint odour of camphor, Ellin Rimmer smelled of garden flowers, of orris and rosewater. 'And oh my poor doctor, witness the lengths to which a rational man may go to distort the truth he professes to hold so dear!' (For Rafe was too honest to continue with such facile self-pretence.) 'And was your heart really so unaffected?' he asked himself. 'Or did it swell within you when she so confessed her feelings? And your body, you arrant hypocrite? Did that remain unstirred? Confess it, you know as little of your bride's faults and merits as Aunt Drusilla does – your notions of female worth as unfixed now as ever they were. As a serious man you cannot be attracted to Miss Rimmer's lightness of character. You are not here this afternoon at this church simply to oblige the lady, are you now? Admit it. No, nor even to protect the future of your family line. No such worthy conceits for you, you monstrous fraud!

'You are here because you *desire* her. And not for her naïveté neither, nor yet her candid mode of speech. Not for her mind at all. 'Tis her *jeunesse*, her perfumed warmth, the soft mortises of this young woman's body which have brought you hither. Another kind of duty, Sir, and to quite another master!'

Or to put it more simply, Rafe Corbyn had finally fallen in love.

* * *

In this modern century, as in all preceding it, the advantage of choice in marriage was a man's. A girl might bait the line, but the fish must hook and land himself. And certainly in Ellin's case there was little room to doubt that Mr Corbyn represented a profoundly better catch than she had any right to expect. As a child she'd never been indulged, never spoiled into expecting all her dearest wishes granted.

'Dear life, Ellin Rimmer – what on earth do you suppose?' she'd inwardly demanded. 'No one but a simpleton would expect her own lady's maid and a carriage and four *and* romantic behaviour from one and the same bridegroom. It wouldn't be reasonable.'

No indeed, after her experiences of the previous months it was quite enough, she assured herself, that Rafe Corbyn was a man with all a man's essential parts. She was bound to him in gratitude for what he'd performed for her father, as well as by inclination. 'And for my side of the bargain, I'll make him a better wife than he ever dreamed of,' she cheerfully avowed, 'if God will only grant me the grace to accomplish it.'

* * *

The Almighty's co-operation thus far at least had been apparent since the dawn of her wedding day, when a pale October sun had risen out of the mist to gild the topmost branches of the oak behind the church. The air was crisp and clear, the breeze off the Channel no more than fresh. Up before seven to scan the heavens from her window, the prospective bride decided early that her fashionable new wedding gown must certainly go uncovered for her walk to the church. The simple classical lines of these *robes en chemise* were never intended for smothering beneath joseph cloaks or pelisses. And hers must be displayed to very best advantage, to be sure it must – even if the worse came to the worst and she had to succumb to a chill of it on her honey-month!

The gown had been made up by an émigrée dressmaker of some repute in Lewes, from a length of saffron-dyed ninon which Mr Corbyn had generously sent to Bond Street for, and to a style promoted by Madame Rose Bertin herself. Ellin's wardrobe had never boasted anything half so fine. And bringing it forth to drape across a chair in the first thin rays of the sun, she thought her wedding dress the loveliest, quite the most elegant garment she'd set eyes on. It was of a clear golden shade that the Frenchwoman described as *souffre* – a colour that seemed to light up the room, with a low neck and a high waist, pulled in tight with draw-strings above and below the breast and draped in a demi-train at the back. A garment to be worn *au naturel* strictly without diddy-doublers, hoops, stays or bum-pads; without anything indeed but the finest of lawn shifts beneath.

That her father and the greater part of his congregation should consider such apparel unsuited to a virgin bride was naturally a foregone conclusion; for new fashion was seldom if ever to be approved by the unfashionable. Ellin had hopes though that her bridegroom would admire it. His aunt too, if when it came to the test that tiresome lady could show but half of the urban sophistication she laid claim to.

Miss Drusilla Corbyn had in fact paid another of her rare visits to Sellington Parsonage on the day immediately following her nephew's astonishing announcement – descending from her carriage *en grand tenue* without waiting to be invited.

"But what an inconveniently small room," she'd declared from the parlour doorway, lowering her spy-glass to compress her skirts with both hands as if she quite expected the chairs and settles to crash in on her like the Symplegades on her way through to the hearth. "And but a single maidservant, do I hear? I am sure I can't pretend to imagine how you endure it, Miss Rimmer."

And it was only after Ellin had faithfully set forward every practical advantage of the modern modest-sized parlour, that she perceived the trap into which she had fallen.

"Exactly so," Drusilla observed from the high-backed chair she'd selected by the fire. "As I anticipated, Miss Rimmer, you reveal yourself to be satisfied with a cottage existence which any lady of genuine quality must find cramped to a degree." She adjusted the ruffles at her own thin neck. "Or to view the matter from another angle, you have just now confirmed your own lack of aptitude either by temperament or experience to preside over an establishment a quarter the size of Chalkdean Manor." She smiled her disdainful wire-drawn smile. "Come now, I'll hear no denial."

But Ellin was not the girl to be frightened or deterred by a dried up old maid, however bold and high she might set herself. From the cradle upwards she'd been instructed to consider Woman as an afterthought on the part of the male Divinity. A superfluous rib, to be justified only by marriage, as a helpmeet for Man and an envelope for his children. And although she herself had inclined to an heretical consciousness of her own worth, she couldn't help but share her Age's harsh judgement of spinsters as defectives and failures to their calling. No woman should be without her own man. It said so in the Bible. And it followed that Mr Corbyn's aunt was rather to be pitied than feared.

"Miss Corbyn, I prefer no claim to qualifications such as yours to manage a large household," she'd confessed, bravely seating herself opposite the lady and summoning a smile of her own that she hoped and believed to be disarming. "But truly Ma'am, I have every willingness to learn, if you will only be kind enough to guide me. Indeed I am sensible that the greater folly on my part would be to allow a simple want of experience to prevent me from embracing a situation in life which every unmarried female must envy."

But oh dear, how very *un*-sensible one's own tongue could be when it chose! What a sly and underhand tendency it had of selecting the very words one would most rather not have uttered! Ellin had intended to appease the woman as best she could, but thanks to her provoking tongue had succeeded only in blowing on the coals of her resentment. And here she was now on her way to the altar, laying hold of the occasion to flout her splendid new wedding dress in Miss Corbyn's unhandsome face, and likely end up making matters worse still between them.

'Well if so, it can't be helped,' she thought defiantly, refusing to let anything dampen her spirits on this day of days. 'I'd lay that old Minerva would censure any bride of her nephew's as a matter of principle, whatever her complexion or style of dressing. And at least she'll not fault this one on point of fashion!'

In town she'd heard that young ladies of rank had taken to wearing veils of silk gauze or lace at their weddings, in the manner of Eastern brides. But Ellin and her dressmaker had agreed that in her case a bandeau of yellow organdie bound *à la grecque* around he dark curls would be infinitely more telling, reserving the net for an *echarpe* cloak, a little negligent drapery only between the elbows. And if the ultimately fashionable effect had proved quite as chilly as Ellin feared for the short walk to the church on her father's arm, then the look of startled disapproval on the face of the old coachman at the gate more than compensated for the goose-bumps.

"Married in yeller – married in yeller!"

A couple of young ragamuffins from the churchyard wall had scrambled up onto the Wenham tomb to bait the peaching parson and his scantily clad daughter as they paced slowly by them toward the garlanded church door. "Married in yeller – ashamed of the feller!"

Although as things had fallen out, shame was the last thing Ellin felt. She could even afford to smile a little at Papa, balancing precariously on his good leg to flourish his stick at the urchins. For she was as proud as the very devil of her daring *souffre* chemise; and prouder still that this time the gentleman who stood waiting at the altar rail, was waiting for her.

Chapter Nine

"Dearly beloved, we are gathered together here in the sight of God and in the face of this congregation to join this man and this woman in holy matrimony, which is an honourable estate instituted of God in the time of man's innocency . . ."

They might have been any village man and maiden standing before him, Rafe thought, for all the personal sentiment the parson allowed to his voice as he forged their marriage bond. ". . . an honourable estate – and therefore not by any to be enterprised nor taken in hand unadvisedly, lightly or wantonly to satisfy men's lusts and appetites – like brute beasts that have no understanding . . ."

By the Church's definition bride and groom were both guilty it would seem. Although perhaps their real problem lay less in the natural appetites they shared, than in their separate perceptions of them. For whereas Ellin could look forward with thrilling trepidation to a final release from the bonds of chastity, Rafe saw marriage more as a further means of control than as an emancipation in itself. The 'brute breast' of the Christian ethic he identified with Plato's wild stallion of desire – a refractory beast which, according to the Greek philosopher, might yet be trained to run in marital harness with the gentler emotions of love and respect.

Thus it was that while his young bride nervously flushed and fidgeted her way through their long wedding feast at Chalkdean, Rafe found the patience to pay off every arrear of civility that the occasion demanded. To reply in kind to all the traditional wedding discourses; and through it all, for hour after hour, to calm and encourage the volatile young woman at his side.

Ah! when will this long weary day have end,
And lend me leave to come unto my love?
How slowly do the houres they'r numbers spend!
How slowly does sad Time his feathers move!'

Yet somehow the time passed. And however slowly it might seem to the groom, however interminably to his bride, in reality at quite its usual pace. Until at last a little after midnight Ellin was free to leave the derelict feast and retire above stairs. To be waited on by her new husband in due course, swept up to the door of their bedchamber at the head of a roistering company of guests. Although – thanks largely to Queen Charlotte, who'd put a stop to more barbarous conventions – to be followed beyond it only by their vulgarities and the lewd extravagance of their imaginations.

She was already abed when he entered, stretched out with the covers pulled up to her chin – her hair confined within a plain night mob, and her grey eyes wide with apprehension. So slight and slender that the curves of her breast and thigh barely showed beneath the quilting. Like a mere child, Rafe thought, his own secret longings automatically diminishing before the realities of his bride's youth and innocence.

"There I have locked them out, and now not even a maid may enter," he said, hastening to break into that first difficult moment of silence.

She smiled shyly. "Nor leave neither I suppose, Sir?" A tremulous attempt at flirtation which under the circumstance he found a little shocking.

But of course, she was wearied to death, poor child. And fearful too, trembling on the brink of some dark mystery which no doubt she'd heard transformed the most civilized bridegrooms into brutal despoilers of maidenheads.

"My dear," he said gently, "I'd like you to know . . ."

"What the devil you waiting for, Jack? Want 'elp to thread the needle, do ye?"

The interruption was Sam Ashby's, unmistakably, directed through the keyhole on a plangent blast of alcohol, which effectively conveyed the sentiment a further twenty yards through the night air beyond the bedchamber – to the ears of his daughter Ann and one of his own paid labourers, Jarvis Copper. (A couple who for their own part were in little need of such encouragement.)

For Rafe though, the contrast between the suggestion and the reality of his wife's appearance produced a reverse reaction. And by the time he returned from clearing the stairhead of the drunken farmer and his bacchantes, he had come to a remarkable decision.

"My dear, this has been a long and taxing day for both of us," he said from the doorway. "And whatever those rude fellows may be disposed to expect of us, I think we should try to sleep."

And was it relief he perceived in her fading smile? Or merely surprise at his apparent complaisance? "We have years of marriage ahead of us after all, in which to attain a very handsome knowledge of one another," he continued in the same solicitous vein, as he crossed the room to her bedside, "to allow intimacy to grow naturally as it should, my dear, out of mutual affection and respect."

The tester and hangings of the great bed shielded the girl's face from the candlelight and the dying embers of the fire. Her eyes in the shadow of their lashes were unfathomable, dark as charcoal; the change in their expression too subtle for a husband as new to his business as Rafe to interpret. So when she silently nodded her agreement, he simply turned from her to snuff the candles one by one – all but the single flame he carried with him into the dressing closet.

* * *

The new furbishments for Elizabeth Corbyn's old four-poster were of printed cotton, illustrating a vaguely classical theme of Phaethon and his ill-fated sun chariot. From between a horse's prancing hooves and the rays of Helios himself, Ellin watched the candle shadows of Rafe's movements against the pine-panelling of his closet – as first wig then dress coat, weskit, shirt and breeches were removed in orderly progression. To be followed by the sounds of washing and the purging of urine in the appropriate vessels. Until presently he reappeared before her, self-conscious in his cap and night-shirt, to pinch out the last taper and climb into the high bed beside her.

The succeeding night they were abed, the pair of them, well before eleven. The house was quiet this time and intimate. But for the rest it was disappointingly the same; the sag of the mattress to accommodate her husband's large and decently shirted form, the brush of his lips on her forehead as he saluted her with a chaste 'goodnight'. Then nothing, just as before. Ellin could hear his breathing – great heavy breaths, feel the drag of the covers as they lifted to each intake. She could even feel the warmth of his body, because its weight had drawn her down to within a few inches of his left arm and thigh, close as two wax figures in an old fashioned picture frame. But how long, oh merciful heaven how long before he'd reach out and touch her? How long before that helpful little slope could be allowed to bring her down to meet him?

* * *

Had his wife but known it, Rafe was quite as acutely aware at that moment of the position of his own arm and the precarious incline of the mattress above it, even of the cadences of his own breathing – for he held them all within the same heroic control. He'd sworn to grant her time, to subjugate his own needs if necessary for weeks together, until Ellin was ready to come to him freely of her own accord. So he too lay unmoving in the great bed, like Tristan in the legend, with only the sword-blade of his honour to separate them.

He'd lain awake that second night long after she had slept, dry mouthed and faintly perspiring. And somehow as he lay there his right hand had found its way into the open neck of his nightshirt, fumbling tentatively as it might be her hand, to feel the contours of his own chest – the bristling hair, the steady beat of his own heart. To tease a useless nipple into phantom arousal, while all the time his inward eye tormented him with visions of posturing succubae and copulatory acrobats. Until in his imagination his arms were already round her, his flesh against hers – as much of it as he could press against her. Yet only the right hand could move still. Because to move the left but a little, no more perhaps than its own span, would be to touch her. And to touch her would be to lift the invisible sword from between them.

Then Ellin herself had stirred in her sleep, turning away from him to curl embryo-fashion, hugging her legs in to her soft woman's body. Only to extend them again almost at once, bracing back as if at Rafe's express command, down through the rising curtain of her nightrail, backwards and downwards into warm collision with his redundant left hand. And not all the philosophical volumes in his library could have saved their student then from his Promethean fate.

He was never afterwards to know whether Ellin had been awake or asleep at the actual moment of her body's invasion. So acquiescent, so open had it come to him. Nor, to his shame, could he recall if he'd sought her permission in words, or merely thought to do it and then shed the thought like a superfluous item of clothing as he raised his own knees behind hers. He knew because his body knew that she moved beside him as he pressed down, hard down on her shoulders. But whether she resisted, whether indeed he'd forced her, he was unable to tell. He knew only that she cried out. That he'd heard her cry and ignored it, ruthless in his passion. That despite every resolution to the contrary, he'd deflowered her from behind and beneath with no more consideration than any lumbering stock bull might feel for the heifer he serves. Without a vestige of abnegation or restraint.

Yet it was a measure of Rafe's true character that the first practical thoughts to emerge from his self-recriminations, concerned the course of his immediate duty as he now perceived it. And in a little while he'd risen to pull on a bedgown and light fresh candles, to fetch clean linen from the chest and to prepare a sedative draught for his wife, while she attended to her own toilet and to the bloodstained bedding.

"Drink it while it's yet warm," he advised her on his return. "'Tis a sack-posset with the addition of a little laudanum to induce sleep – and to help soothe your . . ."

His professional manner faltered before the brilliance of her smile and something tightened in his throat. "That is to say, 'twill ease any discomfort you may still be experiencing," he concluded huskily.

"Thank you."

She took the cup from him without hesitation, holding it in both hands to sip at the milky wine posset – her slim fingers translucent, rosy-tipped in the candlelight. "Thank you, Rafe," she repeated, awarding her husband his Christian name for the first time; and thereby increasing Rafe's own discomfort a hundred-fold.

He stared at her stupidly. A stranger in his bed. A parson's daughter, a sheltered innocent of but nineteen summers – but recently subjected to a brutal and degrading act – in pain perhaps even now, with the impression of his body still upon her. Yet smiling up at him implausibly over the rim of her cup, for all the world as if it were he and not she who needed comforting! As a physician who'd attended the parturitions, the complaints and the deaths of more women than he could recall, Rafe was well aware – had even recorded in his case notes – that despite every convention to the contrary, the female was invariably the more resilient of the sexes. But like so many otherwise intelligent men, he saw nothing inconsistent in the exclusion of his own circumstance from any such professional observation. Patients were one thing, personal relations quite another. Was he not after all eleven years this girl's senior? Educationally and venereally experienced as it was impossible for her to be? A man, with a man's privileges of intellect and emotional control? But of course he was! The guilt he now felt for his abuse of such advantages, blinding him to the fact that Ellin's suffering at that moment was in reality a good deal less acute than his own.

"My dear, you shame me!" A juvenile confession that he instantly regretted; blurting it out at her, as he had, more in the way of an accusation than an admission of failure. "I mean that the grossness of my behaviour cannot possibly deserve either your thanks or your smile," he felt bound to explain with a kind of desperate pedantry that to his own ears sounded hardly less objectionable.

He tried again, forcing himself to hold fast to those pellucid grey eyes of hers by way of a penance. "Below stairs in the dispensary just now I determined to beg your forgiveness," he said miserably. "Not to condone or exonerate, but only to forgive me if you could."

"To forgive you, Sir? For claiming your due as a husband?"

The girl's surprise at the idea was clearly unfeigned. And that of course made things even worse.

"No, but you must not," he found himself almost shouting in

his agitation, "you must not forgive me so easily! Not at least until you've heard me out. My dear girl, don't you see that I can only look you in the face on the understanding that there will never be a repetition . . . that I can place my hand on my breast like this and swear that I will never touch you but when you tell me that I may, never treat you but with courtesy and a very proper . . ."

He was dripping candle grease on the turkey rug. And in the midst of his self-abasement he saw a spasm pass across his wife's pale features.

"My dear, what ails you? Are you well?" He started forward anxiously to assist her.

"No, oh no," she gasped. "Oh dear, I'm sorry . . .!" as helplessly she began to laugh.

*   *   *

No really, it had been too much for her sense of the ridiculous. And so different to anything she could have imagined. Like the time at Sellington Gap when she'd started out on a catalogue of abuses for that abominable brother of his, and ended up laughing like a hyena at her own fraudulence. Unforgiveable, intolerable to laugh at her dear Mr Corbyn, and at such a time! But then how could anyone be expected to keep their countenance when the man was so determined to place himself in the wrong? And to look so droll too while he was about it, with his hand on his heart and his dripping candle! – the majestic effect of his Indian silk bedgown offset so comically by his want of wig or slippers, by his tufty cropped pate and great bare toes!

"Dear me, I fear 'tis I who should apologise for my monstrous rudeness," she'd contrived in the grip of another paroxysm. "You'll think me a dreadful giddy-head, Sir, as a fact. But oh dear, there is laughing room in our situation, you must agree?"

'And now surely he has to laugh as well,' she thought. 'He'll laugh in a minute and make us friends again.'

But her husband it seemed was unable to find any of the laughing room that she'd discovered. And slowly, unwillingly, Ellin's own smile retreated from her face, confronted as it was by the very portrait of embarrassment that was Mr Corbyn's.

'And dear heaven, how do you propose to tell the man you never slept?' she demanded of herself, with one of those little reflex shudders that sometimes follow involuntary laughter. 'How will you now tell him that you were awake from first to last and all along?'

The answer was plain. She could not, could never – no, not if she lived a thousand years!

* * *

A single horseman climbed the chalk track out of Jevington village, his *étui* of surgeon's instruments at the saddle, his hat pulled well down against a westering sun. It was July. A malty fragrance of making hay drifted across the combe to him from the steep meadows of Oxendean, and from the garlands of white clematis along his path the hint of a more delicate perfume. 'Bethwine' they called it in Sussex, this chalk-loving vine, 'Tom Bacca' or 'Traveller's Joy'. Though little enough joy in it today for the gentleman doctor, plodding homeward by Long Brow from the most ill-conditioned assembly of patients in all the five parishes of his practice.

More than one villager had muttered that there must have been a witch's curse on Jevington that summer of 1797, there justabout must. Or why else should misfortunes pile so one upon another? A wet haymaking, an epidemical outbreak amongst cattle or Christians, these things anyone could understand; for such natural disasters were commonplace within any country community. But in a fine season to be so afflicted? And in place of typhus or the smallpox this summer, by such a bewildering variety of ills? A witch's curse, it was the only reasonable explanation.

Rafe Corbyn of course held no belief in witches, nor in any of the other superstitious explanations for the ills that afflicted the downland villages. For all their horrid diversity, the outbreaks of fever and consumption, the scrofulae, scurvies and digestive distempers he'd lately been called on to attend might rather be traced, he thought, to the debilitated state of the villagers who'd contracted them – to the destructive combination of another fruitless war, of two years of disastrous harvests and of the hardest single winter in living memory.

In January of 1795 unprecedented frosts had frozen the chamber pots above stairs at Chalkdean, the Thames in London and the Ouse and Cuckmere rivers in Sussex, decimating livestock and exhausting local food reserves. So bitterly cold was it that downland folk declared they must have left the weather-gates open at the final Lewes sheep fair in September. Across the Channel in Flanders the British troops, for the most part without anything more substantial than flannel weskits to keep them warm, had suffered greater losses from sickness and exposure than from enemy action. In Holland the freezing of the Texel had enabled the revolutionary armies to complete their conquest in original style, by sending out their mounted Hussars to surround a helplessly ice-bound Dutch fleet. And back in England meantime, gales and floods had followed the great freeze to ruin spring planting. Despite government imports, bread and fresh meat were already in short supply even before the failure of the subsequent harvest. The Corbyns, the Gages of Firle, even the Ashbys of Sellington had distributed such corn as they could spare. But it wasn't nearly enough. Over the Cuckmere at Blatchington, provision riots amongst the regiments quartered there had ended in the looting of local shops and flour mills. In London, where the poor were dying like flies, the windows of the State Coach were smashed and King George himself petitioned by a rabble chanting, "Bread! Bread! Give us peace and bread!" And to make matters worse still, national ballots to raise men for a Supplementary Militia the following year had left fatherless households everywhere, to support themselves on a shilling or two a week out of army allowances or overtaxed parish funds – with wheat as high as twenty-eight shillings a bushel and quarter-loaves selling nowhere for less than ninepence.

Part way up the hill out of Jevington, Rafe turned in the saddle to rest his eyes from the glaring reflection of the chalk. Below him the track descended directly to the village street, its thatched and ivied cottages dwarfed into miniature by the great bare breasts of the mother hills, by Combe Down and Bourne Hill beyond. A scene worthy of the pen of a Thomas Gray, some might say, or the brush of a Gainsborough? If they could but steel themselves to ignore the hunger, the filth and the disease of its human occupation!

Rafe turned back wearily from the sight. He did what he could. As a landowner he contributed corn and helped to fund the Poor Relief out of his taxes. As a physician he scaled his fees to his patients' means – seldom charged his one and sixpence for a visit, and never pressed for payment. Because the truth was that more often than not his prescriptions failed to cure. For of what use were vomits, purges and suppurations, or all the remedies of the Apothecaries' Hall to a body already so hopelessly weakened?

The sun had already touched the chalk summit of Long Brow up ahead; a golden ball of fire poised as it seemed to roll over and away out of sight, down by Lullington and its notorious racetrack to the Cuckmere and the sea. Gold then for Lullington on the weather side of the ridge, shadows and sickness for poor Jevington in its lee. An appropriate enough contrast when one considered how mighty rich Harris and his Lullington gang had now become out of war shortages and rising taxes – with Aaron as their agent in Normandy still, busy feathering a nest for himself in some grand merchant's establishment at his own countrymen's expense.

And was it for this that he'd saved the boy from an ignominious death from exposure or pneumonia with the British troops in Flanders? Was Aunt Drusilla in the right after all? Had honour indeed lost all meaning for Aaron? Rafe frowned and prompted the horse onward with a nudge of his heels. If only he could simply leave his brother to find his own way to the devil by the shortest route and then contrive to forget him, as he knew most other men would have done in his place – to forget poor Mamma on her deathbed, parchment-faced, gripping his hand in hers: "See after your brother, *will* you Rafe? See after Aaron for me – please . . ." That memory in particular had refused to fade, prompting him in June to send again for the prodigal's return.

Chalkdean.
Tuesday June 13, 1797.

Sir,

Or is to be 'My Dear Aaron' still? As I write I find myself in the curious case of one who hardly knows how to give title to his own brother, so estranged have we now become. And yet the mother we both loved, the years we have shared together beneath this roof must still make their claim, must they not? There is so much malice, envy and nonsense in the world, perceive my true affection, Brother, however I may choose to preface it.

It has been a good while in my head and my heart to tax you with some further correspondence, for all that I've yet to receive an answer to my last letter. And believe me, I'd willingly set down my pen and take ship to you in France, if only I could think it would help to bring you to your senses. In the past I have tried to reconcile myself to your enterprises abroad as to those of some temporary adventure which would be detrimental in effect to no one but yourself. I could not have forseen then, I think, that the war would last so long, nor that a little loose trade with the Normandy coast could materially damage our country's interests. But now, Sir, we all see things with a different face. It is asserted in Westminster, and even in our own courts, that what began as a diversion for profiteers and adventurers has now become a traitorous felony. You know as well as I that England's prosperity depends on gold. Yet our reserves of that commodity are now so diminished that the banks must issue paper notes of small denomination, while bullion they say is still transferred in large quantity to the French. ('Smugglers' gold', to purchase contraband and finance the forces of the enemy.) I have even heard it told that French soldiers are now clad in Lancashire cloth, with Nottingham boots on their feet!

Hitherto Aaron, you have always represented this business as standing between so many of our poor villagers and the workhouse. But that metal no longer rings true. Because now they go hungry I tell you, while that vagabond of Lullington grows fatter and more arrogant with every day that passes. His pack-horses still run untaxed. He even buys substitutes for his men to meet the militia quotas. He laughs in the Commissioners' faces. Yet unwisely I assure you, for the tide is turning against the trade in Sussex, and they've sworn to bring him down.

A man may be brutalized all too easily by greed, if I may term it so. But from the degree of sense that you have, Brother, and knowing you to have come into the world too greatly favoured by nature and fortune to have need of such trade, I am persuaded that you will see the folly of siding with these felons against the interests of your own country. Indeed I cannot conceive that at the last you will choose to forfeit your heritage and waste away the promise of your youth in such a cause.

I fancy you are wearied of this. But you who know me so well will surely comprehend that I have your best interests at heart. For the last time I put it to your conscience, Sir. Return now to the right side of the water before it is too late. Become a Voluntary Patroller or train as a militiaman, list with a fighting regiment if you must – but only return!

For to see you yet where you belong with your two feet firm on Sussex chalk, is the most earnest wish of your affectionate brother,

R. Corbyn

PS: I am placing this letter in the hand of one you know, Sir, who has assured me of its safe delivery within the week, and without interference of the seal. And indeed I trust he has not deceived me, for the sake of all I put at risk by sending directly to you again in France. R.C.

Chapter Ten

The familiar roofs of Chalkdean were visible at last to the returning horseman, settled like another little village within their own downland combe. Soon now the precarious tip-tilting descent, the enveloping animal odours of the cowsheds and stables, the boy setting aside his tack and polish to hurry forward for the bridle . . .

It was a game Rafe often played at homecomings such as this, riding on before himself in his own imagination, anticipating every homeward step. Until finally he attained the flags without his own drawing room window – no longer now the eager anticipant but in his phantasy a stranger, looking in as a stranger might on the charming sheltered world of the Corbyns of Chalkdean Manor.

Someone had lit a bonfire earlier in the day, up beyond the wall of the herb garden. Now though it was dying. Its smoke drifted hazily across the brick frontage of the old house flattening its perspectives, increasing for Rafe its sense of unreality. In an elbow chair in the window like a cut-out in a ha'penny peepshow, sat Aunt Drusilla, gaunt and ill-favoured as ever in her lace pallatine and ruffled turkey-tail bonnet; yet immeasurably improved to the eye of any observer by the presence just now of a tiny white-clad child at her knee.

'And what if that little miss were not your own dear Lizzy?' her father teased himself. 'What a perfect model for an angel you'd suppose her then, in her grown-up silk and muslin. And what would you not give as a stranger, Rafe, to hear that fluffy little moppet cry out "Papa!" and run into your arms?'

Before he could indulge himself with any further such nonsense, however, the child had flung herself up onto her great-aunt's lap, working with determined knees and elbows to a position from which she might snatch the spectacles from that irresistibly prominent nose. An act of reckless piracy which for any other mortal would surely have been attended by the most fearful consequences. Whereas in this event the lady not only smiled as she retrieved her endangered opticals, but actually reached out to hug the little vandal to her disappointed bosom. And from the flags outside the window, the watcher too had smiled. Miracles still happened, it appeared, even in 1797!

Beyond the modern miracle a small brown and white terrier sat prick-eared and intent, backturned to the window. And beyond the dog on the far side of the room, a young woman in a blue silk gown was coaxing an air from the ivories of a harpsichord. It was the sound that had attracted Rafe to the window in the first place. And as his gaze came to rest on the white neck beneath the piled Grecian-crown of curls, on the straight back, on the soft curves of the girl's seat on the stool, he could no longer imagine how any man might feel as a stranger to such delights. For the days when Rafe Corbyn could so regard his young wife had long since passed.

If Ellin's laughter had seemed misplaced to her husband the night he'd consummated their marriage almost three years before, her obvious contrition at the time had soon convinced him of its hysterical origin. Shock at the degrading nature of the act had temporarily unhinged her, he decided. (His fault of course, not hers – no blame attached to Ellin.) And when a few nights later this sweetly forgiving girl voluntarily reached out for him across the bed, Rafe had gently put her from him, unflinching in his determination to spare her feelings and subordinate his own unruly desires.

Yet disgracefully the chief of Rafe's thoughts as he now beheld her, as the tinkling notes of the harpsichord drifted out to him on the evening air, concerned themselves still with the vital currents of his own virility, and its most obvious application to that soft young body. For the truth was that the more he toiled to subdue his physical appetite for his young wife, the more he was enslaved by it. From the early days of their marriage he'd frequently denied himself the pleasure of her society, making work for himself in his dispensary or at his escritoire, only to quiet the cravings that nagged and gnawed at him so obsessively. And every once and again when the demands of the flesh had become too persistent to be suppressed, he'd made certain to observe his own rule most scrupulously; never taking her but with her verbal acquiescence, disburthening himself always in the minimum time, deliberately reducing the act almost to the level of those other unavoidable evacuations to which all mortal systems are subject.

But despite heroic efforts – however he might strive to confine the monster in its lair – it continued to plague him with obscene urges for exhibition and debauch, for visual as well as tactile excesses, which he knew must disgust his young bride beyond measure if ever he permitted her to guess at them.

* * *

'Here the rosebuds in June and the violets are blooming,
The small birds they warble from every green bough . . .'

Ellin crooned the words of the lilting Sussex ballad barely above her breath, picking out the accompaniment on the instrument which she'd persuaded her husband to have re-tuned and carried down from his mother's old music room above stairs; staring sightlessly at the wall before her as she did so.

'Here's the pink and the lily and the daffydowndilly,
To adorn and perfume the sweet meadows in June . . .'

Such a simple and pleasing little celebration of summer, she thought, for all its botanical inaccuracies. And not a trace of sadness in the thing to excuse her tears. Surreptitiously Ellin brushed them from her cheeks and lashes, remained for a moment with her hands resting on the keys, and then rose from the stool with a freshly determined smile.

"Come along, Lizzy my love," she said brightly, beckoning to the child on Aunt Corbyn's lap, "bedtime!"

At which of course the other woman must feel compelled to be obstructive. "There child," she said, tightening her own thin arm around the little girl, "it wants another hour at least 'til dinner time, and to be sure it will do you no harm to wait up a little longer for your father."

And was it ever to be thus between them, Ellin thought wearily. Duels endlessly over Lizzy, over Rafe's affections and the management of his household? Tussles even for the keys of the tea chests and linen cupboards?

"Aunt Corbyn, I'd take it kindly if you would give me credit for knowing what is good for my own daughter and what is not," she said loudly and slowly to make sure of being heard. "And to avoid confusing the child, I really must insist, Ma'am, that you leave such matters to me. "Now then, Lizzy." She held out an uncompromising hand to the child. "Henshaw will be down for you in two shakes of a lambkin's tail, and we mustn't keep her waiting, my love, now must we?"

It had been a close-run thing though. Lizzy had come with the greatest reluctance at a slowish alderman's pace, and Aunt Corbyn might have rivalled Medusa herself for her petrifying stare. Yet neither had actually defied her, which was in itself she supposed a kind of victory. And by the time Ellin had returned the little girl to her nursemaid and made her own way back to the drawing room, she was in a mood to be conciliatory.

'For what can a little polite dissimulation signify one way or the other in the cause of a peaceful evening?' she reasoned with her pride. 'She's a possessive and jealous old maid who's bound to resent you whatever you do; you may as well accept it. And there's nothing to be gained by provoking her more than you can help.'

She took the plunge. "If I appeared rude just now, Aunt Corbyn, then I'm sorry for it," she said pacifically. (If only the need to raise one's voice wouldn't lend the words such a false emphasis.) "Believe me, I am only too delighted that you and Elizabeth should take such pleasure in each other's company. But as her mother, I also happen to think that her health and the proper formation of her character must suffer from too much drawing room society. An apprehension I should think you'd understand, Ma'am," she added significantly, "for I'm persuaded that you yourself could never have been permitted such liberties as a child, any more than I was."

And there, she'd done it again! With whatever good intentions she began, something unworthy in Ellin, something not wholly unconnected with mischief, always seemed to finish up deliberately goading the woman into a contradictory statement. As if some immutable law of nature declared them bound to cross swords whenever they conversed.

"My infancy and what I was or was not permitted to do is hardly to the purpose," Mistress Corbyn remarked without looking up from the stitchwork in her lap. "What is plain to me, however, is that you have determined to exclude that child, to her certain ruin, from the only influences that are at all likely to civilize her. I mean of course those of myself and her father. And furthermore, Madam . . ."

But Ellin could not wait for the further thrust, the desire for a satisfactory riposte of her own had been far too great. "By what right pray, do you tell me how to manage my own child – and within my own household too?" she struck in with the most effective weapon she could lay her hand to. "Do me the favour to recall, Ma'am, that Lizzy *is* my daughter and not yours. Nor ever will be!"

"I will tell you by what right, by the right of superiority! Do you understand me?" Drusilla enquired of her mending needle. "By right of superior birth and upbringing and superior experience – qualifications which, as a mere parson's daughter, you can never aspire to." Her mouth clamped shut in a long hard line of contempt and the frills of her cap trembled. But still she refused to look up.

"And I say the only rights you have in this house are those that my husband chooses to grant you out of the kindness of his heart!" The temptation to hit her, to drag off that ridiculous goffered bonnet and send the woman sprawling to the floor, was well nigh irresistible.

"*My* husband, Aunt High-and-Mighty – my daughter and my house, d'ye hear Not yours but MINE!"

Notably though, it was the younger and not the elder Mistress Corbyn who then turned in a phrenzy to run from the room. And it was not until she could hear her own feet pounding the hollow treads of the staircase, that Ellin perceived the absurdity of retreat at such a moment. Her rights and her house, or so she claimed. Yet here was she halfway up the stairs, and there was that insufferable woman in calm possession of her own drawing room! Impetuosity again, Ellin – reckless, ruinous impetuosity! Two and twenty years of age, married for almost three of them and already the mother of a two-year-old child. But the years had brought her little enough, it would appear, either of wisdom or maturity. She checked herself on the first landing-place, beneath the portrait of Rafe's mother in panniers and a powdered wig, then slowly began to descend again.

"So what now, Strap?" she asked disconsolately of the little terrier who'd followed her out into the vestibule and now stood waiting at the bottom of the forbidden stairs. "Must we now return in ignominy to the strains of the 'Pink and the Lily'? Or hazard a little Mozart, perhaps? And very like to an accompaniment of quite another kind from Madam Face-ache in the window! Or shall we retire to repair our dignity in the Master's library, and make him seek us out there when he returns?"

Despite his youth, the terrier's intelligence was as acute as any of his breed. And at the very mention of the word, he bustled off across the hall flags to stand quivering at the library door, every sense focused on its unattainable brass handle. Ellin smiled in spite of herself. Of all the terrier whelps in the hunt kennels, her little Strap had been the only one bold enough to approach her as she knelt in the straw to examine the litter, squirming forward on his fat little belly to lick her hand. Perhaps some instinct had told him even then that they were to be friends? And ever since, he'd loved her as only a dog can do, entirely without reserve. The most engaging and least complicated affection, Ellin sometimes thought, of all her life to date.

Once inside the room the dog hurried over to the empty hearth and flung himself down beside it, first to scratch and then to wash every part of his anatomy within reach or reason, while behind him Ellin listlessly perambulated the bookshelves. It was a ritual so frequently performed that she very nearly had the titles by heart. A collection, as she'd long since discovered, entirely untainted by the type of sentimental or gothic novel to which she so unworthily inclined. Nothing here by Mrs Parsons or Charlotte Smith. Few enough fictional works by any writer – neither Walpole, Fielding or Smollet, nor even Defore. A little of Richardson only, and Fanny Burney's *Cecilia* (which Ellin had already read three times). But there again, more Shakespeare, Milton and Bunyan, more English historians and French critics in more editions than anyone could possibly hope to benefit from! She looked at the gold-stamped titles but barely troubled to read them, asking herself instead as she moved on past Plutarch and Gibbon, Chambers, Wiseman's *Surgery* and *Elementa Medicinae* by the foot and the yard, whether she could ever really hope to make a fit wife for a husband as serious-minded and scientifically inclined as hers.

Not that Rafe himself had ever been so discourteous as to criticize her for her narrow parlour education. On the contrary, he seemed very nearly as convinced as her father that women were temperamentally unsuited to erudition. And when Ellin had teased him for such old fashioned notions and begged him to instruct her, to read over to her the passages that most interested him in these worthy volumes of his, she'd merely proved his point for him by wandering off into reveries of her own while he so obliged her. She had listened enthralled to the timbre of her husband's deep voice, to the undercurrents of warmth in the voice itself rather than to the ideas it framed. She had watched his strong fingers turning the pages, remarking the little tufts of hair above his knuckles, his clean spade-shaped nails. Her own man, a dream fulfilled – and yet . . . Only to realize with a start that Rafe had stopped reading to ask her opinion of something she hadn't heard, smiling down at her with the fond amusement of a man to whom even his young wife's lack of application was charming.

In Chichester Ellin had heard women talk indulgently of their husbands as 'great big babbies, bless 'em – and oftentimes more trouble than kiddies and all!' But no one could ever see a husband as mature as hers in such a light. In their marriage it was she rather who'd become the child, Ellin thought ruefully. That her husband was proud of her – of her appearance, and of the obvious effect she had on other men at the social functions they attended – she was well aware. But when it came to the more practical duties of a wife, she'd found herself frustrated at every turn. In the running of their household at Chalkdean Mistress Drusilla contrived somehow to be always there before her, ever ready to assure Ellin that her interference was neither appreciated nor required. And Rafe too, gently advising her to leave such humdrum business to his aunt. A nursemaid, Mrs Henshaw, had been engaged from East-Bourne to care for Elizabeth, and for any other children Ellin might elect to present him with. And even in the bedroom, her husband had made it clear to her that a gentleman should expect little more from his wife between the sheets than the passive reception of his body every once in a while.

At the time of their wedding Ellin had gaily promised herself to be bountiful, to be everything to Rafe that he could possibly need in a woman – never dreaming that he'd actually demand so little of her. Men were born and remained free and equal in rights, or so he assured her. But what of poor women? To be possessed with such gentlemanly restraint – to be subjected to such briskness and vigour when all one's body cried out for caresses, and afterwards to mere affection when only violence and passion would have served.

Three years earlier, Ellin had truly believed that marriage and the blessing of children would cure her of her impetuosities and all her secret longings, to complete her as a woman. Now she had a kind and generous husband, a real man. Now she had affluence, an allowance for her clothing and all the daily necessities for a comfortable life. So much one would have thought to be grateful for. Yet here was she, as hampered in spirit, as confused and restless, as much in need of entertainment and stimulation as ever she had been in the old days of Chichester and Sellington Parsonage.

"And is that only to be gained from buying dresses in Lewes, or from driving out to an assembly or a charity ball once in a way? Or from scratting with that possessive old beldame in the drawing room? Well, and what do you say? Are they now to be my only diversions?"

She put it to Strap in the tone of voice she always reserved for her smallest friend and greatest ally in the house. And by way of reply the little dog abandoned his toilet to lavish on her a look of concentrated devotion, and to thump on the floorboards with his inconsiderable stump of a tail.

* * *

By the time Ellin shepherded his daughter from the drawing room, Rafe was already feeling distinctly uncomfortable in his role as spy. And he was belatedly preparing to make an entrance, when a violent movement in the window caught his eye. It was not simply that his aunt had dropped her mending – for in Rafe's experience dropped mending could be relied upon to travel for short distances only, and then generally at something below shoulder height. Nor was it even the force with which she'd hurled the offending garment from her. It was the expression on her large features as she crossed the window embrasure to retrieve it that froze him where he stood. For a moment Drusilla's face had been in clear profile to the garden. And in a single shocking impression of twisted mouth and glaring eye, Rafe perceived there an intensity of emotion that he'd never suspected in the woman – not through all the years of her complaints and bullyings and her petty squabbles with his brother.

In the next moment, however, Rafe's attention was again distracted. This time by the clamping of a horse's hooves on the path through the smoky herb garden above him. It was a short cut to Friston Bottom and the coast; a route expressly forbidden to all riders by his aunt, and only ever used in defiance of her rule by a single member of the family.

"Aaron, good God!" His brother had known to expect him even before he emerged, gathering substance out of the bonfire smoke like a rider from the apocalypse.

"'Good God,' Ray? Now surely you mean 'good evening'?" Aaron's own greeting held as much ironical amusement and as little significance as any other casual homecoming of the past years. For all the world as if he was simply slipping in through the garden after a day at the Lewes raceyard or an afternoon of coursing on the Dencher. "And how very civil of you, if I may say, to run out to meet me, Sir, like this."

* * *

Unshockable himself, Aaron loved to surprise, never tired of the spectacle of emotional conflict in others – his brother's in particular. Poor old Ray, struggling now to accommodate shock and pleasure and resentment at being so teased, all at the one moment – reactions chasing each other like cloud shadows across his countenance. Yet he would not have been Ray neither, if natural affection had not shortly triumphed over all to produce a smile to correspond with his own.

"By my word, Aaron, it *is* you!" he at last declared, striding forward to seize the horse's bridle and clasp his brother's free hand, as if he quite expected him to fade back into the smoke again and out of sight.

"The very one, Brother. But why so amazed? Your dearest wish, as I recall it, was to see these feet of mine firm on Sussex chalk." Aaron raised himself in the saddle to disengage a stirrup and wave one boot absurdly in the air. "So here you have it then, nothing simpler!" With which he swung back over the horse's rump to spring nimbly to the ground.

Chapter Eleven

"And are we now to assume that Aaron expects to return to Chalkdean as if nothing has happened?" Drusilla Corbyn enquired of the dining board at large. "And are we to be prepared to feed and to house him, might I ask – to admit him to our stall in the church without so much as an apology for the injury he has done to our characters? Without any indication, for the matter of that, of his intention to reform?"

"But how wonderfully well you put it, my dear Aunt." Aaron smiled fondly across at her. "And may I add that the graciousness of your manner is only exceeded by the heartwarming affection of your welcome. I'faith, I see no help for it but to oblige you to the fullest and stay forevermore!"

Knowing that she'd never ask him to repeat an impertinence, he'd purposely pitched it too low for her insensitive ear. And while his aunt glowered impotently, and Rafe hastened to divert the conversation to a safer topic, Aaron turned the warmth of his smile upon the other female at his brother's table.

Her blush was rather charming, he thought, wickedly raising his own red brows to see how much deeper he could make it go. The extra flesh that child-bearing had added to her figure was also becoming to his little sister-in-law. A girl worth looking at, by jakes! And spunk enough to raise her voice to old dragon Drusilla withal, from what he'd heard from the garden. Yet for all, that she hadn't changed so greatly. Motherhood and three years in his brother's bed had failed to rob the parson's daughter of the quality he best remembered. No indeed! It was there in her grey eyes still, clear as a trade card for any man who *was* a man to read.

* * *

When a little later both ladies had withdrawn to leave the gentlemen to their brandy, Rafe returned doggedly to the question that lay between them.

"See here Aaron, 'twas unhandsome of you to so tease our aunt at dinner," he began, aware of his own pomposity, yet somehow unable to evade it. "In truth she has every right to call you to account, as I have myself, Brother. After so long an absence even you must see it would be unreasonable to expect aught else."

"Oh indeed, unreasonable to a degree." Aaron put up his feet and crossed his booted ankles, see-sawing in his chair. "And whatever else we may do, my dear Ray, we must ever strive to be reasonable must we not?" He smiled again broadly to show white teeth, uncommonly regular, all but the pointed canines.

"Yes, Sir, I think that we should. And will you now begin perhaps by favouring me with an explanation for this visit of yours? One I can believe, Aaron. Are you now come, as I am hoping you have, to tell us that this war has brought you to your senses at last? That you've finally done with French trading and those blackguards of Lullington, and are ready to return now where you belong?"

"Where I belong?" With a sudden burst of energy that reminded Rafe of the irrepressible child he'd once been, Aaron crashed his chair back to the boards and strode off across the room to the close-stool in the corner between the sideboards. "And where in cockoo's name d'ye suppose I *do* belong, Sir? At Lewes with the whop-straws, trading last year's mouldy corn for twice its natural worth? Or up on the downs at Bright'on, is it – playing at toy soldiers for the Prince of Wales? Or sitting like a castrated puss in a corner of my aunt's parlour while she tells the world how greatly she prefers my brother? Is that what you have in mind for me?"

He lifted the lid on the spode chamber pot, unbuttoned and used it noisily, holding down his breeches-fall with one hand and taking aim with the other. At ease with his own flesh in a way that his inhibited brother could never be.

"I meant in England," Rafe persisted awkwardly, "the land that gave you birth, Sir. For whatever blows or disappointments you've sustained, Aaron, you can hardly blame England for them. Like it or not, this is your country, and your first duty . . ."

"Duty – back to duty, bigod!" Aaron shook himself vigorously, flicked down the mahogany lid and turned to face his brother at the table. "And what of challenge and opportunity and all the daily hazards that give flavour to a man's life? Really Brother, 'tis wonderful to think you can have reached the great age that you have and still remained so utterly unworldly. Why I doubt even now you could be trusted to recognize a good opening when ye saw it – no Ray, not if it had hair round it!"

"Damn it Aaron, you grow too wild! There's no occasion for such coarseness."

"But tell me truly, Ray," the young vulgarian continued blandly, "d'ye never tire of tight and tidy morals, of that infernally straight and narrow way of yours? D'ye never miss excitement in your life, nor think to take a shorter route to what you want?"

"No Brother, not if it involves the wilful exploitation of others to reach it. That is the way of the barbarian of the dark ages, not of the enlightened man. We are trying to improve ourselves, are we not? That surely is what our civilization is all about."

But Aaron did not appear to be listening. In a few more rapid strides he'd reached the dining room door. Behind it, in a grimy heap, lay the saddle-bags he'd kept within such close sight since parting from his horse. Stooping to wrench back the straps of the nearest, he extracted a bulging leather sac and returned with it to the table.

"Five hundred guinea here alone, Ray!" he exclaimed in sudden triumph, releasing the contents in a glittering cascade onto the table cloth. "And four more over there of the same." He waved the empty sac in the direction of the saddle-bags. "You need gold, you say, to help finance Pitt's war for him and to feed our starving villagers. All very fine, so take it!"

Scooping up a fistful of coins, he lifted Rafe's hand and trickled them, chinking, into his palm. "Take it Ray, and use it for whatever philanthropic purpose you like. Use it for Loyalty Loans, or for pills and potions, or on bread for the poorhouse if that's your fancy."

But this time when his mouth smiled his eyes remained in earnest. "Think of it, if you like, as a step forward for civilization," he said with a note of eagerness in his voice that was impossible to ignore, "the gift of a dark age barbarian to the noble cause of enlightenment. Only take it, Brother – please."

He seemed about to say more, but changed his mind. For a full minute they stared at each other in silence across the table, while Rafe once more recalled the boy in Aaron – bright-eyed and freckle-faced, so anxious always for approval . . .

"Race me, race me home, Ray! Your horse against my pony – and still I'll win, you'll see . . .!"

"Contraband gold, Sir? Tainted coin for patriotic loans?" he said at last, dropping back the shining discs without taking his eyes from his brother's face. "Are you really such a child still, Aaron, that you imagine I could even consider such a thing? Do you not understand that to take this gift of yours would be to condone the system of greed and brutality it represents? And that I'll never do, Brother, not even for you."

"God's blood, Ray, you can't be as great a fool as you pretend! 'Tis the same coin, for pity's sake, whoever's hand it's passed through! Man alive, 'twill buy the same whether it's crossed the Channel a dozen times or travelled no further from the mint than to the coffers of the Bank of England. Can't you see?"

"And can't you see how tall I've grown? Look, look now Ray! Up to your second weskit button, can't you see? And soon I'll be taller yet . . ."

"Maybe it will buy the same," Rafe said gently, responding still to the eager child he remembered. "But would I be the same d'ye think, if I took it? The same in my own estimate, or yours, Aaron?"

He withdrew his hand from the contentious gold to trace a fold of the linen cloth with his fingernail – down and up, up and down, as if to nerve himself for something unpalatable. "I am rejoiced that you have come home to us, truly so," he added at last. "And for my very life I hope that this time you'll remain; because that is the best gift you could give me, Brother. But let us have this clear between us for once and for good. Whatever you may have chosen to bring over from France with you, you have brought for yourself, Aaron, and not for me. For yourself alone, Sir. I'll take no part of it."

* * *

Near the middle of September, with the first frosts of autumn threatening and the barn-swallows mustering forces for their coming migration, Ellin Corbyn announced – and for once without fear of contradiction – that it was time and past time for the honey to be taken from the hives in the apple orchard.

"If you will only be good enough to dig out the pits for me tomorrow, Rafe," she'd boldly requested of her husband in their bedchamber the previous evening. "I will show you which hives. And then we may smoke them down at dusk together, to be ready to bring them in and break out the comb on Tuesday forenoon."

It was an event Ellin looked forward to, the annual wresting of the honey from the Chalkdean bees. In part, she cheerfully acknowledged, because Rafe's officious aunt had revealed herself unwilling to undertake such a hazard, being fearful of the stings (or 'bites' as the old Sussex bee-masters indifferently called them). And for the rest because she herself demonstrably was not! In Chichester the Rimmers had kept bees for many years; ever since Ellin had happened on a stray swam in the jasmine beneath her window at the Bishop's Palace, and hived it herself in a wooden wash-pail. Beekeeping she'd quickly discovered was a deal simpler than most bee-masters implied; for the insects themselves did by far the greater part of the work. Indeed she had missed her bees when she and her father had come to settle in Sellington. And when in the year following her marriage to Rafe his principal bee-master was ballotted into the militia, she'd willingly offered to take charge of his hives – those few that had survived the great frosts of the previous winter. It was something she could do for a change, which Aunt Know-it-all-Drusilla could not!

Rafe's personal presence was not in any real sense necessary to the operation of honey-taking. There were more than a dozen men on the estate who could have excavated Ellin's pits and lifted down her skeps for her to quite the same effect. But the truth was that she liked to have him there beside her. It boosted her confidence immensely to feel so capable in her husband's presence, to take the initiative for once in a business that was alien to him. Nor it seemed was Rafe anything loathe to act as her assistant. It did them both good, she truly believed it.

Before dusk on the appointed day then, Rafe had so far obliged his lady bee-master as to dig her a neat row of smoking pits in the chalky soil of the orchard, and to prepare to her specification a sufficient store of sulphur-papers for the hives she'd selected. Only to disappoint Ellin at the last by deserting her in favour of an urgent summons to Friston village. A laden waggon had overset there on the bank near the mill, to strangle one horse in its collar and pin the unlucky driver beneath it. A young Barton, so they heard, one of Sam Ashby's sister Susannah's great brood from East Dean.

"Cutting the corner too darn close, 'e were, and not for the first time neither," the Friston messenger had breathlessly appraised them. "Still breathing when I left 'im, Mister Corbyn, Sir. But white? Ye never seed nothing whiter! As white as any clout I guarantee – and safe to be church-yarded for a certainty, no error, an you doan't look deedy, Sir."

"So it seems there's to be no help for it, my dear," Ellin's husband had informed her in the preternaturally calm and collected manner he invariably reserved for such times of emergency. "I must naturally do what I can for the poor fellow. But in the meantime perhaps we can persuade young Aaron here to loan you a share of his muscle in my place? "Will you not, Brother? And to collect my portion of the stings for me while you're about it!"

'Though the Lord only knows 'tis none of my seeking,' Ellin repeated to herself, as she and Aaron left the house to climb up through Aunt Corbyn's flower and herb gardens to the walled orchard beyond. 'If he were not my brother-by-marriage, if Rafe himself had not suggested it, I swear he's the last man on earth I'd have chosen to venture abroad with after dusk, the very last!'

But was he really? Or was there not something about the fellow even now that intrigued her? For the fact was that after almost four years in Sellington, Ellin knew very little more about Aaron Corbyn than she had when she first beheld him in this same garden, in retreat from another of his aunt's polite drawing room teas. His brother she'd come to understand a little at least during the time they'd lived together as man and wife. Rafe had become real to her for all his heavy armour of obligation and reserve. She could see weaknesses in him as well as strengths – the stubborn will beneath his courtesy, the occasional lapses of control that made him only human. But Aaron remained incalculable. From the early days of their marriage, her husband had made it clear to Ellin that his brother's whereabouts and the rumours which constantly attached to Aaron's name were not topics that he cared to discuss. If anyone had enquired after him within her hearing, they were simply informed that the young man was completing his education abroad, touring in Switzerland or in Italy. And thereafter either Rafe or his aunt had seen to it that the subject was turned as soon as possible.

Only once, when recounting to Ellin the tragic history of their mother's fatal illness, had Rafe thrown any further light on his younger brother's character. Aaron had taken it desperately hard, he told her. All through her last long struggle he'd insisted on sitting at his mother's bedside, holding tightly to her clammy hand – urging her constantly to throw off the fever, and to live. And when at last the poor lady had lost that final battle, her fifteen-year-old son had refused to accept defeat. For the whole of one day and night he'd repulsed all efforts to make him leave her corpse – departing abruptly and without a word early the following morning, to ride away over the downs like a shot out of hell. Only to return days later – filthy, unshaven and reeking of cognac – in time to intercept her funeral cortège on its way to Sellington church, and publicly to abuse his mother in her coffin for the faithlessness of her betrayal. A desecration for which her sister-in-law, Drusilla Corbyn, had never forgiven him.

But all that had been eight, nine years before. After his brother's unexpected arrival home earlier in the summer, Rafe had impressed it on everyone that Aaron's future and not his past was what concerned him now. There was much, he said, that required the young man's attention on the estate and its tenantry farms, a vital harvest to be gathered in. And afterwards, with corn now at such a premium, more land than ever to be put down to cereals. Over at Glynde, John Ellman was using a modern threshing machine and a seed drill to speed matters forward; and Aaron could do worse, Rafe told him, than to follow the Duke of Bedford's example and make his own study of that excellent agri-culturalist's methods. The talk whenever the brothers met that summer of 1797 was largely of agrarian concerns. And if Rafe Corbyn wondered, as his wife did, why Aaron sometimes rose so mighty early or stayed out of doors so late – if ever he asked himself, as Ellin frequently did, whether his brother could always be over at Glynde with Mr Ellman when the farm bailiff came searching for him – then she never heard her husband speak of it.

Nor was Aunt Corbyn disposed to be any more forthcoming on the subject of her younger nephew. For if she spoke of him at all, in his absence or to his head, it was only in the most broadly abusive terms. Leaving Ellin to speculate as best she might as to whether the sensitive adolescent who'd grieved so extravagantly for his mother was still to be found in Aaron, somewhere beneath that confident exterior – while at the same time to wonder if the more recent tales her maid whispered to her over her morning chocolate might also possibly be true. Could her disreputable brother-in-law really have been living in France like a prince these three or four years past – and out of the proceeds of smuggled brandy and tobacco? And had he returned to Sussex now, as they said, only to make some new arrangements for its transport to the capital?

Was it possible? Aaron's French mode had certainly impressed her most particularly that day in Sellington when he'd caught her spying on him a second time, from the window . . .

Which was of course the other thing that made the fellow so unsettling – the check on Ellin's own conscience, with the know-ledge of those earlier encounters lying between them still like the guilty secrets that they were. He had only to look at her with those damnably knowing eyes of his, to smile as he was smiling at her now in the light of the candle-lanthorn he carried before her through the garden, to replace in her mind any lingering images of that pathetic orphaned youth, with others – more vivid and a great deal more embarrassing.

It was warm still for September. The bees had continued to forage amongst Aunt Corbyn's blue scabious and livelong sedums late into the afternoon. And it was not until after sunset that Ellin judged it safe to move the hives. Even then in the gathering dusk there'd been no more than the faintest tang in the air to betray the advance of autumn. The rustling leaves, the crickets in the grass, the drowsy bell-music from the sheep folds sounded no less permanent than they might have done a week or a month earlier, the perfume from the white tobacco plants behind the sedums no fainter. Yet they affected the man and the woman in the garden as if they had been, for they could feel the shift of the season within their own bodies. Death and decomposition for the leaves and the crickets and the white petals of the tobacco. And with it an unavoidable sense of nostalgia.

Behind them the rectangular bulk of the house was already receding into darkness. Even the blue of the sky was dimming at last, draining back into the land. Over Exceat Hill long banners of drifting cirrus showed scarlet and amber in the rays of an invisible sun; and as Ellin watched, a flight of gulls dropped through them, planing down through their fading colours to dissolve into the shadow of the hill.

The light from Aaron's lanthorn illuminated the plaited straw domes of the hives, ranged on a series of benches and tables at the southern end of the orchard. But as the young man stepped in behind them to where his brother had dug the first pit, Ellin hurried forward to intercept him, pulling down the veil of her hat and tying the tapes around her collar as she did so.

"Not yet," she whispered. "The first thing is to tell them, or they'll give us trouble for certain. Stand aside, Sir, if you please, it won't take but a moment." With one clumsy gauntlet she fumbled out a small metal object from the trug basket on her arm, and prepared to use it. "I have only to warn them what we intend."

"Jove, is that a fact?" He crowed with incredulous laughter. "And will they appreciate such a warning, d'ye suppose? 'Dear bees, we have come stealthily by night to destroy you – to massacre your queens and lay waste your colonies, and to steal your precious honey. You won't object, now will you?'"

"Oh hush, they'll hear you!" she hissed, mortified that he could think her capable of such absurdity. "Not *those* hives – 'tis the others we must tell, the new swarms. Oh you can laugh all you like, Aaron Corbyn, but they'll never work well for us next season unless we take the trouble to inform them of all that's important. Ask anyone who knows aught of beekeeping and they'll tell you the same."

"*All* that's important? My oath, but there's a responsibility! And do you really tell them all, Nelly? In your wedding gown as a blushing bride? Did you come then to seek their blessing?"

"To be sure, everyone does," she said primly, ignoring the insinuation.

He coughed into the white ruffles at his wrist. "And in your shift, Madam, on your wedding night? And did you steal out then to tell them what was purposed?"

"For shame, Sir, you forget yourself!" So he did too – with all the delicious arrogance of her favourite fictional villains. 'And oh Ellin, you know you should not have come!'

"But what of the black sheep's return to the fold?" her brother-in-law relentlessly continued. "Was that important enough, I wonder, to warrant sharing with the bees? And your own feelings for the young reprobate? Does this hive hold their secret? Or this one? And will it tell me if I ask?" He stooped beside the nearest skep to listen with exaggerated attentiveness to the droning of the insects within. "Oh buzzing busy-body bee," he intoned facetiously, "pray tell us what she thinks of me."

"Don't be so ridiculous!" He could hardly have seen her smile in the darkness and through the veil, she thought – thank the Lord. But even so her response must have been inadequate to say the least in the face of so obvious an extravagancy. An omission Ellin now hastened to rectify.

"And I'm sure that I can speak for the bees when I say that we all of us think you an exceedingly impertinent young man," she added with freezing formality. "Kindly follow the apostle's advice, Sir, if you wish to remain, and study to be quiet!"

Difficult, though, to maintain one's dignity in such an operation and before such an audience as hers, required as she was to rap on the top of each hive with the doorkey she'd brought with her for the purpose, and to address its occupants aloud:

"Now listen, my dears, you're not to be inconvenienced, do you hear me? Your honey's your own for the winter, to see you through safe to another spring. 'Tis only the heavy hives we'll be taking – three old colonies who've done their work. More room for you, my dears, more honey for your brood." And so to the next. A tap with the silver key, and: "Now listen, my dears, you're not to be disturbed . . ."

And all the while to be so acutely aware of his eyes on her, of the rogue's obvious amusement. And of something else – something which had more to do with the nostalgic atmosphere of the autumn evening, with Rafe's absence and her own unsettled state.

'Mild manners and thin talk,' that's what the old bee-masters prescribed for their charges. 'And never you go tarrifying 'em, my dear, with anything sudden or onreasonable.' But could the bees really tell, Ellin wondered? Were they really so sensitive to human feelings that they could detect a tremor in the voice or a quickening of the pulse, despite all one's efforts to conceal them?

And could he, the young devil?

Aaron planted the first sulphur-papers on their wooden cross within the pit, and crouched to light them. Leaving Ellin with the demonic impression of a face like a Vauxhall mask, underlit by their blue flames; for he'd declined to wear either hat or veil. Then together they lifted the skep down and banked the loose earth around it, to seal in and suffocate the colony complete. Inevitably some of their victims had yet contrived to escape, to hover distractedly through the stinking smoke that rose around the hive, yellow-stained with unburnt sulphur. But no more than a few. And Ellin was already congratulating herself on a first successful taking, when the whine of an angry guard bee sounded in her ear. To be followed in immediate sequence by a sharp exclamation of surprise and pain.

"Wherever it's stung you, Sir, I suggest you leave it be." She heard a voice as mild and thin as you please, which at first she hardly recognized to be her own. "There is a way, you see, to remove the barb," she added, a little ashamed with herself for feeling so pleased with the poor bee, "which may largely prevent the wound from smarting and swelling, if 'tis only performed quickly enough."

"Ah, but would you perform it for me, my dear Sister – that is the question? And *wherever* it has bitten?"

He lifted the lanthorn from the grass beside him and raised it slowly, teasingly, up the contours of his breeches and his ruffled shirt to his face. The smile had returned, widening as she watched to expose the satanic canines. Such danger in that smile, such danger for a woman! – reminding Ellin of those old legends of the Devil's visits to the country girls in the shape of their mortal sweethearts.

'From his brimstone bed at eve of day a-walking the Devil goes . . .'

"Oh 'pon my life, but 'tis here after all," Aaron exclaimed at last in mock surprise. "See here – a dead shot between the eyes!"

He indicated the place above the ruined bridge of his nose where the bee supposedly had stung. "So come now, won't you, and show me how you operate? Or are you afeared perhaps that I too will bite you, Sister Nell?"

It was a dog's trick to say so, for truly she was afraid – though hardly of bites and stings. Sooner than allow the rogue to perceive it, however, Ellin briskly put off her gloves and untied her veil, stepping forward as bidden – to discover the sting where he'd said it was, embedded amongst the little sprouting triangle of red hairs between his brows, its poison sac adhering still and very near intact. With the sticky point of the knife she'd used earlier to free the skep from its propolis cement, she hastily removed it.

"And the other?" he demanded. His eyes relentlessly consuming, on a level now with hers; and looking through them Ellin felt, directly through them and down into the very depths of her soul. "The bee that stung old Adam and set all mankind so furiously a-jigging? Could you cure me of that itch too, Bopeep? And would you, d'ye suppose, were you now free to do so?"

Even through the sulphurous fumes from the pit she could smell the sweet-yeasty male odour of his breath. So close – so tantalizingly close was Aaron Corbyn's mouth to hers.

Chapter Twelve

The sycamore avenue made a dismal spectacle after the rain. A tunnel of dripping leaves – tattered and tarnished, leprous with decay. Yet the day was improving. As the chaise drew clear of the trees Ellin glimpsed an arc of windswept sky above the high bank of the Chalkdean drive, and her spirits rose a little. In a few minutes she'd hear the gulls and feel the salt wind whistling through the landau's hoods – out of the house and off the estate and away from that red-headed devil, even for a few hours – the sheer relief of it!

Four weeks almost had passed since they'd robbed the bees of their comb. The last of the honey had been strained clear and safely sealed in its pots, the comb-wine casked, the beeswax boiled clean of its impurities. All it had wanted was a break in the weather, a single morning without the sound of rainwater gushing in the downpipes, for Ellin to announce her intention of driving over to Sellington with Lizzy and Strap and her father's share of the bounty.

"I'd feel happier, I think, if I could take him the honey myself," she offered Rafe, as if any explanation were needed for a visit to her parent. "Papa would never say so, but I do believe he misses me in his way. And to tell the truth, Rafe, I should like to see if that random Mrs Mary is going forward in the house any better since my last visit. You know the state I found the linen in then; and I'm afraid she's already entirely ruined Papa's bed quilt for washing it."

It was the truth, but by no means all of it. Because how could anyone inform so kind and obliging a husband as hers that she longed for the chance to escape his house and family? That any chance to do so would be as welcome to her just now as a spar to a drowning man? How to explain to Rafe the way things were? How his brother had brought provocation to an art – lounging before her in the tight-knitted outrageously revealing breeches that masculine fashion still licensed its followers to wear, lifting those Mephistophelian brows of his, stretching the tension between them like a cord, to tweak and jerk at her responses whenever he chose to do so. And Aunt Corbyn with her interminable mending, grimly stitching while she quizzed the pair of them over her spectacles, watching and waiting for her moment like one of those frightful creatures in France who sat knitting or making lace beneath the guillotines. And even Rafe himself, her gentlest most near-sighted husband, adding further to her distress and confusion by refusing steadfastly to see what was going on beneath his very nose.

"But of course, my dear," he'd assented with his usual forbearance. "By all means deliver the honey and the wine yourself, and stay for luncheon if the horses are not wanted. Your father will be glad to see you, I'm sure, and for the chance of a visit from our little Lizzy. Just so long as the child's well wrapped against the chill, and you have Gabel with you to see you safe from harm."

And his eyes as he looked up at her from his prescriptions had been so calm and kind, so totally devoid of suspicion that she could willingly have struck him! Ellin had only to look at her husband to feel guilty nowadays. (And human nature being what it is, she could not help but blame him for taking her loyalty so very much for granted.)

'Not that I've really done anything to be ashamed of, nor even contemplated it,' she told herself stoutly. 'And whatever the Bible may have to say about adultery of the mind being near as bad as the real thing, that's clearly nonsense. Why surely to goodness, every man and woman in the land at some time must have . . .'

"Wabbit!"

Ellin's further self-justification was interrupted by her daughter's high voice, piping up from her nest of rugs and woolly outer garments on the further side of the chaise. "Wabbit – nuvver wabbit! Look Strap!" She reached out a fat little mittened hand to seize the terrier by the collar and drag him bodily toward the window.

"Oh do have a thought for the poor dog, Lizzy! You're like to hurt him if you hold him so tight."

But Ellin had to smile at the look of determination on one small face and pained resignation on the other, as the little girl forced the terrier's unwilling muzzle against the pane.

"Wabbits!" Elizabeth Corbyn repeated after the disappearing white scuts at the roadside. "See Strap? Wabbits!" Her intention translated immediately to action, regardless of her mother's objections. Impulse and impetuosity, just like Ellin's own.

'And which of us the more infantile?' she wondered, disengaging a hand from her fox muff to loosen her daughter's grip on the long-suffering Strap. 'Lizzy with her "wabbits", or me and my fascination with a young Lothario who amuses himself only at my expense.'

But already the rabbits were passed. Released from his stranglehold, the little terrier hurried back to the shelter of his mistress's skirts – only to be recalled almost at once to share with Lizzy her first sight of the Channel.

"Sea – the sea, Strap! Look!"

A moment that signified their arrival at the Gibbet Cross, and a consequent opportunity to change their seats. (For it was Coachman Turner's invariable practice on the drive to Sellington to pause for a spell at the crossways, to rest the horses and apply the skid, and allow the ladies to re-arrange themselves if they cared to, with their backs to the shafts for the steep descent of Sellington Hill.)

With this ritual duly completed, Ellin rapped out their readiness to proceed on the oiled leather of the hood above her head. Thinking as she did so of Papa awaiting them at the Parsonage door in his dreadful malodorous old wig, his formal speech of welcome at the ready. She smiled and rapped again a little louder.

"Turner?" The landau remained stationary. "Did you hear me, Turner? Why aren't we moving?" she demanded.

"Soldiers, Ma'am." The coachman's disembodied voice floated down to her like a pronouncement from heaven. "Best to let 'em pass." And as he spoke a corroborative clatter of hooves could be heard from the roadway beyond.

"Soljers! See Strap? – lots!" Lizzy was enchanted. And this time so was Strap – so far forgetting himself as to take advantage of the precious child and her mound of coverings as a convenient platform for his own observation of the troopers, ears and tail-stump all a-quiver.

In the three years since the Duke of Richmond had reported to the Ordnance Board that Seaford Bay represented quite as likely a place as any other for a prospective enemy invasion, the Sussex coastal ways had reverberated to the movement of troops. To the marching feet of artillerymen returning to their batteries at Seaford. To mounted fencibles *en route* to South-Bourne barracks or their new signal station at Beachy Head; and in the autumn months, to great noisy mobs of militiamen on training manoeuvres from Blatchington and Bright'on Camp. Soldiers everywhere, blocking the roads and crowding the pavements of the towns. Even in the local assembly rooms, where officers' scarlet had now become a commonplace.

Ellin was familiar then with the breed. But for all that, she remained as susceptible as any other young woman of three and twenty to the spectacle of a passing cavalry troop in blazing tunics and tossing cockades; and so far denied all but the most unsatisfactory view of this parade, she lost no time at all in securing a better one.

"You stay there, Lizzy," she instructed, "Mamma won't be but a minute." And before the child could object or Strap could bid to follow, she'd thrown off her rug to unlatch the carriage door, gathering the folds of her mantle around her as she leapt down into the roadway.

"Who are they, Turner?"

Despite her improved position by the shaft-horses, the envigorating effect of the wind on the plumes of her turban bonnet made it difficult at first for Ellin to discern anything much beyond an oscillating blur of red and white. (While it has to be said that at the best of times the differences between one military uniform and another had never been entirely clear to her.)

"Royal South Gloucester Militia outter Blatchington, Ma'am."

The coachman's authority on such matters was unimpeachable. "And a regular old gaggle of special constables, for the matter of that," he added lugubriously, jerking his chin down the column. "Making theirselves userful for a change."

"Constables – where?" Ellin stood up on tiptoe for a better

view over the plump haunches of the bays, supporting herself on the carriage shaft with one hand and holding back her wayward feathers with the other. "Surely our parish constables haven't taken to exercising with the military now, have they, Turner?"

"Well if they 'ave, 'tis a middling queer way they got of going about it," Gabel remarked from his high perch as a horse trotted into view with the body of a soldier slung like a wool-sack across its saddle.

Ellin stared after the apparition in horror. At every movement of the horse's quarters the man's head bobbed and bounced about – with something dark and viscid dripping, trailing from it in the wind.

"Oh dear life, that man! Turner, he's . . ."

"Deader'n a soused mackerel," the coachman helpfully supplied. "Brains blowed about, Ma'am, something spiteful."

He regarded her impassively from beneath thatched brows. "Reckon 'ere's the varmints what's done it, or I miss my guess," he announced with rather the air of some poker-faced fairground conjuror about to cap one successful trick with another.

As Ellin watched, a group of eight or ten men in cocked hats and plain greatcoats with constables' staves in their hands succeeded the ranks of brilliant dragoons. Like a covey of brown partridges, she thought, at the tail of a flock of dashing cock pheasants; the Sellington constable, Amos Caldwell, amongst them, his normally cheerful features clamped into an expression of almost unrecognizable severity. And following behind the constables came three surly prisoners with their hands cuffed and their feet lashed securely beneath their horses' bellies, their faces bruised and bloody.

"Looks like a fair old start-up at Lullin'ton 'smorning," Coachman Turner observed conversationally. "And they said ye could never catch a weasel napping, neither."

He honoured the drama of the occasion with a sepulchral cough. "That smutchy old tun-belly at front's this 'ere Tolly 'Arris you've 'eard tell of," he added, directing his chin at the most prominent of the three bound men. "Weaselest son of a doxy in four counties I'd say – and as safe to be 'anged, Ma'am, as is salt bacon."

One of the man's eyes was puffy now and swollen, the old whip-scar obscured by a trickle of fresh blood. But Ellin would have known him anywhere for his bulging neck and distinctive Egyptian profile, leave alone the great belly that rode before him. Her father's assailant from the causeway – so *he* was the notorious Tolemy Harris! And only to think that she'd attacked him herself that fateful afternoon, and with her bare fists. Why for heavens sake, she was lucky to be alive!

Simultaneously tugged in three different directions at once – by revulsion, by pity and by a rapidly expanding pride in her own audacity – Ellin watched the man in helpless fascination; defenceless for the moment against further assaults to her feelings, as the villain turned to stare back at her, and the tangle of hair that covered the lower half of his face parted into crimson utterance.

"Never ye fret, parson's daughter, this meat's not for 'anging. B'ain't a juryman in Sussex would send old Tolly down!" he bawled out at her for all to hear. "Back afore the dog can lick 'is arse, parson's daughter, and you better believe it. Tol 'Arris will be back!"

"Ah, and I reckon 'e justabout will and all," Coachman Turner affirmed with the utmost complacence as the column moved on over the hill in the direction of Seaford. "And I've a thundering good notion that's where we'll see 'im, a-riding of the 'orse what the acorn foaled." He pointed the butt of his whip at the great oak gibbet-post on the far side of the crossways. "Mark me, Ma'am, that's where you'll see that old diddi-moosh next – in a chain 'arness and the tightest black suit 'e ever did wear, or ever will I daresay."

A prediction to be realized in due course, when one raw and frosty morning the following February a new crossbar was fitted to the gibbet-post on Sellington Hill, and a sticky, unhandy object hauled up to it from the back of a farm tumbril. Thinner by then after four months in irons, unrecognizable beneath its puckered skin of tar as the remains of Tolemy Harris, onetime Horsemaster of Lullington Heath.

Even as Ellin Corbyn busied herself in her father's pantry at Sellington Parsonage, stocking the wide shelves with sufficient honey and comb-wine to last him through to the next taking (and all the time living over in her mind her thrilling encounter at the crossways), Harris and the other two prisoners were conveyed to the military barracks at Blatchington, and from thence to the House of Correction in Lewes. As it later emerged, the original warrant for 'One Thomas Harris, called Tolemy' had carried but a single bill of indictment, for horse theft. An offence for which in the past that same individual had been acquitted more times than the Petty Sessions magistrates cared to recall. But as Rafe had already warned his brother, the tide of opinion was fast turning against the Trade; and this time the law was not to be cheated.

Why a wily old dog like Harris should have been so rash as to expose himself to a charge of armed resistance was never afterwards explained (for the prisoners' own claim that pistols had been forced into their hands, was scarce to be credited against evidence that the Horsemaster's natural son, Wester Harris, had then promptly discharged his into the face of the nearest dragoon). As things stood, fifty-six separate offences carried the death penalty under English law, including those of horse theft and of armed resistance. But although any court could try a man for his life, the murder of a King's soldier was something of a special case; and one which the examining magistrate at Lewes had no choice but to refer to the higher authority of His Majesty's Court of King's Bench on circuit. Even then Harris might still have fulfilled his boast at the crossways and contrived to escape the noose. It was young Wester's hand after all, not his, that had pulled the trigger. Nor was he himself without friends and associates in East Grinstead, where the first Assize Court of the new year was to be convened. In another time the jury might still have been influenced to find in favour of so celebrated a local rogue. But not, as it fell out, in that January of that year of 1798.

Since the previous May, when Austria had finally withdrawn from the European conflict, Britain found herself standing virtually alone against the menace of the new French Republic – which already commanded Italy and the Low Countries in addition to Savoy and the Rhine. And when in October, Admiral Duncan decisively defeated the Dutch fleet at Camperdown, a new and desperate mood of patriotism had found expression in celebrations and victory bonfires in towns and villages throughout the country. In the face of crippling war taxes and continuing predictions of enemy invasion, the British rallied as they had so often in the past, and would again, with their backs against the Atlantic wall. In the very month of the Lullington contrabanders' arraignment more than two million pounds were raised by public subscription: 'To drive into the sea all French scoundrels and other blackguards'. And when it came to the point, the prosecuting counsel at East Grinstead had only to remark the defendants' unpatriotic association with France and French trade, to ensure the attainder and subsequent execution of all three. Their bodies to be preserved and variously exhibited in chains at Felbridge and Crowborough and at Sellington Cross; suspended like pigeons over cabbage patches as a warning to all who might think to follow their example. Folk heroes no longer, but traitors now, to be reviled and assaulted by a newly virtuous population. Even in Sellington, where the children of men who'd landed and ported for the Lullington gang were urged by their mothers to run up the hill and fling stones at the dangling carrion that had once been its leader.

But all that was in the melting pot still on the day Ellin Corbyn transferred her honey and her wine to the shelves of her father's pantry in Sellington, while her daughter played ball with the little dog Strap on the flags of the parsonage kitchen. The Lullington Horsemaster was yet alive at Blatchington; and when the Corbyns returned home by Sellington Cross that afternoon, the gibbet-post was still untenanted. Just a tall oak post silhouetted like a pointing finger against the sky.

* * *

Toward evening the wind veered round to the north, banking the clouds across the Channel to ensure another of those moonless autumn 'darks' so helpful to the illicit professions of the night. And when a little before nine a solitary rider traversed the hilltop in the direction of Newhaven and the sea, he passed unthinking through the long shadow of the gibbet post.

Later in the pearly light of dawn a sharp eye might have identified the same man departing from Newhaven harbour in the bow of a two-masted ketch – in place of his caped greatcoat and tall beaver hat a fisherman's jersey, with a knitted cap to conceal his bright red hair.

Aaron's thoughts as he stared out to sea were concerned exclusively with the problems of the present. With the possibility of Wester Harris turning King's-evidence against him in the hope of saving his own worthless neck. But more imperatively, with the need to prevent a certain dutiable cargo from leaving the quai at Fécamp; until such time as he could arrange for its diversion, that is, to Hastings or Lancing Stade. Both excellent good reasons in themselves for an immediate crossing to France. For in spite of everything dear Brother Ray might have hoped or assumed, Aaron had never intended to remain in Sussex for longer than it took to gauge the strength and temper of the new military dispositions along its coast, and to agree with Tolly the best means of evading them. Now circumstance had forced him to remove himself from the theatre of action until the outcome of that old limb of Satan's latest arrest and its effect on the Lullington operation were known – to charter a vessel and crew from his friends at Newhaven, and to run out with the herring fleet. The only practical course now open.

For Aaron Corbyn was above everything a practical fellow, or so he chose to think. And if anyone had presumed to suggest to him that October morning that his motives for leaving England included within them any more complex emotions concerning his brother and his brother's wife, he'd have turned from his scrutiny of Channel shipping, at very least to smile and more than likely to laugh aloud in their faces.

BOOK 2

(1798–1805)

Chapter Thirteen

The new pregnancy suited Ellin. By the fourth month most of her earlier feelings of nausea and internal heaviness had dispersed. A little plumper and a good deal more settled within herself, despite an occasional showing of blood she fairly glowed with health; and it was only at her husband's insistence that she could be persuaded to lie abed of a morning, even until ten.

She looked about her room with pleasure. Wonderful to think even now that all this was hers, that she actually belonged here in this splendid great tabernacle of a bed. Since Rafe had left her a little after seven, she'd watched through its open hangings as the sky lightened. The first rays of the sun refracted from the snow outside to strike up into the bedchamber at a novel angle, illuminating the shaded side of the beams, the cobwebby corners and the smudges of candle soot that normally escaped detection. Snow-covered and pink flushed, the downs looked larger, nearer and somehow more solid than before.

'Swelled out with new life as you are yourself, you little pumpkin,' Ellin thought yawning, with one hand on the curve of her belly and the other idly weighing-out the growing substance of her breasts.

'January – January 25th. But by June 25th when this new child of yours is born, those hills will be green and gold and covered in wildflowers.' She smiled a small, contented smile. Thursday, January 25th, St Paul's Day. 'And if Paul's Day be bright and clear we'll have good luck through all the year!' Winter sunshine on snow. A warm bed and a fire in the hearth, the protection of a kind and gentle man and the little fishlike stirrings of his child within her. She felt fortunate, indeed she did – happier than at any time she could remember – certain that for her at least the traditional St Paul's Day forecast would come true.

In spite of the stringent new taxes on windows, on male servants, on horses and carriages that were to cost her husband so dear this spring; despite wild rumour's of gargantuan seventy acre rafts in construction even now at Calais and Dunkirk, she could not feel personally affected by this war. British defeat at French hands was unthinkable. Everyone affirmed it from Mr Pitt down. Nor, for the matter of that, could Ellin feel seriously threatened any more by those other emotional conflicts that had formerly made such a battleground of her nerves. Her erstwhile tormenter had long since removed himself from his brother's hearth and home, to France as everyone supposed. Beyond the disruptive influence of his brown eyes, she could afford to view Aaron with at least as much charity as Rafe did, as a young man who chose to cloak his true worth with flippancies and random provocations. While, as far as their own relationship was concerned, from the moment she'd informed him of her condition Rafe had forbidden himself all but the most platonic physical contacts with his wife – a touch on the arm, a kiss on the cheek or brow. An attitude with which, curiously enough, Ellin had found herself in complete accord. During her first confinement she'd demanded all the bodily comfort and reassurance her husband could give her, hating and resenting his damnable rule of abstinence and doing everything in her power to help him break it. But this time she felt differently.

Looking back, it seemed to Ellin that the confused little parson's daughter to whom that basic human function had proved such a trial and distraction, no longer actually existed. When she called to mind those so vivid memories of hers of Aaron and Ann Ashby in the grove behind the church, jerking and jiggling like a pair of jointed marionettes – or of all those subsequent occasions in this very bed when she and Rafe had clung to each other with such set faces and straining bodies – why how else could she now regard that act but as the greatest of absurdities?

'And what with all this conceiving and resting and lying-in for months at a time,' she thought, slipping out of the bed and into a pair of fur-lined mules laid ready on the rug beside it, 'I can only say 'tis a mighty wonder we women are ever permitted to stand on our feet at all!'

"Oh ma'am, for gracious sake, you're never thinking of getting out so soon?"

The footman had knocked and then opened the door to admit Ellin's maid, just as she herself was in the act of crossing the room to where her peignoir had been hung to warm before the fire. And immediately setting down the breakfast tray she carried, the girl ran forward to assist her. "Not that it's for the likes of me to say anything at all, Ma'am," she continued, holding up the garment for her mistress and preparing to say a very great deal more.

"All forbid I should pretend to give you advice, and me a mere servant and all. But 'tis a sight too perishing cold and bleat for a lady in your condition to be running about in a rail and not much else besides, that much I will say. And the fire not laid above an hour, Ma'am! 'Cold?' I says to Footman on the stairs, 'Justabout cold enough to freeze an Eskimoo, that's 'ow cold it is,' says I. Why upon my word, Ma'am, you know I'd as soon cut out my tongue as offend you – but what would the Master say, I should like to ask, if I were to let ye catch a chill in your own chamber? 'A *pest* on you, Ketty,' that's what 'e'd say. Faith, I'd stake my life on it. 'A pest on you girl, to let your Mistress come to this when I charged ye so particular to keep 'er warm and snug.' And now look at you, Ma'am, look at your poor arms – as quilly as any 'edgepig's I do declare – and as like to catch cold as anything I ever did see!"

"Now Ketty, that will do! I vow I never heard such a prodigious rattle of nonsense."

Although it was only with the most strenuous effort that Ellin succeeded in keeping the laughter from her own voice, as she collected her dish of chocolate from the breakfast tray and carried it with her to the dressing table in the window. Not that she had anyone to blame but herself for the girl's garrulousness. Heaven only knew, little Keturah Gubbin had been quiet and meek enough when she'd first employed her above stairs. A round-eyed scullion wench who'd scarce have dared to say boo to a goose if she'd met with one out in the yard. But in her own need for female companionship, for someone more amiable to gossip with than her husband's maledictory aunt, Ellin had encouraged the girl in all sorts of conversational liberties. A policy which at times like this made a proper sense of respect next thing to impossible to re-capture.

She compromised. "But so long as you're determined to run your tongue out on wheels at my expense," she added with a realistically feeling sigh, "then I suppose you may as well plague me with the latest tittle-tattle from below stairs while we try what is to be done with my hair. Come, what's the word down in the kitchens, Ketty? When is Ann Ashby to be delivered of her by-blow, have you heard? And what news of the Lullington villains' trial? Is a verdict yet decided?"

"Glory yes, Ma'am – ain't you 'eard?" Ketty exclaimed, passing over the first question to give the second the attention it deserved. "Guilty as the Devil and soon to swing, all three, that's the short and the long of it. And a proper good job too, I say. For there's three scurvy brewers of mischief as long deserved to be drowned in their own mash-tubs, Ma'am, same as I said to Footman. 'Furies, 'anging's too good for 'em, Willum,' says I. 'If you asks me they want their insides pulled out like they done in the olden-times, and then all their bits cut off, and then their arms and their legs, and then . . .'"

"For pity's sake have a care, girl, you're pulling my hair out by the roots!"

Beneath the maid's demure mob cap the expression in the mirror on her high-coloured countryfied features was shockingly gloating, greedy for blood and pain. And Ellin hastened to return the conversation to a more civilized plane. "Nor does it at all become you, Ketty, to speak so unfeelingly of others' misfortunes," she said primly. "Hanging is a barbarous enough death for anyone I should think, and whatever his crime I cannot imagine that any man deserves a worse one."

"No indeed to be sure, Ma'am, my own very thoughts. Why I'm sure I dislike 'anging as much as ever you do yesself," the girl returned with a flexibility of persuasion that would have done credit to any attorney or politician. "No Ma'am, whatever you may say I can't take to the noose, no sense, and never could.

"But there, will ye look at your pretty 'air in that there sun," she deviated without drawing breath. "As fine as taffety silk I do declare, and all of your own growing too! So will I fetch over that little cushion, Ma'am, to pad it out a thought? And shall we 'ave the blue ribbons for a crown-piece? Ye know they suit you to a marvel. Or is it curls you've a mind to, Ma'am, and a band? I dare swear the iron's 'ot enough to serve by this."

"No, the cushion I fancy, Ketty – but not the blue ribbons. Perhaps the red? And just a few curls on top like this, don't you agree?"

But less than half of Ellin's own attention was on the coiffure. Because she was thinking still of the prisoner at the crossways, the man from the causeway with the great belly and the glittering black eye . . .

> *'Gordamme!'* – and the terrible crack of her father's double-thonged whip – and *'Never ye fret, parson's daughter, this meat's not for 'anging. B'aint a juryman in Sussex would send old Tolly down!'* – and the crack . . . *'Gordamme! Gorr-damme!!'*

"So have you heard when the execution's to be then, Ketty?" she enquired with elaborate unconcern as the maid bustled up behind her with the hair cushion and the ribbons. "Does anyone yet know?"

"Well as to that, Coachman Turner's 'eard nothing as a fact from the toll-keepers what generally 'as the first of it." Ketty Gubbin paused to draw in a little oxygen, a rare concession. "But to be sure there's something I could tell you, Ma'am," she added slyly, "if I weren't afeared of Mister Rafe getting to 'ear. But ye know me Ma'am, I'm nobody for gossip. You might as soon tear a fee from a lawyer as coax an idle word from my lips. And all forbid I should let out anything to put the Master in a fret." She paused again artistically for a second superfluous breath. "But there again, if you'd be sure not to mention it after me, Ma'am . . ."

"Oh for goodness sake stop beating the donkey round the post, you provoking creature – you know as well as I do that you intend to tell me!" Ellin's patience had its limits, even in the mid-term calm of a second pregnancy. "So what exactly is it that you've heard?" she demanded abruptly, turning from her glass to face the girl. "Speak out then, Ketty, I'm waiting."

An open invitation and on no account to be wasted. "'Pon my word, Ma'am, 'tis only in the nature of a whisper, and 'ardly to be spoken of, I'm sure," the voluble maidservant began, preparing to cram the room from floor to ceiling with her speech "'Twas from my sister Sal I first 'ad it. She's with Squire Bridger down Blatchington way, Ma'am, if ye recall? And Sal she 'ad it of a lass who's calling cousins with a barrack sergeant there. Sergeant 'ad it of a special constable who 'ad it of a turnkey as one of that traitory Lullington crew only went and turned evidence on our Master Aaron as a gentleman-trader, didn't 'e?"

Ketty's continuing avalanche of words effectively smothered any sound her mistress might have made. "Dear life, I swear 'tis fit to sink ye what some folkses won't do when they feels thet 'emp about their throttles," she exclaimed. "A written confession, so they say. Too late of course to earn 'im the King's mercy. And I doan't pretend to know 'ow far true it might be, neither, Ma'am. But you can be sure the word were round the villages before ye could say jerry-go-numble. And warrant's out, and 'arf the downland set to see 'im in iron bracelets anywhen Master Aaron should show 'is nose! Parson Rimmer, your own father's seen to that . . .

"Why fancy now, if you ain't as white as a lenten lily, Ma'am!" At the sight of her mistress's upturned face the girl interrupted one spate of words with the counter-surge of another, equally devastating. "I vow and protest I've never seen you so white, Ma'am. Leastways, not since the Master opened up Miss Lizzy's gums to let 'er new teeth through, and they bled such a fright. D'ye mind it? All over 'er short-coats and all!

"And though I'm no one to advise you, I'm sure," she added as an afterthought, "red ribbons will never do justice to ye in that complexion, and I wonder you'd consider 'em, I do really. Far better 'ave the blue, Ma'am, same as I said before . . ."

There was more of the same.

"To be plain, Daughter, I am surprised – nay, I am astonished that you can even consider such worldly business as this after so recently receiving the Host."

It had been some weeks now since Rafe had first declared the jolting ride over to Sellington church to be inadvisable for anyone in his wife's condition. And the Reverend Rimmer's arrival at Chalkdean to administer the Sacrament privately to his daughter on the morning following her maid's revelation, provided Ellin with all the opportunity she needed to discover the truth of the matter. Nor on this occasion had her father found himself able to evade a confrontation as he had so often in the past.

"There's really no call for astonishment, Papa," Ellin said, astonishing herself somewhat by her own directness. "For surely 'worldly business', as you call it, is the very stuff of which our lives are made? And you'll never convince me that God in His wisdom would wish us to be less than frank with each other in its pursuit, before or after Holy Communion."

Papa detested her speaking of God within his hearing, she'd always known that – as if his personal claim on the Almighty extended even to the pronouncement of His name. But the time had passed for humouring him on such matters.

"So will you please tell me if 'tis true what they say, that you've set your own parishioners to watch for Aaron's return from France?" she persisted. "To betray him to the authorities, Papa, and as a common felon?"

Her father had been folding the white cloth she'd provided to convert the gaming table in the little winter parlour at Chalkdean into the semblance of a communion board. An activity he now abandoned to scratch irritably at a fresh flea-bite beneath his wig.

"Because if it is true, then I think I have a right to know," she said. "Whatever you may think of his character, Papa – whatever he may or may not have done – the man is my brother-in-law. He's of my flesh now, and you must see that I owe it to Rafe to consider his side of the case as well as yours."

"*His* case? He has no case," the little man snapped, withdrawing a snuff-stained finger from behind his ear. "You speak of betrayal, Daughter, as if that young delinquent has not himself betrayed every law of decency and right behaviour. He has called down a judgement of his own head I tell you, and must now answer for his transgressions. Whatever a man soweth, that shall he reap . . ."

While he hesitated, rummaging in his biblical armoury for another textual example with which to dignify his prejudice, Ellin seized on her chance of forestalling him. "Well maybe that's true," she conceded, "but I believe there to be something worth saving in everybody, including Aaron. He's not a monster, Papa. Why when his mother died he was broken-hearted, everyone says so. And only think of the consequences of a trial, and of an arraignment if it should come to that. He could be sent for transportation you know, or even *hanged*! Rafe's own brother, only think, Papa!"

"Then he should have reflected on that earlier, should he not? I tell you God's laws are not to be mocked . . ."

"But we are talking of man's laws, not God's; that is my whole case. And you cannot think it just to take a healthy young man's life for contrabanding. Or to condemn him to the hold of some fearful convict ship, to a life in chains at Botany Bay, while others may grow as rich as they please out of piracy and slave trafficking. No Papa, whatever the law of the land has to say, I'll never believe that God's justice ever could be so partial!"

But if Ellin was no longer to be intimidated by her father, the days were also long gone when she or anyone else could hope to moderate him in his own judgements. In recent months the attainder of Tolemy Harris and the dispersal of his gang from Lullington Heath, had coincided with the new upsurge of nationalistic sentiment to cure souls in many an unexpected corner of Sellington parish. In his sermons the Reverend Rimmer had not hesitated to remind his congregation who it was that had first spoken out against French trade, who had endured ridicule and sustained injury in the cause of God, of England and the right. And now men and women who'd once have scorned such nice distinctions, were positively scrambling to repent of their involvement with the Anti-Christ and hail their sanctimonious little parson as a hero.

"I am willing to believe your interference in this matter to be well-intentioned," the hero now asserted without troubling in the least to appear so. "But make no mistake, 'tis Satan himself who's put these sacriligious notions into your head, Daughter. Take heed, and guard thyself against the contaminations of this man!"

On familiar ground once more, her father's already rather high voice rose an octave and became strident. "The contaminations of greed and of covetousness. Aye, and of worse – of the sins of licentiousness, lust and fornication! Lust and fornication,' he repeated, wet-lipped, unconsciously contorting his features into a grotesque reflection of the very vices he decried.

'And what of jealousy, Papa, your own especial sin?' Ellin thought with a sudden flash of insight. 'Because that is what you are, is it not? Dried up and frustrated, eaten up with envy like old Aunt Corbyn – at war with life and the world and everyone in it, just as she is!'

"Or perhaps you've not heard yet that the Ashby girl is with child?" her father demanded, leering at her still from behind the lenses of his spectacles. "And soon to be delivered of the bastard your worthy brother-in-law has sired on her!"

"Indeed I've heard it repeated – who has not? But that hardly proves such gossip to be true."

Nor did it, despite her own recollections of their activities behind the church. And even if it were, the girl was quite as much to blame as he; of that Ellin was certain. For in her current maternal frame she could see Aaron only as the poor young man who'd grieved so desperately for his mother. A man who'd surely love again some day for all his masculine bravura – if only he was spared to do so . . .

"And besides, I have also heard that Ann's refused to swear a father before the magistrates," she heard herself point out. "Not Aaron or any other." Yet even as she spoke, Ellin could feel the hot blood rushing to her face to betray her own interest in the affair.

"Ah yes, and may you blush 'til you burn to so defend a lecher and a fornicator!" the little parson crowed at the sight of it. "But think again if ye think to deceive me, Madam. I have heard the truth of the case you see, from the slut's own father. Farmer Ashby has her own confession of the rogue's part in the affair, and swears to be revenged on him. The instrument God has chosen to punish Aaron Corbyn for his sins! Next week, we are informed, he intends to run a cargo through the Gap. And when he does, our people will be waiting."

Parson Rimmer pointed at his daughter's crimson face. "And take good heed, Madam, because I'll not tell you again," he cried. "If you dare to interfere with God's purpose in this matter, you'll do so at the peril of your own immortal soul. For don't imagine for one moment that as His Minister I could ever defend you against His wrath!"

Chapter Fourteen

A mild spell and one or two heavy showers had all but obliterated the last of the January snow. Here and there patches of white still lingered under hedges and on the sodden thatches of the cottages; but for the most part the downland had reverted to its more familiar winter livery of bronze and grey-washed green. Between the buildings of the Ashby farm the trampled slush had long since absorbed the character of the mud and dung it overlaid, gleaming wetly. And as Ellin's horse picked its way between the puddles, a noisy group of ducks in their pond by the cowshed wall proclaimed their satisfaction with the weather. From the strawyard the milch-cows watched the rider with bored incurious eyes, swinging their tails like pendulums; while from the flint barn beyond, the rhythmical jingle and thump of the threshing flails sounded through the damp air like the pulses of a great heartbeat. Which in a way they were.

The dairy-house was another flint building abutted to the northern gable of the cowsheds and overhung by the limbs of a great beech tree, whose function in warmer seasons was to shade it from the sun. This afternoon its door was open wide. A well-nourished black and white cat sat washing its face in the band of yellow lamplight that shone out over the sill. Behind it a shadow moved across the floor. A pail clattered, metal clanked on metal and someone hummed the snatch of a tune, someone working within.

"And please God let it be her, let it be Ann," Ellin muttered fervently and as much to herself as the Almighty, as she disengaged her knee from the side-saddle and made ready to dismount.

She had come to Bury Farm against her own better judgement,

it was pointless to deny it – on another of those random impulses that so frequently complicated her existence. For despite everything she'd said to Papa that morning in the Chalkdean parlour, she knew him to be right. Whatever sympathies, real or imagined, that she might feel for Rafe's brother she had no business with him now, or with anything he might purpose. If Aaron should be rash enough to return to Sussex in the knowledge of his associates' attainder, then it was not for her to shield him from the consequences. And if Rafe had not already caught wind of Farmer Ashby's agreement with her own father to inform the authorities of any such landing, it could serve no purpose that Ellin could see to burden him with the knowledge. For what could anyone do at this late date, with the warrants already out and the troops at Blatchington alerted? Papa was right. Nothing but harm could come from interference now.

Or so she'd succeeded in convincing herself – until this morning in bed it had occurred to Ellin that the girl, Ann Ashby, might yet be unaware of her father's attitude and of Aaron's intended visit. In which case, surely, it would be no more than an act of charity to acquaint her of it? To give Ann the chance of warning her lover of the danger? A pair of disgracefully prejudiced questions which Ellin again put to her conscience after luncheon, when Rafe had embarked on a round of cottage visits and Aunt Corbyn retired with her stitchwork to the parlour fire. It was no more than two miles to Sellington when all was said, but a stone's throw beyond to Bury Farm and its dairy. And if she took the old dappled mare, Tabitha, and proceeded at a slow foot pace, why certainly she'd take no harm.

'Our Lady herself rode further than that on a *donkey*, and a deal nearer her time than I am!' she assured herself. 'There'll be no one but the grooms to see me go; and if only I leave now and without delay, I'll be back in time to take tea with Lizzy and Henshaw just as usual. To be sure I will.'

The ride had been longer and more uncomfortable than she'd allowed for, nonetheless. And as she slid from the saddle to the muddy cobbles without the dairy door, Ellin found that perforce she must stand for a moment to catch her breath and regain what she could of her composure, before stepping forward to put the black and white cat to flight.

The place smelled delectably of milk and cream, and of the cheeses that ripened in the rafters above it. To Ellin's relief its only occupant looked up from her cream-skimming with as little surprise as if the younger Mistress Corbyn was still a daily visitor to her dairy. Placid, capable, herself immensely pregnant beneath her enveloping white apron, Ann Ashby calmly proceeded with the task she refused to entrust to her dairymaids – while the other girl laboured to explain herself – pausing only to ease her back or to rinse her tin skimmer while she bestowed on Ellin the candid attention of her round blue eyes.

"Well as to that, I confess I'd 'ave been noways concerned about the villain myself, if you 'adn't a'thought to mention it," she remarked prosaically when Ellin had at last justified herself to a standstill. "For saving your pardon, m'dear, 'e's a sight too artful a beggar to snare 'isself in any kind of wire my old grout-'ead of a Pa might think to lay for 'im, I give ye my word."

The girl's gown sleeves were rolled above the elbows to reveal a pair of forearms that would have done credit to a young blacksmith. But in her large hand the skimmer delved beneath the yellow heads of the cream in the scalding pans with a surprising grace, deftly lifting and flicking it over into the waiting bowl.

"But there, I daresay 'twouldn't do no 'arm neither to give the kiddy the benefit of a word of caution," she acknowledged, returning from her final rinse to reach behind her for the strings of her apron. "And for the matter of that, I'll lay I know the very fellow for the job and all – if you'd care to step over to meet 'im for yourself, Ma'am?"

Coarse-grained she might be, promiscuous Ann certainly was. Yet it was difficult to think of anyone so open of attitude and expression as truly sinful. And as Ellin followed her through the yards, holding her riding skirt up out of the mire over her arm, she felt a comforting sense of comradeship with the farmer's daughter. A feeling she vaguely supposed to relate to the expectant condition they shared. At the flint barn she waited while the other girl disappeared within, to reappear a few minutes later with a companion at her shoulder.

"This 'ere article's our Jarvis," Ann Ashby announced, pitching her strong voice above the continuing racket of the flails, and at the same time thrusting the article forward for Ellin's inspection.

A muscular, bandy-legged little man, with the pale dust of the winter threshing floor still clogging his nostrils and eyelashes and the intricate gaufer-stitching of his round frock. He jerked an unshaven chin at her, automatically edging backward as he did so – only to receive another encouraging shove from the farmer's daughter at the rear.

"And Jarvis 'as it there's a lugger in the Gap as 'ud run over a note for us any tide we care to pay 'er charter," the girl prompted. "Ain't that the truth, Jarvie? Well, tell the lady!"

"Ah – oh aye, reckon it could be and all," Jarvis muttered in response to a further manual inducement from behind.

"Aye, so there you are,' Annie confirmed, folding her brawny arms out of temptation's way for the moment, "and didn't I say so?"

'But it can't be – it can't be that simple,' Ellin thought. She could pen the necessary letter of warning to her brother-in-law, of course she could. But where precisely in France to send it? Did Ann Ashby know, or this dusty little gnome of a Jarvis? She could trust the girl, she felt sure. But what of the others? Could any commercial freebooter be relied upon to deliver a message safely and without disclosing its contents to the authorities? And then how much was the charter to cost, for heaven's sake? She was not without funds; she had money put by from her dressing allowance. But would it be enough for such a venture?

"Lord save ye, girl, there ain't no sense in making a great 'arvest over a little corn, is what I say," the philosophical Annie vouchsafed in reply to the questions and objections with which Ellin now bombarded her. "'Tis no more than common knowledge as to where to send to Aaron Corbyn, anybody 'ereabouts would tell ye. Bless us, I doubt there's a fisherman or tide-waiter atwixt Bourne and Bright'on who ain't 'eard tell of 'Jack Cur's Castle' in Faycom. And as to the cost of the posting, well I reckon as twenty guineas would cover it and 'andsome. Wouldn't ye say, Jarvie? Allowing for 'is poison-pated Lordship to match it with twenty of the same.

"Always supposing you think 'e's worth so much, m'dear," she added with a look of frank enquiry in her blue eyes. "For I doan't know as I'd rate the fellow so 'igh myself, and that's the truth."

"Why yes to be sure I do! My husband's brother – but to be

sure he's worth twenty guineas, anyone would be!" Feeling herself begin to flush again, Ellin hurried on to pose her final question. "But are you certain we can trust such people, that is my concern. I mean how can we be sure they'll not take the money from us and then go on to sell the information to the preventivemen? Or to your father, or to mine?"

Ann Ashby smiled in genuine amusement. "Because they know full well that Aaron Corbyn of 'Jack Cur's Castle' will pay better than my old tight-purse of a Pa or any beggarly Revenue man living any day of the week, that's why! Take it from me, m'dear, you generally-always get what you pay for in this life." The girl shifted her weight, bracing back to ease the strain on her spine while at the same time giving a fine prominence to its origin well to the fore. "Aye, and most-in-general pay for what ye get and all," she added with an affectionate pat for the dome of her belly. "Reckon I should know, eh?

"And you needn't go fretting that this 'ere article will snitch on us neither, Ma'am. Not our Jarvie!" She gave way to temptation and again applied lustily to the looped-up frocking that curtained the man's hinder part – this time with sufficient force in the blow to envelop the pair of them in a cloud of grey briffen-dust. "No, you 'ave your letter and the twenty pieces ready for 'im before tide-turn tomorrow, and Jarvis 'ere will see to the rest, never you fret."

If only it could really have been as straightforward as Annie envisaged – the restoration of one's peace of mind for the mere time it took to pen a letter, the paltry sacrifice of a new gown or two. But Aaron Corbyn was after all too deeply entangled in Ellin's affairs to be extracted from them so easily, it seemed. For when she slipped out of the house the succeeding afternoon with her sealed letter and her little cache of guineas in her reticule, to convey them to Jarvis Copper in the orchard behind the herb garden as arranged, it was to discover her messenger in a far from hopeful frame.

"'Tain't no use, Ma'am," he informed her as soon as she was within earshot. "Skipper won't put on so much as an inch of canvas without ye fee 'im double. Forty pieces of gold, Ma'am, fair and square."

"Forty guineas? But that's wholly impossible. Twenty is all I have to spare!"

"Ah, that's what I telled 'im. But 'e doan't care nothing about it, Ma'am. 'Forty – and a middling lean job at that,' 'e says. 'Crossing's a sight too busy these bouts to sail for less, t'ain't feasible.'"

"But has he not understood that my brother-in-law will make it up to forty just as soon as the letter's delivered? I've written to instruct him so. The man has only to wait for him to read it."

"Aye, so I telled 'im."

"And what did he say?"

There was a pause for mental process. Jarvis Copper detached a flake of yellow lichen from the orchard wall and considered it minutely. "'And we shall catch larks when the sky falls down.'" He cleared his throat apologetically. "Begging your pardon, Ma'am, but i'fackins they's 'is very words."

Ellin watched him busily crumbling the lichen, scattering it like seed on the damp earth at his feet. So was this to be the end of it, her brave initiative? And must she now seek Rafe's help after all to save Aaron from his own recklessness? To reveal to her husband the depth of her own interest in his brother's affairs and set the entire matter on a different footing? Or else to keep silent and abandon Aaron to the vagaries of fate? Were these now to be her only choices? Or was there yet another? She thought of the young man in the shallows of Sellington Gap – pristine, gleaming wet – then of another across the saddle of a pony, streaming blood . . . Immediately beyond Jarvis Copper she could see the orderly row of orchard hives sleeping out their winter sleep, and the muddy depressions behind them where the pits had been.

'And the other? The bee that stung old Adam and set all mankind so furiously a-jigging? Could you cure me of that itch too, Bopeep? And would you, d'ye suppose, were you now free to do so?'

"Tell me Mr Copper,' she said aloud and with a sudden resolution, "where exactly is the lugger you speak of at this present?"

The man hesitated and furtively glanced around him. "At anchorage still, so far as I can tell," he offered.

"Yes, but where?"

"Out in Sel'ton roads, Ma'am, near Brass Point."

"Then you must take me to her, Mr Copper, I see no help for

it. Row me out there while the tide's yet full, and I'll interview the fellow for myself."

Madness, she knew it was. But with Rafe at his lecture club in Lewes, the opportunity was simply staring Ellin in the face. 'And heavens, I have to try what I can do at least,' she thought wildly, striving still to justify the racing excitement that she felt – the intention to save her brother-in-law, and at any hazard, that was already forming in her mind.

* * *

"Well lookee 'ere, Mistress, I'm not saying as twenty would even serve to take us over. But supposing it did, it'd never stretch to no fiddle-farting with billies and messages and the like, ye can be 'nation sure of that!"

The lugger's captain was a grizzled, bullet-headed little freebooter with a hard eye and a take-it-or-leave-it attitude to the business which demanded a straight answer, even from a lady. "No Ma'am, you make up your mind to this," he said uncompromisingly, "if I take ye for twenty, you'll carry your own letters, and deliver 'em yourself and all. Aye, and reckon to pay the same again for a passage 'ome. I'll not be out of reason with you, Mistress, and that's my final word."

A simple choice then had confronted her. It *should* have been simple. And too late afterwards to perceive the world of difference between an impulsive gesture, a flight of fancy, and an irrevocably foolish act.

Too late indeed for the woman who shortly found herself in a fishing lugger, heading out to sea – away from the safety of her home and her husband and everything in life she valued! Faced by such a choice, Ellin should patently have refused the captain's unreasonable terms and bade Copper row her back again to shore. The thing was self-evident. So what idiocy, what fatal flaw of character had prompted her instead to board the lugger with her letter and her precious bag of guineas? To send the man back to Chalkdean with the horse, and with a garbled explanation of events that must surely drive her poor husband half-distracted with anxiety? Oh Judas, why – for what? For some obscure maternal impulse? For a crazy romantic idea that had entirely dissipated before the vessel had been at sea for the bare quarter of an hour? Her father had warned her repeatedly of such follies. Her years of marriage to a civilized and reasonable man had taught her better ways. Yet neither warnings nor experience had availed her in her moment of decision; as once again the impetuous girl in Ellin rushed forward to confound them all.

On the deck above her canvas slapped and cracked and crackled in the wind. Men shouted, timber creaked. And in the narrow little prison Ellin had made for herself and her conscience in the cabin down below, a clanking candle-lanthorn played crazy games of light and shadow with the column of the rear mast, with the silver buckles of her riding shoes braced out before her on the boards. An overpowering stench of fishscale and tarred oakum combined with the tilt of the lamp and the rolling of the boat itself to sicken her to her stomach.

Ochreous light and ink-black shadow. Light and shadow, shadow and light – pressing the heavy deck beams down toward her, throwing up the buckles of her shoes. Pain and nausea in her head and in her belly.

'And now you foolish, you unforgiveably foolish woman, just see to what a desperate pass you've brought yourself!'

Ellin gritted her teeth, then tried and failed to rise. The images began to blur, then doubled. Two pairs of shoes, four silver buckles – down and up, back and forth the lanthorn swung . . . Until she heard a cry – her own voice crying out at something that clenched and stabbed at her inside . . .

And then her skirts were wet, her stockings wet and warm – and in the swinging light her shoes dyed red. The silver buckles red. Dear God, blood red!

She cried out in panic, tried again to rise. But then the beams came down again. The light swung back, and back – away back into blackness.

Chapter Fifteen

Through the heaving darkness shadows came and went. Ellin could hear voices and the clanking of the lanthorn still from somewhere far above her. In one moment she saw the captain's weatherbeaten face swimming toward her through the shadows, and smelt the brandy on his breath: "'Old fast now, maidy – 'old fast to me . . ." Then in another she felt his hands, his arms beneath her – pain dragging through her body. Her own voice protesting, rising to a scream, as once again the lamp swung back and darkness blotted in.

But then at last the black began to lighten. A glowing ring began to form with yellow tendrils reaching outward, unfolding like a flower – and from its centre a patch of azure summer sky, expanding rapidly as Ellin's lashes parted, to reveal . . . Why bless us all, how odd! . . . a party of flying wrestlers, with portly matrons and rosy cherubs in attendance – all floundering unsupported through the banners of their own escaping clothing! Ellin watched them listlessly through half-closed eyes, too tired and weak as yet to bring her mind to focus. So was this heaven after all, she wondered? Could angels ever really be so overweight and underclad? And why no sound of harps, no stirring breeze, no feathered battery of wings?

"It depicts the Greek prince Endymion, so they tell me – hurtling through the upper ether to the waiting arms of Morpheus."

A drawling male voice from somewhere close at hand reduced her dreams to paint and plaster. "And if you think this ceiling tasteless, just wait until you see my dining salon down below," the voice continued. "'The Apotheosis of Louis Quattorze', that one

– with the curliest little chicken-hammed dand of a King ye ever did see, cavorting amongst the most prodigious array of loins and rumps this side of Smithfield fatstock market."

With an effort, Ellin turned her head, to discover Aaron on a chair beside the bed. Aaron with his flaming hair and coat of mulberry superfine – lounging in a shaft of sunlight, as unreal and brightly coloured as any of the empyrean revellers up above him.

She stared, uncomprehending. '*My* dining salon,' was what he'd said. 'So is this Aaron's own house?' she thought confusedly, 'and am I now in France?'

"You have been ill," he said, correctly interpreting the doubt and bewilderment in her face. "First on the boat from England and then here in Fécamp. Do you not recall it?" A jewelled pin winked at her from the folds of his cravat. But the ironic smile had given place to something more earnest – something watchful and alert.

Ill on a boat, a boat from England? What did he mean? Ellin tried desperately to think. But still her mind refused to grasp it, shied from the knowledge like a nervous horse. A boat from England must mean that she had crossed the Channel. But why? And why could she not remember? She closed her eyes again, unable to concentrate with that red scoundrel sitting there, watching her like a dog at a sink-hole.

Then suddenly she *knew*. She heard again that dreadful clanking lanthorn and saw it swinging up to light the cabin floor – the rear mast rising gleaming wet . . . wet boards, wet cables coiled and black, and silver buckles to her shoes. Her smart new riding shoes wet too. Her gown wet too . . . Oh God, soaked through with blood!

'Dear Lord, the baby!' Her eyes sprang open, all at once awake, aware now of pain and of an alien wadded shape thrust in between her thighs. Awake to fear. "The baby?" she said aloud, struggling to raise herself in the bed. "My baby, have I . . .?" Her mouth and lips were parched, so dry the words came croakingly.

Aaron moved awkwardly in his chair and looked away. And oh to stop him there, to make him leave things as they were! But abruptly he turned back to face her.

"I must tell you that you've lost the baby," he said with a brutality that covered something else. "It miscarried."

Lost it? But how like a man to put it so. Lost it, miscarried it carelessly like an ear-ring or a glove. 'Your child is dead.' That's what he should have said. 'And you have killed it with your schoolgirl notions of adventure and romance!'

For days each time she woke her sense of loss came to Ellin all afresh – an empty, unfixed kind of loss with nothing to attach it to. No memories, no child to grieve for, no knowledge even of its gender. For Aaron had not thought to tell her, if he knew, and now she would not ask. Nothing left for Ellin but the grief itself – and guilt. She'd killed her child and Rafe's. The fault was squarely hers. And now that she needed Rafe himself so badly, she felt too desperately ashamed to face him – even to write to beg for his forgiveness. She'd die first, she told herself, beneath the fat uncaring deities of his brother's bedroom ceiling.

"Oh Lord," she prayed, "I can endure no more. I know I'm not deserving, but if you'll only let me die, God, I swear I'll never ask another favour."

"It's what they all say – but they always do, you know."

She had not intended to speak it out aloud, was scarce aware that she'd done so. Not until Aaron answered her.

"And you'll forgive me my presumption," he continued smoothly, "but I think I may safely speak for God and all his angels when I say that we none of us have the faintest intention of letting you die. To be sure I've already sent to my brother, to inform him of what has chanced and assure him of your safe return as soon as you are well enough to travel. We'll hear from him I daresay, by the next boat out of Cuckmere."

Through all those early days and nights of grieving he'd remained beside her in his chair, he or the woman who brought her food and changed her bandaging. And now while she begged for death, he had the nerve to sit there in his velvet and his spotless linen to tell her that he planned to have her posted back to Chalkdean like a parcel! Before she died, before God struck her down, she wished briefly for the strength to throttle him.

"How dare you . . . dare you promise my husband any such thing," she stuttered, helpless to control her anger. "I cannot, I will not go back there now. I'd sooner die, I tell you!"

He looked at her with maddening detachment. "Yes, I think that perhaps you would," he agreed. "But then so long as you're sounding so determined on the point, I'd say you stand every good chance of living to be ninety-five. And whether you want to or no, my dear Sister, let me assure you here and now that you are going to live – and to return home safe to my brother's house where you belong. I know you see, because I personally intend to make certain that you do."

And so, surprisingly, he did. For the next several mornings Ellin was woken to the hateful prospect of a silver goblet filled to the brim with lukewarm claret wine; with Aaron's hand to press it to her lips and Aaron's watchful eyes beyond, forcing her to drink while she was yet too weak and sleepy to refuse him. And when she'd drunk, each time, he immediately refilled the cup to make her drink again. The same at noon, and then again at dusk.

"You need it to replace the blood you've lost,' he told her. "Six goblets every day until you're strong enough to stand and walk downstairs."

Sometimes she argued. Frequently they slopped the wine between them, to wet her night rail or stain the sheet and *traversin* with pink. Once she'd choked, and then vomited ignominiously into the chamber pot he held before her. But Aaron mopped up for her with his own fine linen handkerchiefs and remained to all outward appearances unmoved. "Six goblets every day," he repeated, " 'til you are strong enough to stand and walk downstairs." And nothing Ellin could do or say would deflect him from that purpose.

Nor as it appeared, was the woman who attended her any the less resolved to see Ellin well again and fit to travel. (Though whether this sprang from a genuine interest, or from some darker motive of her own, Ellin herself was unable to determine.) Marthe Lefèbre by name, the woman was neither young nor particularly handsome. Yet there was a natural opulence about her in her verbena scented black silk that had its own appeal. And watching her rustling through her duties in the house, Ellin could not but wonder if warming Aaron's bed was one of them.

"Vous allez mieux?" Each day the Frenchwoman saluted her charge with the same repeated phrase, patently more in the way of an instruction than an enquiry after health. And if Ellin showed the slightest disinclination to eat the breakfast that she brought her, Madame Lefèbre would merely cast up her fine black eyes and proceed to feed her spoon by spoon like any wayward child.

With two such wills in opposition, the patient could do nothing but capitulate, and improve. At first Ellin had barely recognized the symptoms in herself. A little more bone, less aspic in her limbs, as she eased herself from her bed to the *chaise-percée* alongside it to answer the calls of nature. Then gradually the development of an appetite for Madame's aromatic *bouillons* and *ragoûts*, and with it a growing impatience for her confinement in the chamber. Even with its casements tightly closed against the winter air, she could not be unaware of the port of Fécamp out there beyond them. Its salty odours seeped in around the leads, the constant keening of its gulls intruding even to her dreams. And propped on pillows by Madame, she sat for hours watching the birds' white shapes slicing up the sky between the panes. Sometimes she could see the masthead of a ship above the sill, so close it almost seemed to touch it; and from her chaise-seat more masts and sails, with rows of smoking chimneys and a distant line of cliffs beyond.

'Not that I care what's out there,' Ellin told herself each time she felt her interest in her surroundings begin to quicken. 'The way I feel, I shouldn't care if every inch of water out there were crammed with spouting whales or British men o' war!' She felt too weak, too utterly downcast to feel aught for anything ever again. Or so she daily told herself.

Which made it all the more remarkable when, less than two weeks from the night of Ellin's arrival in Fécamp, the woman Marthe Lefèbre entered the chamber to find its occupant standing at her window in fascinated contemplation of the harbour down below.

A little later on the same morning Aaron himself arrived with the detested claret, and a suggestion that his sister-in-law might today bestir herself to descend a floor and view the 'Apotheosis of Smithfield' whilst dining in his salon. And it was only after she'd loudly and ungraciously refused him, that Ellin began to realize how much stronger she'd become. Four days later she accepted, negotiating a stairway to the lower floor at some risk to her neck in a too large borrowed gown of Madame's; and feeling more guilty, more traitorous to her grief with every step she descended.

"The house is something above three hundred years old," Aaron informed her in the formal manner of a guide, as he matched Ellin's slow progress down the stairway. "Built as a *comptoir*, so they say, for a fellow by the name of Jacques Coeur. Perhaps you've heard of him?"

'Jacques Coeur. But of course – so this is "Jack Cur's Castle",' she thought, unable to disguise her interest. And if Ashby's daughter was to be believed, not a contrabander between Bourne and Brighthelmstone who wasn't familiar with it!

"And if you're wondering how a young barbarian like me might have come by anything so grand," her brother-in-law continued, handing her through into a salon that positively blazed with gilt and satinwood, "then I must tell you that mansions like this are three-a-tester now in France, with aristos so scarce and their estates all parcelled out. So far as the local *comité*'s concerned anyone who'll stump up their rent is more than welcome to 'em, including English traders and other stateless outlaws."

She looked up at him sharply, to meet an expression so blank and courteous, so patently remote from his former character, that she naturally assumed him to be laughing up his sleeve at her – odious man! And it was not until they'd finished more than one meal together beneath a ceiling every bit as ostentatious as he'd promised, that Ellin could permit herself to believe his improvement of manner to be sincere. In Sussex Aaron's capital had been irresponsibility, or so she'd always thought. There he'd cared for nothing and no one, snapping his fingers in the face of every convention – a charming traitor to his class and country. But here he was the master of a great establishment, with half a score of horses in his stables and as many servants at his beck and call. Stone-built, a full three storeys high, with paved courts and pierced balconies and terraced gardens on the hill behind, his *Maison Jacques Coeur* stood in impressive isolation across the harbour from the town. Everything about it proclaimed the wealth and respectability of its tenant. A role which Aaron, as it now appeared, was more than ready to assume.

In the early days of her recuperation, when he'd laboured to force on her the hateful claret wine, Ellin had cursed him, unfairly blamed Aaron for much of her misfortune. Now she was just enough to see that he was acting only for her benefit. As her strength returned, she found herself wondering if he'd ever thought of his dying mother as he sat beside her bed. And for her own part she began to look forward to their intimate dinners together in the salon. Not by this time for any inquisitive or prurient motives. Not even out of any especial partiality for the young man himself. But as respites only from the feelings of guilt and despair that filled her days and made her own company so objectionable.

As time wore on their discourses extended to an occasional stroll in the damp gardens behind the house, or even to the windswept quays – walking together with formal politesse, talking impersonally, looking to right and left but seldom at each other. And never mentioning, not even once, the letter from England that they both awaited.

All her life, ever since she could remember, Ellin had been aware of the contraband trade. Over the years the tidal estuaries to the south and west of her home in Chichester had seen their share of illegal landings, of captures and scuffles with the Revenue; and contrabanders had never been strangers to the local assize courts. But the trade to Ellin, in Sellington as in Chichester, had always been a cloak and dagger affair, to be undertaken with some semblance at least of secrecy. None of which had in any way prepared her for the *contrabandiers* of Fécamp. For here a very different custom obtained. Here no one troubled to black their faces or lower their voices, or even to wait for nightfall to load their cargoes – as was all too obvious to Ellin from her first expedition onto the quays at Aaron's side.

"Not so much trafficking with Sellington and Cuckmere these days," her brother-in-law frankly informed her. "Poor Tolly's indiscretions have seen to that, I fear, at least for the time being. But there's plenty of demand still from Hastings and Bexhill, and from Lancing Stade. More than we'll ever satisfy." He waved a hand at a pair of huge black painted luggers which lay ahead of them in tandem against the dock. "Fifteen hundred casks of brandy and six hundred of geneva on those two alone, each time of crossing," he said, "if you can believe it?"

"Indeed Sir, if you say so." She'd not sound impressed, she was determined. "Though I do wonder that they can feel free to conduct such business so openly," she felt compelled to add, as they watched the vessels loaded from a row of standing tumbrils on the quay. "For surely such traffic is illegal, even in France? Or am I misinformed?"

"Not at all, Ma'am, you are informed correctly," he assured her. "All official trading links between England and France were naturally severed by the war. But what you must also understand is that Fécamp is *not* France; and those who suppose it so are mistaken – my brother and his aunt included." (And now at last a glimmer of the old challenge in the brown depths of his eyes as he turned toward her.)

"Not France?" But had he run mad? It took all Ellin's will to return her own eyes to the loading kegs, bouncing and clashing together as they passed from hand to hand on their way down to the holds, to maintain in her own voice the same even tone as his. "But if not France, Sir – what then, pray?"

"A 'free port', Madam – and has been these thirty years past, ever since the old king, Louis Quinze, issued an edict to open it to traders. Which makes us internatioanal, d'ye see? Like the lighthouse on the rocks at Ushant: 'Committed in war and peace,' as they say, 'for the benefit of all'." He smiled, his face a mask again. "And as much a part of British commerce I' faith, as Chatham is – or Newhaven, or Plymouth for the matter of that."

To further illustrate the point, he escorted Ellin on another day across the long quay that spanned the tidal harbour and into the town itself – to the great *entrepôts* of the Quai Vicomté, where a further surprise awaited her.

From without, the warehouses were tall lime-washed buildings, as blank faced and utilitarian as others of their kind. Inside they were vast and brilliantly lit emporia – covered marketplaces hurrying with buyers and sellers, redolent with the distinctive odours of spirits and tobacco. Pillared bays around the walls were filled with kegs and barrels stacked by their hundred, and shiny oilskin packs arranged in towers and pyramids. Lamplit walkways pierced racks of bolted fabric – India silks and gauzes, lace, velvet and glittering tinselled muslin. Others displayed a range of finished goods from Leghorn hats and Italian leather gloves to Swiss clocks and German automatons; with space for books and paintings – and for copper-plate engravings of such a scandalous nature that Ellin could barely bring herself to stroll around a second time to study them more closely.

It seemed to her astonished gaze that everything that was highly taxed or difficult to obtain in England was here openly displayed.

Wherever Aaron took her men called out to him in French or English, or in a slurring guttural tongue that Ellin took for Dutch – exchanges over prices or consignments that made little sense to her. And through it all she wandered in a kind of daze, her pose of indifference long forgotten. Like a street urchin in a comfit shop, too overwhelmed to take it in.

"They say no people was ever ruined by trade," Aaron remarked as they returned across the quay, and not without some pride. "But I would go further and assert 'tis trade that *makes* a people. Trade – not ideals that feed and clothe 'em and pay their taxes."

He gestured to the sailors and the dockers of the quayside. "Most people in this place are involved in English trade, if not directly then in our boatyards and packing-houses, or in the manufactories we've set up for the kegs and dry-packs. So where would you say their first loyalty lies? How many red shirts and tricoleurs have you seen amongst 'em, eh? And how many d'ye think ran out to join the revolutionary armies when they came recruiting?" He raised his red brows interrogatively. "Come Sister Nell, how many? Fifty, one hundred? Two hundred would ye fancy, to fight for their fine new French Republic?"

"Really Sir, I'm sure I couldn't say." In this strange topsy-turvy world of his anything she supposed might easily apply.

"Eight," he pronounced triumphantly. "Eight wretched vagabonds who'd lived on the charity of the Benedictine Abbey the Revolution shut down. Eight out of eight *hundred* families! Hardly the reaction of a town loyal to Barras and Buonaparte, would ye think?"

Confusion upon confusion for poor Ellin. Enemies in London and Paris, allies and trading partners in Sussex and Fécamp! Two worlds, two separate moralities. And was she the only traitor after all, for crossing the divide between them? Oh, if only she could cross back now to Rafe and the world she understood! If only he'd send to her, write to her, build for her the bridge of forgiveness and goodwill that she needed now to reach him.

And then, just when she'd convinced herself that he would never write – that she must remain here as an exile for ever, a ketch flying Dutch colours had run into port from Newhaven, and on it the long awaited letter! Aaron himself brought it to her in her bedchamber – the first time he'd ventured there since, her illness –

entering without so much as a 'good morning', to toss the folded wafer on her bed.

"For you," he said curtly, his face unreadable. "From your husband, I collect?" And he turned on his heel again without another word.

Hauling herself up on the pillows, Ellin stared in disbelief at the rectangle of cream coloured cartridge with its superscription in Rafe's hand. For three interminable weeks she'd waited for this letter. But now that it was here within reach she felt a craven desire to kick it from the bed, to pull the coverlets up over her head and hide from whatever truth it contained.

'Ellin Corbyn, Fécamp.' The writing of the superscription so elegant – so controlled and passionless, so unforgiving . . .

Abruptly Ellin leant forward, snatched up the letter from the bed, and broke the seal.

Chapter Sixteen

Chalkdean
Ash-Wednesday,
February 21st 1798

My dear – my own dear wife,
The sincere assurance of my affection is the first and most important message I have to send you . . .

The letters shimmered, then swam. Ellin closed her eyes as relief swept over her like a tide. And when she opened them she saw the sun was shining; the world was whole again.

Around my feet beneath my desk (where poor Strap now lies disconsolate) a dozen crumpled pages witness the difficulty I have, have always had I suppose, in recording the feelings of my heart. And although I have no reason to expect that this attempt will succeed better than the others, I am resolved to have done with procrastination. This time I will force my quill to complete the piece, however ill-expressed; and as soon as it is sealed I will bear it down myself to the young rogue who awaits it in the stable yard. It has been well said that time and tide wait for no man, because in this case it is no more than the literal truth.

My dear, I cannot endure to think of you in such distress and so far beyond my comfort and protection. You must know that all my care is for your wellbeing – although I own that your actions have wounded me most grievously. (And Ellin, why could you not have confided in me, your own husband? Did you think me so unfeeling that I'd have forbidden you your concern for my brother's safety, or denied Aaron himself the warning you proposed?) But there, already I accuse you, when I am myself at least as much to blame as you are. Had I studied as earnestly to know your thoughts as I have to know my own, I believe that you would be here beside me now. Forgive me my omissions; and believe me, my dearest wife, when I tell you that neither distance nor circumstance have the slightest power to lessen my regard for you. I do love thee most truly. The tears stand in my eyes as I write it (I who was never the sentimentalist). I confess it openly to you.

My brother in his letter not only records good hopes of your recovery, but undertakes to bring you safely home to me as soon as that may be. I have always known there to be more to Aaron than he chooses to reveal; and for all my faulty judgement I think I can trust him now to honour such a promise, at whatever risk to himself. If our public papers are to be credited, these rumours of invasion may yet become reality. In which event, the sooner your crossing is made the better. Indeed the vessel that brings you this has already been paid to offer you passage to Newhaven by return. Avail yourself of it, my dear and with expedition. Or, if you do not yet feel strong enough, do everything I beg you to advance the time when you may. Rest well, eat healthily and take good heart. Assure yourself each day, each minute of each day, of my true love and affection.

Our little Lizzy asks for you most constantly. She misses you so much. And in your loss (our loss Ellin, yours and mine) only consider how much you have still to your account – and come home safe and soon to us, my dearest love. To your daughter, to your abject Strap, and to the man who is and ever will be,

Your loving husband,
R.C.

And so he truly loved her after all! Rafe, who'd always been so careful to avoid that term within her hearing. He loved her, forgave her, begged for her return.

'Oh Rafe, dear Rafe I love you too,' she thought with a sudden rush of gratitude. 'And if we sincerely love each other then we can start afresh, I know we can!'

She would make the crossing back to England immediately on the first tide, and without her brother-in-law's escort; Ellin was insistent. After all she'd sacrificed to prevent his earlier return, it would be the sheerest folly for him to risk himself now. She wouldn't countenance it. No, not for one minute.

Yet in the end she was not too difficult to persuade. During her weeks in Fécamp she had come to depend on Aaron more than she realized – to draw from his strength when she could find so little of her own. And when he assured her that the coast patrols between East-Bourne and Seaford were undermanned still beyond any hope of effectiveness, that he himself would return to France directly he'd seen her safe beneath his brother's roof, Ellin was ready enough to believe him.

* * *

They put out of harbour a little before high water to take advantage of the ebb. The best possible time for the run, so Aaron maintained; for despite the lack of cloud cover there was a helpful sou'westerly to beat them over, if it held. And if he personally chose to remain on deck 'til after nightfall, he encouraged Ellin to believe it to be no more than a need for occupation that inspired him.

In reality Aaron knew the Channel to be alive with shipping. Word was that Citizen General Buonaparte had already assembled a veritable armada of invasion craft in the ports of Dunkirk and Ostend. And since no one supposed the British to be ignorant of the danger, the risk of an encounter with an Admiralty sloop or a patrolling cutter was a real one. Not that Aaron himself entertained the slightest doubt that night that they'd evade them all. No God with so celebrated a weakness for lost sheep could afford to let him fail. Not this time, he thought. Because this time, as anyone could see, he was doing what was right.

In Aaron's bold instinctive world any woman was marked for exploitation by any man with the spirit to exploit her. In Fécamp, as he well knew, Ellin had been his for the taking. However unwillingly she may have given it, he'd seen the permission in her face long before – that night amongst the bee skeps in the Chalkdean orchard. In Fécamp he had only to withhold Rafe's letter, to treat her civilly and await her full recovery; and he knew that sooner or later she'd have ridden with him to the Horn Fair, and without any great show of resistance. But instead, the resistance had been his, and for once in his life he'd undertaken to deny himself. For Aaron a novel experience.

When Rafe's wife had looked up at him from his own bed in Fécamp with those tragic grey eyes of hers, he'd glimpsed something familiar – something that still hurt – which he refused to acknowledge even to himself. And instead of sparking life into them, instead of forcing into her eyes a reflection of his own dynamic appeal, he'd looked away, demure as a whore at a christening! And when he held the wine for her to drink, he'd forced himself to concentrate only on the transfer of the fluid, the tilt of the goblet – to ignore the yielding softness of the lips he pressed against its brim.

'A dog I may be, Sister Nelly,' he'd thought as he watched her then. 'But never such a disloyal and ungrateful dog I hope, that I'd permit my own brother's wife to come to harm.'

And when later Ellin consented to walk beside him through his terraced gardens or out onto the quays, deliberately he'd shut his eyes and ears to the provocations of her body in Marthe Lefèbre's borrowed silks – transferring his phantasies instead to Marthe herself, and to their violent nightly essays in her verbena-scented bed.

But now he could feel proud, now that he'd done what was right; and underneath his pride that little burr of niggling pain that made it all so Christian and worthwhile. Instant virtue and automatic maturity. For once the demands of honour and of fraternal affection coinciding with the need to demonstrate his own virility. In a few more hours he'd stand before his upright brother and this time he'd look him squarely in the eye. "Your wife, Sir," he would say, with that sense of real achievement that he'd craved so long and now at last merited. "You see, Ray, I've brought her home to you, just as ever I promised."

One gift from France and from his brother that Rafe could not in any wise refuse.

It was an hour or more after midnight before Aaron judged the proximity of the Sussex shore and called for the lead to be cast. At five fathoms, peering through his Dolland glass, he could just discern the pale smudge of the cliffs across the water. The Channel flood had carried them something to the east of their destination, on a level with the chalk pits of Hollywell twelve miles or so up the coast from Newhaven; and while they worked downshore, Aaron had the gig hauled in alongside and baled for landing. There was always a spare mount or two to be found in the outer stables of Bury Farm, as every trader and tide-porter in the locality was well aware. And in the circumstance, he reflected, it would be a pleasant irony to put into the Gap and avail themselves of that facility!

His sister-in-law's tale of old Sam's plotting with the parson to see him clapped in irons was hardly to be taken seriously, Aaron thought, for all the harm it had done the girl herself. God knows, the farmer had seen many a batchelor's baby before Nan's – had likely fathered more than one himself if truth be told. By this his temper would have cooled. And after a spate of chilling sou'-westerlies, there wasn't a Bury man that Aaron knew who'd stick to any kind of sea-watch through the night. The beach would be deserted, and so would the Bury yards. He'd hazard his life on that.

* * *

When Aaron left her the second time, Ellin herself extinguished the cabin lamp, unable to sustain its tilting beam or the memories it evoked; crouched in darkness for the final hours of the crossing, shivering with coldness and anticipation. After the stale confinement below decks, the sharpness of the Sussex night refreshed her. Aaron carried her ashore for the last few yards from the gig, before wading back for the halfankers he insisted on bringing with them for his brother, whether Rafe liked it or no. Then together they climbed the slippery path from the beach – where on another early morning in another season a naked young man had given chase to a fool of a girl who'd gone now for once and for good. This time she felt entirely sure of it.

They found the horses and all the tack they needed exactly where

Aaron had predicted, and within a short space were on their way again. Even at a foot pace the clatter of the horses' hooves sounded deafening to Ellin's nervous ears. At any moment she expected a challenge, a raised voice or a barking dog. But the yards were deserted. In the light of a moon like a silver coin the limbs of the great beech tree by the dairy glimmered with crystalline frost.

Faraway to the east over the slates of the farm buildings a faint violet flush gave warning of the coming day. And as they passed the dairy, the magpie cat which Ellin had disturbed there once before shot sideways across their path and halfway up the tree – round eyed and fluffy tailed, peering down at them with crazy feline humour. Aaron pulled in his frightened mount and then heeled on without a further glance. But Ellin smiled back at the skittish creature, reminded somehow of herself by the way in which its wild ascent had ended so ignominiously in a clumsy backward slide.

Above the histrionic cat a light glinted through the frosty branches of the beech; and realizing that it came from a window of the farmhouse up beyond, Ellin automatically quickened her pace. Someone was up and abroad already, perhaps even Farmer Ashby himself – and that meant danger. Yet how welcoming and forgiving that window looked. One little yellow square of warmth and light in all this icy darkness. It called to mind the warmth and safety of her own home. So near to Chalkdean now, only a hill between them. So near to little Lizzy, asleep now in her cot – and Rafe, her own dear husband. God bless him in his generosity!

For how could she have known that at this present Rafe was nearer still? Not over the hill in Chalkdean, but here and within that very lighted window, even as she hurried past beneath it.

* * *

Inside, the warmth and welcome of the lamplight was considerably less apparent. The room was cold and unventilated, stinking of chamber pots and stale perspiration. Its principal inhabitant lay exhausted, motionless for the moment amid a welter of soiled sheeting, with the Sellington midwife sleeping peacefully in a chair beside her.

At the sound of a creaking stair-board the old woman stopped snoring to open an enquiring eye; and perceiving it to be Doctor Corbyn in the doorway, immediately snatched up a sodden rag from her lap and leant over with it to mop at the girl Annie's perspiring face.

Sam Ashby had taken his time in calling out the doctor to his daughter. "Justabout best thing for all I reckon, if this ill-begotten nipper never saw the light of day," he'd confided to the midwife, perhaps as much in the way of a hint as an observation. "Best thing, Verity Cheal. Blamed if I doan't think so."

But after Ann had laboured painfully for eight and thirty hours, asking for Mr Corbyn all the while, her father had grudgingly agreed to send for him. Not to say that he approved of male 'finger smiths' any more than Mrs Cheal did. But if the trull died without recourse to a physician – as God only knew she well deserved to – it occurred to him that Rafe Corbyn might have something to say on the matter which would do nothing to enhance his local reputation. And to Sam Ashby, who persisted in considering himself a gentleman in the face of all contrary evidence, his own standing in the parish was not a thing to be trifled with.

Now he lingered self-consciously in the doorway to hear the doctor's diagnosis.

'Awkward as a cow in a cage, just like any man,' Midwife Cheal observed to herself with all her usual scorn for anything male within spitting distance of an accouchement; while at the same time assuming an obsequiously obliging air for the benefit of the college doctor.

"'Er waters discharged yester afternoon – proper old flood and all, Sir," she advised. "Babe's there and in 'is proper place all right. But will 'e make that breach? No Sir, 'e will not – not by any manner!"

"'E just doan't seem to want to come, Doctor," the girl herself appended as Rafe entered her line of vision from the bed. Her hair was soaked with sweat despite the chill; her eyes large, dark-ringed with pain, intensely blue. And somehow she contrived a smile.

Rafe smiled back, impressed by her stoicism, and reached for her pulse. He found it remarkably strong still.

"Well let's see if we can't discover what it is, then, that's keeping him from his business," he said – speaking as grooms and stockmen speak, less for the words themselves than for the soothing effect of their tone.

"'Tis only a mighty marvel to me that she've borne it thus far," the midwife confided loudly from behind his shoulder, unwilling to be excluded. "I've seen some first confinements in my time, Sir, believe you me. And there's plenty I've attended who'd 'ave up and died, upon my word, sooner than suffer as this one 'as."

For two straws, thought the rational and civilized Mr Corbyn of Chalkdean, he'd have picked up the ignorant old witch and strangled the life out of her there and then.

"Then you should certainly have sent for me earlier, should you not?" he said without raising his voice or his eyes from his patient. "When will you people ever learn to apply for assistance when you need it, I wonder?

"And I include you in this, Samuel Ashby," he added, ignoring the midwife's scandalized objections to his examintion of the girl without covers. "You should have appraised me of how things stood six hours ago at least. And you her own father! I'faith man, I find myself astonished at your want of feeling."

"Astonished are you? Dang me, I'm just about blazing astonished and all, I doan't mind telling ye!" the farmer roared, flustered by the turn events were taking into a fine defensive rage. "My eyes and limbs, a fine thing for a Corbyn to sermonize to an Ashby on family feelings, I'd say. She'll not swear it before a magistrate, but the brat's your brother's work, of that you may be sure – one brother to plowter the strumpet's furrow, and now t'other to reap the bleddy 'arvest. There's a middling astonishment if ye like, Sir!"

And blowing like a grampus, Sam Ashby turned from the unnerving prospect of his daughter's private anatomies wide to the world, to thunder off in search of a restorative draught of one kind or another.

In any normal circumstance there was no aspect of the female constitution that could have discountenanced Rafe as a practising physician. At the squalid lying-in hospital at Westminster and more latterly in the scattered habitations of the downland, he'd been called on to attend countless women in childbirth, with haemorrhaging or cystitis or any number of other female disorders. And at such times the proper detached frame had always come easily enough. *Cases*, that was all that any of them were to him – the differences between the individual women more limited from an anatomical viewpoint than any of them would have cared to suppose. But this morning with the Ashby girl he felt differently. Perhaps because of Ellin and what had befallen her? Or because of Aaron and Sam Ashby's recent accusation? Or maybe simply from something in himself after all his months of enforced celibacy – something which refused any longer to be denied?

Whatever the reason, when it came to his manual examination, Rafe found himself for once without his armour of professional detachment, at a sexual disadvantage. For Annie herself, such scant inhibitions as she'd ever possessed had long since fallen by the wayside of events. Like a caricature by Rowlandson, she sprawled back with inelegantly parted thighs. And as of necessity Rafe reached between them to press aside the swollen labia, something base within him recalled a graffito he'd once seen cut into the door of the notorious Golden Lion brothel in London:

'Trade beef for mutton – feed the dumb glutton!'

The glutton, the Moloch that swallowed men, and women too for the matter of that, along with all their best intentions. The female principle at the root of this poor girl's distress, as he now viewed it – and of Ellin's, and of all the malicious rumours that now circulated to link her name to Aaron's.

Bad news certainly flew apace. It had seemed to Rafe that half the downland knew of his wife's defection almost before he did himself. And naturally all credited her with the worst possible motives, despite the obvious limitations of her condition. Her father had ranted like a man possessed and threatened to disown her publicly from the pulpit. Her maid, Gubbin, burst into noisy tears at the news and proclaimed her mistress ruined – while old Gabel had merely shaken his head with the prophetic resignation of one who'd seen it all before.

"Females, Mus Relph," he observed sadly. "Anybody who knows a bee from a bull's foot would tell ye – they generally always goes by their hinstincts, do females. Ah, and wrong a score of times outter twenty."

All presumed the worst. Though only Aunt Drusilla had been tactless enough to show an active pleasure in the scandal.

"Worthless! Have I not always said so?" she demanded with more than a note of triumph in her voice. "But you wouldn't have it, would you, Nephew? Oh no, you had to jump up and wed the creature as soon as she crooked a finger in your direction. But I knew, you see – your aunt was never taken in. I made sure she was a fortune-hunter the moment I first set eyes on her. And by my word, now that she has the measure of your brother's style of living across the water, I can assure you that you'll not see her back in Chalkdean this side of Judgement Day. On that you may depend!"

And although he'd retaliated with energy to defend his wife's good name; assuring them all as he daily assured himself of Ellin's virtue and Aaron's ultimate loyalty to the family, Rafe's own mind had seethed with mistrust and resentment. The village women smiled and bobbed at him as usual as he passed them in the lanes. But he well knew what it was they whispered behind his back. Young Mistress Corbyn had left poor Doctor for his brother – slighted him, diminished his authority as a husband and a man. And however he might strive to trust her and rationalize her action, the bellowing green-eyed spectres of jealousy and affronted pride pursued him still through all his inner thoughts. Even after the arrival of Aaron's note with the tragic news of her miscarriage and the promise of Ellin's safe return from France, even after all his own assurances of love and forgiveness – the women still whispered at the roadside, Drusilla remained as certain as ever of his wife's intention to remain in exile, and Rafe himself as inwardly tormented.

But for all that he was a physician still, and for his time a good one. And no sooner did Rafe's fingers encounter the cranium of Ann Ashby's child, so far advanced it seemed to require but two or three contractions to bring it into the world, than he was recalled to the problem of the moment. Gently introducing his hand a little further, he found the cause of the obstruction almost immediately – a 'dystocia', a constricted ring of uterine muscles between the head and shoulders of the baby – and with the discovery the clear determination of its solution.

"The position is good, and I believe the child to be yet living," he was glad to reassure the girl, conscious as he spoke of a ragged clatter of hooves below her window. A distraction he vaguely associated with Sam Ashby and the farm, and one he had no difficulty in dismissing at the onslaught of another violent spasm in his patient.

"He won't be long in coming now," he told her, "if you will but allow me to take a little of your blood to help him on his way?"

At first he wasn't sure she'd heard. Squirming over onto her side in the grip of the contraction and pulling up her legs beneath her, Ann had replied just then with a great lusty bellow of pain. But afterwards her blue eyes sought his again. And again, miraculously, she found the strength to smile.

"Glory, Doctor – take as much as you like," she panted. "'Tain't 'elping where 'tis, that's certain!"

As a general rule Rafe placed little reliance on bloodletting and never used leeches, not even on children. In this he was unusual in a profession that for the main part considered the lancet and bleeding bowl as indispensible to the cure of every ailment from asthma to apoplexy. Nor were such instruments limited to doctors and apothecaries. Barbers, blacksmiths, even gardeners advertised their benefits and plied them enthusiastically at every opportunity – very often with fatal results. For a few patients of congested and plethoric habit, however, Rafe had found this most over-utilized of all remedies to be of real advantage. Also as it chanced, in cases of uterine dystocia like Ann's.

Normally it was necessary to bleed such patients to the point of fainting before their muscular spasms could be relaxed sufficiently to release the child. But not so with Ann Ashby. Before Rafe had extracted more than eight ounces of her blood, the girl's pains recommenced; and he'd barely time to bind up her arm before a series of strong contractions produced a crown of plastered, lardy hair. To be followed by the crumpled features of an angry living child.

It was a girl – puny of body, but mighty of lung like all the Ashbys. And as Rafe examined it, laughing at its waving fists and at the outrage in its tiny purple face, he was reminded for a second time that morning of his brother.

Chapter Seventeen

"My dear Aunt, your face!" Aaron exclaimed with unimpaired cheerfulness as he flung himself back into the lady's own chair alongside the Chalkdean parlour fire. "The face to sink a thousand Frenchy rafts and the Corsican with them, I do declare."

Miss Drusilla Corbyn inflated her narrow chest, drawing herself up to an altitude from which it was possible to look down her nose at her hell-begotten younger nephew. From the outsize linen mob she'd pulled on over her nightcap a fringe of curling papers protruded. Without stays or padding the form beneath her bed-gown was sexless, flat as a pipe-stem; though not entirely unsupported – for the lady had frustration to tighten her sinews, and anger to stiffen her spine.

"If you are sensible of your own good, Sir," she rejoined from between rigid lips, "you will leave your brother's house this instant, before he returns – and take your doxy with you!"

"What? For my good do you say – or for your own, Aunt?" Aaron kicked one booted and muddy leg up over the chair arm, to dislodge an embroidery frame and ball of coloured silk and send them tumbling to the floor. "And do you really think old Ray so harsh and unforgiving that he'd turn his own wife from his door? Or disown the brother who risks life and limb to bring her back to him? Or are you fearful after all that he will welcome the pair of us with open arms?

"Is that it, Ma'am?" he repated loudly in case she hadn't heard. "I am well aware of how greatly you've always favoured my brother, but does it displease you so much to see me deserving of gratitude for once? Or is it the thought of his young wife returning to Rafe that distresses you? To his *bed*, Aunt – is that what hurts so much?"

And this time he'd struck the spot, of that there was no doubt. "Never, you – you fiend!, he'll never take her back," she cried, so far forgetting her dignity as to run forward and stamp her large foot at him like a gaunt and angry sheep. "Nor forgive you neither, Aaron Corbyn, for your part in her debauch!"

Aaron laughed outright. "Oh, and bye the bye," he added delightedly. "If I might be permitted to offer you a word of advice, Ma'am, I think you would do well to avoid that term of 'doxy' in my brother's hearing. 'Tis hardly flattering to his consequence, d'ye see? And I venture to suppose would do your own cause more harm than good."

For a long moment the woman regarded him speechlessly, white to the nostrils. "Do you intend to leave this house, Sir, or do you not?" she finally enounced with slow precision.

"My dear Aunt, you know that I do not." He tilted back his red head, still smiling broadly and closing one eye as if to consider her discomfiture the better. "But won't you take a seat to keep us company 'til my brother returns? I declare it cricks my neck to look up to you at such a height. And we must have such a deal to discourse, I'm sure an hour or two would hardly serve to do it satisfaction."

"Satisfaction," Drusilla snapped. "The only thing that would give me satisfaction now, Sir, would be to see you, Sir, higher by the height of a hangman's cart!"

And before he could utter another word, she spun around and set off at a furious pace across the vestibule.

* * *

Above stairs Ellin knelt beside her daughter's bed, stroking the fluffy hair, weeping quietly so as not to wake the child. Downstairs Aaron threw another log upon the fire and stirred the embers with a poker. Outside in the cold March dawn, Footman William stealthily closed the out-kitchen door to slip through the shadows down the hill toward the stables.

Within a short space Aaron was asleep, his tight-breeched legs stretched out before the blaze, his face relaxed and youthful despite the rusty stubble on his throat, peaceful now and strangely innocent in its expression. Ellin, returned from the nursery, sat watching him across the hearth, pulling at her little dog's ears. Watching Aaron, but thinking of his brother. Her fascination with Aaron's complex character already part-forgotten. For an hour or more she sat there stroking Strap, listening to the crackle of the pine logs and the patient ticking of the parlour clock, waiting for her husband. Until at last she heard the whinny of his horse.

Strap growled. But even as his mistress rose, the clacking of Aunt Corbyn's cork-soled mules sounded on the tiles outside – first to the door as ever, the old tattle-tale!

'But no matter,' Ellin thought. Whatever his aunt might find to say to her detriment, she knew Rafe had forgiven her. He'd said so in his letter, had he not? And he'd never go back on that. In a moment he would be here in the room reaching out his hands to hers. 'And oh Rafe my darling, I'll make it up to you. I swear I will!'

And now she heard the door – the bolts, the creaking hinge – the woman's voice, his boots upon the tiles. So soon to see his face and feel his arms about her! To lay down the burden of her grief, and her stupidity, and begin to live again . . .

. . . But then the chink of spurs and more boots – oh Jesu, more boots than Rafe's alone!

Ellin stood as she had risen, one hand to her throat, as the parlour door burst open and crashed back to hit the wall behind. The dog barked wildly, Aaron, galvanized from sleep, leapt to his feet and fumbled for his pistol. But all too late – all far too late! For through the doorway the carbines of three uniformed dragoons were pointed at his chest.

The picture froze and no one moved; the young man and the terrier dog absurdly alike, as both stood on their toes to face the enemy, taller than nature made them and rigid with aggression. Then, very slowly, Aaron removed his empty hand from the flap pocket of his coat.

"Armed resistance?" he queried softly. "No I think not, gentlemen, not on this occasion." His smiling mask of cynicism back now in its accustomed place.

* * *

From his old London student lodgings in Paternoster Row, Rafe forced his way down Ludgate Hill through a noisy traffic of pedestrians, chairs and hackney coaches – a man apart, and one for whom the press made passage as much for the desperate resolution of his manner as for the oak cudgel that he flourished in their faces. From the corner of Old Bailey he strode up toward the modern Sessions House, past the Surgeon's Theatre where he himself had practiced – converted now in time of war to a barracks for the City of London Militia. And so on to Newgate crossing, where for the space of several minutes he was obliged to wait while drovers bound for Smithfield cleared the pavements of their cattle.

'Newgate' – the very name struck chill. Over the course of five centuries a series of prisons had stood upon this site. None grimmer than the modern penitentiary, rising sheer in a brooding cliff of granite to cast the street below in shadow. Near the centre of the building a callous ornament of festooned chains and leg-irons adorned an arch still blackened from the fires of the Gordon Riots eighteen years before. And beneath the arch a flight of narrow stairs gave access to a door like a crevice, set deep within the thickness of the walls.

With sinking heart Rafe climbed the steps, to rap with his cudgel and state his business through the grill.

"'Frough the chapel to your left, Sir, for the Master Side where we 'ouse them as 'ave been so careless as to run theirselves to debt," the turnkey informed him as he conducted his visitor by a labyrinth of passages and stairways to an upper floor. "Over yonder's the State Side for scholars as can afford to pay for their own apartments," he added, unlocking another door and waiting for Rafe to pass through. "Up there, Sir, for the Common Side, where our poor pupils 'ave nothing to depend on but the charity of the Foundation. And right 'ere, Guv'nor," the turnkey indicated a tall window ahead of them and grinned evilly, "'ere we 'ave the young ladies of our Academy, as you might say. Take a squint, Sir, if you will, and see 'ow nice we likes to keep 'em."

Rafe could already hear and smell, for the window lacked a pane. Yet still he was unprepared for the sight below. Seen from this high angle the women felons' exercise yard seethed like a snakepit. Its occupants to a woman were matted and grey with grime – female from the breasts they raggedly exposed, yet barely recognizable as the same sex as the most wretched of the whores and beggarwomen in the streets without. Women fighting, shouting, screaming with laughter. Or was it simply screaming? From their clawing hands and shrieking mouths it was impossible to tell. Some sprawled around the walls, sick or drunk or nursing babies. One squatted on the flags while others paddled barefoot through her urine. And from them all rose up the farmyard stench of farrowing sties. Women who stank like sows!

The turnkey grinned again at the sight of Rafe's revulsion. "Genteel?" he said, well pleased with his effect. "I doubt you'd find a sweeter set of ladies, Sir, at Vauxhall or the Palace of St James itself."

At the end of a further flight of stairs they came to Ellin's cell. Plank-lined, it measured twelve by seven feet and provided its own small window on the yard – too high, thank heaven, to give a view, but vented with a grill to catch its sounds and odours to perfection. She sat directly in the window's light, striped with the latticed pattern of its bars. Her head was bare, her brown hair cut in a rough Titus bob like a child's as a precaution against vermin, her eyes enormous. She looked up as the door swung back and tried to smile.

"Oh my dear . . ." He started towards her.

"No Rafe, don't touch me please." She held out a hand as if to fend him off. "I do not think I can bear it if you do."

And so he stood a yard away to see her clench her fist and lift her chin, like some gallant little swimmer struggling to breast the flood of her own emotions. A pulse fluttered in her slender throat; and watching it Rafe ached to take her in his arms, selfishly longing to tell her what he felt, to feel her cling and sob against his chest. Yet knowing he must do nothing now to overset her fragile self-possession.

* * *

Ellin dug her small teeth into her lip and opened her eyes wide to stop the tears from forming. A trick she'd learned long since. 'Oh look at him,' her soul cried out. To find her here – to stand as he had stood in court to see her tried, his own wife, as an accessory to his brother's crime.

The court and its judges rose before her as so often they rose in her nightmares; and in the crowded well, excited upturned faces, craning and whispering, eager for the spectacle of a lady brought down – to their level, and below it to annihilation.

'You, Ellin Corbyn, not having the fear of God before your eyes, but being moved and seduced by the instigation of the devil, have been convicted on full and satisfactory evidence . . .'

"We heard the bell of St Sepulchre's ringing this afternoon," she said aloud to Rafe, lifting her chin again and straightening her back in the chair. "The women thought it meant another execution and set up such a commotion in the wards as you never heard. But then they fired the cannon at the Tower; and now the turnkeys say there's been a victory, that all the French are sunk."

"Well not quite all, perhaps." His turn to try to smile – a conscious lifting of the facial muscles, and another signal failure. "But a great victory for Admiral Nelson and for England, nonetheless, that much is sure. 'Tis just now published in the *Evening Post*, the Yarmouth mail packet brought intelligence of it from Hambourg. This day in August last, they say, our warships came up with the French battle fleet in the Mediterranean near Alexandria and destroyed or captured all but two of them. To leave Buonaparte marooned in Egypt and all his ambitions for the Orient in ruins."

"I am very glad to hear it." But she lied. She had lost the capacity for gladness, wanted only to turn from him and escape this farce of conversation. Two people discoursing from the bare surface of their feelings, as if their hearts weren't breaking!

"I have more news," he said with resolute composure. "First, I think you should know that my aunt no longer lives with us at Chalkdean. For whatever provocation my brother may have given her, however she may now regret her action, I hold her responsible for what has befallen you and can no longer endure to see her in my house."

She nodded gravely, yet thinking how strange it was that Rafe should imagine she cared aught for Aunt Corbyn, or whether she left or stayed or flew to the moon on a broomstick. He assumed that she at least must hate and despise his aunt for her betrayal. But when she thought of that woman in the box, bound over as a witness for the Crown – losing Rafe's affection, losing Chalkdean, unable to halt now the process she had started – all Ellin could feel for her was a dull kind of pity. Aunt Corbyn's life in ruins just like theirs.

"But there is more," Rafe was saying. "My dear, I fear that I have more drastic tidings to bring you." She saw him swallow.

"More drastic?" Something in her drawing in, battening down – refusing to feel more. Instead she sought refuge in details and irrelevancies – in the titles of the books he'd brought her, in the miniature reflections of her own face in the brass buttons of his coat.

"It concerns your father," he said gently. So courteous and careful of her still in spite of all she'd done to him. "You know he was to have attended the assize court at East Grinstead?"

"I looked for him. I thought he was to testify in my behalf."

"We all wondered at his absence. But as it now appears . . ." He paused, his eyes on her face. "It now seems, my dear, that he met with an accident along the way."

"A riding accident?"

He nodded. And the rest she somehow knew, even before he told her.

"It seems his mare stumbled on the hill up out of Whitesmith's Green near Laughton," he said. "A child there in a cottage garden saw it happen. Your father was thrown, but the stirrup held him. They found the leather afterwards entwined around his leg."

"Afterwards?" She bent her head to examine more closely the sprigs of blue forget-me-nots upon her muslin sleeve.

"Before anyone could reach him the horse had already drawn him a hundred yards or more – and by then he was beyond assistance. My dear, they bury him tomorrow."

* * *

He watched her anxiously, but her face showed nothing. Her eyes when finally she raised them were as clear and remote as lakewater. And how could it help her now the man was dead. Rafe asked himself, to discover that so far from rallying to her defence, her monstrously unnatural little parent had intended to stand against her for the Crown?

* * *

If Ellin envisaged her father's terrifying fate between the flints and Betsy's pounding hooves, it was but for an instant. Glimpsed, then thrust away from sight and memory, not to be thought of. She had not loved her father, however much she might have wanted to. She saw that clearly now. And now his trials had ended with his life, poor man. So too she felt had hers. She'd used up her emotions, squandered them on worthless dreams, and now no more were left to her. Time and reality had lost all meaning – like the sky through the bars of her window. If you stared at it for long enough the images transposed – iron turned to air and air to iron . . .

"I love you, Ellin, and will stand by you whatever comes."

Rafe's voice as if from a great distance; the love and pain in his face reduced to something small and unremarkable. But what if he'd confessed it sooner? And what if he had shown it?

'Would I then have boarded the boat to France? Could I have done it then?' she thought dully. Purposeless, futile questions. For what mortal difference could they make now one way or the other?

'Ellin Corbyn, a verdict of guilty has been passed against you as an accessory before the fact of the felony for which your brother-in-law, Aaron Corbyn, has been convicted. The intention of all prosecutions is not so much to revenge and punish what is past, as to deter others from committing like crimes. And I cannot here omit taking notice of the unhappy cause of this judgement. I refer of course to those impudent confederacies which have been formed these many years past in Sussex and its neighbouring counties, and in enemy France . . .'

She could see now the judge's cruel reptilian face with its drooping eyelids and lipless mouth – all sympathy eroded by hundreds, nay by thousands of verdicts and automatic convictions like hers.

'Nothing remains but that I pass that sentence upon you which the law of your country, in conformity with the law of God and the practice of all ages and nations, has already pronounced. The court doth therefore award that you shall be transported beyond the seas to such place as His Majesty, with the advice of Privy Council, shall be pleased to appoint . . .'

To be transported like Aaron on the sworn testimonies of an unknown Revenue officer and a jealous woman; on the evidence of the cognac he'd so recklessly insisted on carrying ashore. On two halfanker kegs of spirit – and when you thought of all the contents of those vast Fécampois warehouses of his across the Channel!

'His Majesty King George the Third has therefore appointed that Ellin Corbyn be transported for the minimum term of seven years to the east coast of New South Wales, or to some or other of the islands adjacent . . .'

To Botany Bay; since the loss of the American colonies the inevitable destination for a transported convict. To be 'abroaded' to Botany Bay where there were already ten men to every woman, so they said – where females were needed desperately for convicts and officers alike. To be dispatched half across the globe to serve out her sentence as a whore. For Ellin Corbyn the ultimate justice.

* * *

The turnkey slammed the door of Ellin's cell and performed the function for which he was named with a practiced flourish.

Rafe closed his eyes and leant back against the wall beside it to fill his lungs with air. Exhausted by the act of standing still.

Chapter Eighteen

On a damp November morning, in mizzling rain, a force of constables formed up on either side of a line of delapidated hackney coaches and left Newgate Gaol to rattle down to Ludgate Hill, and thence south to the river. On Blackfriars bridge the procession halted. And ironed in pairs, like entrants for a three-legged race at a fair, their occupants descended. Several slipped and stumbled on the steps; and one would certainly have fallen, had not his companion caught him by the arm to help him down to the waiting lighter. A curiously ill-matched pair, as several watchers on the bridge observed – a sick and tattered starveling quite clearly from the Common Side, leg-fettered to the quality. And not only to the quality, but to a State Side scholar of the most affluent sort. immaculately turned out in a laundered stock and well cut greatcoat of cinnamon broadcloth.

After months or even years of confinement few 'pensioners of the Crown' embarked on their river journey to the transport ships in anything but a lethargic and demoralized condition. Not even the bustling highway of the Thames itself could quicken the interest of the men in the Newgate lighters. They stared dully at the water, at the river barges, the towering masts, the warehouses and boatyards that lined the banks – huddling in the rain, instinctively seeking comfort as they had in prison in the proximity of each other's scrawny bodies. And you'd never guess to look at them that most were under thirty still. 'Two-legged cattle', that's how their warders saw them. Kine to be driven and shipped and worked in a herd – those who survived to work. The red haired young scholar in cinnamon the only obvious exception.

From the first Aaron had set himself apart from the others. At Horsham and at the convicts' clearing-house that was Newgate he'd paid in gold for separate cells. He'd purchased fresh food for himself, and clean linen and private access to the yards, in the calculation that his chances of survival on the voyage must depend to a great extent on his physical resources. And now on the river while the other men huddled and shrank from the elements, he could lift his head proudly to feel the rain in his face. A prisoner in body, but free still where it counted most.

Sometimes in his cell at Horsham, in the darkness of the night or early dawn, Aaron had experienced the cold pangs of fear that any man, young or old, must feel in the shadow of the gallows. He'd seen a light-built fellow dance out his life that way and knew how long it could take to die at a rope's end. Yet always with the sunrise his natural confidence returned. His days might be many or few. But each one was for living, of that much he was certain. And when for lack of more damning evidence they'd marked him down for abroading after all, he'd faced the sentence cheerfully. There was nothing for him now, he knew, in England or in France. But he'd not waste time in remorse or self-reproach. He had his life still, and with it a new challenge – a fresh chance to set his wits and courage againt the worst they could devise for him, and to prove himself again the better man.

'Aye Ray, better than you, Brother. For I'm to play the man's part am I not, while you must languish back at home with your books and your potions, and your big empty bed. Survival, Ray – you'll see, I'm made for it! Never made to sit in a library chair like you, or on the back of some plodding old cob while life passes me by at a slow snail's creep. A man to prosper in adversity, that's me. With God's help, Brother – or else I fancy with the other fellow's!'

At Woolwich the lightermen turned their vessels into a narrow reach between the shipyards, close by the rotting carcases of the once proud warships, *Prudentia* and *Stanisklaus* – now converted to prison hulks, with ramshackle deckhouses, chimney-pots sprouting from their bulwarks and sodden washing strung between their masts. And there beside these fallen giants, dwarfed beneath their hulls, lay the craft that was to carry the Newgate men sixteen thousand miles across the ocean to the penal settlement of New South Wales.

An ugly little blunt-nosed barque scarce larger than a river boat.

As the first of the prisoners were disembarked from the lighters, a working party of hulk convicts on the wharves beyond sent up a loud derisive cheer; to be followed by another as the new arrivals shuffled aboard the transport, driven two-and-two like Noah's beasts along its steeply sloping gangplank.

"Dear oh dear – can't 'e keep 'is yards square without your Lordship's stays to brace 'em then?' a sailor called out rudely from the rat-lines at the sight of the red haired young felon actively assisting his companion in through the gun deck port. (A remark which for good reasons of his own Aaron had smilingly let pass.)

On the gun deck itself, where the space beneath the beams was so limited that many had to stoop, the fifty Newgate convicts were mustered with their bundles and their boxes for an address by the ship's surgeon.

"Men," that individual shortly and somewhat nervously announced from the companion ladder to the open deck above. "For be assured, I judge you to be men no less than I myself, despite all your offences and the unhappy situation to which they've brought you. But to introduce myself, my name is Surgeon Mascall, and my function is to ensure the health and wellbeing of all aboard this vessel during the voyage to New South Wales which under providence she is about to undertake."

In his elevated position on the ladder he'd been visible to the majority of his audience only from the waist downwards. But when at the commencement of his address the surgeon ducked briefly down again below the level of the deck to check that all were present and attending, Aaron had glimpsed a shock of pale hair above a face that boasted but little of character and less of manhood. As well-meaning and pettifogging a fool, he made certain, as any he might himself have selected for the object he had in view.

"The purpose of my addressing you at this time," the surgeon now proceeded to explain, "is to call your attention to certain regulations which I have myself drawn up for the guidance of all convict passengers aboard this ship."

A printed sheet of paper fluttered briefly on its way aloft to Mascall's line of vision. "REGULATIONS," he read portentously. "Item One: You are on no account to fight, quarrel or steal from one another, or to use obscene or blasphemous conversation."

"Bleeding arse'oles," a dismal voice exlaimed from somewhere in the assemblage below, "so where's the Goddamned profit in that then?"

"Item Two: You are at all times to be polite and obedient toward the officers and guards set over you," the surgeon hastily continued. "A faithful report will be made of each man's conduct in this respect. And those who behave well, though they may have joined us with the worst of reputations, will be favourably represented on arrival in the colony. Item Three: A standard of personal cleanliness being essential to the continued health and comfort of all on board, the strictest attention should be paid to this on every occasion. At the considerable expense of His Majesty's government each convict is to be provided with a suit of clothes and a change of linen and stockings, besides a pillow, a blanket and a sanitary bucket (one bucket between four persons). Item Four: The prisoner that shall dare to defy or break through any of the aforesaid items will not only be punished severely as an example to others, but must never expect to be recommended to the notice of the Governor of New South Wales."

On this dire note of warning the paper rustled down again and into view. "You will find that copies of these Regulations have been placed in conspicuous positions in your prison quarters below," their author concluded proudly. "And men, I would recommend them most seriously to your attention. For I apprehend that your future condition may well depend on them to a greater degree than any of you can at present conceive."

Which was perhaps not so wide of the fact as might be supposed. For truly those prisoners most attentive to the rules for personal cleanliness which the flimsy sheets promoted, found the papers themselves a more than useful adjunct to the sanitary buckets provided.

The orlop, or 'overlap' deck to which the Newgate men were now consigned, occupied the full width and a great part of the length of the ship immediately beneath the gun deck, and thus also below the laden waterline. Without benefit of portholes, limewashed against the worm and illuminated by nothing brighter than tallow glims, it looked like a cellar rather than a deck – an underground wine-store, with narrow wooden racks on either side more suitable for kegs and bottles than for living men.

To the amusement of the marine guards who'd escorted them down, several pairs of shackled men knocked heads or scraped spines while attempting to reach their berths in a stooping posture; for the beams on this deck in places gave a clearance of less than five feet.

"There y'are then lads, make the most of the space while you can," one departing marine advised unkindly as he prepared to douse the glims. "Because if ye think you're tight with fifty, wait 'til you're two *'undred* and fifty down 'ere, and then see 'ow brave you feel!"

He climbed the ladder, taunting still. "And another fifty of your Newgate whores up there above you to piddle on your 'eads! Three 'undred, that's the number – that's what she's booked for, see? Three 'undred of you scum of the earth, packed in like bleeding 'errings in a barrel!" And a moment later the after-hatch grating had slammed down behind him to leave the orlop and its human freight in almost total darkness.

Aaron lay back staring sightlessly upward. The deal boards of his berth were as rough and unyielding as rock. His ankles pained him where the basils of his iron cuffs had chafed them raw. But the discomfort he knew was as nothing to what would follow. Alone of the prisoners he'd made it his business to discover all he could of the transport ships and their modes of operation. There was more than one old lag or second-timer in Newgate who'd made the trip to the Cape before, or even to Botany Bay and back, at His Majesty's behest. Men all too willing to recount the horrors of their experiences to anyone with the time and patience to listen. From them Aaron already knew something of the overcrowding, the inevitable infestations and epidemics, the extremes of heat and cold that were to be met with on such voyages; and he'd laid his plans accordingly.

Above him as his eyes became accustomed to the gloom, he could just make out the rim of the upper berth, and beyond it the deeper blackness of the deckhead. Soon, tomorrow or the day after, the Newgate women would be dropped down with the tide from Blackfriars and crowded into the small prison ward reserved for them on the gun deck up above – amongst them the girl who one way or another had brought him to this – Rafe's pretty little wife.

"Ellin is now to be of that party; do you understand me, Brother? They have confirmed that you are to sail together on the *Lady Augusta*." Rafe's own voice in the State Side common room at Newgate.

Aaron pressed one hand to his forehead and closed his eyes, even in the darkness, the better to recall his brother's face.

"Aaron listen, I have this day received an answer to my petition to the Duke of Portland – and Brother, they've agreed! Seeing it's to be a matter of months before the next female transport is due to depart, they have fixed on sending a party of women ahead aboard a men's ship – your ship, Aaron. And Ellin is now to be of that party; do you understand me, Brother? They have confirmed that you are to sail together aboard the *Lady Augusta!*"

"Really now, and is that a fact?" The old compulsion to barricade himself with flippancy. Feelings too strong, too full of resentment ever to be revealed – least of all to Rafe.

"I think you've heard me say so, Sir."

"Well Sir, how very kind and civil of them that was, i'faith. Is that what you've been waiting to hear me say? And have you a picture perhaps of the pair of us strolling at our leisure on the quarter-deck, to view the wonders of the deep – and to marvel to each other at the clemency of British justice even as it bears us away to years of servitude?"

"Aaron, I'll allow that you are bitter, and maybe with reason. But there is good in you still. Your action in returning Ellin to me from France has proved it. And however you may care to disguise your virtues and your loyalties, I believe that I can trust you to do the best that you can for her now, when she most needs your help."

"Dear Brother – from where I'm sitting it would seem you have no choice."

Aaron smiled again. But only at the memory of his brother's earnest face. The man on the berth beside him moved restlessly, dragging at the chain that stretched between them.

"Listen to me, Aaron." Rafe's voice again – quiet and slow and steady in its final efforts at control. "When we were younger our mother charged me solemnly to see after your safety, you know she did – to protect you from the dangers of the world and those within yourself. A task in which it seems I've failed and all too comprehensively. But now I'm charging you – entrusting you with the safety of the person I hold most dear – and you must not fail, Brother. She is to be listed in the Indent Register as Ellin Corbyn; and additionally I have paid them to record her as *your* wife Aaron, not mine, d'ye see? The way things stand 'tis the only certain means of guaranteeing her your protection in the colony."

Their eyes met again, and likely for the last time. "Look after her Aaron, if not for her own sake then for mine." Brown eyes reflecting brown. Brothers in flesh with nothing but memories of a distant childhood, of a dying mother to bind them in spirit – and now the protection of another woman, passed in that last long glance from one brother to the other.

* * *

If the male convicts had been for the most part sullen and subdued on their arrival at the *Lady Augusta*, the women were another case entirely. Unhampered by shackles, they clambered aboard like monkeys by the permanent sea-gangway affixed to the ship's sloping side; using the occasion to shrill obscenities at the sailors in the rigging and to hoist their tattered skirts above their knees.

Had she not sat alongside them in the closed carriages and open lighters, and heard the way the women spoke amongst themselves, Ellin might well have judged them as Rafe had in the prison yard – as creatures long since lost to every female tendency. But as it was she saw them rather as they saw themselves, as victims in a world of ruthless men. Men who seduced them and set them on their course of theft and prostitution – men who arraigned and judged, and sentenced them to cross the world in servitude for other men to use. In the lighters they'd hugged their bundles of possessions and their children, staring across them at each other with round and fearful eyes. But on the ladder to the ship they'd winked and laughed and flashed their grimy thighs, reaching pathetically for the one weapon in their female arsenal that was proved and proved again to carry with a man.

Ellin, in the second of the boats, held back until the last – climbing then with the barest economy of motion, her eyes fixed to the batons, each baton as she gripped it. On the prison Ordinary's advice she travelled in her oldest weather cloak, bareheaded with her short hair blowing about her face. And if the men above had whistled all the same and shouted down to her to show a leg, she gave no sign of hearing. Curiously she could feel for the other women, crude and strident as they were, in all their frightened necessity for male support. But for herself – for Ellin Corbyn of the parish of Sellington in the county of Sussex, about to be transported as a convict to Botany Bay – for herself and her own situation she felt nothing still.

She left the Newgate lighter without looking back.

* * *

Toward the end of December and just four days before Christmas, when the yule log was brought in to be kindled on the eve of St Thomas, Rafe Corbyn stood like a martyr behind the draped pine table of his kitchen at Chalkdean. It was his duty as Squire of the Manor to distribute gifts and ginger wine at Thomas-tide to the poor women of the district come 'a-goodening' to his door. A seasonal task he'd first undertaken after the death of his grandfather, and had performed faithfully every year since – initially with his aunt at his elbow to hand out the gifts and exact her toll of gratitude from the recipients; and thereafter with Drusilla and his wife, one on either side of him, to compete for the role of Lady Bountiful. This year he stood alone, but for Ellin's little terrier and Cook at the dresser with the wine.

"Good afternoon, Sarah, what is it that you'd like? What can I give you, Mrs Armiger? And you, Mrs Pyecroft, have you chosen?" Over and over again he repeated the formula.

"Art'noon Sir. One of they 'ot mince tarts, if ye please."

"A candle Sir, and thankee."

"Thankee Sir, a bobbin would come in 'andsome Sir, I'm sure." Each woman smiled and dropped a curtsey as she took the gift and moved along the line toward the dresser. And Rafe smiled back at them each one, as if he couldn't feel their curiosity; while beneath the table Ellin's little dog sat watching, sniffing at each passing cloak and petticoat, each pair of boots, for one that never came nor ever could.

The women saw, of course, exactly how things stood at Chalkdean. For months the Corbyns' affairs had topped Nan

Ashby's bastard and the parson's accidental death, even run close to Nelson's victory of the Nile as the favourite conversation piece for the taverns and churchyards, the threshing barns and cottage parlours of the downland. And if through all that multitude of words the women had retained their good opinion of the doctor, they'd still come to his kitchen on Goodening Day, as Rafe himself well knew, less for his gifts than for the spectacle of his suffering. He knew and understood. The poor things were attracted to the drama of it all, much as they might have been to a strong perfume or a bright colour, as a welcome contrast to the drabness of their daily lives.

'So why deny them? Why deny any of it, Rafe? And why not stumble down to them looking as you feel – haggard, physically ill, red-eyed and unshaven? What object in pretending, when they know in any case that all your dreams and fine ideals are crashing about your ears like so many toppled castles?'

But in truth he'd contained his feelings too long and too successfully to allow them expression now. Like Ellin in her prison cell, control was all he had to hold to – control and occupation. In some obscure way he was fighting for his own life, or what remained of it. Sickness was rife still in the downland, with more patients than ever needful of attention. In the Chalkdean barns there was corn yet to be threshed, to be milled and distributed to the needy. There was an estate still and a household to be managed, a child to be comforted and distracted – and letters, vital letters to be written and received. So much around him demanding of attention.

Since his wife's and his brother's removal from Newgate Gaol, Rafe had engaged agents to report on their vessel's slow progress down the Thames estuary and around the Channel coast – agents in the Transport Office at Deptford, at Woolwich, in Deal and most recently at Portsmouth. For four days, he was informed, the *Lady Augusta* had been stormbound in the Downs harbour near Deal; and by the time word reached Chalkdean that she'd sailed again in company with a naval convoy bound for Portsmouth, he knew she must already be at anchorage somewhere off the Isle of Wight. The last news of her had come indeed from Portsmouth. She'd lain nearby at Mother Bank for a full three weeks, it was reported, to make up her numbers from the local convict hulks, and await a second convoy to protect her from French privateers to the latitude of Gibraltar. A number of feverish convicts had been sent ashore at this her final English port of call, so the agent's letter informed him – all men and not one of them a Corbyn.

But still the village women came smiling and bobbing, stretching out their calloused working hands.

"Well now, Mercy?" he heard his own voice enquiring with a physician's professional concern, "and how are those rheumatics of yours this afternoon?"

"No more'n middling, Sir, ye know me. But I'm scratching along somehows – and none the worse for your asking, Sir, that's sure."

"So what's it to be then? A silk bobbin, or a candle?"

"A candle if ye will, Sir."

He felt the unshed tears behind his eyes, hard little knots beneath them.

"And Mrs Copper, what for you?"

"Aye, a candle if ye please, Sir."

And all the time their eyes were on his face, watching for the outward signs of his despair. And all the time her ship was sailing southward carrying his Ellin from him, churning his thoughts behind it in its wake.

Chapter Nineteen

Christmas Day found the *Lady Augusta* battling through galeforce south-easterlies and towering seas in the Bay of Biscay. Even with her hatches battened, a deal of water still penetrated the vessel's lower decks through her hawse-holes and, for want of better caulking, from the seams of the timbers themselves. In the women's prison abaft of the gun deck it cascaded from the beams and sluiced from side to side across the floor. Frightened half out of her senses, wedged in an upper berth with her feet against a bulkhead that creaked ominously beneath them, Ellin felt certain that the little ship was about to break up.

"Oh Lord, who stills the raging of the sea, hear us – hear us and save us," she repeated through chattering teeth.

Yet waiting for the moment when the oakwood splintered and the boundless volumes of the ocean gushed in to claim them, she found her father's prayer-book God impossible to visualize. She tried, and tried again.

"Oh most powerful and glorious Lord God, at whose command the winds blow and the waves lift up – save us Lord out of the jaws of this death . . . help us Lord, or else we perish . . ."

But perversely the only image she could form was of the all too mortal features of a man – an image, of all things, of her brother-in-law's irreverent face smiling at her through her prison bars!

Curiously enough, when the pilot had first come to lead them out from the river to the open sea, Ellin had fared better than the other women in adapting to the heave-and-tumble motion of the vessel – contriving, as those who'd smuggled gin with them into the prison wards had not, to retain both her feet and the contents of her stomach. In their early days at Woolwich, the strongest and most aggressive of the Newgate women had reserved for themselves the open area between the berths and the view it offered through the grilled doorway of their prison, repelling all trespassers with hard words and harder fists. But as one after another they'd succumbed to seasickness, Ellin had found herself at liberty to walk the floor – to breathe through the grill the wider atmosphere of the after deck and watch the guards on their endless circuits of inspection. If she stood close enough to the bars she could see the companion ladder to the officers' cabins on the quarter-deck above, with the after hatch down to the orlop and the shaft of the mizzen mast immediately behind it.

In the mornings when the air was cold she could thus observe what at other times she merely smelled, the foul vapours rising from the male prisoners' grating. She could hear the men's chains and the deep groundswell of their voices. And in the evenings when the glims were extinguished, she'd listened to the shanties they sang to each other through the darkness – ballads bawdy and soulful, of 'Spanish Ladies' and 'Bollicky Bill', and of the 'Lament of Botany Bay':

'Come all you men of learning and a warning take by me,
I'd 'ave ye quit night walking and shun bad company –
I'd 'ave ye quit night walking, or else you'll rue the day,
You'll rue your transportation lads, when you're bound for
Botany Bay!'

She knew of course that Aaron was somewhere down there amongst them – posing as her husband, so Rafe had told her, to ensure their eventual domicile together in New South Wales. Probably his voice was one of those she'd already heard, if she could but separate its accents from the rest. Her chances of seeing him, however, this side of Botany Bay seemed blessedly remote; for the for'ard orlop hatch from which the men emerged for exercise was obscured by the main mast from the only women's window which faced in that direction.

In the meantime, Ellin's own daily excursions to the crowded little upper deck had merely served to confirm her in the pointlessness of her existence. For the handful of other females willing to face the swell and brave the wind above decks, there were silver coins to be extracted from the off-duty sailors who awaited them on the foc'sle – and to be earned with their bodies on the boards or against the walls of the cramped little galley beneath it. For the children hale enough to accompany them there were the escorting warships to be shouted at and waved to from the gangways. But for Ellin neither satisfaction – nothing for her above decks but a melancholy reminder of all she'd lost. She stood apart under the eye of the sentinel, ignoring the men's coarse invitations and the women's jibes – watching the English coast slide by the gun ports, straining her own eyes for any scoop or indent in the cliffs that might be Sellington. Her remembrances as she watched returning like homing birds to Rafe and Lizzy, to the leafless sycamores of Chalkdean and her dog Strap, waiting vainly for the mistress who never came.

Paradise Lost – a gold-stamped title from her husband's library.

Below decks at mealtimes she was required to serve the weaker women with their rations; tepid oatmeal in the mornings, hard ship's biscuit with peas or salted meat at noon, and again in the afternoon at four. While the decks were being sanded after breakfast she carried out the sanitary pails to the sewer-men, and turned the thin mattress they'd given her for bedding. Occasionally she'd nurse a fretful baby for its mother or help to occupy the older children with games of dice and hucklebones. But for most of her time she lingered near the door, purposelessly watching the sentinels and listening to the ceaseless rumble of the men's voices from beneath her feet.

Until one morning early, while she waited for the breakfast overseers to arrive, an altogether different sound demanded her attention.

"Guard! Guard, ye poxy snailcreep – guard I say!" The voice of one man pitched like a crier to silence all the rest.

In less than no time half a score of marines converged upon the after hatch. And all the women who could stand had scrambled from their berths to crowd around, engulfing Ellin in the rancid odours of their bodies.

"What's up Milady – what's the story? 'Oo's been murdered, eh?" They jostled and shoved at her from every side, their eyes bright with interest. "Let's 'ave a sight. Move over can't ye, gel?"

But curiosity, it seemed, was not quite dead in Ellin, because she held her ground. By now a number of red-coated guards had disappeared below. The ship's surgeon and a small crowd of officers and sailors stood peering down the hatch, with handkerchiefs clasped to their noses against the stench – waiting as the women waited for the first head to reappear above the deck. Predictably, when it came it wore the cockaded felt hat of a marine – to be followed by another of the same alongside the close-cropped pate of the felon they hauled between them up the ladder. A second unconscious body, still chained by its leg to the first and supported by two further marines, completed the group. And with the raucous encouragement of the women at the door, the pair of them were somehow manhandled out around the mizzen mast and deposited on the deck before their prison.

Ellin would have known him anywhere for the living colour of his hair, despite its brutal cut. It was Aaron, indisputably – Aaron with his coat gaping and his shirt sodden, its once fine linen plastered to his skin with sweat and vomit – so close that she could see the scatter of freckles across his cheekbones and his broken nose. The other, the man he was chained to, was already beyond help. That was obvious to all from the unnatural angles of his limbs as he sprawled there on the deck, even before the surgeon hurried forward to confirm it.

"But this one's alive right enough, Sir," one of the marines vouchsafed, stirring Aaron's body with his foot. "You take my word for it, Mr Mascall, nobody bawls like this feller did without 'e 'as a proper working pair of lungs!"

The surgeon patently agreed. At his behest a smith was quickly summoned to strike off the chains that bound the living to the dead, and two sailors detailed to bear Aaron's body aft to the sickbay.

Distracted by the catcalls and the ribald comments of the women at the door, they lifted him clumsily, trailing one arm and allowing the young man's head to hang back unsupported. His chin stuck up, sharp and unshaven, and his mouth gaped open – curving to an inverted shape that Ellin, watching, could not but liken to a grin.

'How strange,' she thought, 'so like a smile.' Until she realized with a sudden shock that his eyes were open too and smiling directly at her! Aaron smiling through her prison bars! His eyes in the grime of his face the same clear warm colour that they'd always been. The vital, shocking image that she clung to now while waiting for the ship to founder in the gales of Biscay.

* * *

From his hammock in the sickbay Aaron could hear the chain-pumps working night and day to keep the barque afloat. Above him the storm-trumpets screamed orders to reef and brace against the gale. Beneath him shackled men in feet of filthy water cried out in mortal terror of their lives. Yet here was he, unchained and dry – that was the chiefest thought in Aaron's mind. He was up here and those poor fools were not. Thus far at least his plan had worked.

In the Newgate press yard he'd been at some pains to pick out the likeliest fellow to share his irons; a sickly shambling scarecrow of a man who looked as if a stiffish breeze might waft him to eternity. For it had occurred to Aaron that whoever was shackled to the first man to die aboard the transport, would be himself by definition the first to lose his double irons. And if at the same time he could contrive the symptoms of a sickness of his own, the mariners' fears of infection would surely leave them no course open but to remove him from the other men? The first step as he saw it, to a passage unconfined and free of chains.

'So die, why can't you – die tonight,' he willed the wretched man each time the guards pinched out the glims to leave the orlop deck in darkness. 'You'll die in any case you know, you have no chance. So why prolong it? Why not die tonight and do us both some good?'

Yet morning after morning he'd awoken to the sound of laboured breath from beside him in the berth. To see the fellow's skinny hand stretch out for his oatmeal ration – to watch with disgust while he squatted on the bucket and somehow propelled his wasted body up two flights of ladders to the upper deck. His face set in a stubborn determination to live on, and to thwart Aaron in his gamble for an early release from irons.

The morning after they'd boarded the transport at Woolwich, two further consignments of prisoners from the *Prudentia* and

Stanisklaus alongside had trebled the population and considerably worsened the condition of the *Augusta*'s orlop deck. For the hulk convicts to a man had been as filthy and verminous as the most wretched specimens from the Newgate Common Side. With every day he spent amongst them Aaron knew his chances of contracting some or other of the distempers they carried with them from the prison ships must inevitably increase. And were he to find himself confined still to this lowest deck when the *Augusta* put in to Portsmouth, the odds against him could scarce be improved by the addition to their number there of another hundred felons (and hundreds of thousands more lice) from the hulks in Langstone harbour.

Well, if the disobliging fellow refused to make up his mind to die, then his mind must be made up for him, that was all. No place on a convict ship for sentimental notions.

'The game, not the rules, Ray. Not if you want me to see her safe.'

The new plan was bold, and relatively simple for a man without scruples (and if you cared to see it from the pestilent fellow's point of view, more merciful at least than nature) – a balled handkerchief for his mouth, a peg stolen from the laundrymen waisters for his nose, and a blanket overall to smother out his cries. The last watch before eight bells would be the time, Aaron decided, when most of the convicts were in their deepest slumber. And on the night he'd chosen for the deed he forced himself to stay awake to count the half hour bells through all the watches – and to defend himself against any unwary notions of guilt or sentiment that might assail him.

At the last stroke of the final bell he'd moved with the efficiency of repeated mental rehearsal – to feel for the man's face, to fasten the peg and force the rotten teeth apart for the kerchief – the blanket dragged swiftly into place, his own body weighting down the other's; and all the while the echo of the bell still ringing in his head. All undertaken and complete before his brain could interpret the message of his hands, his ears, his trembling outstretched limbs. For through it all his victim had lain quiet and cold and unresisting – dead already.

'Which is one good way, maybe, of inducing a fit man to vomit like a weakling,' Aaron thought ruefully a few minutes later, wiping his mouth on his own filthy sleeve as he leaned across to remove the peg and kerchief from his dead companion.

* * *

For Rafe Corbyn's ills work was the only remedy, or so he told himself. Each day he set himself to ride out further through the downland in his search for disease and deprivation – to distribute more bread, prescribe more draughts and powders and return home more exhausted than he had the day before.

Each evening when Lizzy had been coaxed from his knee by Mrs Henshaw and borne away upstairs to take her nursery supper, her father remained alone, too tired himself to eat. Too tired at last to think of Ellin and her fearful journey? If only he could be! He longed for sleep, yet dreaded his empty bed; for there it was that thoughts came crowding in on him of Ellin with his brother. Ellin and Aaron – married in name and soon, he must accept, in fact. Monstrous thoughts of guilt and jealousy – and somewhere in amongst and underneath them, creeping on its belly, the little gnawing creature of his own unsatisfied desire.

'Marriage has many pains, but celibacy has no pleasures,' the modern cynic, Doctor Johnson, had once been heard to say. A view which tended to ignore that little creeping beast – that thing which fed on pleasure and drove lonely men like Rafe to pace the floor at night; to read, to work by candelight, and too often to see the sun rise through the window of his surgery.

At one such chilly dawning, Rafe dozing in his chair had raised his head to see those first thin rays of light search out a scrap of yellow in a corner of the window; the folded wings of a dead butterfly lying on its side. A piece of life's jetsam, blown in perhaps from the ivy outside. Without quite knowing why, he reached out to touch it with his finger, probing at the legs tight-folded to its abdomen. Searching for life? Had he been? And was he surprised when the insect itself reached out to grip him, clinging tightly to his hand? Rafe only knew that when he raised it, so tightly gripping, and saw the quiver of its veined and yellow wings, he'd felt a remorseless stirring of that part of him he'd striven so hard those past weeks to ignore.

In a moment the butterfly fluttered from his finger toward the light, beating against the frosted window, dusting the ice crystals with the yellow of its wings. Yellow on the pane – sulphur, brimstone and damnation . . .

With a cry of anguish and frustration, Rafe snatched the palpitating creature from the glass – Rafe Corbyn, that most temperate, rational and civilized of men – to press it still living to the hardened ridge of his own body; smearing its fluids, tearing the delicate fabric of its wings, brutally rubbing its life away in company with the last remnants of his self-respect.

And afterwards he'd bowed his head and wept for the emptiness of his existence.

* * *

In the first week of January 1799, fifteen days out from Portsmouth and already within sight of the island of Madeira, the ship's company of the *Lady Augusta* were assembled on deck to see to the decent disposal of two more of her convict cargo.

"Man that is born of woman hath but a short time to live and is full of misery," read the captain in the hollow voice he reserved for such hollow occasions. "He cometh up and is cut down like a flower . . ."

Which was about as close a description to the truth as any Surgeon Jeremy Mascall could think of himself, watching from the ranks behind as in swift succession the stitched and weighted rolls of sailcloth plummeted to the deep.

'Cut 'em down!' That had been the captain's order at the termination of the punishments that killed them – though less like flowers perhaps, the surgeon considered on reflection, than something lowered from a butcher's hook! He winced again at the memory. Three years as a doctor and five in training had inured him to a great extent to the sight of blood, and to the sounds and symptoms of the pain that normally accompanied it. But he was a man of sensibility still, and wanton cruelty had always distressed him.

When the gales of Biscay had moderated sufficiently for the crew to leave the pumps, it was discovered that in the expectation of drowning on the flooded orlop, four of the male convicts had somehow succeeded between them in severing the links of their shackles. A crime for which all were automatically condemned to five dozen lashes at the gratings. And this despite Mascall's own earnest representation that two of them were near fifty – the upward age limit for fourteen-year men – and as such unlikely to survive the punishment.

One blow had been sufficient to draw blood and knock the breath out of the first man's lungs; by the second or third the blood was running freely, by the sixth it clogged the knotted tails of the cat itself and spattered the arm that wielded it. By the twelfth stroke the flesh of each man's back had been cut and cross-cut into a crimson pulp – by the fortieth or fiftieth the bone laid bare. Men brave enough to hold their tongue for the first dozen were howling like animals by the third. Of the offending convicts, one was already dead before his punishment had finished. Another was cut down with a damaged kidney, to die soon afterwards. The others had endured all sixty lashes and might perhaps survive. That was for their surgeon to determine, said the captain.

Jeremy Mascall groaned with exasperation. Responsibility without authority, that was his situation on the *Lady Augusta*. Approved by His Majesty's Board of Transport Commissioners as a man of reputation with a published monograph to his credit, appointed official surgeon by the ship's owners for the duration of her voyage – yet unhesitatingly ignored whenever his ideas conflicted with the captain's own! Certainly that had been the way of things at Langstone when he warned against the fever that he found there on the hulks. Even the Inspector General of Health, Sir Jerome Fitzpatrick, had agreed with him that the Portsmouth convicts were in no fit state for abroading. But the captain wanted numbers, and numbers he would have. Mascall could send back any men he judged unfit so long as they were in harbour, he allowed.

"But we're chartered for three hundred, Sir, and three hundred is what we're sailing with, make no mistake about it. Convict transport, that's my business, Mr Mascall. Yours is to doctor the buggers, and for preference to keep 'em alive 'til we put into Sydney Cove."

"But how can I prevent an epidemic if the hulks they come from are over-run with goal-fever, with typhus?" the harassed surgeon had complained – not to the captain, who'd long since vouchsafed his last word on the subject, but to the red haired young man in the sickbay who'd already responded so well to his own ministrations. "I have sent a dozen cases at the least back to the hulks. But for aught I can tell the others have already brought the infection on board, within their bodies or without them. I've no facilities here for cleansing these men adequately – no authority for improving their conditions. The captain has even forbidden me access to their deck. Did you know that? He says my visits may give rise to dissatisfaction and unrest!"

In his agitation the surgeon had forgotten to whom he was speaking. "But then if I cannot even examine them," he cried, "how in conscience can the man expect me to keep them alive?"

"Perhaps he doesn't, Sir. Have you thought of that?"

In spite of his convict status, the young man was obviously a gentleman – as well mannered and politely spoken as anyone could wish. Which was why Mascall himself had spoken as he had, why he hesitated even now to declare him fit and send him back to the overcrowded conditions of the orlop.

"Not wish me to keep them alive? I'm sure I can't tell what you mean, young man. The entire purpose and justification of this voyage is to deliver convicts to New South Wales."

"No Sir. To *take* them, I agree – but not necessarily to deliver. That is your business, Sir, as the captain says."

"But the Transport Commissioners have agreed to pay a bonus for each man landed alive; I have that on authority."

"A bonus of four pound ten per living man, Sir; as against a fee of twenty pound to ship him out from England. So far as the Commissioners are concerned, the main thing you see is to dispose of us – to remove us from civilized existence. 'The refuse of society, to be evacuated like the vicious humours of the body'. Have you not heard that said of transported convicts?"

The young felon's face was impossible to read. Yet he spoke without apparent bitterness toward the Commissioners. Extraordinary, Mascall thought, for one who'd already suffered such hardship at their hands.

"Six thousand pound, as I understand it, is what he's paid to ship us over. But if as much as half our number perished, he'd stand to lose no more than seven hundred pound in bonuses," the young man continued in the same even tone of voice. "A sum, Sir, that I am persuaded he would more than recover for the owners from the extra cargo he could take on at the Cape. Mark me, Sir – if but fifty of us died, our good captain would move the women down a deck and fill up their ward with stores and livestock quicker than hell could scorch a feather. Economics, d'ye see? 'Tis the only language these charter captains clearly understand."

"But that would be madness," the surgeon exclaimed. "How would we manage? Where would we treat the sick in event of an epidemic of that magnitude? And who would help me? My hospital and dispensary are entirely inadequate. Why, they haven't even given me a loblolly boy to run my errands."

For the first time since they'd recovered him from the orlop, a light kindled in the other's eyes. He smiled a small and deferential smile.

"Well as to that, Sir," he said, "as it chances I may be in a position to help you there. My brother, you see, is a physician. He trained at Cambridge and the London hospitals – and through him I have learned a little doctoring myself. Nothing out of the way, Sir, you understand. But enough I believe to be of some assistance to you with your work. If you were only able to keep me here at hand, Sir, in the sickbay?"

And assist the young man had indeed, in every way he could. When they carried in the bleeding carcases of the convicts who survived the flogging, he nursed them with the tenderness of a mother, even picking out the maggots that later on infested them. And when in due course the first of the fever cases joined them from the orlop, the captain made no difficulty in having the man assigned as convict assistant to the surgeon. Not if it saved a sailor for more useful business above decks.

"Then if the worst comes, Mr Mascall, and the contagion spreads – as upon my word I pray to God that it will not," said Aaron Corbyn, "you know that my own wife is aboard the ship, over yonder amongst the women – the little one with the curly hair and the eyes like saucers. And if I say so myself, Sir, she has some skill with healing that 'twould be downright profligate to waste in an emergency."

And again he smiled that charming deferential smile of his.

Chapter Twenty

He thought immediately of Ellin when he saw the woman at his door – of how he'd found her on the stormy afternoon her father's leg was broke – leaning against the porch, soaked and bedraggled, beseeching his assistance with those great grey eyes of hers . . . But this girl on this February evening stood solid and unsupported. And her eyes as she lifted them to Rafe's were indisputably blue.

"We've come to 'elp keep 'ouse for ye, Sir, me and my Sary Ann," Sam Ashby's daughter announced, coming directly to the point as usual. She held out her arms towards him, and Rafe saw that she carried the child he'd delivered within the protecting folds of her cloak.

"To keep house for me?" he heard himself repeating stupidly as he leaned forward to see the baby's face.

"Some as ought to know better 'ave 'ad the nerve to call the precious mite a traitor's bastard, all-along-on-account-of this 'ere raddle-pate of 'ers," the girl explained, pushing back the cloak to reveal her daughter's crown of reddish hair. 'Marched down from Sel'ton village this afternoon they did, large as life, Sir, and twice as ugly, to tarrify the stock with all the pots and pans they could lay their 'ands to, and play rough-music 'neath my poor beni'ted father's parlour window."

Annie smiled reflectively at the memory. "Create?" she asked herself to save Rafe the trouble of a comment. "My word, raging about like a fire in an 'aystack, 'e were. Reckon you could've 'eard that man 'oller from 'ere, Sir, allowing for a fairish wind. 'Daughter,' 'e cries, 'you've brought shame on this 'ouse and on my good name, so you 'ave!' So fine a gentleman 'e thinks 'isself these days.

"'Well I know a gentleman when I sees one, Pa,' says I, 'and you're not it! No Sir, not by a long mile you ain't. And if my child's not wanted 'ereabouts, then I'll take 'er to 'er natural uncle over Chalkdean, so I will. For 'e's a *proper* gentleman and there's the difference. Short of a woman now to do for 'im and all. 'E brought my Sary Ann into this world in the first place, and I reckon 'e'd not begrudge 'er the right to a share of it. Now would 'e?'"

* * *

As the *Lady Augusta* sailed south from Madeira and the Canaries on a course headed for the Cape Verde Islands and Ascension, the cold winds of the North Atlantic gave way to the warmer air and glassy seas of the tropics. And with the change in climate, the typhus which the Langstone convicts had inevitably brought aboard, developed swiftly into the epidemic that Aaron anticipated and Surgeon Jeremy Mascall so feared. The floodwater of Biscay had served to float the stinking contents of the men's sanitary buckets the length of the orlop deck. And now in the dark and humid conditions that so suited them the vermin multiplied and seethed on every slimy surface, carrying the fever with them from man to man. Within days the little sick-bay to the aft of the gun deck was full and overflowing. Men were laid in rows before the door of the female prison, and after that amidships on the deck beyond it. A number of the women and children themselves contracted the contagion. And at Aaron's instigation the surgeon petitioned the captain to have Ellin removed from her ward, ostensibly to nurse her own kind with the proper regard for decency and convention.

'As if such things could possibly matter on a ship like this,' Ellin herself thought, wondering at their sense of logic. And if she'd also worried that her own qualifications for doctoring might fall a good way short of Aaron's claims for them, she soon saw that to be equally unimportant. There was little enough that anyone could do for the victims after all, beyond carrying their rations and their slops for them, or sponging them with clean seawater from over the ship's side. Most died within a week – sunken-eyed and dehydrated, raving like bedlam lunatics – to be committed to the deep without shroud or ceremony, without the slightest regard for either decency or convention. Tossed naked to the waiting sharks – man, woman and child alike.

Ellin's back ached painfully from constant bending. Her body streamed with perspiration. Her clothes and slippers reeked of the stinking yellow flux that seeped and spurted from the restless bodies all about her. Though where it all came from she could never understand – they drank so little and sweated so much. Yet in spite of all its horrors, she was grateful for the exercise and freedom that the activity brought her. Whenever the atmosphere of the gun deck became too vile to bear, she could take a bucket and climb topside, with no sentinel to let or hinder her. On the main deck she could stretch and straighten, to clear her lungs of filth and fill them with soft clean air – to feel the sun on her skin and look out across the shining miles of ocean for the first sight of Ascension Island. Small freedoms which on a transport vessel one came to value simply for themselves.

Moreover, there was Aaron now between decks, to demonstrate to her that life existed still and flourished, despite every degradation. They seldom spoke but often exchanged glances. Each time she met his eyes Ellin found herself searching them for some reflection of the grief and fear she felt herself, for the comfort of a shared emotion. But the support he offered her was of a different kind. For his eyes as they smiled back at her spoke only of the strength and courage that she lacked, and he possessed in such abundance.

* * *

On Easter Sunday a dozen or more unmarried girls from Sellington and Friston village, and from the Chalkdean estate, rose from their beds before dawn to venture out in their warmest hoods and mantles to see the sun dodge the Devil from the top of the downs. They stood in a solemn group to watch it shiver off its crimson veils; then linked hands in the glow of its rays to pace around the strange little mound of chalk that crowned the hill above the Ashby farm.

"Hey diddle derry, dance round the Bury," they chanted loudly. (And it should be confessed, with something less of grace than vigour.) "Hey diddle derry – da-ance to the man!"

No one now recalled quite why so blatantly a pagan custom should be celebrated on a day of such obvious Christian significance. Nor could anyone be sure that its performance in any way increased a virgin's chances of exchanging her unsatisfactory condition for that of a wedded and bedded wife. Indeed there was more than one old woman in the downland who swore that such magic had lost its potency back in the days of her youth, when His Majesty's Government had elected to alter the English calendar to suit some interfering foreign notion of time – and in so doing, to put all of nature's seasons out by a clear eleven days.

But if any of the modern generation felt as doubtful of the charm's effect, the likelihood of an illicit male spectator or two crouching in the furze nearby was more than sufficient reason in itself to justify the attempt. Giggling and pink cheeked from their exertions, the maidens descended, negotiating the steep little sheep trods in heavy agricultural boots that were never made for dancing and prancing about on the hills – waving their arms and swaying their hips with exaggerated instability, and glancing behind them every now and again in the exciting certainty of being followed.

On a bank near the old beech tree on the periphery of the farm buildings they stopped to gather a few thin posies of early violets and primmy-roses, and to pass the time in gossip while they waited for the tardiest of the village boys to come up with them.

"All forbid I should speak ill of anyone," declared Ketty Gubbin without even the suggestion of a blush, "but I say she'll be in 'is bed afore Witsun, with another Corbyn bastard to 'er name by this time next year – and see if I'm not right."

"Glory Ket, ye doan't say so? My word, I'd never of thought Mister Rafe . . ."

But in truth Ketty had hardly begun to say; and a dozen hasty words were as much as any other girl could reasonably expect to crowd in edgewise.

"Well I'll say nothing more," she said emphatically, "but let me tell you, Joanna 'Ebden, she've got 'im around 'er small finger all right and no mistake about it, as all the servants in the 'ouse will bear me out. Such goings on ye'd never believe! Why what d'ye think the Master says to Farmer Ashby when 'e comes up to take 'is daughter 'ome? 'No Sir,' says 'e as cool as ye please. 'No Sir, I'm sorry but this lady's now seen fit to name my brother as the father of 'er child; and so long as she seeks it there's an 'ome 'ere for the both of 'em and always will be.' And my Lady Lightskirts 'erself standing and smiling behind 'im all the while like the cat that got the cream. My eyes and limbs, ye should've 'eard that farmer swear! Properly jacked-up 'e were. I declare I couldn't 'ardly listen to the man for very shame!

"Now I'm mild as a milkmaid myself as you all know, and I'm not saying as some folks 'ave that the slummocky wench should be whipped at the cart's tail, 'arfway to Bright'on and back," Ketty added with commendable charity. "No, nor even made to stand up on a stool in church with nothing on 'er but the men's eyes, to confess 'er wickedness afore God and 'Is congregation – same as your Dad recommended in the Lamb last week Sue Langshaw, if all we 'ear be true." The other girls tittered appreciatively.

"To be sure I'll never be one to speak of a body be'ind 'er back," continued Ketty, stooping virtuously to gather a violet from beneath Nan Ashby's dairy wall. "But give some folk an inch and they'll take a yard, soon stretch it they will! And I vow and protest 'tis justabout more'n I can bear to see that wicked strumpet fixing to take the place of my poor little Mistress at Master's board and in 'is bed. That much I *will* say."

Not, as it would appear, that things were moving near so fast at Chalkdean Manor as that critic had implied. For though it's certain that the farmer's daughter would not have scrupled to make her host and employer a gift of her body in repayment for his kindness, as yet he'd shown her not the slightest encouragement or sign of interest in that way. And as a matter of record, her domestic duties in Rafe Corbyn's household still excluded Ann Ashby from all but the most superficial encounters with his curtained bed.

* * *

On Easter Sunday, while the Sussex village maidens consolidated their marriage charm in an exchange of blandishments with those of their swains bold enough to venture after them over the hill, the *Lady Augusta* was lying at anchor off the coast of South Africa, at Simonstown.

During the sixteen weeks of her voyage from Portsmouth, and despite Surgeon Mascall's printed regulations for good health and personal cleanliness, more than thirty of the transport's orlop deck occupants had already perished (together with two marines, a sailor, four children and six of the women on the gun deck). Forty-five deaths already overall.

To the south of the Cape Verde Islands, as the temperature rose steadily to an equatorial heat, conditions below decks matched or exceeded those of the infamous slavers that still plied between the Guinea Coast of Africa and the West Indies. Writhing naked bodies clanked their chains as they fought for oxygen within a dark and putrid effluvium that blackened the brass buttons on the marines' uniforms each time they opened up the hatches; the very picture of Hell. Water was restricted to scarce more than a pint a man per diem, despite the thirst that salt rations inevitably induced. Rats familiar and foolish enough to inhabit the suffocating subhuman world of the orlop were killed and sucked of their blood – the ribs and overhead beams of the deck licked dry of condensation. But then, as the ship moved further south into the freezing currents of the Antarctic, men who'd bartered their clothes for food or water on the equator had died of exposure where they lay, with nothing to cover them but their irons. And such was the state of the *Lady Augusta* when she finally arrived at the Cape – so saturated had she become with death and with disease, that the inhabitants of the Cape Town settlement swore they could smell the convict transport across a mile or more of water, even before they could see the broad arrows stencilled on her sails.

Prominent in the first party to put ashore in the *Augusta*'s whale boat was the ship's surgeon, Jeremy Mascall, with a letter from the captain to the Acting British Governor at the Cape to request hospital accommodation for upwards of a hundred of their sick. But when it was realized that gaol-fever, the dreaded typhus, was the principal complaint from which they suffered, Governor Dundas sent out a pilot instead to conduct them to False Bay on the far side of the Cape Peninsular. They'd be sheltered there he assured them from the south-easterly gales that were due at this time of year. And doubtless they could find places for their sick besides, in the naval hospital at Simonstown.

A town in name maybe. But in reality little more than a supply depôt for passing shipping. A quay and a jetty with barracks and warehouses alongside, a couple of dozen prim dutch-gabled buildings straggling along the lower slopes of a range of barren mountains – that was almost all there was to the place, as the *Augusta*'s company were to discover when they arrived there the following afternoon. But as the Governor had pointed out, there was also a small hospital in Simonstown, built originally to cater for the naval vessels and merchantmen that put in to False Bay *en passage* to India. And this time when Surgeon Mascall went ashore to make arrangements for the sick, his convict assistant, Aaron Corbyn, was permitted to go with him.

"No Sir, I regret that there can be no question of risking the introduction of a typhus infection of this scale to our settlement," the Commandant of the military barracks that faced the wharf formally asserted. "I should like to be of assistance, naturally. But as a physician, Sir, you must see that in the absence of a direct order from General Dundas, I could never authorize an action that would involve such a hazard to our civilian population."

"But man for pity's sake, there are human beings out there dying by the minute! Does that mean nothing to you?" The strain of the voyage had taken its toll on the surgeon, and poor Mascall's voice quavered with emotional exhaustion. "Men like you and me, Captain Collins," he insisted, "and women too and little children, God help them – dying in conditions that none of His creatures should be permitted to endure."

"It seems I must remind you that they are also convicted felons," the Commandant said drily, with a briefly contemptuous glance at Aaron's kersey jacket and close-shorn head. "I cannot possibly think of putting their welfare above that of our own people. No Sir, for the common good I can have no option but to place our hospital out of bounds to your sick, and likewise our graveyard to your dead."

He rose to dismiss them. "I'm sorry Mr Mascall, but I fear that in this case you must contrive to make your own arrangements."

"Which in effect must leave us no alternative but to cast the bodies overboard into your harbour. Is that what you intend, Sir?" the convict Corbyn's voice struck in unexpectedly from behind the surgeon's shoulder. "Because if so, with the south-easterlies we've been getting these several days, I can tell you that they're like to make it back to shore again damn near as quick as if we sent 'em in by whale boat."

Still standing behind his desk, the Commandant examined his fingernails and heaved a sigh. "Your felonious assistant appears in need of a lesson in good manners, Mr Mascall," he remarked with perfect composure (while at the same time covertly registering the good sense of the young fellow's observation). "A lesson that I would suggest we are well fitted to administer here and now, if you will allow it? Perhaps you noticed the flogging triangles on our parade ground as you came in?"

"On the other hand, Sir," Aaron continued with a coolness that the officer could not but admire, "unless I am mistaken, your Governor did promise us a safe haven in Simonstown. And it's my belief that he could not refuse you if you were to seek his permission to make use of the old stables on the hill yonder as a quarantine hospital for our sick, and to dispose of the corpses elsewhere. In a communal grave, shall we say, at some convenient distance from your settlement?"

* * *

The probability of letting the cat out of its baize bag for a little more flogging exercise at his expense had naturally occurred to Aaron before he spoke. But regrettably Mascall was too weak a vessel to be relied upon to force the issue on his own. They'd heard of the derelict stables from the natives on the bumboats that came out to meet the *Augusta* when she first dropped anchor. And aware that appreciably fewer of their number could expect to reach New South Wales alive if the epidemic were to continue unchecked, Aaron had weighed the odds and allowed the sacrifice to be justified. A decision that was fully vindicated five days later, when a company of dragoons turned out to conduct the transport's surgeon, his assistants and more than a hundred of their sick to the empty stables on the hill behind the barracks. It had been but a token of a dozen lashes in any case, when it might well have been fifty. Pain passed and skin healed eventually, Aaron reflected. Life offered only once.

Since the commencement of Napoleon's middle-eastern campaign, and the consequent removal to India of the greater part of the British garrison forces at the Cape, the military stables at Simonstown had fallen into disrepair. In the gales of the previous winter the thatch of their roofs was breached in several places. And with insufficient bedding straw remaining even for the few horses that still occupied them, the sick from the *Augusta* were laid out on mats of dessicated vegetation cut from the hillsides round about and covered over with sailcloth. But winter was again returning to the Cape, and the nights were cold. In their first twenty-four hours ashore it twice rained heavily, to soak a number of the convicts where they lay. And within the inside of a week ten more of them had died.

It could be said with justice – indeed *was* said by Surgeon Mascall, and on more than one occasion – that the new conditions for his patients offered little in the way of advantage over the ship itself. The reverse, if anything. But Aaron Corbyn, who'd paid for the convicts' removal with six dozen bleeding weals across his own back and shoulders, was by no means dissatisfied with the bargain. So far as he was concerned, the main object was to excise the infection from the vessel, to allow her decks to be cleansed and those with the strength to recover to do so. To save his life and Ellin's, in other words – not the lives of the pestilential creatures they attended in the stables. The fewer of those to return to the *Lady Augusta* the better, he thought.

Aaron's was a selfish and a brutal attitude, one he knew that Brother Ray would never have adopted, whatever his personal situation. But that he couldn't help. Life was for living, Aaron's only rule – every nerve and muscle, every waking thought an expression of his instinct for self-preservation. He used himself at least as ruthlessly as he used others. He always had. And perhaps at the final reckoning, God would grant him credit against all the sins he'd committed along the way, for preserving Ellin's life beside his own?

Chapter Twenty-one

Aaron looked across the tangle of human forms that littered the long galleries of the Simonstown stables, to where his sister-in-law was in the act of emerging from a stall – a wooden pail in one hand and a dripping water scoop in the other. In four months Ellin's hair had grown again almost to her shoulders. Somehow she'd contrived to wash it since coming ashore; and released from its customary knot behind, it had begun to curl again as if to demonstrate some inner resilience of its own. If she'd been slim before, now she was downright thin. Thin and straight, with sharp little collar bones and breasts like those of a girl of twelve.

'Well the closer to the bone the sweeter the meat,' thought Aaron unromantically. And her grey eyes were fine still, larger and more expressive than ever. They regarded him now with that look of special concern which she'd shown for her brother-in-law ever since his flogging. A look which, even as he struggled to dismiss it, released in Aaron unwanted feelings of another woman from another time and place. The demands of his body playing tricks with his emotions; something he'd sworn would never happen again. Soon, he knew, they'd find themselves together in the tack room – he without his shirt and she with her gentle tentative fingers, so like his mother's – so anxious to spare him the very pain he found such pleasure in controlling. His brother had charged him with her care, entered him in the Indent Register as her legal husband. And although Rafe had made no mention of whether he expected him to consummate this 'marriage of convenience', he must surely have known that it would happen? For how else could it be with a woman of her looks and a man of his credentials?

But now she was waiting anxiously to see what progress he'd made with his stripes, waiting for him at the tack room door. Just an anxious woman. Just another woman after all! Aaron shrugged with mock resignation, bending his head to conceal a smile as he picked his way between the bodies to meet her.

* * *

It was a curious trick of irony, Ellin thought, that when at last she'd come to touch his body – with no one, not her father, not her husband, not even her own conscience to prevent her – it should be like this. No longer pristine and beautiful, but hideously scarred by the tails of the cat. Six tails despite its nine-tailed appellation – six tails, twelve times applied. Seventy-two knot wounds and as many cuts and stripes.

"Oh I'm sorry, does that pain you?"

His involuntary movement, the sharp intake of his breath convinced Ellin that it did, as she gingerly applied the salve of nettle and hazel that Mascall provided for the purpose. But in another moment her patient expelled his breath again in a little snort of laughter.

"Pain? D'ye think the touch of a woman's soft hand could pain a man after the attentions of the cat? Not on your life, Nelly! Lay it on, girl, and as hard as ye please!" And he shot Ellin a glance over his lacerated shoulder that reminded her uncomfortably of the night she'd ventured to extract the bee sting from between his red brows – and of that other occasion when he'd pursued her on the horse in all the pride of his naked youth.

'Hey sweetheart, but why run now after such a long and teasy wait?'

She'd known how it would be, of course, from the moment she saw where they were expected to sleep as man and wife, in the disused tack room of the Simonstown stables. Had anticipated it long since. Yet when she applied the salve and felt his injured muscles flinch beneath her touch, when she heard him laugh that low excited laugh again and saw the clear intention in Aaron's face, Ellin found herself retreating from the inevitability of what was to come. Over the past weeks she had seen at close quarters everything there was to see of the male anatomy. Everywhere she looked men sprawled about her in their own filth, naked and stinking, their flesh green-tinged like mouldy cheese. And now with Aaron's body beneath her hands at last, she felt . . . why nothing but pity and a vague unease. God had a sense of humour after all!

* * *

No such reservations for Aaron. He too was on familiar terms with the bodies of other men, it being his function to dispose of them in the granite quarries behind the Simonstown settlement as soon as Mascall pronounced them dead. A task that was not without its own grim satisfaction for such as he. For each time his pack-horses toiled to the lip of a quarry, each time he tipped a body over and watched it tumbling like a boneless doll, he felt his own strength and confidence increasing. Hyenas ate those wasted bodies, bones and all. But his body, when he returned to cleanse it at the stable well, remained in starting trim. And that despite the punishments of the lash.

It was dark on those occasions at the well and far too cold to linger long. But the sensation of his own hands on his own spare form had never failed to bring him satisfaction. Everything here for use – the skin taut-stretched, his muscles and sinews standing out over the bones like roots writhing over shallow soil – the bones themselves, hips, ribs, shoulders, the sharp angle of his jaw, the geometric hollows beneath his cheekbones, the orbits of his eyes . . . His fingers traced their hard familiar forms. Someday they would be all that remained of Aaron Corbyn, these bones beneath the flesh. But not yet, by heaven!

* * *

Ellin lay in the tack room on the pile of mouldy chaff sacks that served her as a bed, listening to the furtive rustlings of some rodent in the darkness across the chamber, to the moaning of the sick and dying beyond her door. Listening and waiting as she had for each of their previous three nights at the Simonstown stables – for the moment that he'd choose to cross the room.

'And oh Papa, if you can see me now and read my thoughts,

you'll know I've done with those besetting sins of mine. Nothing unconsidered or impetuous in Ellin Corbyn now!'

And when at last the door opened, she knew intuitively that this was to be the night. His face was invisible – his eyes, his mouth, his pointed canine teeth concealed from her in darkness. But she could hear his breath and sense the urgency of his movements. She knew well what to expect.

* * *

The religious and the superstitious may hold that no such thing as chance exists. For others, coincidences do happen in life as well as fiction. Longitudinally the Cape of Good Hope was but a matter of some sixteen degrees east of Sellingtion in Sussex, no more than an hour advanced in time. It was one of the clock on the morning of April 5th when Aaron Corbyn crossed that chilly harness-room at Simonstown. And thus when at a few minutes past midnight of April 4th the panelled door of his brother Rafe's bedchamber at Chalkdean also swung open, the two events could be said to be as nearly simultaneous as makes no difference.

But unlike Ellin, Rafe was unprepared. He'd been sleeping soundly within the curtained fastness of his bed when four strong limbs, persistently applied, had woken him again to love. Or to something that for the moment served him quite as well.

* * *

They neither of them made a sound. Nor did they kiss or touch as lovers. Ellin lay motionless, passively accepting Aaron as she'd accepted Horsham Gaol and Newgate and transportation on the *Lady Augusta* convict ship. Hoping perhaps for more, but no longer willing to expect it. And in the event he'd brought nothing new or unexpected to the entry of her body, for all his enterprise and red haired vitality – for all the mystery of his character. He took what he wanted, just like any man. Yet even so he had the power to cheat her, in witholding from Ellin the sound of his pleasure – the audible proof of her conquest which, without realizing, she'd taken for granted as her female right.

A violent movement that increased in violence and then abruptly stopped. A swallow, a single deep breath, and then an impatient withdrawal. That was all he communicated to her. No cry and no surrender. Nothing for her to hold to. The conquest Aaron's and Aaron's alone.

* * *

Not so with his brother, or with the girl, Ann Ashby, who stole beneath the hangings of his great four-poster bed at Chalkdean. With no more love between them than that other couple so far away in Simonstown, both Rafe and Ann had taken and given pleasure unstintingly.

"Reckon we'd all go sour like the cream if we 'ad to stand too long," the girl remarked prosaically. "So take what ye want, Sir, 'ere's the way – no bounds."

And thus surprised, both by her frankness and by the opulence of the gifts the farmer's daughter proferred him, Rafe had accepted with a gratitude and an enthusiasm that brought to the pair of them its own rewards.

* * *

And afterwards while Ellin in her harness-room lay shivering and listening to the rats, and to the silence beyond the rats, and Aaron yawned ungallantly while he thought how very like she'd been to every other woman that he'd plumbed – that other couple in that other place fell unprotesting into sleep.

* * *

It was almost the end of May before the *Augusta* had been ready to put to sea again. Of the sick convicts quartered in the stables, a further thirty-five had died ashore. And just as Aaron foretold, the ship's carpenters succeeded Surgeon Mascall in his makeshift fumigations, partitioning the orlop to make way there for the women and children who'd survived – and to clear the decks above for other more profitable cargo. As the *Augusta*'s captain was only too aware, virtually any commodity purchased at the Cape could be sold at extravagant profits to the Government Commissary or the notorious military buying-ring in New South Wales. In place of the coal therefore that he'd shipped out to the Cape colony as ballast, he now took on building materials: clay tiles, softwood timber, and lime mortar in sealed containers. He took on grain, gambling that he could keep it from rotting or fermenting in the hold. In addition to the water and supplies he needed to keep his sailors and convicts alive for a further eight weeks at sea, he took on a quantity of tea and sugar from an East Indiaman anchored alongside them in False Bay. (For both commodities were retailing in Sydney for more than three shillings a pound, so he was reliably informed.) He also took on cheap rum and dessert wine from the local vineyards for selling to the merchant officers of the New South Wales Corps garrison. But above all he took on livestock. Pens for cattle, sheep and hogs were hastily constructed on the gun deck and in the waist of the vessel. Crates of chickens and guinea fowl, ducks and geese were stacked on the quarter-deck, even stowed in the ship's boats. And instructions were issued to all hands to give precedence to their four-legged and feathered cargo over the felons below them. For in plain fact, at the rates the Transport Commissioners offered, it would be more profitable now to put a crate of hens ashore in 'Terra Australis' than a living convict.

Aaron's attention was not held by the crated fowls or the nets of struggling sheep, as he watched the loading operations from the hill above the quay. Nor even by the bellowing cattle, hoisted from the longboats in their ungainly cradles of canvas and rope.

"Gad's life, Nelly, will you look at that!" His voice rose unconsciously in its excitement. "Just look at that smart piece of flesh!" And following the direction of his gaze, the woman who'd come to join him at the gate of the old stables was in time to see a tall chestnut horse led out onto the granite setts of the jetty below.

"A blood horse, but what a famous thing! A warranted thoroughbred, d'ye see, to sail with us to New South Wales!"

Ellin looked back at him, uncomprehendingly. "No Aaron, I confess that I cannot see," she said wearily. "I cannot see of what possible advantage to any of us a horse might be aboard our ship."

Down on the jetty the animal moved like a dancer, the winter sunlight gleaming on its polished flanks. They could hear the men's cries of alarm as it reared and curvetted in defiance of the water and of the precarious ramp with which they'd sought to bridge it.

Aaron chuckled with amusement. "Not just a horse Nell, but a *blood* horse and a beauty," he repeated. "And you can take it from me as a fact that wherever a horse of that quality goes, by land or by sea, there's money to be made and aplenty for the fellow who knows what he's about."

And when it came to horses (or to money for the matter of that) Aaron himself of course was just precisely such a fellow.

By the time he and Ellin had embarked with the surviving convicts from the stables, those who could now walk and those who must still be carried, it was to find the chestnut stallion installed in a purpose-built compartment of his own on the gun deck between the for'ard hatches. An area which already sounded and smelled more like a farmyard than the deck of a ship. The animal, as Aaron soon discovered, was the property of a paying passenger aboard the *Lady Augusta*. One Cameron Blair, a hard-bitten little Scots lieutenant who'd sold his commission in the 91st Regiment of Foot in South Africa, tempted by the promise of a free land grant and convict labour, to stake his savings, his acumen and his energy – all he possessed – on settlement in New South Wales. The stallion he'd won in a game of cribbage from another officer, who'd had it shipped out to the Cape from England only three years before; a warranted thoroughbred, as Aaron inferred, sired by the British racehorse Rockingham. And on an impulse he could afford to back with cash, Blair had decided to take the animal with him to the new colony, along with a local mare of Basuto and Spanish jennet breeding and his share of the other more traditional farm stock.

"I hear the Corps officers out there are near as partial to horse-racing as our fellows of the Cape," Aaron himself had overheard the Scotsman remark to an interested marine on one of his innumerable visits 'tween decks to check on the welfare of his livestock. "Or would be if they had the mounts for it. No more than a hundred or so nags in the entire colony to date, so they say. And if we can only get him there in one piece, I'll lay five pound to a crown that Young Rockingham here 'ud pay for his passage out of stallion fees within a month of landing."

Lieutenant Cameron Blair was a stocky man of middle years

with a red neck and a pock-pitted skin, and a direct approach to life that encouraged his eavesdropper to seize the chance that offered.

"In which event, Sir, you'd be well advised to hire yourself a good man with horses, to protect your investment for you on the way," he put in quickly. "The mare too I'd say, if she's as far in foal as she appears."

He had gambled on his own effrontery before, still bore the fresh scars across his back to prove it. But when the other man turned about to face him, he knew he'd judged aright.

As Aaron had forseen, every last ounce of strength and stamina that he could muster was required to see Blair's horses through the trials that still lay ahead of them on the two month voyage to New South Wales. From the Cape the *Lady Augusta* turned southward into Antarctic waters once more, crowding sail as she bravely cast herself into the path of the Roaring Forties. Rain lashed her stem to stern. The wind rose to punch out her canvas and roll the little barque from one beam end to the other. And below decks Aaron worked manfully to keep the frightened horses on their feet – tightening and adjusting the web of braces that held them upright, stroking, soothing, talking constantly to calm and reassure them.

Considering the nature of the liquids that seeped down to them from the topside sheep and pig-pens, and of the powerful odours in circulation between the decks, the hatches had been left open for as long as possible. And both watches had been called aloft to reef the sails, with massive waves already breaking over the poop and flooding down into the waist of the ship, before orders were given to close and batten them. The first freezing deluge from above hit the thoroughbred, Young Rockingham, with a force that wrenched his braces from their fastenings in the bulkhead and flung the stallion bodily across his pen – to set the mare beyond him squealing with alarm. Retching, half-drowned himself and festooned with sodden straw, Aaron was barely in time to catch the horse's head before a fresh torrent engulfed them. And two more had followed in swift and wet succession by the time the waisters attained the hatches and slammed them down.

From that moment, and until the vessel rounded the south-east cape of Van Diemen's Land six weeks later, the *Augusta*'s gun deck remained firmly sealed. In cold and in darkness, near-asphyxiated by uric fumes, Aaron continued to massage the horses' muscles, to prepare them mashes to tempt their appetites, and to talk.

"That's it, there's the lad. Oh yes you know what it's about, and no disputing. You and I, Rockingham – we know what it's about bigod! We'll show 'em eh, my lad? . . ."

He repeated the same words over and over again with a thousand minor variations. His voice against the roaring of the wind – his hands on the satin muzzle, the long lean muscles of the neck, feeling the strength of the great beast at his side. Through it all, day after day and week after week, Young Rockingham stood foursquare, braced in stoic endurance. And Aaron attending him received back his own assurances from the horse, and with interest, as he could never have done from another man. Still less, he told himself, from any woman.

Chapter Twenty-two

At a little after noon on July 28th 1799, the *Lady Augusta* convict transport at last dropped anchor in the waters of New South Wales. Not in Botany Bay, as most aboard her had been led to expect, but twenty miles up the coast in the great natural harbour of Port Jackson, at Sydney Cove. During the voyage from the Cape of Good Hope another twelve men and three women had died of fever, of malnutrition or exposure, together with all five of the babies born at sea. Exactly one hundred deaths since leaving the docks at Woolwich, with more no doubt to follow in their first weeks ashore in the new land. It was notable, however, that of the patently more valuable furred and feathered creatures taken on at the Cape, the majority had survived – including the little crossbred mare and the warranted thoroughbred, Young Rockingham. Another survivor was the intrepid Scots free-settler who'd imported them – two more his convict groom, Aaron Corbyn, and the woman whom the Indent Register recorded as his wife.

In the southern midwinter the penal settlement at Sydney was at best an uninspiring sight. Only a little more than eleven years had passed since Captain Arthur Phillip had brought his First Fleet into harbour here. And in contrast to the wild beauty of an anchorage which Phillip himself dubbed 'the best of all the world', the convicts' town was an ill-conceived affair of boxy daub and clapboard buildings set in unimaginative straight lines along its southern shore. A larger, cruder version of Simonstown – its modest Governor's House in contrast to the massive triple row of military barracks above, which illustrated the true nature of government in New South Wales.

"But never look so glum, Nelly," Aaron said encouragingly, as together they watched the ugly utilitarian little town draw closer. "Blair's agreed to take us on, has he not? And depend upon it, we could scarce have hoped for better. Assigned-servants, that's what we'll be – not slaves like most of these poor wretches – the house for you my girl, as soon as we have built it for the man, and the paddocks and the horses for me!" He laid a hand on her thin shoulder, for Aaron an unusual gesture. "A new beginning, Nell. A new chance for us, d'ye see – and by God we're going to take it!"

A new beginning in a hard new land. For Aaron there was novelty and challenge in everything that he saw in Port Jackson harbour; in outcrops of yellow sandstone streaked with iron, in timber – forests of it – and in the proud and primitive appearance of the natives who'd paddled out to meet them in their bark canoes.

"If you will only strive to conduct yourselves with propriety, I can assure you that every facility will be afforded to you to become settlers and useful members of the colony here," Surgeon Mascall had impressed on the surviving convicts in his parting address to them but a few hours earlier. It was clearly not propriety though, but courage and enterprise that would carry in New South Wales. A man would be valued here not for his past, not for his meekness in adversity, but only for what he could make of himself and the land that he came to. Aaron had realized that from the first; and all things considered, he was glad.

But to Ellin beside him at the rail, her own scrutiny of the shoreline conveyed a very different message. She felt Aaron's hand on her shoulder and heard the excitement again in his voice. But she did not respond. For where the man had seen novelty, the woman saw only the alien features of an inhospitable landscape. She saw poverty in the sandy soil and the strange contorted shapes of the native trees, hostility in the sad eyes and pouting lips of the aboriginals who stared up at her from the water. Where Aaron saw challenge in New South Wales, Ellin could see only hardship and more human misery, and the likelihood of failure.

* * *

It was impossible for Rafe not to recognize and applaud in Ann the single virtue which he himself had always lacked – and that was honesty. Because the earthy farmer's daughter was honest in a way the enlightened physician now saw he'd never been. There might be nothing remotely ladylike about the pleasure she'd taken in snapping her fingers in the faces of her family and all her many critics in the downland. But there was nothing sham or petty either in Ann Ashby's attitudes. She followed her instincts and spoke her mind, as uncritical of others' behaviour as she was of her own. She took life largely as she found it. And in consequence she found it good.

"'Tain't wrong because ye like it so," she told Rafe, smiling from the pillow. "Why should it be, for gracious sake? 'Tain't wicked neither, Sir, because you'd rather 'ave your little wife in 'ere alongside ye than old Annie. Glory Doctor, there's some things in this world you've got to take the way they come. You wouldn't shave your belly, would ye now, to make your breeches fit?"

And thus the educated man learned humbly from an illiterate girl that history after all was better to be consulted for facts than for principles. Rafe had let the bookish old philosophers in his library dictate to him the kind of wife he needed, he saw that now. Old men's ideas on marriage. Oh yes, he saw that now through Annie's eyes – denying himself his own youth, and Ellin hers, and with it so much for them that was natural and was good.

And paradoxically, in the face of his own real suffering and the tacit disapproval of all his household, Rafe's adventure with Sam Ashby's daughter succeeded where all else failed to restore to him a measure of his masculine self-respect.

* * *

John Hunter, the Scottish Governor of New South Wales, was pleased – delighted even – to grant his countryman Cameron Blair a hundred acres of cleared land some seventeen miles inland from Sydney at Parramatta, the second settlement of the colony. A generous grant, with additionally generous allowances on implements and seed. And one deriving, if their recipient had but known it, as much from the Governor's detestation of Parramatta's biggest independent landowner, John Macarthur, as from any more philanthropic motive. The official Superintendent of Convicts at Sydney made a further allowance to Blair of ten working felons with overseers to cultivate the land, in addition to the Corbyns – whom he'd eventually been persuaded to assign to the Scotsman on receipt of the appropriate ex gratia payment.

At first they'd all been set to work on the construction of Blair's house, on the gentle rise he selected for it half a mile above the river to the south of the main Parramatta settlement. A long single-storeyed edifice it was to be – of the 'bangalo' or bungalow pattern originally imported from India – with wide verandahs on three sides to keep the sun from its outer walls, and separate buildings behind for kitchens and for servants' quarters. The necessary lime mortar, Blair had already purchased and transported from the ship. But the water to mix it must be laboriously carried from the river, every drop – the bricks and sand sent up by packet-boat from Sydney to the Parramatta wharf, and from thence by bullock cart to the building site. And with the further necessities of digging out obstructing tree stumps, of cutting and shaping by hand each piece of hardwood timber for the framing, their progress on the building seemed infinitely slow. Cameron Blair himself, meantime – together with his assigned-servants, his convicts and their overseers – maintained a curious gypsy style of existence in an assortment of military tents and temporary bark shelters set up between the foundations of his new house and the stockades where his animals were penned. A relatively level area which at some later date was to be cultivated as his kitchen garden.

Sunrise, and with it the commencement of the convicts' working day, came something before seven in the southern winter season. But as house-woman – albeit of a house as yet unbuilt – Ellin must be up betimes to strike life into the camp fire, to brew Blair's tea and bear it to him in his tent.

It was the time she liked the best, this dark chill of the pre-dawn, when the silence of the surrounding bush was broken only by the rustling of the wind in the tall gums and the restless shiftings of the livestock in their pens. The stars in the southern heaven were brighter, she'd swear they were, the smell of earth and fallen gum leaves more pungent, the sense of vast remoteness more tangible than anything she'd known; she and the guard set to protect the stock against night-raiders, the only folk to witness it. Later, as the sleepy camp began to stir, she'd sometimes watch the grazing kangaroos fly off like bounding shadows through the trees – or listen to the calling birds, the flute-like native magpies and loquacious parakeets. And after the constant crowding, the fear and oppression of her time in the *Augusta*, the mood of calm and of detachment that the place inspired had come as a balm to her battered soul.

While Ellin worked steadily at the house-site, carrying water and mixing up the precious mortar for the bricks, Aaron expended his energies recklessly beneath his employer's approving eye – digging post-holes, splitting rails, fencing paddocks for the livestock in his charge; and returning exhausted at the end of each day to the rough bark shelter that he shared with Ellin. His physical demands on her in those strenuous pioneering days were brief, infrequent, and sadly without especial significance for either. A fact which Ellin told herself was doubtless for the best. Because she'd long assumed from the way he watched her, that it could be a matter of time only before Blair himself fulfilled the expectation of all free-settlers to whom convict house-women were assigned, and made bid to assert his *droit du seigneur*.

"Devil take it, 'tis hardly of any great consequence if he does, is it? A small enough price to pay, I'd have thought, for the man's protection and all it can bring us in this place," declared Aaron – who wouldn't have to pay the price. "Hardly of consequence," he repeated loudly.

And Ellin failed to notice, because she'd never thought to look, that his hands in the pockets of his baggy convict's pantaloons were clenched impotently in fists.

* * *

It came to Ellin, the thing she expected, in the third week following their arrival in the settlement – by which time an improved diet and the more settled routine of her work in the open air had combined to restore a little colour to her thin face. As she ducked in through the flap of Blair's tent with his tea one early morning, the Scotsman had simply reached up from his blankets in the way she'd known he would, to pull her down beside him.

"Come here." It was all he said or had to say. A plain statement from a man in a position to command. And calmly, surprising herself by her calmness, Ellin set down what remained of his tea and allowed him to do what he would with her, unresisting. An equally plain response from a woman who no longer really cared.

Afterwards, appalled by her coolness, the man felt compelled to apologise and explain. "Well I know young Corbyn passes for your husband," he said defensively. "But I've watched you – heard you speak together. I made sure 'twas but a convenience for the shipboard?"

She looked at him expressionlessly, neither confirming nor denying.

"And in a place like this where you women are so far outnumbered by the men, there's no shame attached to what we've done," he insisted, "no sense in making an object of it, girl. We are all of us realists are we not – we'd have to be. Your 'husband' as much as any of us, I make no doubt."

"Aaron a realist?" She smiled a twisted smile. "Oh yes that, Sir, certainly."

"And only reflect, if I'd not troubled to bargain with that scurvy Superintendent down in Sydney, he would have assigned you to the Corps in no time, and to worse men than me, girl. Looks like yours are worth a deal in grog, you know, to villains such as he."

"Yes I do know," she said, "and I'm sure we're properly grateful for your care of us." A set to her mouth now and a hardness in her grey eyes that had not been there before.

And something lacking in the nature of Ellin Corbyn's gratitude must have been apparent, even to Cameron Blair. Because less than a week later he engaged a second female convict from the town. A young Irish girl with a generous figure and a mass of near-black hair. To assist Mrs Corbyn with the lighter building work, so he said, and later in the house. But also for other more personal duties, it would appear. For from that time forward he'd avoided Ellin studiously – never so much as resting a glance on her body, leave alone a hand.

* * *

In 1799 the little township of Parramatta still looked quite as crude and incongruous as Sydney on its wild and beautiful harbour, or Simonstown in the mountains of the Cape. But whereas those other settlements existed primarily as ports still, built on rock and facing out over the water that supported them, Parramatta was envisaged from the first as an agricultural centre. There was fresh water here, good loam soil and direct access by river to Port Jackson. Predicting a great and prosperous future for the town, Governor Phillip had laid out a grand mile-long mainstreet from the hill on which his own house was to stand to a convenient landing place at the head of the river. A great boulevard more than two hundred feet wide, to put London's Pall Mall and Portland Place to shame. And if the wattled and thatched huts that fronted this splendid thoroughfare were as wretched as any others erected in the colony, if the mainstreet itself was over-run with barefoot children and mangy curs, then at least the land beyond had realized expectations. Across rolling country in which the stumps of a thousand stubborn gum trees still stood sentinel, fields were put down to wheat and Indian corn, potatoes, tobacco, and even to grape vines. That enterprising farmer, John Macarthur already had two hundred acres under cultivation, with his own dairy and stables, and a thousand grazing sheep besides. Parramatta was clearly on its way.

As surely was its newest landowner, the Scotsman, Cameron Blair. For one hundred acres freely granted in such a place must guarantee success. Provided only that the officers of the New South Wales Corps, the ruling clique in Parramatta as elsewhere in the colony, were disposed to permit it.

Formed nine years earlier for special service in this remotest and most primitive of British colonies, the Corps had originally found themselves so ill-supplied with the necessities of life in *Terra Australis*, that their officers were virtually forced to import their own supplies from the Cape and India. An initiative, once taken, which had laid the foundations for their eventual monopoly of the colony's trade – and through it, for a number of personal fortunes. By 1799, and in defiance of its Governor, the Military were already living like merchant princes in New South Wales – with Blair's neighbour, Macarthur, amongst the most powerful of them. At the age of thirty-two the man was not only a captain in the Regiment, its Paymaster and the official Inspector of Public Works at

Parramatta; he'd also become the colony's leading agriculturalist. And it followed that his opposition alone would have been more than sufficient to blight all Blair's hopes and future plans. Yet far from obstructing his newest neighbour, John Macarthur had gone out of his way to assist him with his building and planting programmes; entertaining him at his own table, even loaning him a horse and a ploughman for his cultivations. A concession that was all the more remarkable in the light of that gentleman's well known hostility toward previous competing settlers.

The reason, of course, for Macarthur's uncharacteristic magnanimity, the key indeed to Blair's future in Parramatta, rested – as Aaron Corbyn had predicted months before in Simonstown – on four long and finely boned equine legs. Because Young Rockingham, as it transpired, was not only the first bloodhorse that Parramatta had yet set eyes on – he was, at that precise moment in its history, the *only* warranted thoroughbred in all of New South Wales.

It was hardly surprising then that the horse's transportation by water on the *Rose Hill Packet* from Sydney had created such a sensation on the wharves at both ends of its journey. Nor that Macarthur, as an obsessive livestock breeder himself (and owner of a stable of twelve horses – all of them of disappointingly base parentage), had waived every other consideration in his eagerness for the new stallion to cover his mares in the shortest imaginable time. And within a bare four and twenty hours of their arrival in Parramatta, Blair and his red haired stockman were bidden over to their neighbour's property at Elizabeth Farm to show him the horse's paces. An unexpectedly extended visit from which Aaron returned flushed and grimy with dust and sweat, but confident as a Yorkshire carrier. A look of the boy about him, even now, with his tousled hair and wicked grin.

"Well, did I or did I not say, Nell, that money was bound to follow a beast like that?" he demanded triumphantly. "Impressed?" Captain Paymaster Macarthur would line up his mares tomorrow if he could for our Young Rockingham's pleasure – that's how impressed he is! Aye, and willing to pay handsome for the privilege.

"But we'll not let him run with 'em, ye may be sure of that," he added with a wink. "'No Sir, make him send the fillies down to our paddocks,' that's my advice to Blair. 'Keep the monkey on a chain, Sir. Decline to charge him for the service, whatever he bids to offer. And that way he'll shortly be worth more to us in goodwill than all the stud fees in the book. I guarantee it!'"

And despite all she knew of him, however, she might deplore his methods, Ellin could hardly forbear to smile at the rogue for his sheer outrageousness. A moment of amity between them.

Even for the convicts, there were opportunities aplenty to be found in the growing settlement of Parramatta. And 'opportunity', as Ellin had always been aware, was Aaron Corbyn's middle name. In winter months the daily term for bonded labour was from dawn until three each afternoon. For the remainder of each weekday, however, from noon on Saturday and for all of Sunday, the convicts' time was their own to dispose of as they chose. During the early establishment of his property and the back-breaking work of its initial cultivations, Blair had been keen to buy as much voluntary labour from the Corbyns as they were willing to grant him – and to pay well for it. So well indeed, that between the pair of them they'd found they could accumulate near as much in a single week of overtime, as either might have earned from the government paymasters in a six month term of bonded labour. A profitable enough venture in itself. But with the main building and fencing work completed and Blair's early fields all sown, Aaron felt able to divert a little of his surplus time, and Ellin's, to a still more lucrative trade. And that was rum.

From the earliest days of Governor Phillip's founding colony its luckless inhabitants had seized on alcohol, and rum especially, as the one means by which they could escape the wretchedness of their existence. Officially the sale of liquor was banned to convicts. But as the only inducement guaranteed to make them work, it soon became a ready source of profit for the merchant officers of the Corps – acting themselves as wholesalers and importing the spirit in quantity. Thus for a man who in his years at Fécamp had mastered the delicate art of 'dilution', the retail opportunities that such a trade afforded had proved a deal too good to miss. Aaron could tell to within a few drops the exact degree to which a spirit might be watered, not only to escape detection but actually to inebriate more quickly (knowing, as the majority of his customers did not, that a correctly diluted spirit is swifter to take effect than a neat one). And between his practice of the art and the preferential terms Macarthur and his colleagues were prepared to offer him as Young Rockingham's groom, he was very soon able to sell as much rum as he and Ellin could physically carry to the town each afternoon – and at profits of as much as one hundred and fifty per cent.

It was Fécamp all over again. Within two months Aaron had established his own illicit grog-shop in a bark hut at a point where the new highway to Sydney cut across a corner of Blair's property. And in another two he'd cleared sufficient profits to risk a further investment. Not this time in a warehouse or a lugger, but in a horse of his own – a little buttermilk-coloured mare that some Corps officer had shipped over with a boatload of livestock from Calcutta, and then re-sold cheaply as the result of a raceyard fetlock injury.

* * *

To Ellin it seemed the greatest possible extravagance, the purchase of that lame little mare. But as always Aaron remained unshakeable in his optimism.

"Damn it all, look at her neck," he said, "look at the carriage of her tail. She has Arab or Barb blood, I'd take my oath. And if Blair's willing, as he says he is, to let our Rockingham have a sniff at her, I tell you we'll have a thoroughbred out of this old girl within a twelvemonth, or near as makes no odd's."

"But Aaron you know 'tis years before a foal can race or breed," she remonstrated. "And even if it could, what then? Of what use would such a horse be then to assigned-servants, convicted felons such as we?"

"Of what use, woman? Do you *still* not understand? Blood horses have yet to arrive in this godforsaken land, that's the point. Scrub stock and half-bred hacks were all they knew in New South Wales 'til Rockingham. We're at the beginning of it all, Nell, don't ye see – the very place to be!"

He was like a child in his enthusiasm, and looking younger than he had in years, his fair skin tanned, his freckles more pronounced than ever. The youth from the sea at Sellington. The naked rider again who'd chased her up the cliffs. "Felons or freemen, it makes no difference here," he said with shining eyes – no trace now in them of mockery or laughter. "We'll breed and race the devils, that's what we'll do. And win, Nell – hang me, we'll make 'em win!"

Chapter Twenty-three

In Janary 1800, the first summer of a new century, Ellin's child by Aaron Corbyn was delivered, at Blair's own insistence, in a back bedroom of his new house at Parramatta. It was a boy – and in those early days of life when likenesses are often so pronounced, the very image of his father.

Possibly there'd been no need to write of it to Rafe, for Ellin had long since discharged her duty of sending word to her husband of their safe arrival in the colony. Yet something basic in her recognized an obligation to present him with the fact of it. If only to sever for once and for good the last fragile links that bound them still – he in Sussex and she in New South Wales.

Blair Farm, Parramatta
January 22nd 1800

My dear friend,
And yes, I believe I must now call you so, for I can no longer claim the right to name you 'husband'.

Ellin paused to brush away the tormenting flies, and to stare through the open doorway of their hut while the ink dried on her pen. Nothing moved in the white dazzle of the yard outside. Hogs, fowls, even the goose that supplied her quill, lay panting in whatever shade they could find. The cicadas filled the air with their ceaselessly shrilling paean to the sun, as again she bent to dip her pen.

Your brother and I are both in good health, and I trust that this will find you and my dearest daughter Elizabeth in a like condition. You must know that I think of you both and pray for you each day, and have done since I last beheld your faces.

Things go on here as well as may possibly be, considering the situation in which we find ourselves. Mr Blair's new homestead is now completed, his vines planted and his first crop of Indian corn near ready for harvesting. As for us, we have our own cottage now behind the horses' stables – a neat little place for all its simplicity . . .

Neat for Parramatta maybe. But for Rafe at Chalkdean, reading her letter at his inlaid escritoire? How could he see such a habitation as anything but squalid – with its earthen floor, its unglazed windows and fly-speckled walls, its insects and invading dust?

We have grown our own vegetables for the past months, though water just now is scarce and the kangaroos must constantly be watched for. No fence will keep them out. You may also be surprised perhaps to hear that your brother has purchased a little Indian mare, which he expects to foal sometime toward the year end to the stallion Mr Blair brought with him from the Cape.

We are credibly informed that Buonaparte is back in Paris and now in the position of First Consul. Will he hazard again to invade England from Boulogne, do you suppose? . . .

Again she paused to do battle with the flies – to look up into the rafters, to look down at the floor – to look out across the glaring yard to the powdered gum trees and the vivid blue line of the distant mountains. And then to turn aside and for the hundredth time to peer through the muslin swathing at the boy-child sleeping in the crib beside her stool – his face hot and flushed, irresistably pouting, so like his red haired father still . . .

But to come to the main object of my sending to you (her pen wrote on at last in defiance almost of her inclination). Rafe, I must tell you that earlier this month I was delivered of a child. Your brother's son, undoubtedly; and a fine boy on whom it is sincerely to be hoped the sins of his parents will never be visited. Under the circumstance you may think me wicked, but I had hoped to name the boy Saul after my father. Your brother, though, refused to countenance the scheme, and I'm afraid was quite angry that I should consider it. So we have agreed instead to call him Michael, after his father and yours – which I trust will give you no offence. I trust too and pray that the receipt of this news will be no more painful to you than it need. Thanks to your forethought and unselfishness we pass in this place as man and wife. No one here enquires too closely as to previous commitments or attachments, since the conventions of England are generally judged too remote to apply in New South Wales. And aside from the protection that this arrangement affords me, at such time as our conditional pardons may come through, the married status will further entitle Aaron to a grant of perhaps twenty or thirty more acres than he could otherwise anticipate.

I cannot expect you to understand or condone what I have become. All attitudes here have been coarsened by the conditions in which we are forced to live. Forgive me, if you can find it in your heart to do so. Give my love to our daughter. (But disguise it as your own, Rafe. Because by any means you can, you both must try now to forget me, along with the shame and unhappiness I have brought upon you.)

May God have care of you, my dear, now and forevermore in the future. You know that none can be with more sincerity than I am, your affectionate friend,

E. Corbyn

A fly alighted on the writing paper beneath her signature, and paused for a moment to rub its forelegs together obsequiously before another sent it buzzing on its way. The quill spattered ink as Ellin allowed it to slip through her shaking fingers to the floor. But on the skirts of her faded indigo gown, not on the precious letter. That she sanded, folded, superscribed on the verso, and finally sealed with a stub of red wax that she'd saved for the purpose.

* * *

"Mr Corbyn, Sir – as vicar of the parish I feel it to be no more than my duty to remind you of the moral example that a man in your position of responsibility must be expected to set . . ."

Words which Rafe himself could well have uttered once in lecturing to his brother. As trite of expression, as earnest of viewpoint then as the nervous young parson now whom his Aunt Drusilla, incredibly, had dared dispatch to save him from himself – and from poor Annie.

"In her letter from Tunbridge your aunt, Miss Corbyn, was in addition most anxious that I personally should represent to you the danger in which you are placing your immortal soul, and that of the woman, by continuing to indulge so openly in this liaison."

"So openly? But do I hear you aright, young man? Can you be telling me then that 'twould be better if I were more discreet? Is that the tenor of your message, and of the Church's?"

An unkind shaft at one so plainly in awe of his distinguished sinner. And a remark that the father in Rafe regretted in the instant he saw the young parson's prominent adam's apple bob up above his clerical neckbands.

"No, but of course I see that you are saying no such thing – unfair of me to suggest it," he put in quickly, pausing for a smile. "But come now, if we are to discuss this in a civilized fashion, let us be clear at least as to the nature of my immorality, and of Miss Ashby's. She was without a secure home for her child, you apprehend? I provided it. I was without the physical comfort of a wife, or of any other woman for the matter of that. She offered it. Neither of us has defrauded the other that I can detect, for we have both given freely. Nor have we wronged another person, I think, by our behaviour – no, not even my poor aunt. Moreover, my own daughter, I would have you know, has become quite as fond of Miss Ashby and her little girl as I am myself. And Miss Ashby's work within this household makes less for other hands."

Rafe smiled again. A comradely smile as he hoped, and not a patronizing one. "My dear young Sir, my best advice to you, if you will permit me to offer it, is to be less quick to judge and to condemn. Not to make the same mistake as I have done and to close your mind to the real virtues of a physical affection. True philosophy invites all communication, witholds nothing. We're all of us in need of affection, and life being what it is, I truly believe that we must be ready to find it where we can.

"But now I've shocked you. You doubtless see me now as an old libertine in love with a young hoyden. Come, is that not so? And if I were to tell you as a fact that I am not remotely in love with the girl? Dear me, then I see that I would only shock you further. Well I can only suggest then that you dismiss us from your mind and prayers. Save your concerns, young man, for someone more worthy of salvation. And if it will make you feel any the better, I will write to my aunt in Tunbridge Wells. Shall I do that? To assure her that you've discharged your duty to admiration – everything she could reasonably expect of you. But that, in spite of all, I remained obdurate in my debasement . . ."

Though as it happened, it was to his wife and not his aunt that Rafe had written first – straightway on receipt of Ellin's travel-stained letter from Parramatta. His own problems with the Vicar of Sellington and the delightedly scandalized parishioners he represented, paled to extinction beside Ellin's news and her apparent desire for release from him. In all their years of marriage, together and apart, Rafe had never been totally certain until now that it was *she* he loved, rather than the sensation perhaps of love itself. But now with another woman in his bed and Ellin's tattered letter in his hand – now at last he knew for sure.

He wrote back to congratulate her unreservedly on the birth of her son, swallowing his pride, courageously hiding his pain. But he wrote also to tell her that the door to her return would never be closed; not so long as he drew breath. He sent to her his unaltered love, his gratitude to his brother for caring for her as he had. And when he'd signed and sealed the letter, he sat by the window of his library, staring out into the summer twilight and fondling the ears of Ellin's little old terrier dog, Strap. He knew now that she was unlikely ever to return to him. Her young son – her relationship with Aaron, whatever that had become – not least the dangers of the voyage home; all were bound to weigh in favour of a future for Ellin in New South Wales, even after she'd received her pardon or served out her sentence. Yet it was true what he wrote. She was his wife. He loved her still, and he could never bring himself finally to close the door on her.

* * *

A little more than three years later, in December of 1803, Aaron Corbyn was standing at the rail of his own paddock a mile to the east of Parramatta township – standing with his son in his arms and Ellin at his side in a gown of glazed and brightly printed calico.

"Look at his forehand if you don't believe me," he was saying. Look at his hind quarters! Now I ask you, Nelly, did you ever see a horse so built for speed?" His red brows raised, his warm brown eyes on hers, stirring feelings she once had thought were dead.

And if Ellin was still no judge of racing form, the beauty of Young Rockingham's colt out of the buttermilk mare could not be lost on her. His coat, a pale chestnut, looked golden in the sunlight – his mane flaxen, near to white. A mount such as they'd found for Napoleon Buonaparte on his abortive Egyptian campaign. The colour that in Spain they called 'Isabella' and in Mexico 'Palomino', so Aaron said. And if Aaron said so, Ellin was now ready to believe him.

She'd found it hard at first to credit his boast that a fine colt or filly, a near-thoroughbred racer, would come of his eccentric purchase of the Indian mare. Nor had she shared his conviction that the Governor was so mighty eager nowadays to grant emancipations, that within a year or two they might expect their freedom and the land to spread it on. And yet he had been right. On the personal recommendation of Cameron Blair, the pardons had come first in June – amongst those granted in honour of the King's birthday that season. Then, with so many unsuccessful grant-holders simply walking off their properties, the land followed shortly afterwards. Thirty acres of part-cleared bush, which Aaron had already fenced and together they'd begun to cultivate. His dreams for the future taking shape before her eyes.

Meanwhile the settlement of Parramatta, larger, dustier, untidier than ever, was fast becoming a real town. Within the last three years a new storehouse and granary, a new Governor's Residence, an incongruous Grecian-style church and a bridge across the river had all been built. A weekly market was established. Plans for a modern stone gaol and a court house had been approved by Macarthur and his successor in Public Works. Houses were springing up everywhere with shingled roofs and glazed windows, unheard of luxuries hitherto. Confidence was growing. You could hear it in the rough strong voices of the place. Voices like Aaron's, as it had now become. And for the first time, in that year of 1803, more than half of Parramatta's occupants were recorded as free grant-holders. A convicts' settlement no longer.

* * *

Aaron had called his colt 'The Pioneer', because that was the spirit in which he'd bought its dam and planned for its conception.

"Did you ever see a horse so built for speed?" was what he asked of Nell. And if her face told him that she only barely understood, he saw that the boy knew. Young as he was, his brave little Michael had laughed and clapped his hands with pleasure, already sharing this latest triumph with his father. A jockey in the making, he'd take his oath on that!

Aaron raised his own red head. A bold, proud movement like the horse's. Watching the colt and noting the child's reaction, exhausted and limb-weary as he was from the efforts of the day, he experienced a moment then of true fulfilment as clear and bright as the great blue sky above them all. He had a right to pride in his achievements. For they were his creations, child and horse – no man could deny it. Even Ellin in a sense, as his wife now in all but British law, and the mother of his son. That he *could* see in her eyes, just as he felt it in her body when they lay together in the cabin that he'd built for her. Whatever his sins, however he might have won her, she was his woman now.

As Cameron Blair's chief stockman, and later as his jockey, Aaron had already achieved some celebrity on the rough race-grounds of Parramatta and the Hawkesbury – matching his employer's now famous blood horse, Young Rockingham, against the mounts of the Corps officers and Macarthur. (Before that notoriously self-willed gentleman had departed for England to resign his commission and seek new markets for the wool that New South Wales was now producing.) With their passion for racing and gaming, the dissipated élite of the Corps were all too easily detached from their money, in Aaron's experience. And now with a two-year-old that was worthy of his aim, with a racehorse of his own, he could almost feel within his grasp the funds he needed to build and plant his property at Parramatta. If all went as intended and 'The Pioneer' lived up to Aaron's hopes of him – well then, there was no reason he could see why Nelly should not be dressed someday in China silk in place of calico; with India rugs upon her floors, and their little Michael conversing in French with some gentleman's tutor up from Sydney. All things were possible for the man who dared!

But first the colt himself must go to school – to be forced on to perform early, superbly, and above all unexpectedly. For as Aaron well knew, his best and only chance of a real killing would be as an outsider – and at his first race – before the Corps could get a sight of the horse's action. For the highest stakes, moreover, the competition must be of the first quality. Which meant his sire, Young Rockingham, with one of the latest bloodstock importations to match him – Major Johnson's new thoroughbred 'Northumberland', perhaps, or the American horse 'Washington', which had already won a number of scrub races down in Sydney. An epic thoroughbred contest was what was needed. A 'champion race' – a three mile run to finish down the broad mainstreet of Parramatta town, with all the colony to see it. That was the match that Aaron planned for his golden Pioneer!

In life you either won or lost, he'd always held it. But as Aaron rose from his naked bed at Ellin's side and set forth to train the colt – by moonlight or in early dawn, on the rough dirt tracks beyond the settlement. As he worked and schemed to stage that crucial three mile race, through Blair and his cronies in the Corps, his thoughts were centred only on The Pioneer's performance. The broader contests of their past, the normal daily hazards of their present survival, for once he failed to take account of. Hazards which for a man of Aaron's time must naturally include the smallpox.

Chapter Twenty-four

In New South Wales, as everywhere in Europe, smallpox was pandemic, an ever-present threat – never entirely disappearing from the ramshackle habitations of the convict settlements, ready at any moment to erupt into full-blown pestilence. An inoculation against the scourge had been known in England since early in the previous century, when Lady Montague had introduced it from the Levant. A system which latterly had been made safe by the substitution of cowpox matter for the inoculum. It was not until March of 1803, however, that samples of this newest discovery arrived in Sydney aboard the convict transport, *Glatton*. By which time the cowpox lymph had sadly lost all potency in its months at sea. The next year the experiment was tried again, with better care this time to protect the precious inoculum against the extremes of heat and cold to which a voyage across the world subjected it. And this time it succeeded. In May of 1804 the *Caromandel* arrived in Sydney Cove with a new sample from the Royal Jennerian Society in London – which a little later was successfully to immunize four hundred of the colony's children against the feared infection. A fact that was of but cold comfort to the parents of those who'd already perished in the smallpox epidemic which had swept through Sydney and Parramatta the previous February.

At first Ellin believed it to be nothing more serious than one of those summer fevers that occasionally afflicted the children of the settlement at times of intense heat. But when she discovered the tell-tale clusters of pimples in the roots of Michael's soft red hair, she began to fear in earnest.

"Though it could well be the measles," she gallantly assured his father when she sent him for the doctor. "At the first there's hardly anything to tell between them, so they say."

But on the second and the third days, when the pimples developed into blisters and then to weeping pustules which smothered the little boy's face – around his eyes, in his nose and in his mouth, there was no escaping the truth. Doctor D'Arcy Wentworth, who attended him daily, bled the four-year-old child from his arm and applied a blister to his tender little neck – to help the fever intermit, as he explained to the frightened parents. But that it never did. On the seventh day, after an agony which for months and years to come would shriek and batter through the dreams of the mother who supported him – blind, disfigured, weeping tears and pus, the little boy had fought his way to death.

* * *

They say that a recent grief usurps all others. Yet the strange thing was that Ellin could still recall how hard she'd found it, that first time at Aaron's house in Fécamp – how hard to mourn an unknown child who'd never learned to smile or laugh, or to command the love of others with his laughter and his smiles. Strange that the empty unreal sense of grief she'd felt in France could find a place to roost still here and now, and after all these years, amongst her present horrors.

If only Aaron's arms had kept their strength. They'd always been so strong, his arms – yet never safe, not safe like Rafe's. No place in them to rest and hide. And now even their strength had gone; Aaron's body slumped beside the cot on which his dead son lay, his breath still reeking of the rum.

"A judgement," he muttered hoarsely, "a life for a life . . ."

But Ellin saw only that he shared her grief, that somehow they must try to help each other. At the nape of Aaron's neck the strong red hair still curled as Michael's had, before the doctor shaved it all away. Unbearably the same. And on an impulse of frustrated need her hand reached down to stroke it tenderly.

"Don't you – don't you touch me!" He reacted like a madman,

leaping from his chair to retreat half across the room from her. "He's caught me once, but He'll not again – not He!"

He laughed wildly at the consternation in her face "A life for a life, Nell," he repeated, "that's His game. My son's life for your father's."

"My father's?"

"Your father's killing, woman – don't ye see? A life for a life, upon my word – a parson for a child . . ."

Somewhere in the aching void the grief had gouged inside her, a new fear began to grow in Ellin. "But Papa's death was an accident," she whispered, "you know it was. He always rode so badly, and his foot caught in the stirrup. Rafe said . . ."

His laughter chilled her with its mirthlessness. "Oh but you're drunk, Aaron, crazed with grief. You scarce know what you're saying."

"Drunk? Yes you're right at that, I am. But then have you not heard, Nell, that a drunkard always tells the truth? *In vino veritas*?" He staggered back unsteadily towards her, his face livid beneath its tan, grinning like an empty deathshead. "Caught in the stirrup, was he? Right again, he was – aye, and bound there too with good strong hemp! He was to testify against us at Assizes, d'ye see – your everloving father! You didn't know that, did you? To expand our conviction to one of treason if he could. That's why he had to die – to save our carcasses, Nelly, yours and mine, from the tar bath and the gibbet!"

Shocked then into silence, she needs must stand and listen while he told her how he'd planned it all from his cell in Horsham Gaol. How Tol Harris's desperados had been sent to ambush the little parson and tie him to the stirrup. How they'd turned a deaf ear to his curses and his prayers, and later to his screams of anguish as they whipped his horse forward over the flints. He spared her nothing. And listening to him shouting, gabbling, stumbling on his own words in his need to confess – to tear down and destroy whatever trust and affection had succeeded in growing between them through their years of toil and deprivation – Ellin remembered in a sudden flash of clarity how violent had been his objection to 'Saul', as the name she'd chosen for their son. She recalled how Aaron looked then with the anger and suspicion in his eyes. And if she could call that so clearly now to mind, that look of his – then had she guessed it at the time? Or always known?

She tried to think. But her mind was overwhelmed by shock and pain, and refused to help her. She'd known him to be ruthless, capable of violence, was even attracted to the aggression in his character – she knew that well enough. But was there more? Had she known then and all along that there was something deformed within the spare young body she admired – something vicious behind Aaron's warm and smiling eyes, his pointed canine teeth? Something she'd recognized but refused to acknowledge, even to herself?

A murder? The murder of her own father. Had she known of it even as she yielded to his killer at Simonstown? And God, if that was true, then she too was damned for all eternity!

* * *

There was nothing Aaron could have done at that late date to prevent the race. The match between the imported horses, Young Rockingham and Washington, and the home-bred two-year-old was already announced in both the colony's newspapers. The officers of the New South Wales Corps had put up a prize of fifty guineas for the winner. And a number of private wagers for a great deal more had already been laid on the horses, and on the street cock fights that would inevitably follow their match. A thoroughbred race, the colony's first, must be an historic event by anyone's reckoning. And on the evening before the horses met – even as the small shrouded body of Michael Corbyn was laid to rest in the cemetery on the southern fringes of the town – Parramatta's taverns and grog-shops were roistering with punters in from Sydney, Toongabbie and the Hawkesbury.

Not that anyone would have been amazed if, under the circumstances, Aaron Corbyn had withdrawn his colt from the running. Indeed, rumours that he'd already done so had circulated for some hours on the morning of the match, before the man himself appeared at the start of the course with set face and glittering eye, his brow already dewed with sweat.

'And if you think you've got me beaten, God, then you've never seen me race,' he thought grimly. 'Or maybe you've forgotten old Mike Mills – the trading man who raced the Devil through St

Leonards forest for the price of his own soul. And beat him too by more than a furlong, so they say.'

His son was dead and buried. His luck too maybe. But not his courage – that Aaron Corbyn would never bury!

The course was right handed. Three miles from the new court house intersection down the broad mainstreet to the wharf – then skirting the military barracks, up through Surgeon Wentworth's property to St John's cemeteŕ where the Corbyns' son now lay –and so down Bridge Street to join Governor Phillip's great boulevard again at its western end for a straight mile-long finish clean through the centre of the town. A five and a half, a six minute race. A long course for a two-year-old, maybe, or so most of the punters were inclined to think. But The Pioneer had Arab blood and the stamina that went with it. And in training he and Aaron had shown each other the way it was to be.

Of the other horses, Young Rockingham appeared first with Blair's new groom, Tom Corrigan, in the saddle – sidling and crabbing down the church street through the crowds of milling spectators, his great nostrils flaring at the overpowering fumes of rum and geneva they exhaled. The Pioneer pricked up his ears and whinnied a greeting to his sire, just as a ragged cheer from the crowd announced the approach of the tall black American, the stallion Washington, from the other direction.

An unprecedented gathering of more than five hundred people had assembled to watch them race. But as the starter raised his hand, the roar of all those voices hushed to a sibilant hum.

"Are ye ready?"

In his excitement and impatience to be off, The Pioneer danced back a little from the line; and for a breathless moment the starter waited silently for him to regain it.

". . . GO!!"

Before Aaron knew it they were away, all three, with a mighty leap and a sound like the roll of a great drum. The older more experienced horses had made a cleaner start. As they flew at a tearing pace past the Red Cow inn they were already a length ahead, shoulder to shoulder like a pair in harness. But The Pioneer was willing. Aaron shifted his weight forward, standing in the stirrups, and applied the whip. The dust from the riders ahead rose up to engulf him, gritting in his eyes and mouth. But under the cut of his whip The Pioneer was pulling hard, pulling up – inexorably gaining . . .

* * *

At the wharf alongside the barracks Ellin stood like a statue to watch Aaron pass by her – his face a glaring mask of concentration, unaware of her presence, blind to all but the race. He'd put everything on it, she knew, every penny they possessed. Their entire future in the colony depended on his winning.

So it should have mattered. She should have turned to watch him take the corner at the barracks and then run with the others through the cottage gardens to see them pass behind. But she hadn't moved. She simply stood exactly as she was, the only one to do so. Alone in the swirling dust.

* * *

Washington had taken the looping bend around the barracks far too wide, to lose ground amongst the waggon tracks that rutted its outer curve. Near the mile-and-a-half The Pioneer caught up with him – ears back, stretched out like a greyhound – to draw level, and then to pull ahead. And from the spectators who'd run through from the mainstreet to see the home bred colt set down the proud American, there rose a mighty cheer.

Now he was travelling – smoother, faster now – through the sweat spray half a length behind his sire – now less than half a length. Then up came his ears as The Pioneer took the cemetery corner on the inside and they swung into Bridge Street together, pursued at a safe distance by half a dozen barking curs. Neck and neck now, Young Rockingham and his son, flank to flank and stride for stride, blowing and streaming lather, shaking the earth with their thunder.

For the turn into the final straight mile of the mainstreet both horses instinctively shortened their stride. Then a lurch . . . As The Pioneer changed legs to lead on his offside into the straight, Aaron sickeningly recalled himself examining the animal a week or two before – and a suggestion of heat behind the fetlock joint. The possibility of a tendon strain like his mother's which at the time he'd chosen to ignore. And God in heaven, not now – it can't go now in the straight, with the post in sight and the race almost in hand!

"No-o-oo!" He bellowed it at the top of his lungpower. Aaron's last protest against losing, he who'd always won.

The colt's ears were back, flat back again. But he was game, he had the heart. He had lost a yard, but soon he'd make it up, straining and gaining with every stride – urged and belaboured, slashed with a bloody spur – gradually, painfully pulling ahead . . .

* * *

From her place by the wharf Ellin was unable to tell which of them led, if either; for they faced her directly, sweeping down the street in a great cloud of yellow dust. Like something in a dream or a vision . . . *'and they that sat on them – through fire and smoke and brimstone, repenting not . . .'*

* * *

The dust in Aaron's throat. His breath rasping and raw. The roar of the crowd indivisible from the sound of the wind in his ears and the beat of his heart. Flames, fire, licking and billowing around him. But ahead now – and so close, so near now to the post!

The horse shifting ground – nose up, muscles bulging, clearly in pain. But ahead still! Still a clear neck ahead, with the post coming up – the final throw.

'And God he's *won* – he has! He's . . . but he's foundered, he's going down – down, the Devil take him!'

Then baked earth and the great sweating body of the horse. And a sound like a pistol shot. The sound of his own neck breaking.

Unknowing, he died.

* * *

As the ligaments tore from the weakened tendon, The Pioneer crashed to his knees. So slowly, it seemed to Ellin – crashing down and over, carried forward by his own momentum. And Aaron's face without fear or pain, almost calm as he fell with the horse, and under it – when she too heard the sound of the breaking neck.

The golden horse rolled on and lay thrashing the air with its dusty hooves. Aaron was moving too when she reached him, his muscles still jerking, his eyes dilated, dark and staring, a fleck of bright blood like a jewel on his lip.

Then he passed into silence with a noise between a growl and a sigh, full of irritability and frustration. His muscles relaxed.

Chapter Twenty-five

It would have been hot in the graveyard but for the breeze that blew up the hill from the river, and ultimately Ellin supposed from Port Jackson and the sea. A young man was working stripped to the waist, throwing up the soil in a pinkish mound beside the grave he was digging. Ellin watched him mechanically – muscles and sinews rhythmically moving, swaggering, posturing a little, conscious no doubt of her eyes. A man watched by a woman. Like Aaron in the sea all those years ago in Sussex . . . bodies, instincts – she could laugh at them now, if ever she could remember how.

Aaron's grave lay beside their son's, piled up with stones against scavenging dogs; each grave marked with a neat wooden cross and a brief inscription:

Michael Corbyn. Born January 11th 1800.
Died February 9th 1804.

Aaron Corbyn. Born October 6th 1773.
Died February 12th 1804.

'Last week! Aaron would have been thirty-one last week,' she thought. 'So I must be . . .' (it seemed years since she'd considered her own age) . . . 'why, I'm still but twenty-nine.'

Which meant she could have another forty, even fifty years ahead of her. She was healthy enough, it was not impossible. Fifty years in New South Wales! And what would it be by then – by 1854, this crude and vital settlement on the underbelly of the world? Would Aaron's dreams for its future be realized by men like Blair – or by Macarthur, if ever he returned to Parramatta? And would they cross the Blue Mountains someday to discover the great continent that Flinders had now proved to exist beyond, with his voyage around its coast. *Terra Australis* – 'Australia', as the cartographer called it – a land for the future? She felt her own unimportance in that future, whatever it might hold. And yet she had her life and all those years to live.

Ellin looked down at the fluffy yellow sprays of wattle she'd laid upon the graves of two Corbyns for whom there were no years. Already their blossoms were wilting in the sun. No life. No child. No father. Nothing for her here but guilt and empty years. Nothing here – but in England . . . in England there was another child, and there was Rafe. He'd written to her after little Michael's birth – such a kind and understanding letter, to tell her that the door lay open still . . .

Ellin looked up quickly and away from the wilting flowers, as a thought she recognized marched boldly through that open door to take possession of her mind. In a tall red gum outside the cemetery a party of marauding cockatoos were stripping the tree's young shoots. To the accompaniment of their raucous shrieks she heard again the clipped tones of the official who'd presented them with their Free Certificates the previous June:

"If you wish to return to Europe, a passage home is permitted. But at your own expense. In which event you may apply for a further certificate to record a description of your character during the term of transportation."

Aaron had laughed at the man's solemnity and told him to save his characters for a ladies' sentimental novel. But Ellin had listened, and remembered what he said, every word of it.

As she closed her eyes now in the graveyard and turned her face to the sun, in place of the harsh brilliance of the southern sky she could see only a rose coloured glow – the candlelit bedchamber at Chalkdean, with a fire in the grate and snow on the downs outside . . . Always before when her thoughts had strayed down these paths she had succeeded in diverting them before they could force a decision. But now it was too late.

With the prize for the race, and Aaron's winnings besides, she already had enough for the passage home. She'd made the journey once; with God's help she could do it again. And if she did? If she herself were to follow on the letter she'd sent to England with the news of Michael's death, and of Aaron's? Would Rafe be truly glad to see her now? As glad as she would be to see his face? And *was* there a future for her still in Chalkdean after all, with Lizzy and with Rafe? She knew only that at this moment and above everything she craved the safety of his arms, his steadiness, his gravity and self-control – all things once rejected, yet needed now so badly!

And if not his arms – if Rafe's arms were too much still to ask of life and of God – then to see his face at least. Heart-weary, exhausted as she was, a journey halfway round the world did not seem too far to Ellin for a sight of the loving kindness in her husband's grave brown eyes.

To the watching gravedigger it was as if of a sudden a new woman had entered the cemetery to stand where the other had stood. He'd never seen Corbyn's little widow smile before, and the change astonished him. Instinctively he tried to catch her eye again, to draw something of its warmth onto himself. But already she had turned to go, running toward the gate.

Ellin was going home!

* * *

Death must have been in the air that October, in Chalkdean as in the Parramatta cemetery. At the very hub of his stable yard domain old Coachman Turner sat propped in a wicker chair astride the central drain, panting his life away in needless instructions to the grooms and stable lads who passed about him. Years of exposure to rain and freezing fogs and dusty summer roads had damaged the old man's lungs beyond all hope of remedy – to swell and congest them for the pneumonia that would shortly take him off. But Gabel had no more time for death than he'd had for tye-wigs in their day, or for domineering women.

"Gaarge – Gaarge!" he rasped in an attempt at the commanding tones he'd once employed here, fighting for the lungpower to urge the boy to action. "Gaarge! 'Ere's the Master back again – and you're, you're never . . ."

But the Master had already dismounted and George run up to do his duty, before he could force the words. ". . . You're never ready for 'im, boy," he whispered at last, blue in the face from lack of breath.

"Oh Gabel, my dear old fellow. What am I to do with you?" Rafe knelt on the cobbles and gently pulled the old man forward against his shoulder to help him catch his wind, patting him like a baby.

"I tell them to keep you in the warm beside your fire – and here I find you courting every random breeze and draught, and without so much as a cape or topcoat to protect you."

But he spoke only for the sake of speaking, to lessen the man's embarrassment. For they both knew that if Gabel were to be denied a central place in this familiar world of his, he might as well be dead.

After a time the old man's battle for air yielded up a series of shuddering breaths. He lay back in his chair with Rafe's own cloak around him, both eyes shut tight against humiliation.

"I be that weary, Mus Relph," he gasped at last. "An old breakdown nag, that's me. No kind of pace at all."

And crouched there beside him on the cobbles, Rafe wished fervently that he could do for Gabel what the coachman himself had done for so many of his faithful old horses – while his eyes remained closed to place a gun against his head, simply to press the trigger and release him in a moment from all pain and all distress. But instead he held the old man's knuckly hands and talked quietly to him of carriage teams and cobs and hunters from the days gone by – of Dandy and Jinny, Tabitha, Solly and his brother's high-bred Nimrod. And while he spoke he watched the mellow autumn sunlight playing on the sycamores beyond the gate. Leaves turning, falling with the season – and memories, grains slipping through the sandglass of the years.

In September Ann Ashby and her child had left him, departing abruptly without a warning or explanation one afternoon while Rafe rode out to draw a patient's tooth in Wannock.

"But though I'd never lend an ear to gossip, as you know yourself, Sir, not for all the gold in the bank," an exultant Keturah Gubbin informed him two mornings later, "some folks are saying as she've taken private lodgings down in Seaford with a Captain of Dragoons. Glory Sir, the very idea! Why upon my word, Sir, I'd sooner be struck deaf and dumb as to give credit to such a wicked tale!"

And although in many ways he'd been sad to see Annie go, missed her little Sary's bright hair and engaging ways about the place, Rafe was now honest enough to admit to himself that the girl's instincts had been true. However he might defend their relationship to parson and to parish, they both recognized its limits – the hard casing round his inner heart that kept it safe for Ellin. He was grateful to Ann as she was to him. But if ever he'd implied more, the girl herself was undeceived.

"I'll tell ye what, you'll never stop loving that wife of yourn, and you may as well believe it," she had affirmed. "'Tis writ all through you, m'dear, as large as life for anyone to read."

So now if she chose to stop competing with the ghost of Ellin Corbyn – to find for herself and her child another masculine protector, removed from her father's disapproving eye and the clacking tongues of Sellington parish – then Rafe was the last man on earth to say her nay. She'd left Chalkdean as simply and as naturally as she came to it. And having once ascertained that she and little Sarah Ann were indeed safe and well cared for in Seaford town, on reflection Rafe found himself content to leave them as they were.

One unlooked for consequence of Ann's departure had been the arrival on Rafe's escritoire the following week of a sealed missive from Tunbridge Wells. Aunt Drusilla wrote, as she'd written before, to assure her nephew of her regard, of her continuing care for his wellbeing. But this time she further beseeched him to permit her return to Chalkdean, at least for a visit – to be allowed to assist Rafe if she could with the domestic duties of his house.

Rafe had no illusions that the woman had reformed in the household of his Cousin Barnabas at the Wells, or indeed was even capable of reformation. But in the years since he'd last set eyes on her, he had come to see his aunt as much in the light of her own misfortunes as of those she had brought on others. He saw her as a woman unwanted and unloved, herself incapable of unselfish affections. In finding it in his heart to pity her, he was already more than halfway to forgiveness. And on the day he walked out to meet his aunt at the Manor garden gate, Rafe saw that she had changed after all – and that for the better. She was older now, like all of them, less self-assertive and somehow smaller. She'd even waited quietly in her seat while the young coachman hurried around to release her from the carriage. A final submission that must surely have brought joy indeed to poor old Gabel's heart – if only he'd been there to see it.

Smiling, Rafe turned from the sycamores to describe it to him, that at least. But before he could speak again, Gabel himself moved to forestall him.

"She'll come back," he wheezed, opening his bloodshot eyes a fraction. And they both knew that it was not of the old Mistress that he spoke. "She'll come back, Mus Relph, I'll give ye my word she will."

* * *

At Polegate Green Ellin alighted from the East-Bourne coach and arranged for her portmanteau to be unstrapped and borne into the inn there, to await the transport she should send for it. She was mortally weary after such a great while on the road, stiff and sore from close acquaintance with innumerable ruts and pot-holes in the highway down from Southwark. A five mile walk and two long hills still lay ahead of her. Yet she was unwilling to rest, unable to wait. For what was a walk of five miles after a journey of sixteen thousand or more? And with Chalkdean at the end of it!

As she made her way down through Jevington village, a woman on a cottage step stared rudely at her worn and dusty clothes, wondering plainly who she was and where she'd sprung from. A dog sprawling in the shadow of a wall rose to bark half-heartedly after her. A child with a tabby kitten on a string snatched it up to run away with it across the street as Ellin passed them by. And two bent old fellows throwing horseshoes by the forge, stopped to push back their hats and stare after the female stranger with the same hard and curious eyes as the cottage woman's.

"But I'm *not* a stranger! I know this place – I've often passed this way before." That's what she wanted to call out to them. "Look – look again you fools, and then perhaps you'll see! 'Tis Ellin Corbyn – the parson's daughter who came to Chalkdean as a bride and left it as a felon. You must remember me!"

But she said nothing (and nor would she now to anyone but Rafe). She merely bent her head and hurried on to climb that last long hill to Chalkdean.

From the top she could already see its chimneys and scent the homely, horsy odour of the stables. ('Home!' How could so brief a word encompass so many complex feelings?) Rather than pass the yard gate and run the risk of meeting with a groom or stable lad, she skirted round behind the coach-house, up through the woods to Aunt Corbyn's garden. They smelled of earth, those woods – wet earth and rotting leaves, just as she remembered. Her feet as she walked made but the faintest rustle in the mould. She felt like a ghost – a forgotten person in an unfrequented place. And then she heard the sound of childish laughter intermingled with the barking of a dog. And on the smooth green lawn beyond the trees she saw a girl in white muslin running to retrieve her ball.

"No Strap, you know you're not to play," the child cried out. "You're too mighty old and fat to chase a ball, you know you are. And look, you're tearing it, you silly boy. Now give it here to Lizzy this very minute!"

And was it really Lizzy – her Elizabeth? So tall and grown, such long straight limbs, and not yet nine! Ellin remained uncertainly within the shadow of the trees. But as her daughter threw the ball again she felt a surge of all her old impetuosity, a childlike urge to run out herself and join the game. That is, until she saw who 'twas that caught it.

Rafe's face, when she'd first beheld it all those years ago, had been quite unremarkable – or so she thought. Later in the daily intercourse of marriage his features had become so commonly familiar that she scarcely paid them heed. But now at last she saw her husband clearly as he was. His face looked older, with a deep vertical crease between his brows and new lines etched about his eyes and mouth. But what a face! So much stronger, calmer and more handsome than she'd ever succeeded in recalling. And so infinitely dearer to her now, as he stepped forward with that look of special tenderness that fathers keep for their daughters, to guide the ball into his Lizzy's outstretched hands.

Through all the long months of her voyage home, Ellin had struggled with every kind of fear; that the house when finally she reached it would be burnt or sold – that Rafe had moved – that he'd brought home with him some fatal fever, that he and Lizzy . . . Yet how unfounded all those fears had been. For here they were both safe and healthy. And here was she.

Ellin had already started for the lawn. At any moment one of them would look across and see her there. One look – one single point of contact, and her life would turn full circle! But then a third figure emerged from the direction of the house, a woman with a tray of cordials. And even before she recognized Aunt Corbyn, Ellin slipped back into the cover of the trees.

'I hold her responsible for what has befallen you and can no longer endure to see her in my house.'

Yet here she came, trampling Ellin's hopes with every step she took. For how could she now, or ever, return to a house where that woman still presided – or dare to re-enter her unrelenting world of birth and precedent? She who'd been a 'guest of Newgate', a convict transported to New South Wales! The ghost of the little parson's daughter she'd just now felt herself to be, might just conceivably have dared to run out to them across the lawn in spite of all. But not the tired and empty woman she'd become. Ellin had suffered and changed too much, she knew, ever to step back into that girl's shoes – whatever Rafe had written in his letter. And she saw now in the midst of her confusion, as Aunt Corbyn held out a glass of cordial to her favoured nephew, that her own presence here in Chalkdean could do nothing but disrupt and destroy the calm and happiness of their lovely summer garden.

"And oh my darlings, I love you both too much to use you so unkindly," she whispered through her tears.

For a moment she lingered, undecided still. Then with one last longing look, she forced herself to turn again and walk back the way that she had come.

Chapter Twenty-six

In November of that same year of 1805, on the anniversary of coachman Gabel Turner's death, the gatekeepers on the Dicker turnpike had spread the news of Lord Nelson's last and greatest victory, off the Spanish coast near Cape Trafalgar. A few weeks later in his absurd oriental pavilion at Bright'on, the Prince of Wales was heard to boast (a little prematurely, as it later appeared) that Napoleon Buonaparte had finally been sent back to the Devil who spawned him. Meantime, across the downs at Chalkdean the yule log was again brought in for lighting; and once again the Corbyn household prepared to mark the Feast of St Thomas with their usual stock of gifts for goodening.

In the spring Rafe had received word from his wife of Aaron's death at Parramatta, and of the tragic loss of their little son. He wrote to her straightway with all the words of comfort he could muster – enclosing details of the passage back to England that he'd secured for her on the returning transport ship, *Andromeda*. And in his letter he tried, he'd tried so hard to explain to Ellin how he himself had changed – how much he'd learned of life from the years they'd spent apart, of what was true and what was false – how certain he now felt of their right to happiness together at this last.

But would she believe him now? And would she care? Those were the questions that kept revolving in his mind. Could she still summon sufficient strength of body and of purpose after all that had happened to make that appalling journey, and to survive it?

And Aaron – what of he?

'Race me, race me home, Ray! Your horse against my pony – and still I'll win, you'll see – I know I will!'

How like his brother, though, to end his life that way. As if the intervening years and all the tragedies they'd brought had never come between. Poor Aaron – defeat in victory at the end. His death, his mother's death before, already now so far away in time and distance that they hardly signified. Little more now than detritus. Life, as Aaron himself had once remarked, was strictly for the living.

* * *

"Ah, Mercy – I'm glad to see you here again this year. And what can I give you, pray?"

"A mince tart, Sir, an' ye will, Sir."

It was late already, and at Rafe's suggestion Aunt Drusilla had taken Lizzy in for her supper while he remained to dispose of the last of the goodings.

"And Mrs Pyecroft. what for you?"

"I'll take a mince tart too, thanking ye Sir – seeing as the candles 'ave all gorn."

One woman who'd come in a little late remained still by the door of the back kitchen after the others departed. As Mrs Pyecroft had pointed out, only the mince pies were left now, each baked into an oval in the supposed shape of the Christmas manger. Rafe reached for one automatically, relieved that it was to be the last, and beckoned to her to step into the light. Her face was hidden from him even now by one of the hooped French bonnets that had come in with the new century and would very nearly see it out. A shabby traipse of a woman, she seemed – nervous of coming forward, with one hand braced back against the wall as if to steel herself to an action that she doubted still. Rafe wondered vaguely who she was.

Strap knew. The little terrier was getting old now, stiff with arthritis – too fat from too many mince pies, and other such illegal treats, consumed over too many years. But his eyes were sharp still, his sense of smell as acute as ever. He began to whine softly, and Rafe looked down in some surprise.

"Strap? What is it? What's the matter, old man?"

For once, though, the dog ignored him, quivering now from head to foot. His master frowned, perplexed – looked up again and met the woman's clear grey eyes.

She didn't speak, and nor did he. Rafe simply felt the hard casing that had formed around his heart expanding, cracking, falling away, as she moved toward him and reached out to place her two small hands in his.